"The pinnacle of near-future science fiction."

—Cixin Liu, Hugo Award–winning
author of *The Three-Body Problem*

"Chen weaves a stunning tale of greed and deftly exposes all the hidden contours of the human heart."

—Maggie Shen King, author of *An Excess Male*

"Filled with wonderful invention, compelling characters, and a whirlpool of story, *Waste Tide* is an urgently needed, thought-provoking wild ride of a novel. I couldn't put it down."

—Lavie Tidhar, author of *Central Station*

"Viscerally gripping action . . . Sheer excellence."

—*Kirkus Reviews* (starred review)

"Already an award winner in China, this book is likely to draw comparisons to Cixin Liu's *The Three-Body Problem* and Kim Stanley Robinson's *New York 2140,* and is a provocative addition to the growing corpus of Chinese speculative fiction and near-future and realist SF as a whole."

—*Library Journal*

"A complex and provocative exploration of the interactions among social class, corporate ambition, cultural identity, environmentalism, and human potential, with enough buzzy ideas to power a couple of novels, and enough violent melodrama to keep the reader plummeting along."

—Gary K. Wolfe, *Locus*

"A sci-fi blockbuster with mob bosses, robots, and a powerful virus . . . Downright prescient."

—*Shelf Awareness*

WASTE TIDE

CHEN QIUFAN

TRANSLATED BY KEN LIU

TOR

A TOM DOHERTY ASSOCIATES BOOK

NEW YORK

This is a work of fiction. All of the characters, organizations, and events portrayed in this novel are either products of the author's imagination or are used fictitiously.

WASTE TIDE

Copyright © 2013 by Chen Qiufan 陈楸帆

English translation © 2019 by Ken Liu

A Tor Book
Published by Tom Doherty Associates
120 Broadway
New York, NY 10271

www.tor-forge.com

Tor® is a registered trademark of Macmillan Publishing Group, LLC.

The Library of Congress has cataloged the hardcover edition as follows:

Names: Chen, Qiufan, 1981– author. | Liu, Ken, 1976– translator.
Title: Waste tide / Chen Qiufan ; translated by Ken Liu.
Other titles: 880-01 Huang chao. English
Description: First edition. | New York : Tom Doherty Associates, 2019.
Identifiers: LCCN 2018050987 | ISBN 9780765389312 (hardcover) |
    ISBN 9780765389329 (ebook)
Subjects: LCSH: Electronic waste—Fiction. | Diseases—Fiction. | Survival—Fiction. |
    Science fiction, Chinese—21st century—Translations into English.
Classification: LCC PL2933.E526116 H8313 2019 | DDC 895.13/6—dc23
LC record available at https://lccn.loc.gov/2018050987

ISBN 978-0-7653-8933-6 (trade paperback)

Our books may be purchased in bulk for promotional, educational, or business use. Please contact your local bookseller or the Macmillan Corporate and Premium Sales Department at 1-800-221-7945, extension 5442, or by email at MacmillanSpecialMarkets@macmillan.com.

Originally published as 荒潮 in 2013 by Changjiang Literature Art Publishing House 长江文艺出版社 in Beijing.

First U.S. Edition: April 2019
First U.S. Trade Paperback Edition: March 2020

Printed in the United States of America

D 0 9 8 7 6 5 4

TRANSLATOR'S NOTE ON LANGUAGE(S) AND NAMES

Waste Tide makes use of a variety of Sinitic languages and dialects (or, to use the more accurate term, "topolects"—more on which below). The speech of the natives of Silicon Isle is based on the dialect of Shantou (also known as Swatow), a variety of Teochew, which is a member of the Min Nan family of Chinese languages that also includes Amoy, Taiwanese, and Hokkien.

The waste people, migrant workers from less economically developed regions in China, bring with them their own regional varieties of Chinese (a majority of which are dialects of Mandarin), but communicate with one another and with the natives of Silicon Isle in Modern Standard Mandarin, the lingua franca of contemporary China.

In addition, due to Silicon Isle's location in Guangdong Province and proximity to Hong Kong and Guangzhou, many inhabitants of Silicon Isle can understand and speak Cantonese (especially the Hong Kong dialect) to some degree and are familiar with Cantonese (including Hong Kong) culture.

People with some education also pepper their speech with allusions and references drawn from Classical Chinese, a literary language.

This linguistic richness, which is part of the everyday experience of many Chinese, presents certain challenges in a translation intended for the Anglophone readership. The rather unfortunate tendency of the Western media to pay attention only to Modern Standard Mandarin and Hong Kong Cantonese, the two prestige members of contemporary Chinese languages, makes it hard to appreciate the experience of navigating a far more colorful linguistic landscape. (In Chinese, the contested distinction between languages and dialects is neatly side-stepped by the word *fangyan*—literally, "regional speech." I've chosen to follow the modern convention to translate this word as "topolect" instead of the problematic and inaccurate "dialect.")

I've limited the use of Chinese words and phrases in this translation to an absolute minimum for readability reasons. To convey some flavor of the linguistic variety, I employ phonetic Teochew in select spots, leaving full tone marks to footnotes to aid readability of the main text. (There is one exception in the text where tone marks are used to distinguish Teochew from Mandarin.) Words that have entered English via Cantonese, such as *dim sum* and *hakau,* or Mandarin, such as *feng shui,* or even Japanese, such as *nori,* are presented in these forms that would be familiar to Anglophone readers. Toneless pinyin based on Modern Standard Mandarin is used for Classical Chinese or contemporary neologisms such as *shanzhai,* which are perhaps in the process of becoming part of the English lexicon.

Chinese names are generally presented with their Mandarin readings using toneless pinyin, surnames first, in accordance with Chinese custom and practice. An exception is made for names of characters from Hong Kong, which are presented in phonetic, toneless Cantonese, surnames last, following the Western convention.

CONTENTS

PROLOGUE

Clouds roiled in the southeast like runaway horses. Typhoon Saola, still three hundred kilometers away over the sea, was approaching Hong Kong.

The typhoon's course, fleet-footed and erratic, was just like its namesake.

A vision of that graceful animal, now existing only as pixels in image databases and stuffed museum specimens, flashed before the eyes of Sug-Yi Chiu Ho.

The name "saola" (scientific name: *Pseudoryx nghetinhensis*) came from a Dai word used in Vietnam. Scientists had to wait eighteen years between the discovery of some unusual skulls and the first reported sighting of a live specimen by peasants; five years later, the species was extinct.

White stripes covered the saola's cheeks. Long, straight horns, curving slightly backward, gave it the nickname "Asian unicorn." The species possessed the largest scent glands among all then-extant mammals—also an important cause for its demise. In the folklore of Vietnam and Laos, it was a symbol of good fortune, happiness, and longevity.

Now all that sounded like a joke.

So damned cold! Sug-Yi gripped the side of the tiny speedboat with one hand and pulled the jacket tighter around herself with the other. The Hong Kong Observatory had issued tropical cyclone warning signal number eight, indicating a sustained wind speed between 63 and 117 kilometers per hour, with occasional gusts exceeding 180 kilometers per hour.

I really picked a good day.

Coltsfoot Blossom leapt, breaking through a series of foam-crested waves, and gained on the 8,000-TEU cargo ship *Long Prosperity*. The cargo ship had crossed the Pacific from the Port of New York and New Jersey. It was bound for the wharves at Kwai Tsing, from where its cargo would be distributed to smaller ports in China.

The pilot gestured at Sug-Yi, and she nodded back. Her face, buffeted by the strong wind, appeared especially pale. The numbers scrolling across Sug-Yi's goggles indicated that the target had decreased its speed to ten knots in accordance with the port authority's regulations, meant to reduce the amount of pollution spilling into the port's waters as well as to lessen the effect of the ship's wake on smaller vessels.

And it provides a good opportunity. She waved at her crew, reminding everyone to be alert.

Coltsfoot Blossom accelerated and converged on *Long Prosperity*'s heading until it was right up against the side of the ship, matching its course and speed. Next to the giant container ship—built by Samsung Heavy Industries, 334.8 meters long and 45.8 meters wide—the speedboat looked like a remora attached to a basking shark.

"Hurry!" Sug-Yi's voice was almost drowned out by the roaring motor.

The magnetic rope ladder shot out like a spiderweb, firmly attaching itself to a spot about two meters below the starboard rail of *Long Prosperity*. The bottom of the ladder remained connected to the speedboat to provide stability. A fully armed member of the assault team nimbly began the climb up. He dangled from the underside of the ladder so that his back was toward the sea to take advantage of the hooks attached to the soles of his shoes as well as to avoid becoming dizzy from the visual impact of the surging waves.

Though he was well-trained, the lone vanguard swayed terrifyingly like a wounded insect on a thread of spider silk, buffeted by the wind and waves. The twenty-five meters he had to traverse looked short but would be arduous.

Hurry, hurry! Sug-Yi's dread rose with every passing second. *Coltsfoot Blossom*'s agile interception of *Long Prosperity* had happened so fast that the crew of the cargo ship had not yet recovered enough to react. But time was running out. Once they reached the shallow water inside the harbor, the waves would become even higher, increasing the danger of the maneuver.

"Are you getting all this?" she asked the young woman next to her, who nodded anxiously, the miniature camera mounted next to her ear bobbing with her head. This was her first mission. Sug-Yi gestured at her to stabilize the camera.

The show must go on.

She let out a laugh. When had she changed from being disgusted by this philosophy to being its loyal practitioner? This was akin to the "nonviolent direct actions" that Greenpeace engaged in: lying down on tracks to stop trains, climbing landmarks, assaulting whaling ships, intercepting nuclear waste . . . time after time, each performance more outrageous than the last, relentlessly challenging the tolerance of governments and megacorporations. While these acts earned her organization a growing measure of notoriety, they also brought public attention to environmental problems and perhaps helped to enact environmental protection legislation.

That's justification enough, isn't it?

She recalled the speech given by her mentor, the founder of the Coltsfoot Blossom Organization, Dr. Guo Qide, at the most recent reception for new members.

The lights had dimmed, and a painting had appeared on the giant screen: amid mountainous waves, a three-masted sailing ship was about to capsize. Some of the panicked crew had escaped on life rafts, leaving behind a few hopeless men to struggle aboard the ship. The chiaroscuro of black sea and white waves arrested the eye.

"This painting, *L'Incendie du Kent,* was the work of Jean Antoine Théodore Gudin in 1827." Dr. Guo's mesmerizing voice captivated the crowd as he declared, "The world we live in is that ship, about to be lost. Some have already jumped on life rafts, but some still remain ignorant and unaware.

"Our job at Coltsfoot Blossom is to sound the drum and strike the gong, to play the clown, to swallow fire, to use whatever tricks we have at our disposal to catch everyone's attention. We must let people know that the ship is on the verge of sinking, but those responsible for our condition think they can get away untouched. Unless we tie their fates to ours, we will be the ones left behind to pay for their mistakes."

A sharp cry interrupted Sug-Yi's reverie. She looked up and saw several crewmen looking over the gunwale of *Long Prosperity.* They were trying to pry loose the rope ladder's magnetic point of attachment, but since the ship's hull was designed to maximize the cargo deck area, the top edge of the hull curved out at an extreme angle. In order to reach the ladder, the men had to lean so far out that their bodies dangled over the side. Fighting ineffectually against the strong wind, the crewmen finally gave up after a few attempts.

The man on the ladder climbed even faster. Only about ten meters left.

A white stream of water lashed out from *Long Prosperity*'s deck and struck his body. The rope ladder swayed like a swing. The man's hands slipped off the rope, and he began the long plunge into the surging waves below.

Sug-Yi's hand covered her mouth but she couldn't look away. The young woman with the camera screamed.

But the man stopped falling. He hung upside down in the air: the hooks on the bottom of his shoes had saved him at the last moment. He jackknifed in the air, caught the rope with his hands, and continued to climb up.

"Nicely done!" Sug-Yi shouted at him.

Long Prosperity's crew continued to spray the man with the high-pressure hose, treating him as a living flame spreading up the rope ladder. The greater danger to the man wasn't the impact of the water against his body, but the temporary deprivation of air due to water filling his nose and mouth. Luckily, he was prepared. Pulling the clear visor down over his face, he continued his upward journey fearlessly. Eight meters, seven meters . . .

A smile appeared on Sug-Yi's face. She seemed to be watching herself from years ago, a young woman who had covered herself in saola scent and then squeezed herself onto crowded buses, subway trains, and ferries, ignoring the angry looks of those around her covering their noses, telling anyone who would listen that the most precious perfume, when made at the price of the extinction of a species, would turn into an intolerable stench.

Countless people had asked her: was it worth it? She had answered countless times: yes, of course it was. Even if the entire world treated you like a troublemaking attention whore, as long as you held on to your faith, it was enough.

The cargo crew shut off the high-pressure hose. *Perhaps they've found a new trick?*

"They're changing course!" shouted the speedboat pilot.

Sug-Yi read the data off her goggles: *Long Prosperity* was turning toward *Coltsfoot Blossom* and simultaneously accelerating to twelve knots. This was an attempt to disrupt the speedboat's mission without drawing the port authority's attention. The speedboat began to bob up and down more erratically from the cargo ship's wake. The rope ladder twisted and swayed in the air like a snake, and the man on the rope was hanging on for dear life.

"Accelerate and match course," she ordered. "Keep it steady."

The man on the rope tried to keep climbing. His body contorted to adjust his center of gravity and posture, maintaining the stability and balance of the rope ladder. Five meters, four meters . . . he was like a skilled yoga practitioner dancing on a rope in the middle of a storm.

Almost there. Sug-Yi held her breath and counted down in her head.

The young man's next task was to use suction cups to climb from the rope ladder's attach point all the way up to the deck while dodging the crewmen. Once there, he'd have to chain himself to a container like Houdini—preferably after having unfurled the flag of the Coltsfoot Blossom Organization somewhere prominent—and then wait until the media and the Environment Protection Department showed up. According to the decision acquitting the six Greenpeace activists in the Kingsnorth Power Station case, as long as Coltsfoot Blossom could provide a "lawful excuse" tied to environmental activism, their actions today would not be deemed illegal. Of course, everything depended on whether the information they were relying on was accurate: that the containers on this ship, originating in New Jersey and bound for Silicon Isle, held the so-called Devil's Gift, toxic waste capable of creating an ecological disaster.

It was not a simple plan, but the hardest part was about to be completed.

. . . two meters, one meter. The man was finally at the top of the ladder. But he didn't put on the suction-cup gloves. Instead, he held on to the rope and swung back and forth, moving his body like a pendulum.

"What's he doing?" Sug-Yi asked angrily.

"Thomas . . . likes parkour," the young camerawoman murmured, and continued to film.

So he's called Thomas. These days, so many skilled and idealistic new members were joining the organization that it was no longer possible for Sug-Yi to know everyone's name. *Being young is a good thing. Most of the time.*

Thomas continued to swing as he anxiously calculated the distance and angle. The maneuver he had in mind would require him to let go when his body was at the top of the arc, leap through the air while simultaneously turning ninety degrees to catch the top of the gunwale. It demanded the utmost of his muscle strength, flexibility, and mental faculties.

"Thomas, stop!" Sug-Yi shouted. "Don't jump!"

Too late. She saw that athletic, balanced body leap into the air, seeming to freeze for a moment in the wind, slowly and elegantly turning through a quarter of a circle, until his hands slapped loudly against the side of the ship. The steel plates vibrated while his body dipped under gravity. All he had to do now was to flex his arms and stomach to pull himself up and complete the beautiful gymnastic move.

Sug-Yi got ready to applaud this daring performance.

Maybe it was the wind, or maybe a patch of water left on the gunwale, but there was an ear-piercing scraping against metal and Thomas's hands slipped off. He began to fall irrevocably. Panicked, he grabbed on to the swaying rope ladder with one hand, but his momentum carried his whole body toward the hull of the ship. There was a loud, crisp crack from his visor, and his neck buckled, leaving his head at an unnatural angle. Thomas's hands let go and he continued to fall.

His body plunged into the sea in a noiseless splash, an indelible image.

The young camerawoman was stunned. The lens next to her ear had captured the entire scene and the accompanying screams and cries. This video would later be played over and over in the media and on countless websites, and internet commenters would dub it a "recruiting ad" for the Coltsfoot Blossom Organization. The campaign slogan? "Youth does not mean stupidity."

Sug-Yi took in the scene, her mind dazed. She didn't give the order to retrieve the body, neither did she move or show any expression.

Is it really worth it? She didn't know if she was asking Thomas or herself.

Long Prosperity continued to accelerate and turn toward the speedboat. Sug-Yi's pilot, having received no new orders, didn't take any action. *Coltsfoot Blossom*'s hull collided with the cargo ship and was pushed up, and the dull sound of metal being deformed filled the crew's ears. They grabbed on to whatever was at hand, trying to avoid being thrown into the water from the tilting deck. Freezing seawater, full of whirling eddies and foamy, white spray, poured into the boat.

Now the boat was really going down.

PART ONE

SILENT VORTEX

The Basel Convention on the Control of Transboundary Movements of Hazardous Wastes and Their Disposal is an international treaty that was designed to reduce the movements of hazardous waste between nations, and specifically to prevent transfer of hazardous waste from developed to less developed countries (LDCs).

The Convention was opened for signature on 22 March 1989, and entered into force on 5 May 1992. One hundred and seventy-nine states and the European Union are parties to the Convention.

The United States, the leading producer of electronic waste, has never ratified the Convention.

—Wikipedia entry on "Basel Convention"

1

The fine, handcrafted wooden model of the junk at the center of the glass display case glistened with the reddish-brown varnish intended to give it an antique air. There was no holographic scene around it; instead, the background was a hand-drawn map of Silicon Isle—really a peninsula connected to the mainland by an isthmus, but everyone talked about it like a true island—and the sea around it. It was easy to tell that the mapmaker strained too hard to show the natural beauty of the local scenery, and the excessive application of colorful paint appeared unnatural.

". . . this is the symbol of Silicon Isle, representing good harvest, prosperity, and harmony . . ."

Scott Brandle was fascinated by the model ship and only half paid attention to the guide's patter. The color and texture of the model, especially the puffed sails seemingly full of wind, reminded him of the steamed lobsters served at the reception last night. He was no vegetarian, and he wasn't a zealous supporter of the World Wide Fund for Nature either, but the fact that the plate held a third claw and that the lobster's carapace had apparently been carefully patched had made him suspicious. The thought that the "wild lobster" with an extra limb might have been raised in the sea farms nearby had taken away his appetite, leaving him to stare as the Chinese officials gorged themselves.

"Mr. Scott, what would you like to study tomorrow?" Director Lin Yiyu, already drunk, asked him in the local topolect.

Chen Kaizong (a.k.a. Caesar Chen), Brandle's assistant, did not correct Lin's confusion of his boss's given name and surname, but translated what he said literally.

"I want to understand Silicon Isle better." Although Scott had been drinking some *baijiu*—the strong distilled spirit unavoidable at Chinese social functions—he remained fairly sober. He omitted "the real" from his request.

"Good, good." Director Lin, his face red from *baijiu*, turned and said something to the other officials. Everyone laughed uproariously. Kaizong did not translate right away. After a while, he said to Scott, "Director Lin says that he will be sure to satisfy your wish."

They'd already spent more than two hours in the overly air-conditioned Museum of Silicon Isle History, and the visit didn't seem to be nearing its end. Without a pause in his torrent of heavily accented English, the museum guide had taken them through all the brightly lit exhibit halls. Using ancient poetry, government correspondence, re-stored photographs, re-created tools and artifacts, faux documentaries, and dioramas made with plastic mannequins, the guide had presented Silicon Isle's thousand-year-long history dating back to the ninth century.

However, the museum's exhibits fell short of the designers' ideals. The intent might have been to showcase how Silicon Isle had progressed from fishing and farming into the modern industrial age and thence into the information age, but all Scott saw were rooms full of boring artifacts accompanied by droning propaganda. The hypnotic effect was about on par with his memory of his drill sergeant's speeches during basic training.

But the interpreter, Chen Kaizong, was fascinated by the presentation, as though he were completely unfamiliar with Silicon Isle. Scott noticed that since the moment Kaizong set foot on this patch of land, the earlier indifference that had seemed too precocious in the young man had been replaced by a pride and curiosity that felt more natural for a young man of twenty-one.

". . . wonderful . . . unbelievable . . ." Periodically, the expressionless Scott dispensed a word of praise like a robot.

Director Lin nodded appreciatively. The smile on his face resembled those found on the plastic mannequins, and his striped shirt was tucked into his dress pants. Unlike the other officials, he still had a thin waist. What he lost in presence, he gained in the impression of efficiency. Standing next to Scott, who was almost six foot three, Lin Yiyu resembled a walking stick.

And yet, this man could make Scott suffer without being able to say a thing, like a mute man forced to swallow bitter herbs.

He says one thing and thinks another, Scott thought. Only now did he finally understand what Director Lin had meant last night. Before he came to China, he had purchased a copy of *The Ignoramus's Guide to China,* which offered this pearl of wisdom: "The Chinese rarely say what they mean." He had added the annotation: "And how is this different from Americans?"

Perhaps the officials present at the reception banquet last night had been told to be there—none of the real decision makers had shown up. Measured by the amount of *baijiu* consumed, those officials had accomplished (or even exceeded) their assigned tasks of creating a jolly atmosphere at the reception. Based on Director Lin's lack of genuine cooperation, Scott was certain that his research trip for TerraGreen Recycling Co., Ltd., would not go smoothly.

The key personnel from the three main clans of Silicon Isle were never going to show up. The best that Scott could hope for was to take a tour of some carefully prepared model street and Potemkin village factory, eat some tasty, refined dim sum, and carry a pile of souvenirs onto the plane back to San Francisco.

But wasn't that why TerraGreen Recycling had sent Scott Brandle instead of someone else? A smile softened Scott's angular features. From Ghana to the Philippines—other than that accident in Ahmedabad— he had never failed. Silicon Isle would be no exception.

"Tell him that we're going to Xialong Village this afternoon," Scott leaned down and whispered to Kaizong. "Make him."

Then he pursed his lips and put on a careless smile as he glanced around. Kaizong understood that his boss meant business and began a rapid exchange with Director Lin.

The museum was too bright, too clean, just like the whitewashed and rewritten history it tried to present, just like the version of Silicon Isle that the natives tried to show outsiders. It was infused with a false, shallow technological optimism. In this building, there was no Basel Convention, no dioxins and furans, no acid fog, no water whose lead content exceeded the safe threshold by 2,400 times, no soil whose chromium concentration exceeded the EPA limit by 1,338 times, and of course nothing about the men and women who had to drink this water and sleep on this soil.

All history is contemporary history, he recalled Chen Kaizong saying when he had interviewed him.

Scott shook his head. The voices of Director Lin and Kaizong, straining to maintain a façade of friendliness but unable to come to agreement, grew louder. If they were speaking Mandarin, perhaps he could converse with Lin using the help of translation software, but they were using the ancient Silicon Isle topolect, with eight tones and exceedingly complex tone sandhi rules. He had no choice but to rely on the special talent of his assistant, whose linguistic heritage was the main reason that the history major fresh out of Boston University had been hired.

"Tell him: if he has objections"—Scott's eyes fell on a group portrait, and he tried valiantly to pick out anyone who had appeared in the documents he had reviewed before the trip; here in this restricted-bitrate zone, he was deprived of access to remote databases, and the Chinese faces all looked the same to him—"we'll have Minister Guo speak to him directly."

Minister Guo Qidao belonged to the Provincial Department of Ecology and Environment and was slated to become the next Deputy Minister for the National Ministry of Ecology and Environment. He had most likely been the one to draw up the short list of companies to bid for the project.

A fox can sometimes invoke the name of a tiger to get things done. Another trick from *The Ignoramus's Guide to China.*

The argument ceased. Director Lin, who had assumed a posture of defeat, appeared even thinner and smaller. He rubbed his hands together. Compared to the threat of Minister Guo, he seemed to worry more about not being able to accomplish his assigned task. But Scott had left him no way out. Lin strained to put on a smile, cleared his throat, and then walked toward the exit.

"Mission accomplished. But we're going to eat first." Kaizong's wide, entitled smile was just what you'd expect from someone who had graduated from an expensive school on the East Coast.

Let's hope that we don't encounter any more dangerous dishes like the "wild lobsters," Scott thought to himself as he passed by the model of the junk. He was glad to leave this museum, freezing cold and full of falsehoods. The model junk seemed to him the perfect metaphor: a play on words was perhaps the sole remaining thread connecting the museum and this island of junk.

He put on the protective face mask from 3M, passed through the mist of condensation near the exit, and entered into the humid, bright tropical sunlight.

Instead of *baijiu*, the restaurant served beer, but the change didn't put Scott at ease. This establishment seemed to respect health and hygiene even less than the one from last night. The private suite they were in was called "the Pine Room," and the ancient air conditioner buzzed like a wasp nest that had been poked. Still, it was unable to eliminate the stench in the air. There was a large wet spot on the wall, looking like the terra incognita on some antique map. The table and chairs were relatively clean, or maybe it was just because the proprietor chose dark colors that didn't show stains.

The food was brought out quickly. Excited, Kaizong introduced each dish to Scott, explaining the ingredients and methods of preparation. Kaizong was a bit surprised that he, who had left Silicon Isle as a child of seven, could still recall those tastes and flavors. Crossing the Pacific seemed to have also carried him back across a gulf of more than a dozen years.

Scott had no appetite, especially after he learned how duck liver, pig lung, cow tongue, goose intestines, and other organ meats had been prepared. He chose plain rice porridge and soup—choices that appeared to offer the least risk of accumulated heavy metals. He restrained the impulse to pull out the field testing kit. As a result of the network-access regulations, it was impossible to connect to remote encrypted databases from here, and thus impossible to determine the composition of food, air, water, soil, and the associated risks. And of course augmented-reality technology had no use here.

Director Lin seemed to detect his anxiety. He pointed to the electric rickshaws hauling water through the streets outside: "This restaurant belongs to the Luo clan. Even the water is hauled in from Huang Village, nine kilometers away."

The Luo clan controlled 80 percent of Silicon Isle's high-end restaurants and entertainment venues. The clan's economic power was based on the largest collection of e-waste-dismantling workshops on the island, including those at Xialong Village, which they intended to visit this afternoon. The power of the Luo clan was such that they had their first pick of all waste containers passing through Kwai Tsing, and whatever was left was divided up between the other two big clans. A real-life example of the Matthew effect, the triumvirate of Luo, Chen, and Lin clans had in effect been reduced to reign by the Luo clan alone. It was even powerful enough to influence government policy.

Scott turned over Director Lin's words in his head, trying to guess at the hidden meaning. Another bit of Chinese folk wisdom came unbidden to his mind: *Once you've eaten someone's food, it's hard to raise your voice at him. Once you've accepted someone's gift, it's hard to lift your hand against him.*

He was growing more and more annoyed at these Chinese tricks, as though he had to constantly decrypt everything that was said while the encryption key shifted unpredictably with the flow and context. He decided to remain silent.

"Come, come, let's drink!" This was the best way to break an awkward silence at a meal. Director Lin lifted his foamy beer.

A few rounds later, Director Lin's face was once again bright red. After the last time, Scott was more cautious. Although the Chinese also had a proverb that translated to *in vino veritas,* it didn't seem to apply to Director Lin.

"Mr. Scott, please allow me to be frank." Director Lin clapped Scott's shoulder, his alcohol-laden breath in Scott's face. "I'm not trying to hinder your investigation and research. I have my own difficulties. But please listen to a bit of advice: this project isn't going to work out, and it's best you leave here as quickly as possible."

Kaizong finished translating and looked at Scott, a trace of annoyance in his expression.

"I totally understand. We serve different masters. Why don't you also listen to a bit of advice from me? This project is going to be a win-win for everyone. There are no downsides. Anything can be discussed. If it succeeds, it will be a model project for Southeast China. This is an important step for China's national recycling strategy. Your contribution will not be forgotten."

"Ha!" Director Lin's laughter had no mirth in it. He drained his glass. "Interesting. Americans will dump all their trash on another's doorstep and then, a few moments later, show up and say they're here to help you clean up and that it's all for your own good. Mr. Scott, what kind of national strategy would you call *that*?"

The sharp retort from Lin stunned Scott. Apparently this man was more than the cowardly bureaucrat he had imagined. He carefully considered his response, struggling to inject sincerity into his words.

"The world is changing. Recycling is an emerging industry worth hundreds of billions of dollars. Maybe it's even the way to control the fate of global manufacturing. Silicon Isle has a first-mover's advantage here. Shifting gears is much easier for you than for developed countries, and you can act without the political and legal burdens they face. What you need is technology and modern management practices to increase efficiency and reduce pollution. Right now, both Southeast Asia and West Africa are hotspots where a lot of money and companies are going in, trying to secure themselves a seat at the table. But I can guarantee that the terms offered by TerraGreen Recycling are the best. We also never neglect to give back to those who help us . . ."

Scott emphasized "give back." Images of those officials from the Philippines hinting for bribes flashed across his mind.

Director Lin did not think this American would be so direct, completely devoid of the typical empty buzzwords and insincere politeness he had come to expect. He hesitated, lifting his empty glass and setting it back down, and made a decision. "I'm glad that you're so straight with me. Then I'll put all my cards on the table, too. The issue here isn't money, but trust. The natives don't even trust the Chinese from outside the island, let alone Americans."

"But Americans aren't all the same. Just like all Chinese aren't the same. I can tell you're not like the rest." Scott now used the trick that, he knew from experience, worked everywhere on the planet.

Director Lin stared at Scott, his jaundiced eyes filled with swollen blood vessels. He looked drunk but wasn't. After a while, he harrumphed and said, "You're wrong, Scott. All Chinese *are* the same. I'm no exception."

Scott was surprised. This was the first time that Director Lin had called him "Scott" instead of "Mr. Scott." But he was even more surprised by Lin's next question.

"Do you have children? What's your hometown like?"

In Scott's limited—but not inconsiderable—experience of socializing with Chinese men, he had found that most would converse about international politics and global trends. Some would talk about business, and a few would bring up religion or hobbies. But never once had he encountered anyone who brought up his own family or asked about Scott's. They were like natural-born diplomats: holding forth about the world and concerned with the fate of all peoples, but always omitting their own private lives as fathers, sons, husbands, or brothers from conversations with him.

"I have two daughters. One is seven, the other thirteen." Scott took out his wallet and showed the creased photograph to Director Lin. "This picture is old; I never got around to changing it. I grew up in a small town in Texas. It's a bit of a ghost town now, but back when times were good it was very pretty. Have you seen the *Texas Chainsaw Massacre* films? It's a bit like that, but not so scary." Scott laughed, and Kaizong joined him.

Director Lin shook his head and returned the pictures to Scott. "When they're older they'll break many hearts. I have only a son, thirteen, in middle school."

A pause. Scott nodded, encouraging Lin to continue. Truth be told, he didn't know where the conversation was going.

"The greatest hope cherished by the people of Silicon Isle is to see their children leave this place, the farther the better. We're old and can't shift from our familiar nests, but the young are different. They're blank sheets of paper, full of potential for new pictures. This island has no hope. The air, the water, the soil, and the people have been immersed in trash for too long. Sometimes you can no longer even tell what's trash and what's not in our lives. We rely on waste to feed our families, to grow rich. But the more money we make, the worse the environment becomes. It's like we are holding on to a rope looped around our necks. The harder we pull, the less we can breathe. But if we let go, we'll fall into the bottomless pit below and drown."

Instead of translating right away, Kaizong grew excited and began to argue with Director Lin in the local topolect. Director Lin kept on shaking his head.

"This is exactly why we came here," Scott said. "My parents were just like you. They wanted me to leave home and go to a big city. But only after I'd been on my own for a while did I realize that responsibility is always there, on everyone's shoulders. You can turn your face and pretend not to see certain things, or you can face them and change them. Everything depends on what kind of person you hope to be."

What a lovely speech, suitable for a Hollywood film. Scott wasn't counting on much support from Director Lin, but right now, right here, if he could avoid making an enemy, it was as good as making a friend.

"It's too difficult." Director Lin continued to shake his head. "I've read your proposal and your bid carefully. I don't know enough to say anything about the technology, though I know that TerraGreen Recycling is a leader in recycling, and the environmental reclamation plan you came up with is attractive. However, there's a big problem: your plan requires the thousands of workshops across the island to be eliminated, and future e-waste would be sorted, dismantled, and processed by you. Do you understand what this means to *them*?"

Scott understood who *them* referred to. The Luo, Lin, and Chen clans monopolized all the e-waste recycling and processing business on Silicon Isle: a yearly processing capacity of millions of tons and an economic output measured by billions of dollars. For a large industry like that to upgrade would result in a redistribution of profits, a process that was certain to be raw and bloody.

"Our plan would create tens of thousands of new, green jobs with full benefits. And due to TerraGreen Recycling's superior technology, the processing would be far more efficient and reduce the losses currently experienced with manual dismantling and processing. Economic output would be increased by at least thirty percent. But most importantly, we will allocate special funds to help Silicon Isle in a comprehensive plan for environmental remediation. We'll return your home to its former glory: blue skies and clear water."

This was basically a recitation of the description in the proposal. Kaizong was impressed by his boss's powers of recall, especially since he couldn't even rely on his augmented-reality gear.

"I know all this." Director Lin seemed to have completely sobered up from whatever measure of drunkenness he had had and ordered a cup of strong tea. "But no one really cares. The natives don't care. They just want to squeeze as much money as they can out of whatever life is left in this place. The migrant workers don't care, either. They just want to earn enough money as quickly as possible to return to their home villages and open up a general store, or build a new house and get married. They hate this island. No one cares about the future of this place. They want to leave here and forget this period of their lives, just like the trash."

"But the government ought to care!" Scott couldn't help himself.

"The government has more important things to worry about." Director Lin took a big sip of tea. His speech was now unhurried, and the red flush had faded from his face. That polite, efficient, but fake smile was pasted back on, as though the sincere father that had spoken earlier never existed. "It's getting late. We still have to get to Xialong Village. Believe me, you won't be staying long."

There are two Silicon Isles, Scott Brandle thought as he watched the scene slowly scrolling past the window of the Land Rover.

Earlier, government officials had taken them to visit Silicon Isle Town proper. Amid the chaotic traffic, Scott had been surprised by the number of expensive cars whose drivers seemed to be always leaning on their horns: BMW, Mercedes-Benz, Bentley, Porsche . . . He thought he had even seen a ruby-red Maserati parked right across the sidewalk, with its young owner squatting next to it, enjoying seafood barbecue bought from a street vendor.

Despite the peninsula's low position on the totem pole of China's administrative regions, Silicon Isle Town was prosperous. Scott saw many boutiques specializing in luxury brands that he had only expected to see in China's largest cities. It was the fashion among the town residents to build expensive, traditional, *hiasuanhoun*-style mansions,[1] but they also liked to add in elements of European influence, giving the whole place a kind of dazzling but incongruous ersatz exoticism. A visitor

---

[1] *Hia⁷suan¹houn²* (in Mandarin "Xiashanhu," literally "downhill tiger") is a traditional house style popular in the Chaoshan (a.k.a. Teochew) region of Guangdong Province. The style is so named because it requires different parts of the house to be situated at different elevations to comply with *feng shui* principles, and the resulting form resembles a crouching tiger.

sometimes felt as though he had stumbled into a third-rate architectural fair: one house showing Mediterranean influence, the next displaying Scandinavian minimalism.

It was just like Scott's China guidebook said: these were the nouveaux riches of contemporary China. They bought the best material goods the world had to offer and used them to fill their own empty lives.

Scott didn't see any pedestrians wearing masks. He knew that prosthetic respiratory systems hadn't yet been popularized here. Silicon Isle Town was located upwind from the rest of Silicon Isle, so the air quality was at least passable, though there was a pervasive stench that made breathing difficult. It was an odor that he had once experienced in a rubber-incineration plant in the Philippines, after which he had felt like gagging for a whole week. But the people here seemed to take the smell in their stride.

The Land Rover lurched slowly through the traffic. From time to time, a three-wheeled electric rickshaw carrying drinking water would cut across the traffic, causing horns to beep and curses to ring out. But the rickshaw drivers, all speaking nonlocal topolects, simply ignored them. A ton of water, costing two yuan in Huang Village nine kilometers away, would sell for two yuan per forty-liter drum once ferried here. The natives didn't care to earn such low profits—but their big business was what caused most of Silicon Isle's surface water and groundwater to be undrinkable in the first place.

That's the price that must be paid for economic development, everyone said. It was a cliché they had learned from TV.

"We're almost at the village," Director Lin, who was seated in the front passenger seat, turned to tell Scott.[2]

"Holy—" Kaizong blurted out before he could control himself. Scott followed his gaze, pursed his lips, but said nothing. Although he had already reviewed a lot of background material on Silicon Isle's conditions,

---

[2] In China, the higher-ranked, more honored, and important passenger is seated in the back-seat of a car.

reading about something could not compare to the shock of reality staring from the other side of a glass window.

Countless workshops, little more than sheds, were packed tightly together like mahjong tiles along both sides of every street. A narrow lane was left in the middle to allow carts to bring in the trash for processing.

Metal chassis, broken displays, circuit boards, plastic components, and wires, some dismantled and some awaiting processing, were scattered everywhere like piles of manure, with laborers, all of them migrants from elsewhere in China, flitting between the piles like flies. The workers sifted through the piles and picked out valuable pieces to be placed into the ovens or acid baths for additional decomposition to extract copper and tin, as well as gold, platinum, and other precious metals. What was left over was either incinerated or scattered on the ground, creating even more trash. No one wore any protective gear.

Everything was shrouded in a leaden miasma, an amalgamation of the white mist generated by the boiling aqua regia in the acid baths and the black smoke from the unceasing burning of PVC, insulation, and circuit boards in the fields and on the shore of the river. The two contrasting colors were mixed by the sea breeze until they could no longer be distinguished, seeping into the pores of every living being.

Scott observed the men and women living among the trash—the natives called them the waste people. The women did their laundry in the black water with their bare hands, the soap bubbles forming a silver edge around floating mats of duckweed. Children played everywhere, running over the black shores, where fiberglass and the charred remains of circuit boards twinkled; jumping over the abandoned fields, where embers and ashes from burnt plastic smoldered; swimming and splashing in dark green ponds, where polyester film floated over the surface. They seemed to think this was the natural state of the world and nothing disturbed their joy. The men bared their chests to show off the cheap body films they had applied. Wearing *shanzhai* versions of augmented-reality glasses, they enjoyed a bit of rare leisure by lying on the granite banks of irrigation canals, filled with broken displays and plastic junk. These ancient canals, built hundreds of years ago to bring water to thirsty rice paddies, now shimmered with the fragmented lights of the process of dismantling the old.

"We're here. Still want to get out of the car?" Director Lin's tone was mocking, as though he were only a visitor.

"Without going into the tiger's nest, how can we retrieve the tiger cub?" Scott struggled to enunciate the proverb in heavily accented Mandarin. He put on his face mask and opened the car door.

Director Lin shook his head and reluctantly followed.

Hot, polluted air assaulted Scott, accompanied by an overwhelming stench. The mask filtered out particles and dust but was powerless against odors. For a moment, he seemed to be back in the suburbs of Manila, two years earlier, except that the smell here was ten times more concentrated. He tried to remain still, but sweat continued to ooze out of him, mixing with unknown chemicals in the air until it formed a viscous film that stuck to his skin and clothes and made taking even a single step difficult.

In front of them stood a stone gate inscribed with the characters *Xialong* in clerical script. Normally, Scott Brandle would have considered examining it for signs of its antiquity and craftsmanship, but at this moment, what flashed through his mind was the beginning of the warning carved on the gate of Hell in Dante's *Inferno*.

Per me si va ne la città dolente,
per me si va ne l'etterno dolore,
per me si va tra la perduta gente.

Scott had read these lines when he studied Italian in college; he had never thought he would need this half-forgotten skill for the rest of his life. But here, the lines seemed especially appropriate. He did his best to put out of his mind the last line of Dante's warning.

The laborers stopped what they were doing and glanced their way curiously. Most of the eyes were focused on Scott. Even though he was wearing a mask, his height, pale skin, and head of short, blond hair already betrayed him. The migrant workers had seen foreigners, of course, but they were confused as to why this well-dressed *laowai* would appear here, like some vision of Jesus of Nazareth passing through waves of heat, clouds of toxic miasma, and streets full of filth.

Then, they all smiled. The smiles spread from face to face like a chill wind, pulling up the corners of everyone's mouths.

"Be careful. There are many addicts here." Director Lin's voice was a low murmur next to Chen Kaizong's ears. Without waiting for a translation, Scott, walking at the front, suddenly stopped.

On the ground in front of him was a wriggling prosthetic arm. Whether intentional or not, the stimulus loop of the arm was left open, and the internal battery, incompletely disassembled, continued to provide power. The electricity flowed along the artificial skin to the synthetic nerves revealed at the broken end, and triggered cyclic contractions in the muscles. The five fingers of the prosthesis continuously clawed at the ground, pulling the broken forearm along like some giant, flesh-colored inchworm.

It then collided with an abandoned liquid crystal display, and the broken fingernails scrabbled against the smooth glass surface but could no longer make any progress.

A little boy ran over, picked up the prosthetic arm, and put it back down on the ground facing a different direction. His expression seemed to suggest that the arm was nothing more than a common toy car. And so this bizarre toy continued its endless journey to nowhere, apparently only to terminate when its battery ran out.

Scott squatted down. The little boy stared at his mask, without fear, without curiosity. "Where else can you find the same kind of . . . hand?" Scott asked in Mandarin. Fearing that his accent was too heavy, he also gestured with his hands.

The little boy froze for a moment, and then pointed to a work shed not too far away. Then he turned and ran off.

Scott stood up. An intense joy radiated from his eyes, as though he had discovered some secret treasure.

From outside it was easy to see that no one was in the shed, but in the middle was a heap of junked silicone products whose electronic components had all been removed. The remaining silicone had to be decomposed using special industrial processes to extract the monomers and silicone oil. The local workshops weren't equipped with the technology for this, so the heap was just waiting to be picked up by a specialized recycler.

Director Lin finished his explanation, and then added, "These days, the rich switch body parts as easily as people used to switch phones. The junked prostheses are shipped here. Most haven't been decontaminated and still contain blood and bodily fluids, which pose a lot of potential risk for public health—" He seemed to realize something and stopped himself, awkwardly changing the subject. "It's too dirty here, Mr. Scott. Why don't we go to the back of the village? That's where the workshops are most concentrated."

Kaizong gave him a knowing look. Director Lin was clearly trying to hide something. He translated what Lin said for Scott, but added his own guess. Scott smiled as though he didn't care, and continued to walk into the shed.

Suddenly, a dark shadow dashed out of the left side of the enclosed space. Scott heard a cry from Director Lin and then felt something with a rotten, fishy smell come straight at him. He ducked, turned to the side, and shoved whatever it was away with his hands.

A few low growls later, Scott saw that his assailant was a large German shepherd. The dog rolled on the ground, quickly righted itself, and prepared to attack again.

Scott raised his arms into a combat stance and focused his gaze on the creature's green, glittering eyes. His whole body was tensed and ready.

But at that moment, a silent order seemed to hit the German shepherd, and the dog lowered its eyes, tucked its tail between its legs, and ran off into the shade behind the shed.

"It's a chipped dog." Director Lin held up his phone. His chest heaved as though he had been the one attacked.

To stop burglars, the villagers liked to keep large dogs with implanted chips. Thanks to an electronically enhanced Pavlov effect, if anyone entered a designated area without sending out a predetermined signal, the chipped dog would attack relentlessly until the intruder was incapacitated. Each village had its own unique signal band, which changed often. Only a few individuals possessed the authority to have all the key frequencies. Director Lin was one of them.

"A few have been killed by the dogs, most of them radical environmental activists." Director Lin smiled. "I have to say, Mr. Scott, I didn't expect you to be so knowledgeable in the art of hand-to-hand combat."

Scott smiled back, his left hand held over his chest. The sudden surge of fear and adrenaline had caused his heart rhythm to become erratic, and he needed a moment for the tiny box implanted in his chest cavity to do its job.

Kaizong tried to hide his surprise. He could tell that Scott's quick reaction and his almost automatic defensive maneuvers were the results of long, professional training. It appeared that his boss was not just a successful business consultant. And the goal of his trip to Silicon Isle was perhaps not as simple as project research.

Scott entered the shed and stopped in front of the flesh-colored hill of prostheses. He squatted and purposefully sifted through the pile. A pungent disinfectant smell assaulted his nose. Translucent artificial cochleas, false lips, prosthetic limbs, breast implants, augmented muscles, and enlarged sexual organs bounced against each other, and the pile collapsed around him. His field of vision was filled with the pink glow of faux health, as though he were trapped in the storage locker of Jack the Ripper. Finally, he found what he was looking for.

The string of letters and numbers, SBT-VBPII32503439, was obscurely etched on the inside of a rigid, mold-cast prosthetic part that resembled half of a strange shell. Glistening with a bone-white light, the empty prosthesis apparently once contained some integrated circuits.

Scott raised this treasure in front of Director Lin's face and tossed it at him. A trembling Director Lin caught it, his face full of disgust.

"Director Lin, I'd like to ask you for a favor." Scott's voice took on a deliberate, courteous tone. "Would you help me find the person who processed this piece of trash?"

"That is not so simple. We're not like you. We don't have modern management processes and databases . . . this might take a really long time." Director Lin pondered the prosthesis. It didn't look like anything that could be attached to a body, or at least not a normal body. "What in the world is it?"

"Believe me: you don't want to know."

There was a noise behind him; Scott turned cautiously. Several laborers ran past the work shed without stopping.

Director Lin nodded thoughtfully. The peninsula was so small that there could be no secret that he wouldn't eventually discover; it was just a matter of time.

"I will do my best to find the man for you before you finish your research trip," he said meaningfully.

At that moment, Director Lin saw more people running past the shed in the same direction as the previous laborers, their expressions mixtures of excitement and fear. He stopped a young man and—because none of the workers here were natives—asked in broken Mandarin, "What happened?"

"Someone got clamped." The young man dodged out of his way and ran on.

Director Lin's face changed, and he chased after the young man. Scott and Kaizong followed. They saw a crowd forming around another work shed, everyone arguing excitedly. The three shoved their way through the crowd to the front, and all drew a sharp intake of breath.

A blood-covered man was lying on the ground, his limbs jerking uncontrollably. A broken, black robot arm's pincers were clamped around his head and neck. Through the cracks between the robotic claws, one could see that his facial features had deformed under the pressure, and bloody foam was seeping out of his orifices. He was no longer coherent, and from his throat emerged the grunts of a wounded animal. His twitching body looked like an assembly line mistake that attached a robot's head to a man's body.

"How did this happen?" Director Lin asked the crowd. The answer, as best as he could tell from the cacophonous responses, was that during the dismantling of the junked robot arm, the man had triggered the backup feedback circuits and got his head caught in the viselike grip. This man was clearly unlucky and had angered the spirits somehow. Everyone shook their heads to indicate sympathy.

Scott rushed over and gestured for Kaizong to hold the man's shoulders still to avoid damaging his spine. Then he carefully examined the robot arm: manufactured by Foster-Miller, Inc., USA, Model "Spirit Claw III" (no longer in production), six degrees of freedom, equipped with embedded microbatteries that could power its servomotors for up to thirty minutes after main power had been cut off. This particular model was a basic, semi-military model widely used for riot control, public safety, bomb squad, and other similar applications.

You're both lucky and unlucky. Scott felt rather powerless. The man was lucky because the maximum force the arm could generate was only 520 newtons. If the robot had been an industrial model, the man's head would have turned into tofu pudding long ago. The man was also unlucky because due to its use in bomb disposal, the arm was made with a special, hardened alloy. Regular tools couldn't even make a dent in it.

"Make way, make way!" The crowd parted at the noise, and two men carrying a plasma cutting torch over their shoulders came into the shed. One of them, seeing Kaizong holding the victim's shoulder, gave him a grateful look, and then glanced at Scott suspiciously.

That's useless, Scott thought. *In fact, it will make things worse.* But he said nothing and stood to the side.

The plasma cutting torch emitted a light blue arc. As the arc struck the joints of the robot claw, there was a hissing noise. As impurities were incinerated, the light shifted through different colors. The cut in the metal turned black, then red, then white. Everyone seemed to glimpse hope and held their breaths. They stood on their tiptoes but also didn't dare to come too close.

The man caught in the claw began to thrash harder, and pitiful, keening screams tore from his throat.

Metal conducts heat really well. Scott turned his head away.

The man's hair began to burn. Shining, translucent blisters appeared over his scalp, quickly burst, and blood bubbled out. The men operating the plasma cutter scrambled to stop and looked for wet rags to put out the fire. White smoke rose along with the smell of burning flesh and then dispersed among the crowd. Some held their noses; others began to vomit.

Oh dear God. Scott knew that at this point, the only solution was to connect to the Spirit Claw through the proprietary interface and issue it the commands to shut down the servomotors. But he didn't have the tools and didn't know if this robot's command-processing module was still functioning. So all he could do was to pray for the batteries to run out as soon as possible.

Kaizong and another man struggled to hold the wounded man down. Kaizong felt the body under him gradually weakening as though some unknown substance was silently draining away. The thrashing ceased. He let go. The man did not move.

The robot claw loosened with a loud bang. Everyone jumped. Then the man's crushed head drooped to the ground.

Scott gazed at the crowd in front of him, at the waste people's expressions: a combination of helplessness, numbness, fright, and excitement. He saw Director Lin's disgust and Kaizong's shock. He seemed to even see himself, a pale white face hovering incongruously among the yellow faces. What expression was on that face he could not see clearly: it was too blurry.

Scott Brandle could no longer avoid thinking of a snippet of Italian: *Lasciate ogni speranza, voi ch'entrate.*

The last line in the warning carved above the gate of Hell.

Partway through a pile of colorful but boring snapshots of daily life and commonplace scenery, Chen Kaizong's eyes lingered on a black-and-white photograph. He found it difficult to believe this was the work of a child.

The photograph had been taken near the recycling workshops, an area that the child's parents, Silicon Isle natives, must have warned him repeatedly not to enter. In front of a chaotic heap of junk, a waste person sat, holding half of a prosthetic limb. The hair and the clothes made it impossible to tell the person's gender. On the youthful face was a strange expression: he or she did not look into the camera, but instead gazed somewhere off-frame, deep in thought.

A rare, beautiful image. Kaizong closed the album of the best student photographs and looked out at the exercise grounds.

The children had been exposed to the blazing sun for two hours already. Their faces were bright red and sweat poured off their heads. Below their squinting eyes were deep shadows. Like worms, they constantly wriggled, shifting their center of gravity from foot to foot, scratching at the forehead or wiping away sweat, but they strained to minimize their movements to avoid drawing the attention of the teachers.

The principal on the dais continued to make his impassioned speech, describing how basic education would change Silicon Isle's future. Two high-powered cabinet-style air-conditioning units stood at each end of the dais, and the cold air they emitted immediately turned into white mist, drifting like clouds over the VIPs seated under the red parasols.

Enough. Kaizong leaned over and whispered in Scott's ear. Scott lifted his eyebrows and whispered back. Kaizong got up and walked over to Director Lin. More whispers. Director Lin frowned, thought for a moment, wrote something on a slip of paper, and asked an usher to hand the note to the principal.

The loudspeaker fell silent, relieving the audience from the feedback whistles caused by the principal's overanimated enunciation. The principal then hastily concluded his remarks. Everyone applauded enthusiastically, bringing an end to the honored guests' visit.

"Mr. Brandle, are you all right?" the principal asked in heavily accented English.

"I'm fine, just a bit of a headache. Maybe it's the air-conditioning. Thank you."

"What's on your itinerary for the afternoon?"

"I'm probably going to cancel everything. I have some work I need to deal with."

Kaizong understood that this last statement was intended for him. He had complained earlier—not hoping anything would come from it—that though he had been back in Silicon Isle for a whole week, he hadn't had a chance to pay a visit to any of his relatives. Though in terms of degrees of relatedness, he and the other members of the Chen clan only shared a great-great-great-great-grandfather.

So the trip to Kaizong's alma mater ended in this delicate and awkward mood.

Since the trip to Xialong Village, Kaizong had become extremely interested in his boss. Google didn't turn up anything that he hadn't already known from Scott's résumé. There was nothing suspicious. He had to settle on the guess that Scott Brandle's combat skills were learned during the two years when he was in the army, but many more mysteries about Scott bothered him.

Kaizong really was starting to get a headache. He was no longer used to the air here, the stench, the noise, and the pervasive lack of order. He couldn't understand the young men in the streets who applied polyimide OLED body film to their bared shoulders so that the electrical currents flowing through their muscles could power the colorful display of flowing text and images. In America, that kind of body film technology was generally used as a diagnostic tool for monitoring patients' bio signs. But here, it had become a part of the street culture of status display.

He couldn't explain to Scott that the character *pu* that the young men exhibited on their shoulders didn't stand for *putong*, the Mandarin word for "common," but was pronounced in the second tone in the Silicon Isle topolect and meant *fuck*.

The Silicon Isle of his memory was poor but lively and hopeful. People were friendly and helped each other. Back then, the water in the ponds was clear and the air smelled of the salty sea. On the beach one could pick shells and crabs. A dog was just a dog, and the only things that crawled on the ground were caterpillars. Today, however, everything was unfamiliar, strange, as though there were a deep gulf in his brain: on this side, reality; on the other side, memory out of reach.

Kaizong remembered what his father had said when he informed the old man that he was going back to Silicon Isle: "Yes, you should go. That's your homeland. But remember: don't get too close. You'll see more clearly that way."

He had once thought his father's words mere useless aphorisms.

Kaizong realized that the middle-aged man standing in front of him, with his high brow ridge, angular nose, and a hint of gentleness at the corners of his lips, looked surprisingly like his father, even though they were only related distantly.

Chen Xianyun, who as a young man had once been Kaizong's father's business partner, was now the Chen clan's executive director. His position in the clan was second only to the clan head, and when it came to the daily affairs of the family and the business, his word was effectively law.

Out of habit, Kaizong opened his arms, anticipating a hug, but this relative whom he did not know quite how to address had already extended a strong hand.

"Uncle Chen, I hope you're well." Awkwardly, Kaizong repositioned his arms to shake hands. "My father has often mentioned you to me, and I'm really glad I finally got to meet you."

"Ha! I trust your parents are well?"

"They are both healthy. Thank you for asking. They're thinking of coming back for a visit sometime next year."

"Good, very good. Why don't you have lunch with me? Given it's a holiday, there's lots of good things to eat."

Kaizong had long noticed the delicious smells wafting out of the kitchen. He was getting sick of eating at restaurants every day and yearned for a home-cooked meal. Gratefully, he accepted Chen Xianyun's invitation.

What he appreciated most weren't the dishes full of meat or fish, but a kind of pastry he hadn't had in years: cakes made with wild *cekêgcao*, an herb.[3] The grass was first boiled into a stock and mixed with lard and sticky rice flour into dough. Then, the dough was filled with a mixture of bean paste, glutinous rice, peanuts, shrimp, and pork. Next, heart-shaped cakes were pressed from the dough with wooden molds. Steamed on a bed of fresh bamboo or banana leaves, the finished cakes were endowed with a unique herbal fragrance. The people of Silicon Isle made them only on special occasions, such as big holidays.

Kaizong and Uncle Chen continued to talk, and before he knew it, Kaizong had already consumed three *cekêgcao* cakes, washing them

---

[3] *Ce⁶kêg⁸cao²* (scientific name: *Gnaphalium affine*) is a plant used in traditional Chinese medicine and also appears in the cuisine of many East Asian cultures, typically as flavoring in sweet cakes.

down with cups of *ganghu* tea.[4] Thanks to the digestive aid from the tea, the greasy cakes didn't feel heavy in Kaizong's stomach.

Uncle Chen seemed in very good spirits as well and asked Kaizong a series of questions about life abroad. He nodded from time to time at Kaizong's answers but never expressed any opinion.

Gradually, Kaizong realized that this clan leader was deliberately avoiding the subject of TerraGreen Recycling's plans for Silicon Isle. Kaizong became curious: he very much wanted to know what this powerful clan, connected to him by blood, thought about the project.

"Uncle Chen—" He hesitated and chose his words carefully. "—I'm very interested in your opinion concerning the proposed recycling industrial park. . . ."

Anticipating the question, Chen Xianyun smiled. He put down his chopsticks and asked a question of his own.

"Kaizong, you study history, right? Can you help me analyze this puzzle: it's almost the middle of the twenty-first century, and yet, why have we maintained this primitive system of clans?"

Kaizong was at a loss. He had read about the clan system of his home in books, of course, but he had never experienced life in the clans: a collective life that was born thousands of years ago in patrilineal societies; rooted in an economy of family farms; based upon a shared family name, shared ancestors, shared clan shrine, and even shared property; regulated by clan laws; and reinforced through all the members worshiping together and being buried together.

"I'm guessing"—he scrambled for an answer—"that it's because the clan system has evolved to adapt to the modern world. The contemporary clan is more like a joint-stock company. All the members are shareholders, and they participate in the profits of the whole in accordance with

---

[4] *Gang¹hu¹* (or *gongfu* in Mandarin) tea is a technique for preparing tea that originated in the Song dynasty (AD 960–1279) and is especially popular in the Chaoshan region of China. The complicated technique imposes strict requirements on every aspect of tea preparation, such as the type of water, the strength of the fire, the selection of cups and teapot, method of steeping and pouring, etc. "*Gongfu*" here does not refer to the martial arts technique, but to the skill and care taken in the process.

their positions. All clan members follow the same set of internal regulations and possess the same company culture. Of course, since all members share the same family name and the same ancestors, there's more of a sense of identity with the joint enterprise, which makes management easier." Kaizong poured another cup of tea for Uncle Chen.

"Very well said. People can tell right away that you've studied abroad. But you haven't touched upon the most key point." Chen Xianyun put his index and middle fingers together, curled them slightly, and tapped the tabletop—a gesture indicating thanks.

"It's about a sense of security," Uncle Chen continued. "If a man is robbed or beaten up, a company employing him has no obligations to help him. Could he seek the aid of the law? If he's lucky, maybe it will work. But when all the legitimate paths are ineffectual, the only people he can count on are the people in his clan.

"Or you can look at the problem another way: as long as you belong to a powerful clan, anyone who wants to mess with you must understand that the cost for doing so may far exceed the gains."

I guess all those rumors about how the people of Silicon Isle behave like gangsters are not without basis, Kaizong thought. He wanted to argue, though. "But we now live in a society based on the rule of law."

"Haha!" Uncle Chen's laugh was gentle, and he looked at the young man with pity and affection. "Remember, from the beginning of history till now, we have had only one society: a society based on the law of the jungle."

Kaizong wanted to bring up more evidence for his position, but he knew, deep down, that Uncle Chen had a better handle on the truth. It wasn't a truth written down in books, but something rooted deeply in the soil, tested by blood and fire.

"Getting back to your question," Uncle Chen said. "What I think about the proposal isn't very important. What matters is how *everyone* feels. If everyone feels the same way, then whatever I think doesn't matter." He stood up and patted Kaizong on the shoulders. "I want to remind you: you're one of us. As long as you stay within the Chen clan's territory, I can guarantee you'll be safe. But when you go over to the Luo clan's territory, be very careful.

"Why don't you relax a bit? This evening I'll bring you to see the celebrations for the Ghost Festival. It will be a lot of fun!"

Kaizong, now deep in thought, didn't respond to the invitation.

He was remembering a scene from two years ago.

On the campus of Boston University, next to the Charles River, he was in a class on world history taught by Professor Toby Jameson. The old man, with his head of white hair that made him look like Colonel Sanders, asked, "Who can give me an example of globalization?"

The young man he called on stuttered for a while before picking up a half-eaten hamburger and said, "Mickey D's."

The whole class laughed.

"Very good," said Professor Jameson. "That answer is better than you might realize.

"This isn't just a cliché from a list: McDonald's, Nike, Hollywood films, Android phones . . . No, when you walk into a McDonald's and order a meal for five ninety-five, what do you get? Potatoes from the Andes, corn from Mexico, black pepper from India, coffee from Ethiopia, chicken from China, and of course, America's unique contribution: Coca-Cola.

"Now do you understand what I'm getting at? Globalization is not something new. It's a trend that has been going on for hundreds, thousands of years. You can see it through the Age of Exploration, through commerce, through writing and religion, through insects, migratory birds and wind, even through bacteria and viruses. But the problem is that we've never achieved consensus, never tried to build a fair system so that everyone would benefit. Instead, we've engaged in a perpetual cycle of looting, exploitation, and forceful extraction: from the Amazon, from Africa, from Southeast Asia, the Middle East, Antarctica, even outer space.

"In this age of globalization, there are no permanent winners. Whatever you've obtained, you'll lose someday, and you'll have to pay it back with interest."

The professor struck the podium loudly, like a judge slamming down his gavel. "Class dismissed."

Kaizong returned to the present. The reality was that TerraGreen Recycling wanted to present the inhabitants of this peninsula with a technological solution to counteract the negative effects of globalization, to save them from this living hell. But the answer the residents gave was: "No, we'd rather live with trash and waste."

Fucking crazy.

His frustration didn't come from the project alone. Kaizong was well aware of the idealized expectations he had built up for this trip home.

For the longest time, there was a gap in Kaizong's memory that covered the transition between his childhood in Silicon Isle and going to school in America. It was as if two film reels had been forcefully edited together in a montage, consciously or otherwise, jumping over the time in between.

It was an intense feeling of confusion. He was a child uprooted from his familiar environment, away from his family and friends, and deposited unceremoniously into a strange world, where the language of his childhood was replaced with incomprehensible, odd syllables, where all he could see was strangers of other races who looked different from himself. He couldn't read, couldn't write, couldn't sleep well, couldn't eat well—even his sense of time and place became disrupted, and he would need almost twenty minutes after waking up to remember where he was. During that half year, Kaizong—now called "Caesar"—followed his parents as they moved from city to city in search of a place to settle down. He had neither the opportunity nor the courage to converse with strangers.

He even stopped speaking with his parents.

The anxiety didn't let up until he was in college, but he continued to feel not fully integrated into the American society around him. He was unlike the ABCs—the American-born Chinese—and he was also unlike the Chinese students who had completed high school in China before coming to America for college. No matter how hard he worked, no matter how he excelled, an invisible wall divided him from the entire world. Kaizong/Caesar felt himself a creature caught in the space between parallel worlds, unable to find a place where he belonged. In the end, he chose to major in history, a world separated from reality by time; he felt safer there.

When he saw the job listing offered by TerraGreen Recycling, he had clicked "Apply" without any hesitation, compelled by a desire he had long suppressed. He yearned to return to his home, to return to the world where he had once belonged, to speak his own topolect, to eat the food of his childhood, to see the familiar land and sea. He believed that he could use his intellect and knowledge to introduce Terra-Green Recycling's superior technology and management experience, and make his contribution to the betterment of his homeland. He believed that the effort would allow him to feel that sense of belonging, to recover that sense of being present in the world, and even, he hoped, to repair the growing estrangement between himself and his parents.

But now, Kaizong understood that what he yearned for wasn't his homeland, but his childhood.

Today, the fifteenth day of the seventh month on the lunar calendar, was the traditional Ghost Festival. The folk holiday was also known to Daoists as Zhongyuan and to Buddhists as Yulan.

Whatever the name, this was the day on which ghosts who had suffered all year in hell were allowed to return to the living world for a brief respite. It was their only chance to enjoy real food the whole year. The living were supposed to prepare all flavors of delicious snacks, ghost money, and joss sticks as offerings to the ghosts. The idea was to build karma, to give relief to lonely ghosts who had no family to care for them, and to commemorate one's ancestors and keep alive the family's memories.

"It's a bit like the American Halloween, I imagine," said Uncle Chen to Kaizong.

In the square in front of the Chen clan shrine, the townspeople had constructed an altar more than a dozen meters high. On top of the altar was a two-meter-tall statue of the Ghost King, the main deity presiding over the festival, intended to intimidate unfriendly spirits and ghosts. In front of the altar was the offering table, filled with neatly stacked piles of fruits, meats, ghost money, gold and silver bullion made of paper, and other offerings provided by all the families. Smoke from giant, two-meter-tall joss sticks lingered and covered everything in a thick fog. Before the offering table stood three papier-mâché artificial mountains decorated with dough sculptures of the Buddha's hands, as well as various Buddhist mantras concerning the suffering of all and the relief brought by the Buddha.

All the temporary buildings were painted in bright colors and decorated with intricate, abstract patterns modeled on flowing clouds, roiling waves, windswept grass. Everything gave off the air of celebratory excitement—the exact opposite of the solemnity that one might have expected for a festival to commemorate ghosts and ancestors.

Through the streets and alleyways, through the purple haze of incense smoke, the noisy crowd converged on the fluttering dragon flags by the altar. Men and women carried children on their backs and held offerings in their hands. Next to the altar, folk opera troupes enacted Buddhist stories celebrating dutiful children, while street acrobats performed their tricks, engineers adjusted and applied body films, and children gathered in front of the booths of various snack vendors laying out their tempting wares.

No, this is nothing like Halloween, Kaizong thought. *It's more like . . . Mardi Gras.* But he kept the thought to himself. He seemed to be seeing double, with the scene in front of his eyes layered over his memories from childhood—no, that wasn't quite right. It wasn't the sight, but the *smell,* the pungent fragrance of incense, that had immediately transported Kaizong back to those long-ago years at the beginning of the twenty-first century.

He seemed to be again with his dead grandmother. She took him by the hand and squeezed through the dense crowd—raising the lit joss sticks high overhead the whole time—until they had made their way before the offering table. There, she knelt, kowtowed three times, and added their offering to the table. Then she closed her eyes and continued to mutter, praying for ancestors and dead loved ones to not suffer after death.

Kaizong's eyes were wet, even though he had never believed in the existence of a world after death.

"We used to hold the festival after it was dark. There would be lights hung everywhere, and it was beautiful." Uncle Chen, the "executive director" of the clan, had to greet an endless stream of clan members as they passed by. But he continued to act as tour guide for Kaizong. "And then, one year, the electric lines overheated and started a fire. So they moved the celebrations to during the day."

Uncle Chen picked up a piece of paper from the ground—a ghost-money bill—and handed it to Kaizong, laughing. "I guess inflation is pretty bad in hell these days. Look at how many zeros are after the one on there!"

Kaizong noticed that a few men were transporting the piles of ghost money, including the paper gold and silver bullion, from the offering table onto carts and hauling them away. "Are they dragging the money away to burn somewhere else?"

"You're thinking of the old custom. In the past, every family would burn the paper offering in a small furnace in front of their home, but now that's been declared a source of pollution. So now they just take all the paper directly back to the factory to be pulped and recycled. It's all about environmental protection, like you were talking about."

Kaizong examined the ghost money more closely: it was imprinted with a serial number and a manufacturing date, including a web address.

"What's the point of the URL?"

"Oh, you can go to the site to do banking for the afterlife. You can open accounts and buy hell money for dead relatives: coins, bullion, and credit cards are all in use over there. Money deposited in the accounts can be used by the dead for any product, housing, or service available in the afterlife—and, of course, to pay all kinds of taxes over there, too."

The Sims, Afterworld Edition. Kaizong wanted to laugh. Traditions that had supposedly been unchanged for hundreds, thousands of years were finally, gradually fading in the face of science and technology. "But why bother paying for this? It's so easy to counterfeit."

Uncle Chen surveyed the scene, filled with incense and the bustling crowd, and his thoughts seemed to be already on distant shores. Slowly, solemnly, he replied, "As long as you really believe that the other world exists, believe that your dead loved ones are living there, and that it's possible to do something to let them know that you're thinking of them—then it's all real."

Kaizong's father had told him that Uncle Chen's wife had died from cancer the year before last. Before she died, she had been in a lot of pain and begged her husband to take her off life support so that she could suffer less. However, Uncle Chen just couldn't do it. During her last moments, she—so ravaged by disease that she'd barely looked human by then—held his hand and said, "I don't blame you. Don't be afraid. I'll wait for you over there." Uncle Chen had then broken down and sobbed inconsolably. He regretted not obeying his wife's instructions. Far more frightening than death itself was to lose dignity before death.

Thereafter, he implemented periodic physical examinations within the territory controlled by the Chen clan. The benefit applied not just to natives of Silicon Isle, but also the migrant waste-processing workers.

Kaizong knew that there was data showing that the incidence of respiratory diseases, kidney stones, and blood disorders among inhabitants of Silicon Isle was about five to eight times higher than in surrounding areas. In addition, the population produced an abnormally high number of cases of cancer. In one village, every single family had at least one member who suffered from terminal cancer.

Strange fish filled with cancerous tumors had been pulled out of many polluted fishing ponds. The number of stillbirths refused to go down, and rumors spoke of a migrant woman who gave birth to a dead baby whose entire body was dark green and gave off a metallic stink. Elders said that Silicon Isle was already a place of evil.

Kaizong watched Uncle Chen's solemn expression; watched the young people taking photographs and recordings of the proceedings so that the files could be sent to the email addresses of dead relatives; watched the silent, praying faces, childish or lined, flickering in the flames from the candles and burning incense—and something deep in him was moved.

Perhaps there would come a day when everything he was looking at would be replaced by virtual reality, by simulation, by technology, but what couldn't be replaced was how people longed for those they loved. They needed some ceremony, some platform, some way to cross the border between life and death, to connect the past to the present, to shape the formless memories and longing into objects, acts, or ritualized performances so that the feelings that had been numbed by the passage of time might be reawakened, so that the pain of loss, once heartbreaking and bone-weary, could be recalled along with the endless memories that followed.

History is the process through which events are bleached of their emotional color. Kaizong finally realized why he had chosen to study history. Perhaps the experience of continuously migrating from city to city as a child had made him extra cautious with his empathy. He habitually held himself at a distance—whether it was his family, his school, any organization or interpersonal relationship. It was easy for him to achieve true objectivity, a desirable trait in a historian.

However, from that moment, Kaizong began to understand the impact and weight of the phrase "one of us."

One face among the crowd attracted his attention: filled with fear, it contrasted sharply against the crowd of peaceful, thoughtful faces. The features were slender and youthful, but it was impossible to tell the owner's gender based on the hairstyle and clothing. The person was trying to blend into the prayerful mood of the crowd, but that pair of alert eyes, constantly looking back over the shoulder, threw the face into even sharper relief, much the way a stone tossed into a placid lake would become the center of ripples over a blurry background.

One thing was certain: this was not a native of Silicon Isle. Even though he or she was making an effort at a native disguise, the facial features and minor details in the clothing gave him or her away.

For some unknown reason, Kaizong experienced a sense of recognition. He had no explanation for the odd impression of familiarity; the topographical features of that face activated some pattern-recognition module in the right fusiform gyrus of his brain, which then began to secrete neurotransmitters that led to an elevated heart rate.

He followed the gaze of the darting eyes and discovered several young native gang members searching through the crowd. Their getup was eye-catching: skintight, white Lycra vests stitched with phosphorescent patterns on the back that lit up like mini Christmas trees as they walked; loose, baggy, bright-colored sweatpants and running shoes; uniform crew cuts into which complex patterns were shaved with specialized razors; limbs and faces bedecked with metallic piercings; and, of course, the sine qua non of gang culture—various bits of glittering body film showing gang signs and names.

Kaizong had already been warned many times to stay away from men like these. Behind them lay a complex web of power that he could not hope to begin to untangle.

One of the gang suddenly turned around as though he had seen something. His lips curled, baring his teeth in a frightening mockery of a smile. At the moment the stud in his upper lip connected with his nose ring, the body film applied over his shoulders lit up with the image of a brightly burning flame. He shouted something and the two others turned to look in the same direction. The three of them began to slowly make their way through the crowd, their expressions the same as those on hunters sizing up prey that had fallen into their trap and devising new techniques for torture.

Kaizong cursed under his breath. He turned around and saw that their prey was actually staring at him. Those gentle eyes were filled with fear, desperation, and a silent entreaty. His heart skipped a beat as he finally realized why the face seemed so familiar: it was the same face that had featured so prominently in the award-winning photo he had seen in the album from his old elementary school.

The prey shoved through the crowd and escaped into a narrow pedestrian lane behind the clan shrine. The young gang members went in right after, hot in pursuit.

If this were back in the U.S., Kaizong would have stayed put and avoided unnecessary trouble because he knew someone was certain to call the police. But here, on Silicon Isle, he wasn't sure if the scene that had just played out was so much a part of daily life that most of the bystanders seemed unmoved. Kaizong gazed in the direction where the gang members had vanished; his hands clenched into tight fists, relaxed, and clenched again.

"Uncle Chen, please wait a moment here. I'll be right back."

The sides of the narrow lane were lined with vendors selling votive candles and joss sticks. The pungent smell from all the incense was overwhelming. Above Kaizong's head was a narrow sliver of slate-gray sky. The lane was filled with festivalgoers, but Kaizong saw no signs of the gang. He asked several passersby and none admitted to seeing anything.

In the end, it was an old woman selling fried spring rolls who, after much thinking, timidly pointed to an inconspicuous shop to the side.

Kaizong looked closer and realized that between the shop and the store next to it was a narrow alley about the width of a man's torso. It was very well disguised.

The inside of the dark alley resembled a sewer, and the rotting effluvium made him gag. He was reminded of the Los Angeles from *Predator 2*, except that this place was ten times dirtier. He thought about calling the police but immediately decided against it.

A scream up ahead made his heart seize up. He hurried, trying to think of a way to deal with the gang members. As a history major, his experience in street fights was sadly lacking.

He was finally sure that the prey the gang were after was a girl. She had been pushed down into a pool of dirty water. A few surprised rats ran away along the wall. She labored to catch her breath, but she did not cry, and also did not speak.

The man with the flame flashing over his shoulders said something to her, and then kicked her hard in the head. Another man unzipped his pants and began to piss on her.

"Stop!" Kaizong had run out of time to think of a plan.

The gang stared at this well-dressed newcomer, uncertain what he was about.

"Any of you know this jackass?" Flame-Man ignored Kaizong and asked his companions.

"He's not a native . . . but, fuck, he doesn't sound like he's from elsewhere either," the last of the three men answered. Kaizong suspected that the man was using augmented-reality equipment to check him out, but the man wasn't wearing glasses, and he certainly didn't seem like the type who could afford to have retina implants either.

"Who *I* am is not very important—as long as you know who Director Lin Yiyu is."

Everyone paused for a moment after hearing Director Lin's name. But Kaizong's happiness lasted only about three seconds.

"*Pu!* I know this motherfucker. He's that fake foreigner, the one who wants to build the factory!" The man whose fly was still unzipped shouted.

Kaizong was shocked. He knew that the local news had devoted a lot of space to cover Scott Brandle's mission, but he had never imagined that street gang members would recognize him. *The price of fame.*

"Oh? No wonder he can speak our topolect so well. Trying to drag out Director Lin to scare us, eh? Ha, now that we know who you are, do you know who *we* are, *sengmukzai*[5]?" Flame-Man mocked him with a term that roughly meant "college boy." The three moved to surround Kaizong, cutting off his retreat.

Kaizong tensed his body and struggled to recall the few sessions of taekwondo he had taken in college. Alas, he had skipped too many classes and could recall only a few useless stances. He held both of his fists up and stared at his opponents with as much fierceness as he could

[5] With full tone marks: *seng²muk⁶zai².*

muster, hoping to create the impression of being willing to fight to the death.

The men pressed closer, closer, and stopped. One even took a few steps back.

It's working? Before Kaizong could react, a heavy hand reassuringly clapped him on the shoulder from behind.

"Knifeboy, you've grown bold. You dare to piss in Chen clan's territory now?" It was Chen Xianyun—Uncle Chen. Behind him were a few other men with equally fierce expressions.

"Ah, Boss Chen! I apologize. But the person we're after was requested by Boss Luo himself. I'm just following orders." Flame-Man, or Knifeboy, nodded and softened his tone. Opened-Fly hurried to zip up his pants, but halfway up, the zipper caught on something, and the man yelped in pain.

"I don't give a damn who wants this person. Not today. Not here." Chen Xianyun's words were imbued with a force that left no room for bargaining.

"Of course, of course! Whatever Boss Chen wants." Knifeboy extinguished the flame over his shoulders. He spat angrily and turned to leave with his two followers. As he was about halfway down the alley, he tossed back a parting shot. "I had no idea that the Chen clan shrine is used to collect garbage. No wonder I could smell the stink from two blocks away."

"*Pu!*" one of Uncle Chen's men cursed as the character for "Chen" flickered to life in blue over his shoulders. He was about to go after Knifeboy and his gang but Uncle Chen restrained him.

"The Chen clan reminds me of the moon on the thirtieth day of the lunar month—dim and fading, haha . . ." Knifeboy's shrill laughter gradually faded into the darkness at the end of the alley.

"Uncle Chen, how did you know I was here?" Kaizong finally dared to relax, and his whole body felt like it was about to collapse.

"Kaizong, I've lived all my life here. How could whatever you noticed escape my attention?"

Kaizong walked over to the girl still slumped in the pool of dirty water. He cradled her and tried to awaken her gently. The girl's eyes snapped open, and she pushed him away and curled herself into a ball next to the base of the wall, trembling all over. Her whole body was soaked in dirty water, like a bag of kitchen trash.

"It's all right, all right." Kaizong switched to Mandarin to reduce the girl's fear. "What's your name? Where do you live? We'll take you home."

It took a while for the girl to recover her wits. When she was finally sure that she was no longer in danger, she answered, "I'm called Mimi, and I live in Nansha Village."

"That's in the Luo clan's territory," Chen Xianyun added in a low whisper. Then he asked, "Why were they after you? Did you steal something?"

"No!" Mimi exploded in anger. "I've done nothing! But today was the festival, so I wanted to come out . . . and take a peek at all this excitement. They were after me the whole way, and so I kept on running, until I got here—"

"Those mad dogs from the Luo clan have gotten more and more brazen." Since Xianyun couldn't detect any signs of lying in her account, he sighed and gave the order to his men, "Take her back to her village. But be careful not to let anyone from the Luo clan see her."

"No!" Kaizong stood up. He was amazed by his own intensity. "Taking her back would be like sending a lamb back to the tiger."

"She's a waste worker who belongs to the Luo clan—" Xianyun looked away, unable to meet the heated gaze of his nephew.

"The waste people who work for the Luo clan are still people! Uncle, this, of all days, is not a day on which we can do something we'll regret. They're all watching." Kaizong pointed upward. He knew that the men of his uncle's generation believed in ghosts, spirits, karma, and fate. It was more effective to talk about retribution in the next life than to give a lecture on moral philosophy.

Xianyun pondered the dilemma. After a while, he finally ordered his men to accompany Mimi back to her place, pick up some necessities, and then to bring her back and settle her in one of the Chen clan workshops. "I hope that Knifeboy was only claiming to be following

Luo Jincheng's orders while indulging in his own brand of craziness. Otherwise . . ."

Seeing the anxiety on his uncle's face, Kaizong realized that the matter was far from over. He began to understand the complexities behind the earlier discussion about "a sense of security." The clans were like independent fiefdoms who made the rules within their own territories. For the Luo clan, a waste girl wasn't a person, but more akin to a sheep, a farming implement, a bag of seeds. If a waste person belonging to the Luo clan were settled within the Chen clan's territories as a result of intervention by a Chen, then the Luos would consider the act an insult and betrayal. And Kaizong, who was responsible for Mimi's betrayal, would be viewed as a thief who was deliberately provoking a fight.

Meanwhile, Mimi was completely baffled by the conversation that mixed Mandarin with the local topolect. It took Kaizong some time to explain to her what they had discussed and decided. Once she understood, she managed to squeeze out a "thank you" with difficulty.

It was getting late. The square in front of the Chen clan shrine was in a state of disarray: the altar, half disassembled, stood in the setting sun like a skeleton; the statue of the Ghost King, a hard plastic shell, lay on the ground with an enigmatic smile on his face; the offering table had already been taken away, but some votive candles and joss sticks remained on the ground, along with a scattering of ghost money mixed with trampled vegetables and fruits; the dragon flags fluttered in the purple breeze; the lonely spirits and hungry ghosts had all eaten their fill and left; vendors counted their money and gave away whatever food they couldn't sell to the chipped dogs, who ate with total concentration, wagging their tails rapidly and mechanically.

Everything would be repeated the same time next year.

"Do you really think that the lives of the waste people are worth less than the lives of the natives?" Kaizong asked his uncle. Mimi's face flashed in front of his eyes like an afterimage. Something in that face had pierced his retina and inscribed itself indelibly into his memory.

Chen Xianyun's shadow was stretched long by the sun. It crossed the square—now bathed in a coppery light and inlaid with glittering golden flickers from the trash left behind. He did not answer his nephew.

Kaizong recalled another alumnus of Boston University, a doctor of systematic theology who had graduated in 1955, who had once spoken of a dream that moved everyone.

That dream remained unfulfilled.

3

In Silicon Isle, even the trash wasn't as simple as people thought. After the boxes full of trash were opened but before processing, those objects that were still in good shape were supposed to be picked out, repaired, and then sold on the secondhand-goods market, but a few pieces always escaped notice. Sharp-eyed waste people spotted them and secreted them away like treasures. Mimi once saw Brother Wen—all the girls called him that because he acted like everyone's elder brother—cut out a silicone component from a junked Japanese adult doll and furtively hide it under his clothes; the square wound he left behind between the legs of the artificial woman revealed a mess of wires and elaborate, fine tubes, as though the body had been abandoned on the sere lawn after a failed operation, and the surgeons didn't even bother to suture up the incision.

Mimi didn't ask why Brother Wen had done that; she was eighteen and understood the facts of life. She listened to her mother and kept her hair cut to a safe length and endeavored to wear loose-fitting clothing that disguised the curves of her body—she had no wish to one day find herself abandoned on the lawn like that doll.

Brother Wen, who was also from her part of the country, had come here a year before her. He didn't appear to work at all, but he earned more than anyone else. Even the natives of Silicon Isle seemed to respect him. He didn't strut around and get into fights like the local hooligans; instead, he acted just like his name—*wen* was the character for "gentle." Though he might appear delicate and mild-mannered, all he had to do was to say the word, and hundreds of waste people from home villages across the country would rally around him.

Half a year earlier, he had successfully organized several riots to fight for better working conditions and benefits for the workers. Of course, the bosses were used to firing unruly workers en masse and replacing them with new hires, but Brother Wen cleverly organized his protests on the eve of government inspections. The overseers, terrified of getting in trouble with the officials, had to give in to his demands.

Brother Wen's reputation soared as a result of these exploits, but rumors began to spread that the bosses were plotting to get rid of him. Just as everyone was getting concerned about his safety, he went to see Director Lin Yiyu voluntarily, and somehow convinced Lin to invite him as well as the heads of the three clans of Silicon Isle to sit down together for dim sum. After that, the rumors of hit men being hired against Brother Wen ceased. Indeed, Wen seemed to transform into a union representative of sorts for the waste people. Whenever the workers were dissatisfied or needed something, they asked him to negotiate with the bosses, and usually he managed to emerge with a solution that made both sides happy. Still, he continued to live in his run-down shack and spent his days picking strange and unusual components out of the trash, adding them to the collection in front of his shack, and tinkering with them as though he were some kind of folk inventor living on a garbage heap.

Brother Wen was a mystery to Mimi. Although they spoke the same topolect, Mimi always felt that he didn't truly say what was on his mind.

"You remind me of Ah Hui, my little sister," Brother Wen would tell her, patting her gently on her head, but when Mimi asked about her, he always changed the topic while his eyes looked elsewhere, adding to his sense of mystery.

Starting at an early age, Mimi had been used to doing everything by herself, but she envied other children who had older siblings to take care of them. Brother Wen's solicitousness seemed to make a part of her wish come true, but there was a voice inside her that warned her, *There's an inexplicable sense of danger about this man. Stay vigilant!*

About a month ago, Brother Wen had shown a bizarre device to Mimi.

At the time, Mimi and a few other young women were goofing around, chasing each other with prosthetic limbs. When they saw Brother Wen approach, the laughter ceased and they stood still respectfully. Wen called a few of the women over and compared whatever he was holding in his hand with their heads, and then shook his head.

"Brother Wen, what are you holding?" Lanlan, who was from Hunan and slept in the same shack as Mimi, asked.

Wen shook his head. "I don't know either."

"Then give it to us!" The young women giggled and shoved each other playfully. "We'll wear it."

Wen grinned. "Maybe your heads are too big and it won't fit!" He tossed the helmetlike object to the women. They oohed and ahhed over it, as though admiring an intricate crown.

"Brother Wen, I'm not sure that's meant for human heads," Mimi said. The "crown" was bowl-shaped and could probably cover the back of the head like a helmet, but there was a prominent ridge down the middle with a corresponding depression on the inside, making it impossible for the object to fit neatly onto any head. The inside bore signs of damage from some part having been forcefully removed, and there were yellow stains from some unknown liquid.

Wen patted his own head. "Mimi, you really are just like my real sister. Got a good head on your shoulders."

"Not only is she clever, she's also the most elegant of us. I bet the crown will fit her." The joking women suddenly reached a consensus and the helmet was placed on Mimi's head.

Her head was still too big for the device, and there was a big gap between her skull and the curved inner surface. Before Brother Wen could stop the joke from going too far, one of the women pushed down hard. With a loud crack, Mimi felt something cold and sharp pierce the skin right under her occipital bone.

She screamed, removed the "crown," and tossed it on the ground.

"What have you done!?" Brother Wen yelled. The women, scared at the accident they had caused, scattered.

"I'm bleeding!" Mimi felt the sticky, oozing wound on the back of her neck.

"Thank goodness it's not a big wound." Brother Wen took a disinfectant wipe out of his pocket and pressed it against her wound. The bleeding was stanched shortly.

Mimi sat on a garbage heap and fiddled with a broken prosthesis. As Brother Wen looked at her, his gaze full of worry, a thought abruptly crossed her mind: perhaps everything Brother Wen did was only superficially for the benefit of the waste people; in reality, all he cared about was satisfying some secret craving. She was surprised that she had come up with such an idea: it was as though she had only seen shadows and reflections of people but never thought about the kinds of souls that lay hidden beneath their faces.

Souls. Mimi pondered the word. She had only heard it in clichéd song lyrics, but had no direct experience with it: a formless, invisible thing that nonetheless existed for certain. If she could see souls, what would they look like? Like shells scattered on a beach? Like the clouds in the sky? Surely different people possessed souls of different colors, shapes, and textures.

Entranced by her own thoughts, Mimi didn't realize that not too far away, a 35 mm Leica lens had captured her image.

"Hey, kid, what are you doing?" Brother Wen yelled.

The boy was a native dressed in a school uniform. The children of the waste people could not afford the tuition of real schools and could only attend the mobile schools organized by volunteers. They had to share textbooks, and school uniforms existed only in dreams. The camera appeared comically large in the boy's small hands. He knew he didn't belong here and remained rooted in place, terrified and mute.

"Do you think you can just take pictures around here as you please? I hope you're prepared to pay."

"I don't . . . don't have any money. My dad . . ."

"I know your daddy is rich. When he finds out you snuck your way in here, he's going to give you such a spanking." Wen walked over with his helmet and forced a kind-seeming smile onto his face. "I'll make a deal with you. If you help me by putting this helmet on, I'll call it even between us. Does that sound good?"

"Brother Wen!" Mimi wanted to say more but Wen turned around and gestured for her to shush.

The boy looked at the helmet and thought for a while, then nodded.

Mimi turned away until she heard the familiar *crack,* followed by the scream and loud sobs. She closed her eyes, took a deep breath, counted to three, then opened her eyes and walked to the boy. She helped him remove the helmet and cleaned his wound. The skin below his occipital bone was punctured by a pin-sized hole, and blood was oozing out.

"It's all right. It's okay." She strained to not look at Wen, because she was afraid that she wouldn't be able to keep the fury out of her eyes. "You're a good boy. Get home as soon as you can."

Mimi gave the boy a kiss on his forehead. When she was little, her mother did this whenever she fell or tripped, as though the gesture would help relieve the pain—and it worked. She gave the boy another kiss. The child lifted his head, and his eyes gazed at her gratefully out of a muddy and tearstained face. Then he dashed away as though running for his life, and his tiny figure vanished beyond the edge of the dusty road.

"What's the big deal? He's just some native brat." Brother Wen raised his voice. "Have you forgotten how they treat us? Or how they treat our children? I'm doing this for you. What if that helmet—"

"But none of that is his fault," Mimi muttered, and then headed for her shack.

"A day of reckoning is coming, remember." Brother Wen's voice followed her for a long time. "It's coming."

———

The day before the Ghost Festival, a month after the incident with the helmet and the boy, in the Luo territory—

The face of the *lohsingpua*[6]—a local witch of Silicon Isle—appeared especially hideous in the light of the green-glowing film applied to her forehead: her eyes seemed to be two bottomless dry wells under the shadow cast by her brow bone, and no light reflected from her irises. Accompanied by an electronic prayer machine, she muttered an incomprehensible incantation in the slow rhythm of some ancient chant like a blind beast. As she chanted, she sprinkled a medicinal potion made from a dozen herbs mixed with safflower oil—including Japanese bloodgrass, *siêngcao* grass,[7] peach leaves, and Chinese fir—at all corners of the room with a pomegranate branch.

Drops of the holy oil meant to exorcise evil spirits also fell on the unconscious body lying in the middle of the room. Crystal globules covered the boy's pale face like teardrops that hadn't been wiped away.

Luo Jincheng watched the scene uneasily, but he had run out of better choices. The specialists had diagnosed his young son, Luo Zixin, with a rare form of viral meningitis, and the virus isolated from the cerebrospinal fluid could not be identified. Although the boy's intracranial pressure was stable for the moment, he remained in a deep coma, and his electroencephalogram was diffuse and slow. The doctors explained that the boy's brain was like a computer in sleep mode—although the status indicators showed no abnormalities, cortical activity was being suppressed, as though his brain-computer was waiting for some command to wake up.

When a problem can't be resolved by the methods of this world, the elders used to say, *it's best to hand it over to gods and spirits.*

The *lohsingpua* had said that little Zixin had come in contact with

———

[6] With full tone marks: *loh⁴sing⁷pua⁶*.

[7] *Siêng¹cao²* (*Mesona chinensis*), a member of the mint family, is best known in the West as the main ingredient of grass jelly.

something unclean. If the boy had clashed with some ghost, then the boy's soul could be lost due to fright. To recover, a ceremony to "collect the soul" had to be held.

Luo Jincheng listened to the witch's hypnotic chant and seemed to return to the scene of the exorcism he had witnessed as a child. Viewed in retrospect, the ritual had resembled the mediation of some economic dispute that crossed the border between the worlds of the living and the dead. Like in the mundane world of men, most problems could be solved with money. After the medium named the price demanded by the ghosts, the relatives of the afflicted collected the paper ghost money and deputized the clan elders to bring it in front of the afflicted, where they knelt, lowered their heads, and presented the fee. They had to kneel as many times as the age of the afflicted, and afterward the ghost money was scattered in the alleyways and outside the village in a ritual called "the delivery." Back then, the government hadn't yet restricted logging, so paper was cheap, and the ghosts didn't seem to demand too much.

If the condition of the afflicted was very serious, then the ritual of "road sacrifice" had to be performed, which required a feast being held at a street intersection. To show piety, the cooking had to be done with purified hands and the cooks couldn't taste the food for flavor. It was taboo for passersby to show surprise or fear, and they had to walk by the scene without another glance, especially without ever looking backward—otherwise the condition suffered by the afflicted would be transferred to them. The natives knew to never touch the food offered to the ghosts in the feast, but now that Silicon Isle was filled with impious, ignorant waste people, it was no longer rare to hear of incidents where men and ghosts fought over the same food. Unable to prevent the offerings from being defiled, the natives had gradually abandoned the ritual.

Luo Jincheng had never imagined that one day he would play the leading role in such a ritual. He was a devout Buddhist, and there was a shrine set up in his own house. At major festivals, he donated large sums of money for incense and offerings to pray for good fortune—although some joked that since Boss Luo had business dealings across the globe, perhaps even the Buddha found it hard to watch over all his affairs. He understood that he was no different from most Chinese: it wasn't so much that he had faith in the Buddha; rather, he worshiped pragmatism. Putting his heart at ease was the greatest practical benefit of his faith.

Is this karma? Luo Jincheng shuddered as though a pair of cold eyes stared at him out of the void, measuring his soul. Rumor had it that the cargo ship from New Jersey, *Long Prosperity,* had caused someone to die while entering Hong Kong. Since the other clan bosses thought the ship unlucky and refused to accept the cargo, he had bought the ship's entire load at a low price. Boldness had always been the foundation of his success as he built the Luo clan's empire, and his son had inherited that trait from him.

His heart tightened again as he thought of his son, as though his chest cavity were connected to some powerful vacuum pump.

The *lohsingpua* seemed to detect some unusual scent and abruptly turned to his son's desk; the character for "edict"—*chi*—on her forehead flashed green as though she was receiving data at a rapid pace out of the ether. She was looking at an elegant photo frame. A line of golden text in regular script was inscribed in the cream-colored mat underneath the photograph: *First Prize, "Green Island Cup" Student Photography Contest, Silicon Isle First Elementary School: Luo Zixin.*

"It's the waste girl." The *lohsingpua* pointed at the person in the black-and-white photograph, her tone absolutely certain.

"Her?" Luo Jincheng picked up the frame. The background in the picture seemed familiar, but to tell the truth, the shacks of the waste people all looked pretty much the same. "What do we have to do to make Him-ri better?" He used the affectionate diminutive for his son.[8]

"You have to find this girl and, on the eighth day of the next lunar month, perform the 'oil fire' ritual."

Luo Jincheng shuddered. He had heard of the ritual in the reminiscences of elders but never witnessed it. It was said to be a rite of last resort reserved for wealthy families with dying loved ones after having

[8] Luo Zixin's name in the local topolect is read as *Lo⁵ Zi² Him¹; Him¹-ri⁵* is formed from the last character of the name and a diminutive suffix.

tried everything else. The witch had to paint her face with colored tung oil, strip, put on a varicolored skirt, hold an oil-filled porcelain bowl charged with a spell, light it, and then run through the alleyways and streets at midnight while wailing loudly, like some corpse candle wandering in the dark. If any frightened passerby cried out, the witch was supposed to smash the flaming bowl of oil against the nearest wall and let out a great shriek. Then the person who had screamed from terror would die in place of the afflicted as a "holler proxy."

It's dusk; the westering sun is about to set,
All the families shutter their doors.
Chickens, geese, even the crows are roosting;
Little child, please come home.

The *lohsingpua* began the chant to retire the spirits, set to the classical tune of "Suo Nan Zhi."[9] The dreary music was tinged with sorrow, and Luo Jincheng felt a chill down his spine. The eerie green glow over the *lohsingpua*'s forehead finally went out, and Luo hurried to turn on the bright incandescent lights to return everything to pragmatic reality.

Mimi was running, but her legs seemed mired in quicksand: the more she struggled, the harder it was to make any progress.

She didn't know how long she had been running, nor where she was. A sense of urgency tugged at her nerves, making it impossible for her to give up the desire to run, but there was no one after her. There was no concrete threat, only a formless, unnamed foreboding that swept over the sea at her from the distant horizon. Out of the corners of her eyes, she seemed to glimpse some indescribable glow, a complex iridescence found in the sheen of metal coating or the luster of crystals, fluctuating

[9] A classical folk opera tune that was already popular by the middle of the Ming Dynasty (1368–1644).

in the manner of waves or racing clouds, devouring the dim, black-and-white space behind her.

Mimi felt the glow touch her body. Abruptly, the world incomprehensibly turned sideways. A moment earlier, she had been running on flat ground, but now she was climbing up a vertical cliff. The source of gravity shifted from beneath her feet to behind her, and swung to some vanishing point on the horizon. She fought to hold on to something, anything, but everything around her was as flat and smooth as the surface of a mirror. She screamed, but there was no sound.

There was only the fall, an endless fall.

Help me!

The free-falling sensation was replaced by the impression of something unyielding. She realized that she was still lying on the musty wooden bed. The blurry light through her eyelids reminded her that a new day had begun. She had been in the Chen clan's territory for a week.

After a man from her home village had lured her to Silicon Isle with lies more than a year ago, Mimi was finally starting to feel that life here wasn't so bad.

Every morning, around seven o'clock, the eight women who lived in this shack woke up within five minutes of each other. There was no need for alarm clocks, crowing roosters, or any other instrument—they woke up as though a beam of light activated the biological clocks buried in their bodies. They lined up, washed, and brushed their teeth in front of the stone trough covered with green moss, and the white foam, following the inclined trough, slowly collected in a square pool, from where it flowed into a waste pond covered by an iridescent oil film, and then, combined with the industrial and residential wastewater from elsewhere on this island after many twists and turns, plunged without hesitation toward the open sea.

It was just like what that swindler had told her mother: *Go south! She has to go south! All the migrant workers are heading south. Why are you even hesitating?*

But it was his next line that had really hurt Mimi:

Look at how much money other families' working kids are sending home every month. What, are you still hoping her dad would strike it rich and come home?

Mimi forced down her rising rage. Even she couldn't tell whether she was angry because the man had mercilessly held up the truth or because the illusion her mother had polished and maintained with such care had been shattered in a moment, like a cheap clay pot.

She had not left home at the age of sixteen like the other girls in the village because her father had said that he was going to earn enough to pay for her to go to college. But over time, letters from her father had grown scarce, and there was no sign of any money. Other villagers told her mother that many men who went to the big cities for work found other women and started new families. It was best for her to accept the truth and get on with her life. Her daughter was already eighteen, and she needed to go out and learn to make her own way in the world.

Her mother had said nothing as she helped Mimi pack—tucking a large jar of homemade chili paste into her bag—and then cut her hair until it was shorter than her little brother's.

Remember, Mimi, keep your hair no longer than this, her mother had said. *If you get homesick, eat a spoonful of my chili paste.*

Mimi had hugged her mother and cried until her mother's sleeves were soaked.

Utterly exhausted after two days and two nights on the train and several bumpy rides on illegal coolie-shipping trucks, she and six others finally arrived on Silicon Isle. Everything here was new and strange, like the future: the air was humid like a saturated sponge—the slightest exertion resulted in sweat all over her body; the night, lit by rainbow-hued neon lights, was bright as day; countless glowing screens filled the streets like disembodied spirits; posters for nightclubs competed for attention side by side with ads for venereal disease cures; pedestrians on the street dressed in such funny clothing that it seemed surreal, but their eyes stared through Mimi and the other outsiders into the void.

None of this, of course, belonged to them. Their place was Nansha Village, three kilometers away, where another world held sway, a world that they couldn't have imagined.

The man had told her such convincing lies: *You'll be working in plastics recycling, the core industry of Silicon Isle. Boss Luo has the biggest workshops and treats his workers the best. Work hard and the sky's the limit.* After that, she never saw him again. Mimi imagined him appearing at some other remote village in the interior, where he repeated his pitch to another mother: *Go south! She has to go south!*

This was how the poor endured.

In front of Mimi was a pile of plastic fragments of various colors, like bones picked out of the carcass of some animal—so what did that make her? A scavenging mutt? The women workers sorted the plastic with practiced ease: ABS, PVC, PC, PPO, MMA . . . if some fragment couldn't be easily identified, they burned it at the edge with a lighter to ascertain the type of plastic by smell.

Mimi widened her nostrils and gave a light whiff—she didn't dare to breathe in too much of the fumes—the smell was sweet, pungent, irritating to the nose, and she felt as though maggots were wriggling in her throat. Mimi quickly dunked the lit plastic piece into water, and a column of smoke rose up. Gagging, she tossed the piece into the bucket labeled "PPO." Here in Nansha Village, Mimi was required to process tens, even hundreds of buckets of plastic trash like this daily. After a full day's work, it sometimes seemed that she threw up more than she ate.

She'd heard rumors of a device called an electronic nose, which could be used to automatically sort different types of plastic based on their odors. However, the price of a single electronic nose was enough to hire a hundred young workers like her, and the machine was unlikely to be as efficient. Moreover, the instrument might break down and require repairs, while workers could simply be sent home with a few yuan if they fell sick, not even requiring medical insurance.

Human lives are so much cheaper than machines, Mimi thought. But honestly, if the bosses switched to using only machines, where would she and the others find jobs? Here, she earned more in two months than her parents did in a year back in their home village, and as long as she lived frugally, she could save a lot. After working for a while, she planned to go home with enough savings to open a store and set up the whole family for a comfortable life. She clung to a vision in which her father reappeared at the door of their home, and she took the heavy luggage from his hands. The whole family then sat down around the table to share a peaceful, comforting meal, a meal that seemed to never end.

Besides, she had gotten to know so many interesting people here in Silicon Isle, to see so many fantastic inventions and gadgets. It was so much better than life back in her remote village, where even the dogs were too bored to emerge from their kennels. *Experience determines how far one can go in life,* Brother Wen always told her and the other workers. She would nod and blink whenever he said that, as though she knew exactly what he meant.

As Mimi lingered over these thoughts, the fumes didn't seem so bad anymore.

"Take a break!" one of the other girls called to her. With a start, Mimi remembered that she was no longer working in the territory of the Luo clan. Since she was here on Boss Chen's orders, everybody was extra solicitous of her and didn't assign her too much work.

Among the waste people, it was commonplace to say that all the natives of Silicon Isle were the same. *They think we're all stinking trash, and they have to hold their breath and get to the other side of the street as soon as they see one of us.* But Mimi didn't quite agree with this opinion. Some natives were different from others. The Luos, for instance, were not like the Chens. However, she couldn't tell if this was because members of the Chen clan really were kinder or if a clan elder had told everyone to be nice to her. Still, an old native man would sometimes grin at her and offer her bottled water, something completely unimaginable in the territory of the Luo clan.

A bit embarrassed at how little she was being assigned to do, she watched as the others cleaned the sorted plastic junk, removing paper labels with metal brushes and carrying the pieces to a nearby work shed, where machines sliced and pulverized them. Mimi hated being near those machines, because they made so much noise that her innards felt on the verge of being rattled out of her throat. The fine white powder generated by the machines stuck to her skin, where the grains seemed to embed themselves deep in her pores, irritating and rash-inducing, and she could neither wash the particles away nor scratch out the resulting itch.

It was said that the crushed plastic would then be melted down, cooled, formed into pellets to be sold to coastal factories, where they would be turned into cheap plastic products the bulk of which were exported to countries around the world so that people everywhere could benefit from the affordable "Made in China" merchandise; when those wares broke down or became stale, they turned into trash to be shipped back to China, and the cycle began again.

The world ran on such cycles, which Mimi found fascinating and marvelous: the cycles kept the machines roaring and the workers busy.

The third day after her rescue, Kaizong appeared outside her shack. He acted awkwardly and spoke stiffly, as if deliberately maintaining some distance from her. He introduced himself formally and explained that he hoped Mimi would cooperate with him by agreeing to answer some elementary questions he had about the lives and working conditions of the migrant workers under the Luo clan's management.

But the very first question he posed was something that Mimi didn't know how to answer. "How do you feel about Silicon Isle?"

"I don't know . . ." Mimi tried to figure out the meaning behind this question. She decided to ask him the same thing. "How do *you* feel about it?"

Kaizong looked to the sides to be sure no one was nearby. "What I mean is: do you want to change your life?"

The superiority implied by his tone angered Mimi. She glared at him. "I work hard for my money. How I live my life isn't any of your business!"

Kaizong looked embarrassed and waved his hands in a gesture of denial. "That's not what I meant—"

Mimi pressed harder. "Then what *did* you really mean?"

For a while, Kaizong pondered seriously how to express himself properly, but gave up in the end. "I guess I don't know what I meant, either."

"Idiot." Mimi couldn't stop herself. She regretted it immediately. She was too used to talking that way.

Kaizong was taken aback. In his limited social experience, people were not so direct—even rude. But somehow, he wasn't annoyed with her.

Mimi turned and noticed her roommates eavesdropping at the door of the shack. Inspired, she said, "I was talking to *them*."

Crisp peals of laughter erupted from the shack. The awkwardness between them was broken, and the hard shell around Kaizong seemed to have been pried off, revealing the soft nutmeat inside. He looked at Mimi, and half joking, half serious, said, "You're much kinder than my classmates. They usually call me a freak."

Mimi giggled. Looking at the handsome face of the young man, she felt her heart quicken. "They're right. You're a bit of a freak."

Before coming to Silicon Isle, the number of men she had come into contact with numbered no more than a deck of cards. Everything she knew about romance had been learned from TV dramas. Her mother had obsessively muttered to her like a mantra, *All men are the same. When they're pursuing you, you are a goddess. But when they have you, they step all over you.* While Mother went on in this fashion, Father would smoke his cigarettes silently in their hut.

How do they get you? Mimi would ask, holding back laughter.

Mother would hem and haw without presenting any specifics, but in the end, she would offer herself as an example of a failure for Mimi to avoid emulating. She told Mimi that it was best to avoid dating, to delay marriage as long as possible until she had found the right one.

Without dating, how am I supposed to find the right one? Mimi would ask.

Mother would then holler and bellow, while Father, unable to hold back any longer, guffawed. Those were some rare moments of mirth in their home. Every time Mimi remembered those times, she would get a lump in her throat and wish she could go home soon.

Mimi began having that odd dream of desperately fleeing from an unknown danger after her injury, and she always suspected that the strange helmet had something to do with it. The iridescent glow that chased her in the dream started at the horizon but eventually expanded to cover the surface of the sea, like a variant of the seasonal red tides in which billions of tiny lives bloomed and multiplied, out of control, until the light caught up to her shadow, to her running footsteps, corroded her body—she felt disturbed and unsettled after waking, even though she knew it was just a dream.

She wasn't sure if she should bring up the dream with Kaizong. He asked so many questions and seemed genuinely interested in her answers. He wanted to know everything about her, it seemed, with no detail being too small or too silly. But if she told him of the dream, she'd have to tell him everything, including what happened with that little boy. Was Kaizong going to think that she was like Brother Wen, harboring hostility toward the natives? She had always regretted not stepping in to stop the boy from getting hurt, and she didn't feel ready for Kaizong to know about what had happened, at least not now.

Why do you care so much what he thinks about you? Mimi shook her head and tried to chase away the chaotic thoughts. *You are nothing but a part of his investigation for his project, an interview subject, a specimen of the waste people. You're nothing.* She thought she understood the source of her own foolish feelings. It was like those cookie-cutter Hollywood films and soap operas: a hero saves a beauty, and the beauty falls in love. However, she wasn't a beauty, and he was no hero—the most one could say was he was a self-righteous rich boy. Yet Chen Kaizong came to see her every few days, inquiring after her safety and posing questions that she found hard to answer—and, after she tossed those questions back at him, he endeavored to give her meaningful answers.

He told Mimi many of the sights and customs on the other side of the Pacific, things that she would otherwise never have known for the rest of her life; to repay him, Mimi took him to secret sights of Silicon Isle that even the natives didn't know about: the coming and going of the tide, the pink-hued sunset, the black, polluted wastewater discharging into the sea, the mechanical spasms given off by the carcasses of chipped dogs as new signals stimulated them.

"Aren't you afraid they'll talk?" Mimi asked Kaizong.

"What about?"

"That you're spending all your time with the waste people, bringing dishonor to the Chen name." Mimi lowered her eyes as she said the last few words. The tide gently lapped the beach, giving it little bites; the water surged over her ankles, encircling them with white foam; there were no shellfish or crabs in the water, only trash, the trash that had been tossed into the sea and then brought back by the tides, giving off a heavy stench.

"Aren't *you* afraid they'll talk?"

"What about?"

"That you're spending all your time with a fake foreigner, bringing dishonor to the waste people." Kaizong maintained a serious expression. Mimi's face lit up with a wide grin.

After Mimi was moved over to the workshops in the Chen clan territory, Kaizong sought her out every day in an effort to understand the lives of the waste workers better. Like everyone else, she had initially reacted to him guardedly, and spoke to him in the same cold, impatient tone one might use to answer some clipboard survey in the street. It wasn't until Kaizong began eating with them, working by their side, filling his nostrils with the stench of burning plastic, and immersing his hands in the chemical-filled basins for cleaning the plastic, that she slowly accepted this fact: the young man's appearance belied his character. He was not one of the natives who forever looked at the migrant laborers through glasses tinted with prejudice. Even his expressions and gestures differed subtly from theirs. It was as if his Chinese skin were nothing but a disguise, and underneath was some other strange race that she could not identify.

Their topics of conversation grew more varied. Mimi had countless *whys*: about Kaizong, about everything on the other side of the Pacific. In response to his slightly dry explanations, she nodded, half understanding, and after an *oh*, she would follow with a non sequitur of a new question.

There were a few mysteries that had been bothering her for a while.

For instance, the dead dog.

The carcass, full of lacerations and gashes, was lying next to a heap of incinerated circuit boards. Due to the hot weather, the belly was grossly distended like an angry pufferfish, threatening to burst open at any moment, revealing the rotting viscera full of wriggling maggots. The fetid stench of the carcass mixed with the odor of trash, forming an unforgettable mélange.

Kaizong was at first confused why no one cleaned up the dead dog, but soon, he learned the reason.

"I used to feed it often. Poor thing. The owner didn't want it, and other dogs wanted nothing to do with it, either." Mimi squatted some distance away, seemingly trying to convey her sorrow via telepathy.

"What is its name?" Kaizong asked.

"Good Dog. I just called it Good Dog." Mimi smiled at her memory. "It wagged its tail at everyone, and that meant no one cared about it."

Kaizong took two steps closer to the dead dog. Mimi was about to stop him, but it was too late. The tail began to writhe about violently like a live wire, and raised up a cloud of dust. The scene was both ridiculous and terrifying. Kaizong, startled, stumbled back a couple of steps, and the tail became still. But as soon as he came closer, the tail began moving again.

"Frightening, isn't it?" Mimi's voice was subdued. "It's as though its soul is still trapped in the body, if dogs have souls. But it was a really good dog—not like those mean dogs who are always pouncing at people, barking and biting—why did it end up with such a fate?"

Kaizong noticed that the waste people subscribed to a simple form of animism: they prayed to the wind, the sea, the earth or the furnaces, hoped for the containers of trash shipped from distant shores to be full of valuable goods, easy to process, and nontoxic, and even felt penitent as they took apart the artificial human bodies—the Japanese products were so realistic that they felt they were slicing apart real flesh.

He quickly figured out the truth about Good Dog: a failed laboratory experiment in cyborg research.

As originally designed, it should have behaved as any other chipped dog and attacked any and all visitors who did not emit the designated signal; however, something had gone wrong during the implant process and instead of attacking, the dog wagged its tail. In a paranoid environment where everyone was on high alert and treated everyone else as an enemy, a good dog was destined to receive no more fairness than a good person.

"Silly! There's no soul. It's dead, but the servo circuits in the body are still working."

Kaizong spent a long time trying to explain to Mimi the principles behind the chipped dogs. She looked dubious as Kaizong took out his phone—Director Lin had given him and Scott temporary authorization codes to prevent another accidental attack. Kaizong sent out the master key signal and gestured for Mimi to come closer. Mimi tiptoed over hesitantly.

Now, Good Dog's tail remained lifeless.

Mimi let out a held breath. Her gaze at Kaizong was filled with a mixture of two parts admiration plus one part dawning realization. It was as if the fog that concealed the world had been dispelled slightly, revealing the truth in one corner, but it was also akin to losing some of the world's sparkle and shine. Kaizong felt a pang of regret: perhaps some things should not be reduced only to mechanistic, materialist explanations, and a sliver of pure and simple beauty should be preserved.

It was always a dilemma whether to allow someone to hold on to the fantasies of childhood for as long as possible or to force them into the cruel realities of the world as soon as possible.

But one night, on the shore next to a sea full of glowing blue stars, Kaizong chose a third path.

They hired an electric sampan and left at dusk. By the time they approached the neat edge of the artificial coast, the sky and the sea in the distance had merged into a dark indigo. The air was filled with a low rumbling, accompanied by the rhythmic slap of the waves against the shore and the cries of occasional passing seabirds. A marvelous sense of harmony filled the scene.

"Is that the power plant?" Kaizong pointed to a few gigantic dome-shaped buildings not too far away. Next to them was a large chimney painted in red and white stripes, like a phallic monument worshiped by some primitive tribe.

Before Mimi could answer, their boatman spoke up.

"That's right! Look at the color of the sea around here: all black. They dumped the wastewater into the sea every day until all the fish were dead. I used to be a fisherman, and now all I can do is pick up tips by hauling tourists around—" Abruptly, he stopped talking, and it was impossible to see the expression on his dark face in the failing light. "Listen: that's the sound of the pump. Every day, they draw water from the sea for the cooling system, and along with the water, they pump in about two trucks' worth of fish and shrimp. Then they sell the toxic seafood on the market—such sins!"

"Uncle—" Mimi interrupted him in a soft voice. "We're just here to see the glowing sea lights."

The boatman had the good sense to stop his complaining. He turned the rudder and cruised until the sampan was at the other end of the coast; here, the sea smelled pungent and felt warm—apparently where the warm water from the cooling system was discharged.

"Look!" Mimi grabbed Kaizong's hand and pointed at the dark surface of the sea.

Kaizong stared where she was pointing. Now that his eyes had adjusted, they were much more sensitive to faint light. In the depths of the dark green, agate-like water, there appeared points of blue-green luminescence. At first, he only saw a few scattered glows here and there, but they grew, connected into lines and patches, and seemed to rise gradually from below the undulating surface until their outlines became clear: hundreds of thousands of translucent bells. They pulsed rhythmically, contracting and then expanding, their motions graceful and gentle like a dance, like countless blue-green LED lights glowing in the sea, like the trembling, whirling starry sky under Van Gogh's brush. The sampan seemed to be floating in a sea of stars and the passengers drifting in a dream, their swelling emotions matching the rolling waves, resulting in a sensation of vertigo.

"It's so lovely." Mimi's face reflected the luminescent glow and her look was one of intoxication.

"I've never seen so many jellyfish." Kaizong recalled the Aquarium of the Bay in San Francisco, which he had visited. "Why are they gathered here? I thought the water is toxic."

"I heard on TV that the jellyfish glow because of a reaction between some protein inside them and the high concentration of calcium ions in the wastewater," the boatman said. "What you're seeing is the second generation already."

"What do you mean?" asked Mimi.

"The power plant discharge warms up the water, and the artificial shore reduces the impact of the tides; so, every winter, the jellyfish breed here. The babies develop into little stalks with feeding tentacles until the next summer, when they bud into multiple disklike jellyfish that grow into adults. Oh, you're looking at the adults."

"I still don't understand." Kaizong pointed to a blue-glowing underwater current nearby. "They're being sucked in again."

The current flowed into some water intake, and they could see the translucent bells swirling slowly, forming a vortex that accelerated as they approached the pipe's mouth. In a moment, the glowing bodies were deformed, torn apart, and vanished. Their lives' journey came to an end almost as soon as it had begun.

"Every year, they have to spend a lot of money to clear out the clogged pipes," the boatman said. "The jellyfish just breed too fast."

Mimi stared at the scene for a while before the meaning sank in. Angrily, she spat out, "What kind of parents leave their babies in such a dangerous, poisonous place? Don't they care about their children?"

Kaizong chuckled on the inside. This young woman was so naive that he felt another wave of tenderness toward her.

"Miss, if they're not born here, even fewer of them would survive," the boatman said.

"I just don't understand. Why can't people be more compassionate and wait until these beings have left the area before pumping water? Wanting more money doesn't make it okay to kill."

"They can't even afford to care about human lives, let alone the lives of jellyfish."

The old Kaizong probably would have launched a lecture about survival of the fittest, culminating in the conclusion that the presence of the power plant provided the impetus for the evolution of this species of jellyfish so that surviving descendants would be better adapted to the environment, quicker to react to changes, and become more fecund. But the new Kaizong sank into silence. The young woman in front of him was a victim of just this type of thinking: she and others like her had left their homes to come here under the euphemism of "economic development" so that they could eke out a living in pollution and poison, suffer the prejudice and exploitation of the natives, and perhaps even die in a land far from home and loved ones. He could not utter the sentiment that *this is all so that your children and their children will have better lives,* even if that was the truth.

"You're right." Even Kaizong was surprised by himself. "Sooner or later, karma catches up with everyone."

"Sooner or later," the boatman echoed.

The undulating blue-green glow gradually faded from Mimi's face until only her irises, reflecting the faint ambient light, remained visible in the darkness like two dim stars not belonging to any constellations, rising and falling gently over the sea. Though he could only see a blurred outline of her body, Kaizong couldn't move his gaze away; it was as if the region around her had been deformed by gravity so that all the other stars had contracted into inconspicuous details in the background.

Mimi raised a hand and pointed somewhere in the dark. "Look."

Kaizong squinted but could not tell what she wanted him to see.

"I thought you foreigners all wore augmented contacts." Mimi twisted around to look at him. "Fake Foreigner, you're a strange one."

"Not everyone." Kaizong awkwardly tried to neaten his hair, messed up by gusts of sea breeze. "My parents converted to Christianity later in life, and their fundamentalist church believes that mankind should only look at the world with God-given eyes. All prosthetic augmentations are thought of as violations of the will of God because the world must be experienced and understood in the original manner in which God had created it."

"Oh . . ." Mimi seemed to be struggling to grasp the meaning of his words. "Then . . . do you believe in God, too?"

"I'm an atheist, but, since I'm Chinese, filial piety is my first duty; I try to respect their beliefs."

Mimi was quiet, as if reminiscing. She turned to gaze at the sea, over which various dark shadows seemed to stick out like the spines of strange beasts. "That's Tide Gazing Pavilion."

She turned to the boatman. "Uncle, would you take us to Tide Gazing Beach?"

"Miss, it's late. Why go to such an unlucky place?" Kaizong could hear how anxious the boatman was.

"Just to see," Mimi answered softly, but her voice did not waver.

Tide Gazing Beach wasn't in the same location as Tide Gazing Pavilion. Silicon Isle extended a long, curved shoal into the ocean like a tentacle, and it encircled a lagoon of a few square kilometers. The pavilion was at the tip of the tentacle, while the crescent-shaped beach on the shoal was Tide Gazing Beach.

As the tide came into the lagoon, the underwater reefs beyond the tip of the tentacle caused the water to surge into a silvery crescent; and as the tide continued on and reached the beach, the breakers formed a second crescent opposite in curvature. The locals called the sight "Dual Tides Reflecting the Moon." Though the scenery was beautiful, few seemed to come to enjoy it.

The sampan gave a light jolt as it crossed over the outer crescent. As clouds drifted overhead, the scattered silver moonlight fell unevenly over the water. The shadows of the clouds moved along with the sampan, and the two passengers experienced the illusion of standing still until the pale sandy beach grew clearer in their sights.

The boatman stopped the sampan. "This is as far as I'll go."

"Here?" Before Kaizong even finished talking, Mimi had already leapt into the waist-high water with a splash. He hurried to take off his shoes and socks, but Mimi jumped up, grabbed him by the arm, and pulled him into the sea, spraying water all around.

"What's that for?" A thoroughly soaked Kaizong emerged from the water and stared at Mimi angrily.

"Be careful, all right? Once you're onshore, just follow the road back to the village." After this quick reminder, the boatman started the motor and returned the way he had come.

Splash. While Mimi was distracted, Kaizong used his arm as a paddle and doused her with seawater.

"Now we're even." He looked smug.

In the moonlight, Mimi's hair seemed to be encrusted with glistening pearls that slid down her wet strands and left sparkling trails on her face. Her black T-shirt was wrapped tightly around her body and reflected the moon like fish scales. A breeze accompanied the parting of cloud shadows, and her moist eyes brightened suddenly, as though underneath her radiant lashes were two shimmering seas. There was a circle of light around her on the surface of the sea, like the halo around the moon. Kaizong caught his breath as he watched this moon goddess stride toward him through the water.

The goddess stared at him, said one word softly, and then turned and waded for the shore.

"Idiot."

Exhausted, they lay on the beach, unconcerned with the sand that stuck to their bodies. Since so few came here, the beach was far cleaner than the other beaches of Silicon Isle. The waves slapped against the sand rhythmically while the starry sky, visible only in torn patches through cracks in the clouds, slowly drifted. Kaizong heard the sound of Mimi's breathing, soft and slow like a sound coming from the depths of space.

This feels different. Kaizong thought back to the women he had known: his well-bred, fashionable, socially adept East Coast classmates. No, it wasn't just a difference of demographic labels, but something deeper, some contrast that he couldn't describe precisely but was sure of. *The soul.* He thought of the word that Mimi brought up often. *It will have to do.*

"What do you want to do in the future?" Kaizong gazed at the stars. He phrased it like a question directed at her and also at himself.

"Make enough money to open a store back home so that my parents won't have to work so hard."

"I mean—what is the thing you most want to do for *yourself*?"

A long silence.

"I don't know . . . I've never thought about that." She paused for a moment. "I want to go far, far away and learn many new things, like you." She laughed. "Maybe in my next life." Her voice took on a forced levity.

Kaizong didn't know what to say.

In the long stream of human history there was one school of thought that resurfaced time after time: a devotion to the hidden order of the universe and a blind faith in the natural balance of the world. God was fair to all of His children, and Heaven took from overabundance to replenish scarcity.[10] Fate ultimately guided all. Faced with signs of unfairness in the real world, people tried to marshal all kinds of evidence to comfort themselves: if Heaven endowed some with status, wealth, beauty, talent, health . . . then it was certain to take away something else as a price. When such evidence couldn't be found, the theory of reincarnation was invented so that there was infinite time to tally up the counters of lifetimes to achieve eventual balance. Kaizong had once scoffed at the theory of conservation of destinies, but perhaps people needed such a theory not because it was the truth, but because it offered solace in their limited lives.

A laughing face interrupted his musings; Mimi pulled him up from the sand by his arm and they ran, together, toward the other end of darkness.

But he's a native! the other girls always said to her. He was a Silicon Isle native who was unlike any other. Although he occasionally appeared foolish, he never called them "waste people"; his gaze was kind and inquisitive, but he was never afraid to look anyone in the eye; he didn't spit in public, didn't curse and swear; and strangest of all, he wasn't implanted with any prostheses and didn't rely on augmented reality. Kaizong seemed like an astronaut who had just returned to the Earth from light-years away: as soon as he stepped outside the sterile landing capsule, he was mired in a filthy living hell.

She had come to expect Kaizong every day, to depend on his visits. The other girls mocked her for it. But as their friendship deepened, Mimi felt an inversely growing sense of panic: what if he just stopped showing up one day?

She knew what she was really scared of. She was terrified that she wasn't attracted to Chen Kaizong, the person; rather, she was attracted

---

[10] This is a quote from chapter seventy-seven of the *Dao De Jing* (or *Tao Te Ching*), a book of philosophy by the sixth-century BC philosopher Lao Tsu.

to his refined manner of dress, his excessively proper Modern Standard Mandarin that sounded odd to her ears, his learning—everything mysterious and exotic that he represented. She was afraid that all these had, together, formed in her mind an idealized illusion of first love, even leading to an unrealistic fantasy that she herself was equally special in his eyes, equally unique and singular.

She recalled her one experience of having a crush on a boy. It was when she was still going to the school in the town near her village. There was a boy in the class next door, lanky and handsome like a character out of manga. Mimi would slow down deliberately every time she passed by his classroom so that she could look at him for a few more seconds. Sometimes, the boy happened to be looking outside and their eyes would meet, and her heart would leap like a tiny rabbit. *Is he looking at me? What does he think? Does he find me pretty? Will we get along well?*

The fantasies tortured her, and eventually she had to ask a classmate to find out from him what he thought of her. The boy's confused gaze showed that he had no idea even who Mimi was, and her meticulously crafted plans were shattered in an instant.

She told herself then that she would never let herself be deluded by such fantasies again. Never. When Kaizong had jokingly referred to Mimi's boyish haircut, for an instant, she had almost impulsively decided to disregard the advice of her mother and grow her hair out for him until it was even with her shoulders, maybe even down to her waist, even though such a decision would bring her endless trouble, just like it had when she had lived at home.

But in the next second, Mimi had answered him coldly, "It's my hair. I don't give a rat's ass what anyone thinks."

Today, though, she had waited more than an hour already, but there was still no Kaizong at that familiar, dirty intersection.

The sense of having been forsaken rose in her heart—a rather ridiculous feeling, she chided herself. She took a deep breath and exhaled slowly, struggling to shake off the anxiety that buzzed around her like mosquitoes. She knew what she needed. Halcyon Days.

She had to go find Brother Wen.

4

Luo Jincheng stood on the rooftop deck and faced the ocean. The sea breeze came through the open pattern in the parapet, bringing with it the smell of change.

Unlike the houses of the other natives, whose windows were covered with antitheft metal grilles so that the inhabitants only saw a sky cut into pieces by a regular grid, the Luo mansion was built on a cliff next to the sea to take advantage of the rugged and steep terrain. With the additional security provided by chipped dogs and closed-circuit TV cameras, Luo got to enjoy the uninterrupted, open view. He could see all the way to the busy harbor of Shantou, and when the weather was good, he could even see the Shantou Bay Bridge spanning the ocean like a strand of spider silk.

If the Chen clan had really gotten into the same boat with TerraGreen Recycling, then the situation was growing complicated. Three years ago, the collapse in international steel and copper prices had struck the Chen clan hard. The Luo and Lin clans had taken advantage of the opportunity and stolen away numerous highly profitable supply sources from the Chen clan. The two families had even conspired with buyers to artificially lower prices in an attempt to bury the Chen clan completely, but members of the Chen clan had rallied and pooled their resources and efforts to ride out the crisis. It appeared now that the Chens intended to collude with these foreigners in a plot to rise up and regain the power lost to the two other clans.

Knifeboy had returned with a report that the Chen clan had intercepted the waste girl named Mimi, and someone from TerraGreen Recycling was even involved.

But why are they going to so much trouble for a waste girl?

Luo Jincheng pondered the question from every angle but could see no answer. He was certain that Zixin's illness was still a secret. The *loh-singpua* belonged to the Luo clan and wouldn't be so stupid as to leak the news, and in any event, this didn't seem like Chen Xianyun's style, unless there was some other secret about the girl. Luo Jincheng told Knifeboy to not act rashly in Chen territory, but if a second opportunity should present itself, he must not fail again.

There was no deep enmity between him and the Chen clan. For him, what happened between the two clans was only ordinary commercial competition, but as soon as foreigners were involved, the matter was different, regardless of whether the foreigners were white-skinned or yellow-skinned. He didn't trust them, and the mistrust went deep into his bones.

Luo Jincheng had visited many countries around the world, and even tried to live in Melbourne for a while, but in the end, he had returned to Silicon Isle. He had never managed to feel comfortable in front of those Westerners who acted almost pathologically polite; he couldn't get used to waiting for the light to change to cross the street, couldn't get used to saying "excuse me" for every little thing, couldn't get used to the strange smiles that were so friendly yet so false. When they heard that he was from China, their faces broke into exaggerated wonder: *Oh, how quickly China's economy is growing! How much the Chinese can buy!* And, every time, *I love Chinese food!*

At first, Luo Jincheng treated these as just meaningless expressions of courtesy, but then he saw the protesters in the streets of Melbourne, and he finally understood that the "praise" for China disguised terror and disgust. At the time, he didn't know enough English to understand the protesters' signs, but the meaning of the burning Chinese flags was unmistakable. The Australians thought the Chinese had bid up the prices of the local real estate and taken away their jobs, and cheap Chinese exports had decimated local manufacturing. They compared the Chinese to locusts who robbed the Australians of their resources and accumulated unbelievable wealth without giving anything back to public welfare and disadvantaged groups.

SELFISH CHINESE! their signs read, and bloody red crosses were painted over the signs.

Like a pedestrian who had been frightened out of his wits in the middle of the night by a bowl of "oil fire" smashed against the wall, Luo Jincheng bought a ticket back to China the next day. He gave up the idea of emigrating abroad, but began to study English. He hired an expensive tutor and read English newspapers every day. Eventually, wielding his heavily accented English, he even managed to negotiate with foreign business partners.

Luo understood, of course, that he wasn't motivated so much by a sentiment of *'Tis not too late to seek a newer world* as by the lack of a sense of security. He wanted to apply the adage of "know your enemy" to the battlefield of business and be in control of the situation, instead of relying on an interpreter. However, what had really raised his alarm was an unexpected visit from a distant relative.

Most of the Silicon Isle natives had overseas relatives. Refugees of the wars of the twentieth century and the disturbances caused by mass Communist movements had smuggled themselves to Hong Kong and thence to Southeast Asia, where they settled. However, they continued to speak the language of their homeland and yearned for the sights of the old country. Those who managed to prosper sometimes returned to Silicon Isle to visit relatives and to invest in businesses, and the locals called them *huêngkêh*[11]—overseas guests.

A cousin of Luo Jincheng's father had emigrated overseas with his family on the eve of the Second World War and settled in the Philip-

---

[11] With full tone marks: *huêng¹kêh⁴*.

pines. After the reforms by Deng Xiaoping in China, the cousin had brought his children to visit Silicon Isle a few times, and Luo Jincheng had eaten with him at the same table each time. However, that was the extent of their interactions.

Thus, when Luo Jincheng saw his second cousin—the son of his father's cousin—waiting for him, alone, on the chair by the eight-immortal table,[12] he knew that the second cousin had come for help.

After exchanging a few pleasantries, Luo Jincheng smiled. *Tell me what you need plainly. We're family.*

The cousin awkwardly caressed the maroon-colored rosewood arm-rest, and then, after some hesitation, forced himself to speak. *Eighty.*

Luo Jincheng was momentarily stunned. He knew that his cousin's father's business in the Philippines had always done well, and this number should have been well within their resources. *Drugs? Gambling?* His mind worked furiously. When local families saw a fall in fortune, the cause was usually one of these two. If his cousin's father was addicted to gambling, then it might be like throwing money into a bottomless pit. However, Luo Jincheng knew that his cousin's family had provided his own family with a lot of aid when they were in desperate straits, and he fully intended to repay the debt.

I'll give you a hundred. He didn't ask for specifics. It wasn't his business, and he was afraid that if he knew the details, it might entangle him even deeper in the web of obligations.

The corners of his cousin's mouth spasmed a few times, but in the end all he said was *Thank you.* For natives of Silicon Isle, having to ask to borrow money was utterly humiliating.

After his cousin left for home, Luo Jincheng found a long, handwritten letter that said everything that the cousin couldn't say in person. His cousin had used pen and paper to substitute for tongue and lips because, one, he was afraid that he would be overcome by emotion, and two, he didn't want to burden Luo Jincheng. When Luo Jincheng found

---

[12] A traditional Chinese square table capable of seating two per side; the name is a play on the Eight Immortals of Daoist legends.

out the truth, he regretted the unkind thoughts he had harbored toward the cousin.

Everything had started with the coming of an American company in the Philippines. They bribed officials in Manila and got the approval to invest and build an environmentally friendly rubber-recycling processing center. The existing rubber-processing factories were forcefully shut down. The rubber factory that belonged to Luo Jincheng's cousin and his father was shuttered, their capital frozen, their machinery confiscated, and their workers sent away. As the legal representative of the business, his cousin's father was arrested and jailed, and the family was slammed with an astronomical fine for the sin of "long-term environmental pollution."

Some segments of the local population seized the opportunity to erupt into the latest round of the long regional tradition of anti-Chinese pogroms and riots. They smashed and burned and looted stores owned by the ethnic Chinese and threatened Chinese families with violence. They had long coveted the wealth accumulated by these industrious outsiders, and now, they had a chance to carry out their robbery and brutality under the guise of "law" and "environmental protection" without restraint.

Luo Jincheng's cousin had come to beg for money so he could pay the government the ransom needed to get his father out of jail, and then the whole family planned to flee from that land teetering on the edge of hell.

The world is grand, his cousin had written at the end of the letter. *But is there anywhere we can be truly safe?* That final question mark had seemed to Luo Jincheng infused with forlorn desolation.

After that, Luo Jincheng never received any further news of his cousin's family. All attempts to contact them rippled away into nothingness like clay figurines tossed into the sea. He dreamed of that distant land he had never set foot on, trekking through the dense tropical jungle until he saw the houses set on fire and black pillars of smoke rising into the sky, and the smoke and fire coalesced into hallucinatory versions of his relatives. He awoke distraught, but could only pray to the Buddha for their safety. He regretted not giving his cousin more money or asking more questions.

But what could I have done?

Luo Jincheng shook his head. This was not the first time something like this had happened to the Chinese, and it wouldn't be the last.

It's fate. Cold comfort, but it was all he had.

And now, the Americans were standing on the soil of Silicon Isle, repeating their exploits in Manila. Luo Jincheng had done his research and knew that TerraGreen Recycling wasn't involved in the Philippines, but he was certain that all these companies were the same. The Chen clan was now closest to the Americans, while the Lin clan had still not clearly expressed an opinion about the foreigners' proposal because of their special relationship with the government; yet, Director Lin Yiyu was working so actively with the Americans that Luo had to be suspicious. The future of Silicon Isle wavered like the path of a typhoon, and he could not tell where it was headed.

It has been almost half a year since the heads of the three clans sat down together for dim sum, Luo Jincheng realized, and he recalled the taste of the *hakau* served by the Rong family restaurant. Before pouring tea for others, one had to have a firm grip on the teapot—this was a lesson he had to remember.

Like last time, when he had been played by that migrant whelp named Li Wen.

Mimi still remembered that distant summer afternoon a year ago, when the air had been stale, humid, hot, like sticky tentacles that wrapped themselves tightly around everyone. Brother Wen asked her where she wanted the film applied. She thought a bit, turned around, and pointed to the skin on the back of her neck, below the prominences of the first few vertebrae.

"Here."

Brother Wen was confused. "Everybody wants the film in the most eye-catching places. Why do you want to stick it where even you can't see it?"

"Others want thrills, but I'm looking for peace."

Wen adjusted her body film to act in the way she wanted. Unlike others', her film would light up with a golden *mi*—the character in her name—when her muscles were completely relaxed. Most of the time, the upside-down triangular piece of film, like undeveloped camera film, remained dim and dark.

She didn't fully understand her own motivation. Was it just to show she was different from the others? Not entirely. She couldn't control the state of tension life on Silicon Isle had caused in her; even while sleeping, she could feel twinges of pain from her stiff back. Mimi had to constantly remind herself to adjust her breathing to relax her body. She didn't even fully understand the source of the tension: perhaps it was the unfamiliar surroundings; perhaps it was the enmity of the natives, which everyone around her returned; perhaps it was the malicious looks from the local hooligans.

"Maybe you need this more," Brother Wen said.

Mimi had seen the device he held out to her before: a pair of augmented-reality glasses. Most people here possessed a pair. They said that folks in the cities had long ago abandoned such outdated equipment and shifted to contact lenses, which were far lighter and more flexible, or even had surgery so that images could be directly projected onto their retinas. However, the waste people here could only afford secondhand goods, and augmented reality meant something different to them than to the residents of modern big cities with unrestricted bitrates. There, for a few hundred yuan a month, one could access any information compatible with the individual's level of access: weather, traffic, impulse shopping, price comparison, simulation games, immersive movies, social media—even tapping into the view of your husband's augmented gear in some exotic locale on business, as long as he didn't object.

None of these trendy uses meant anything for the waste people. They didn't have the yuan to spare, and they had no need for more junk information—they had plenty of garbage to process on a daily basis already.

Silver, dome-shaped ear cups pressed against Mimi's temporal bones; the contact sensors within were capable of reading Mimi's brain waves, and, with the aid of a basic chip, convert them into simple instructions. A thin and light curved lens made of carbon nanostructures connected the ear cups and crossed over her slender nose like an arched bridge, the argon ion plating refracting a faint indigo glow.

After further adjustments, the glasses were able to recognize basic patterns in Mimi's brain waves. Brother Wen grinned.

"Look at that. Only my little sister can look so pretty wearing something like this."

He took out a small black box, pulled a wire out of it and attached it to the glasses. After about half a minute, he detached the wire. "It's done downloading. Newbies should start with Halcyon Days." After hesitating for a moment, he added, "Promise me that if you want more of these, always come to me. I can't keep you away from all temptation, but at least I can try to protect you from irreversible harm."

Mimi nodded, having no idea what to expect next. A kind of white noise filled the ear cups, but she could just make out a set rhythm in it; without any warning, she was struck with a bout of dizziness, as though she were in the midst of an 8.0 magnitude earthquake. Brother Wen supported her and helped her sit on the ground; she looked at him, uncomprehending. The dizziness persisted, but seemed to change as well.

The world, seen through the glasses, took on a sepia tone, as though bathed in a sunset, but subtler; the outlines and edges of everything blurred a bit and sparkled; a powerful emotional torrent surged out of her heart, as though a long-buried underground spring had been tapped. Abruptly, she understood that she was experiencing the taste of nostalgia.

Although the rational part of her mind knew that she was still in Silicon Isle, everything around her had changed to be filled with the flavor of yesteryear, as if two points in space-time had been folded and merged into one. The sky, the trees, the earth, and even the trash seemed to have been given new life, radiating a warm, lovely feeling. Mimi even felt that her mother was right next to her, holding her—somehow she was once again a child—and caressing her; she could smell the faint fragrance of her mother, like bamboo leaves. There was no more anxiety, no more tension; she wanted to immerse herself in this hallucinatory sensation forever.

Equally abruptly, the golden filter endowed with the soul of reminiscence was ripped away from her eyes, and everything cruelly fell back into the dull, banal, ugly, and acrid here and now. Mimi lifted her head and saw that Brother Wen was holding her. She must have fallen, though she didn't remember doing so. A wave of nausea rose in her uncontrollably, heading straight for her throat.

"It's going to be okay," Brother Wen said, still trying to soothe her, giving her a reassuring smile. "This happens. It will pass."

There were no free lunches. Every downloaded dose lasted only five minutes, because, supposedly, extended use could damage the user's vestibular system. Of course, some crazed junkies completely disregarded such warnings. The electronic drugs were created in every corner of the globe, and those desperate to escape reality or yearning for stimulation, most of them the poor of the third world, sought them out eagerly. In the black markets, coding prodigies painstakingly researched hacking methods so that they could get their hits for free or produce more potent, more exotic variants that could be used in combination with traditional synthetic chemical substances. This made the use of such electronic hallucinogens dangerous and unpredictable.

To avoid getting in trouble with the law, electronic drug dealers typically maintained their data centers in server farms on orbiting space stations. From there, the goods were transmitted to ground stations, where they were distributed to end users. Junkies referred to these space-based drug farms as "Lucy's diamonds."

Mimi dared only to buy these "digital mushrooms" from Brother Wen. She trusted he wouldn't give her anything too dangerous. She tried multiple varieties: some induced insane hallucinations; others could be guided by the user's consciousness to some extent, like taking a journey of inner discovery; one flashed the mysterious smile of a Western woman, but produced no other effects (Brother Wen told her that the program was called HEMK Ekstase, and was probably from Eastern Europe, though he didn't know who the woman was, either); some she swore to never touch again. But always, she could not forget Halcyon Days, which brought her back to childhood, back to her home, back to her mother's side.

"The *mi* on your neck only glows when you're using it," Brother Wen told her.

Half a year ago, Luo Jincheng had thought the dim sum sit-down was the idea of the Lin clan, but as soon as the first dishes were brought to the table, that little waste punk called Li Wen showed up. He respectfully greeted the heads of the three clans and asked if he could be allowed to sit. Neither the Luo nor the Chen representatives said anything, but Boss Lin nodded slightly. Director Lin Yiyu, who was also present, appeared ill at ease at this development.

Lin Yiyu was there both as one of the representatives of the Lin clan and also as the head of Silicon Isle Town Government's Office of Investment. The two conflicting roles put him in an awkward position. It was obvious that he was struggling to keep his expression impassive.

Li Wen sat down, smiled, and said that he wasn't there for food and tea. "I haven't been sleeping well, and my nerves are shot. I guess I'm here to beg the bosses for a prescription."

Lin Yiyu coughed, hinting that he should get to the point instead of playing games.

Li Wen stared at the piping steamer full of *hakau*. "I've heard rumors that there's a price on my head. Those shrimp dumplings remind me of me."

Luo Jincheng finally understood that the meeting was really directed at him. He had wanted Knifeboy to spread the rumors to scare Li Wen and stop him from making further trouble, and it appeared that Knife-boy had carried out his intent to a T. This was one of the reasons Luo thought so highly of Knifeboy: all he had to do was to give a few subtle hints, and Knifeboy intuited what he really wanted and implemented his plan with cruel and efficient initiative. Of course there was a bit of self-deception involved here, but Luo Jincheng seemed to feel that this way, he could shift the blame to Knifeboy and avoid bad karma for himself.

However, it was still unclear to him why the Lin and Chen clans seemed afraid of a mere waste man.

Li Wen, taking note that no one was willing to pick up the conversation, went on by himself. "I've been in Silicon Isle for a year and half, but I really like it here and already think of it as home. I've been to many villages around here, trying to straighten out the accounting, but I just can't seem to make the figures work out. Perhaps all the bosses here can help me?"

He took out a notepad with an oily cover and an abacus, and pushed the pile respectfully toward Luo Jincheng.

Luo Jincheng glanced at him askance, and then began to flip through the pages of the notepad. Soon, the contempt on his face was replaced by astonishment. The notepad was filled with columns of data, including the daily quantities and types of waste received at each village, the recycling ratio, length of the processing period, the fluctuating market prices of metals and plastics, cost of labor, cost of electricity and water, rent, depreciation of machinery and equipment, and so on. The whole thing resembled some giant mathematical matrix. Luo Jincheng knew that all the data in here could be obtained from public sources, but no one had ever taken the trouble to organize them and put them together.

The last page of the notepad contained only a few simple figures in red: the amount of taxes that the clans should be paying based on the calculations and the amount of taxes they actually paid—these last were marked with the explanatory note that they were copied from a news release on the tax bureau's website: "Commendations for Our Biggest Taxpayers."

Luo Jincheng understood that the slender young man before him was far more dangerous than his humble looks suggested. He glanced at the representatives from the Lin and Chen clans, and their faces told him that the figures in the notepad were accurate.

"Young man, you're very clever. Why don't you tell us what you want? We can talk about anything." Luo Jincheng pushed the notepad back to him. It was obvious that someone as savvy as this Li Wen wouldn't keep all this data in only a paper notepad.

Li Wen grinned. "All I want is for you to treat us as people, not waste."

An awkward silence descended over the table. After a while, Lin Yiyu spoke in his habitual smooth "official" voice. "Xiao Wen"—he employed a diminutive meant to show familiarity—"many things can be resolved by having all of us sit down together and hold a discussion. We've been working for years to improve the welfare of migrant laborers. Of course, there remain many areas in need of progress."

"I'm glad we share this consensus." Li Wen raised his teacup. "Whatever is recorded in this notepad is worth a lot more than my life, no?"

The cup hovered in the air, waiting, trembling slightly. Then the Lin clan's cup was raised into the air as well, followed by the Chen clan's. Luo Jincheng understood that he was being cornered. The three clans were now like three fish strung together through the jaws—a forceful jerk would split all their mouths. Although the Luo clan now dominated the other two clans, he could not ignore the interests of everyone and make all the decisions on his own. Switching to a different piscine metaphor: when fish got too desperate, they might break the net—the consequences would not be good for anyone.

Luo Jincheng slowly raised his cup and clinked it crisply against the other three cups.

Now, as he recalled that scene from half a year ago, Luo remembered that outsider rascal's eyes: calm and calculating, like some ticking time bomb. But, for now, Luo Jincheng could do nothing about him. If the data he had gathered got leaked, not only would the three clans as well as the tax bureau get in trouble, but the Americans might seize the opportunity to gain leverage. That was what he worried about the most.

Adding his son's illness to the mix made his life far too complicated.

Luo Jincheng piously knelt before the shrine every morning and every evening, praying fervently at the statue of the Buddha that had been blessed by the monks. He prayed for Him-ri, for the Luo family, and also for Silicon Isle. As he gazed at the golden, mysterious smile on the Buddha's face, he silently pledged that if his prayers were answered, he would donate enormous amounts to charity, renovate the temples, and contribute to organizing massive festivals at the Buddha's birthday every year, inviting every resident of Silicon Isle to share in the blessing.

This is just like negotiating a business contract. The thought flitted through his mind, and he quickly extinguished it. The phone rang.

It was Knifeboy. After about one week of searching, he had found that waste girl, just a step ahead of the Lin clan.

"Seize her and bring her to the Hall of Charity and Piety." Luo Jincheng hung up.

Is the Lin clan involved in this now? He knelt before the Buddha, spread his hands on the ground, palms up, and touched his forehead to the ground three times. The corners of his mouth also lifted up in an equally mysterious smile, as though he had received an edict from another dimension.

You have a deal. The voice came from somewhere in his heart.

The LED light next to the hotel room that meant "Please make up room" was unlit. Scott opened the door and turned on the light. The maid had indeed been here: everything was neat and in its place, and the air was suffused with a faint citrus fragrance. He turned on the TV hanging on the wall, chose a channel at random, and turned the volume up. Habitually, he walked around the room with his phone; the full-band scan didn't reveal any unusual electromagnetic emissions.

The place is clean. This was the best local hotel, and it also meant that the Luo clan owned the business.

Scott took out the portable computer that he always carried with him and launched an encrypted chat program with both voice and text modes—he understood that there was no absolutely secure channel here. The men and women on TV, Caucasian in appearance, were speaking in fluent Modern Standard Mandarin and trying to pitch upgraded pet implants that had been launched in North American markets last Christmas.

They can intuit your moods better and build a better relationship with you. SBT is proud to present our latest products for all tomorrow's parties!

Scott was reminded of the chipped dogs. In a few months, the electronics markets of Huaqiangbei in Shenzhen would be filled with more powerful *shanzhai* copies better adapted to local tastes. And then those copies would be exported to the United States to be purchased by SBT's minimum-wage workers who couldn't afford the real thing and then installed in their unfixed mutts.

The frightening Chinese who pirated and copied everything.

The situation was a bit absurd. While the American working class decried the cheap Chinese laborers robbing them of jobs, they were also thankful that the inexpensive Chinese products helped them maintain their dignified standard of living. Meanwhile, in China, the dollars were converted into yuan and filled the pockets of the nouveaux riches, the factory owners, channel distributors, technicians, and low-level bureaucrats who disdained the Chinese imitations and dedicated themselves to the pursuit of replicating the lifestyle of Manhattan's Lower East Side or the San Francisco Bay Area, including their rapid upgrade cycles.

And so, the yuan were converted back into dollars.

Connecting . . . connection established . . . encryption active.

HIROFUMI OTOGAWA: Clean?

CHANG FENGSHA: Yes.

HIROFUMI OTOGAWA: How's progress?

CHANG FENGSHA: There are a few candidates. I'm following up.

HIROFUMI OTOGAWA: Very good. Remember the time constraints.

CHANG FENGSHA: What exactly is this thing? How does it affect the candidates?

HIROFUMI OTOGAWA: You know the rules.

CHANG FENGSHA: I'm just asking.

HIROFUMI OTOGAWA: A minor accident, nothing more. This is just a routine mission of recovery. Focus on your main project, please.

CHANG FENGSHA: It's more difficult than I imagined.

HIROFUMI OTOGAWA: I heard. Well, it's the Chinese, you know.

CHANG FENGSHA: I'll follow my guidebook . . . can you wait a minute?

A light breeze caressed Scott's face. Due to the heavily polluted air, he always kept the windows of his room tightly shut and relied on the central-air system to filter and exchange the air. *Where is the breeze coming from?* He said goodbye to "Hirofumi Otogawa," quit the chat program, and closed the lid of his computer. Gingerly, he stepped to the window and saw that it was open at a minuscule angle, almost undetectable, and the humid, warm summer evening breeze was coming from this tiny crack.

The hotel was built along a horseshoe plan, with the open side facing the sea. According to feng shui principles, this was a good shape for gathering wealth. Scott's room was located at one extreme of the U where the view was wide open, surrounded by the sea on three sides, which meant it was also the most expensive room in the hotel. The opened window faced the inside of the U, so that, from here, one could see all the rooms on the other side.

He squinted; the neon lights flickering across the glass wall of the hotel formed a shifting mosaic, and the sound of the surf against the shore came to him intermittently. He trusted his senses, which had been honed by strict training: there was something unusual about the scene; his consciousness just hadn't caught up to it. Suddenly, a red glow flashed across an unlit window on the other side of the hotel, on the same story as his, disappearing almost as soon as it had appeared.

A laser. For eavesdropping. Scott realized that the open window was intended to create a better angle for the light and to increase the sensitivity of the glass as it vibrated with the sound of his voice.

He dashed out of his room and ran through the long hallway, calculating the position of the room with the unlit window. A man was walking toward him, and as soon as he saw Scott, he turned around and pushed open a set of emergency doors, and the staircase echoed with rapid footsteps. *It's him!* Scott slammed through the doors and chased the man down the stairs.

Twenty-two flights of stairs seemed to have no end. The man showed no intention of slowing down, and the dense footsteps echoed back and forth in the staircase, reverberating chaotically. Scott's heart pounded, as though about to leap out of his chest any second. His breathing became short, and a red warning flashed before his eyes—it came from his pacemaker, the result of another accident.

The footsteps below abruptly shifted direction. Scott banged through the emergency doors and emerged into the underground parking garage. The figure of the man stumbled toward the light at the exit, seemingly exhausted. Scott slowed down and tried to adjust his breathing, waiting for the pacemaker to get things under control again. He estimated that his prey was about five foot seven, which meant that his strides were correspondingly shorter than Scott's. It was just a matter of time before Scott caught up.

The roar of an engine came, and the ground vibrated as though some beast had awakened and sneezed. *Damn.* Ignoring the pain in his chest, Scott opened his stride and ran after the man. But the shrill squeals of tires rushed at him from another direction, giving no indication that they intended to slow down.

The man turned back to look in the direction of the oncoming car, but his face showed no relief or joy. The headlights lit up his pale face, and his expression quickly turned to terror.

Just as the car was about to slam into him, Scott jumped and pushed him out of the way. Momentum carried him rolling forward until he crashed into the wall. The car, however, did not stop, but went up the incline and vanished into the bright exit.

Scott lay faceup on the ground, gulping for air. He couldn't even pay attention to the pain: his heart felt scalding hot, like some engine about to fail due to overload, convulsing uncontrollably. He had made a mistake in judgment, and he was going to pay a heavy price for it.

The man stood up unsteadily, still stricken by terror. He looked at Scott and hesitated.

Scott forced the convulsing muscles of his face into an ugly smile.

"I . . . I don't know. . . ." The man spoke Chinese. "They paid me and told me to run, run as fast as I could. I don't know anything, really. . . ."

Scott understood. He laughed. *The cunning Chinese! They're using the trick known as "lure the tiger away from the mountain," one of the Thirty-Six Stratagems of classical Chinese war and politics.* It appeared that their real goal was to get him out of his room so that they could get at his computer. He relaxed. Based on his experience, it was impossible to break through his encryption within such a short period of time; if they tried to disassemble the machine to get at the hard drive, they would trigger the self-destruct mechanism; and if they tried to steal the computer and bring it with them, they'd be giving Scott a chance to trace them to their lair.

"Can you help me?" Scott asked. The man struggled to lift him, but Scott's huge frame caused both of them to tumble down in a pile, raising a cloud of dust.

The room had been registered under a false identity. The hallway closed-circuit TV recording showed that the person had disguised himself as a member of the cleaning staff and snuck into Scott's room. The hotel could provide no explanation for this mysterious figure, and Director Lin Yiyu was about to explode with anger. The man had taken advantage of Scott's pursuit of the false lure and stayed in Scott's room for three minutes and forty seconds before leaving in a hurry, apparently having been warned somehow.

The lid of Scott's computer was closed and the machine was asleep, though the fan was warm.

The mysterious figure had ridden the cargo elevator down to the lobby, taken off his uniform in the restroom, and then walked out the front door of the hotel and hailed a taxi.

"We've already traced the location of that cab." Inside the VIP suite, Director Lin was keeping Scott apprised of the situation while he communicated with the police on his Bluetooth headset. "Don't worry, Mr. Scott. He won't get away."

Scott nodded. He found the entire situation amusing. *A thief raising a hue and cry to catch a thief. You're clearly an accomplished actor.* He wasn't so worried about data theft, but he was curious how this farce would conclude. The doctor who had been summoned checked his bio signs; his pacemaker was working properly again, and other than a feeling of exhaustion, he didn't suffer other forms of discomfort.

"Cardiac dysrhythmia?" the doctor, a young woman, asked as she drew his blood.

"A chronic problem. Paroxysmal tachycardia. From time to time, my heart rate goes out of whack."

"I heard that before they invented virus batteries, you had to change the batteries every couple of years in the pacemakers. There was a British man with an electronic heart who had to recharge his batteries every four hours, and he depended on the cigarette lighter in his car for his life."

Scott laughed politely. A sting on the arm told him that she had pulled out the needle. Doctors always told jokes with a purpose, even if what she said was true.

For a long time after he had been implanted with his pacemaker, Scott suffered from a nameless terror centered on the virus-enhanced batteries. Scientists explained that the active peptides found in viruses enhanced the nanostructures of batteries, increasing their endurance and the stability of the power supply, but the idea that live viruses were sealed in his chest cavity could not put him completely at ease.

"You'll be fine. Just be sure to get plenty of rest." The doctor inserted the blood sample into the portable analyzer and observed the shifting figures. "Your heart—is it congenital?"

"An accident." Scott smiled and intended to say no more. But the sealed-off memories escaped from their cages and cruelly tore open his wound. He convulsed, as though his flawed, pulsing heart had come into contact with a cold, steel needle.

That old photograph was still lying in his wallet: a stream in the middle of a tropical jungle, two beautiful little girls laughing, the dappled sunlight on their skin tracing out rococo lines like the veins of some plant.

Ten years ago, Tracy was three, and Nancy was seven.

They had been on a trip to Papua New Guinea. A research institute owned by the Rimbunan Hijau Group had hired Scott to research the impact of illegal logging on the environment and native tribes with the goal of forcing the local government to crack down on illegal logging so that the Rimbunan Hijau Group could be given a monopoly on the lumber supplies of Papua New Guinea. The so-called sustainable development was, in Scott's eyes, just another name for legalized looting.

At least the job paid well and the scenery was fantastic, and Scott quickly reached the desired conclusion. As the project was winding down, Scott sent for his wife and daughters so that the whole family could enjoy a tropical vacation.

After they left Port Moresby, Papua New Guinea's capital, Scott found it much more difficult to locate an unspoiled patch of paradise than he had anticipated. The roar of chainsaws filled the jungles, chasing birds and beasts deeper into the interior. The pipes laid down by Oil Search Ltd. were like a web of exposed capillaries, crossing forests, rivers, and villages to suck the black essence of the ancient past out of the rich soil to slake the unquenchable thirst of the developed world. Even the natives were no longer honest and simple. After the destruction of the rain forests they depended on for their livelihood, they had no choice but to sell their labor and join the logging company, wielding electric chainsaws to cut down the mother trees that had once borne the names of their ancestors.

Their furtive glances concealed hatred and loathing, but they did not pass up any opportunity to surround the white tourists and push any local crafts that could be converted into cash.

In the end, Scott found a place called Kemaru, which in the local language meant "bow and arrow." There was a waterfall as well as a crescent-shaped pool formed by the impact of the water. The mangroves on shore extended their dense aerial roots down to the water, and a broad river met the sea not too far from here, where they could see the beach, the gentle waves of the Bismarck Sea, and the archipelago beyond. Kemaru was perhaps named after the bow-shaped pool.

He repeated *no* to the local guide's sales pitch until, pushed beyond the limits of his patience, he snapped and told him to get out of his sight. The little, dark-skinned man gave him one look and then vanished.

Surrounded by sunlight, birdsong, the clear, cool water, and exotic tropical plants, Scott and Susan acted like typical American tourists. They lay down on the giant rocks next to the pool to enjoy the caress of the sun against their backs, listening to their daughters splashing in the water, giggling like angels. *This really is paradise,* Scott thought.

Daddy! We want to go over there, Nancy said.

Don't go too far, and take care of Tracy. Scott had scouted the site ahead of time. The water wasn't very deep, and there were no dangerous creatures.

I can take care of myself, Tracy said.

Of course, sweetheart. But don't stay away too long. We're going to the beach in a bit. You'll really like it. Scott didn't even bother lifting his head.

Ten minutes passed. Susan began to worry. "Tracy? Nancy?"

There was no answer.

"Nancy! Tracy!" Scott took off his sunglasses, jumped into the pool, and began to swim to one edge of the crescent. The surface of the water was empty. He turned around and swam to the other side, still nothing. His growing anxiety was matched by Susan's increasingly frantic cries.

He dove into the water and widened his eyes, looking for any signs of trouble. Finally, he saw something blue caught in the mangroves' dense roots like a flickering, phosphorescent light: Tracy's bathing suit. He took a deep breath and splashed through the water madly. It appeared that the mangrove roots had caught Tracy's feet, and, as she panicked and struggled, had become even more entangled. Luckily, she was so light and small that Scott easily disentangled her and lifted her out of the water.

Tracy's face was bloodless, and her body was completely limp. He handed her to Susan.

"Perform CPR on her," Scott yelled. "Just like the video. Get the water out of her lungs." Without hesitation, Scott dove into the water again.

Nancy must be around. He widened his eyes and kicked hard through the water. On the other side of the clump of tentacle-like roots that had caught Tracy, he found Nancy's doll-like face. Her eyes were half closed and her mouth was wide open—clearly her lungs were already filled with water. Scott forced himself to keep the terror at bay and focused on extracting the stiff body out from the roots. It appeared that she had been caught because she was trying to save her little sister.

Take care of Tracy. Was it because of that admonition that Nancy had not dared to call for help but tried to save Tracy herself? Scott's heart pounded against the walls of his chest, and all the air in his lungs was used up. But the knotty roots refused to give up. His strength alone wasn't enough, and he felt he was about to explode.

Scott erupted out of the water and gulped for air. The little, dark guide stood on shore.

Goddamn it! Get in here and help me!

The guide shook his head impassively, as though he couldn't understand Scott. *A hundred thousand kina,* he said.

I'll give you what you want. Help me!

The guide shook his head again. *I want it now.*

You fucking sonofabitch. Desperately, Scott took off his Rolex diving watch and tossed it at the guide. *The watch is worth a lot more than a hundred thousand kina,* he lied.

The guide examined the watch, and then dove into the water.

But it was too late.

Scott beat the guide until his face was a bloody pulp. Nancy's body lay still to the side, as pale and beautiful as Millais's Ophelia. He could not believe the little girl, so full of life a few minutes earlier, was truly dead. Susan hugged the terrified Tracy and could not stop crying. The native rescue workers who had shown up too late prayed for the repose of the departed soul, and following local custom, put their foreheads against the murderous tree and continued to mutter. The natives were animists, but Scott could not imagine what they had to say to that tree. He felt his heart convulse in pain, as though a part of his life was being carved out of his chest.

The exertions and his rapid gulps of air had led to paroxysmal tachycardia, according to the diagnosis of his doctor. He also advised that Scott be implanted with a pacemaker. But Scott understood that not only had the rhythm of his heart changed, his whole life had been transformed.

Ten years later, Tracy was thirteen, and Nancy was still seven.

Mimi picked up her pace, not even daring to look behind her.

Back in the Luo clan's territory, she rushed to the familiar old shack, but the moment she crossed into the yard, a few natives emerged from the door, holding the photograph in their hands.

Damn! Mimi instinctively veered off and hid behind a pile of trash. She stuck her head out and stole a peek: they were not the goons from the Luo clan. They were all strangers, and dressed differently from those gang members, but there was no doubt that they were all looking for her.

Mimi was trying to decide between waiting and hiding until these men left or leaving immediately, but someone slapped her on the back, and she jumped up like a startled cat.

"Mimi, you're back! I've been worried about you." It was Lanlan, who worked with her in the same shed. Ever since Mimi had left for the Chen clan's territory, more than a week ago, they hadn't seen each other. It was good to see her familiar grin.

The strangers turned at her voice. Desperately, Mimi pushed Lanlan away and began to run, just like in her nightmare. The graveled road surface, shack, and piles of trash shook violently in her field of vision before receding behind her. She could hear the shouts behind her get closer, and mixed with the rushing air, they seemed like the hissing of the tongues of poisonous snakes. Gravel got into her shoes and sliced open the bottoms of her feet, but she extended her strides and put every ounce of her strength into running, hoping to use the pain to dig into her hidden reserves for survival.

The voices of the men were now next to her ears.

Just as Mimi was about to give up, she saw a water-hauling electric rickshaw. Uncle He, who was from near her home village, was the driver, and he had always been friendly to her. She did not hesitate but accelerated and leapt onto the back of the rickshaw. The cart shook and the colliding water drums made muffled sounds. Startled, Uncle He turned around and saw that it was Mimi. But before he could even speak, she bellowed at him:

"Get going! Go!"

The electric motor roared to life and the rickshaw rumbled along the dirt road toward Silicon Isle Town. Mimi brushed aside her sweat-stained bangs and fought to catch her breath, but noticed in the rear-view mirror a few figures pursuing close behind.

The dozens of drums of water on the rickshaw cart slowed down their progress, and those men were in excellent shape. Like a pack of wolves hounding wounded prey, they stayed right on their heels through the clouds of dust, just waiting for their target to make some mistake.

Mimi bit her bottom lip and tumbled one of the drums over on its side and kicked it off the cart. The drum bounced a few times against the surface of the road and rolled toward the men like a bowling ball. The two men in the front agilely dodged out of the way, but the third man, his view blocked by his companions, couldn't get out of the way in time. The drum smashed into him, and with a shriek, he fell down and did not get up.

"My water! Oh, my water!" Uncle He cried.

"I'll pay you back!" Mimi almost screamed at him.

More drums of water were pushed off the cart and rolled one after the other at the chasers. Awkwardly, they tried to get out of the way and had no choice but to slow down; the distance between them and the rickshaw increased. Since only a few drums were left in the cart, the rickshaw sped up, and Mimi felt as if the vehicle were floating, and the ride grew far bumpier.

"Hold on!" Uncle He warned.

In front of them was a stone bridge over a large ditch, a choke point on the way into the town. It was too late to slow down, and Uncle He twisted the handlebars with all his strength. The rickshaw screeched and made the almost-ninety-degree turn sharply, heading for the bridge. This would have been a fairly easy maneuver if the rickshaw were fully laden, but now that Mimi had gotten rid of most of the heavy drums, the light rickshaw lost its balance, and the outer wheel rose into the air as the rickshaw slid across the bridge at an angle like a glider, scattering the street peddlers who had set up booths on the bridge.

Uncle He did his best to avoid hitting the crowd, but the vehicle's weight and speed proved too much for him in the end. Mimi felt a violent jolt and found herself flying through the air. The rickshaw smashed into one of the bridge piers with a loud crack, and Uncle He was tossed against the head of the bridge, where he lay limp like a dish of meat displayed for sale.

Mimi slammed against the road. Pain racked her body and her mouth was filled with a salty, iron taste. Dazed, she seemed to hear the footsteps and the shouts of the men chasing after her come closer. Desperately, she tried to crawl forward, seeking any sliver of hope. She grabbed on to a foot that stopped in front of her whose taut calf muscles were as hard as stones.

"Help me . . ."

Kaizong's face flashed through Mimi's confused mind; she wished that he would appear now, like he had the day of the festival, in the alley. She lifted her face: the man's face was blurry against the strong backlight, but the shifting outline of his face showed that he was laughing. She heard a crisp crack like two pieces of jade being knocked together, and saw a red flame rise from the man's shoulder.

She understood that this time, luck wasn't with her.

5

The weak sunlight traversed the long and dim corridor to strike the jars and bottles inside the cabinet, where it refracted into a turbid yellow-green sheen. Kaizong stared at the objects stored within—animal and plant specimens soaked in aged medicinal alcohol—with some trepidation: a variety of snakes, sloughed snakeskin, and ophidian reproductive organs; stag antlers; bones of the long-extinct South China tiger; black bear gallbladder; giant centipedes; insects he couldn't name; and the stems and roots of plants. The chitin exoskeletons, softened by the alcohol, seemed to drift like miniature spaceships in some indistinct alien landscape.

The natives of Silicon Isle, especially among the older generation, had unshakable faith in the power of the life essence of these animals and plants, mediated by alcohol, to extend longevity and to increase sexual prowess.

Kaizong was terrified that he was going to come upon some glass bottle containing the drifting remains of some disfigured fetus. This was far from impossible: the placenta of the newborn was once sought after as a health supplement, and many nurses and doctors had once profited off of its trade. Kaizong's mother had even partaken of the precious "purple river wheel" derived from her own afterbirth.

This is not a bad idea for a WWF ad, Kaizong thought. *You are what you eat.*

At the end of the corridor was a narrow door with a pale light seeping through the seams. Stepping through the door, Kaizong found himself in a wide-open space, a circular grain-sunning ground surrounded by rough but solidly built brick houses. A thin and small old man sat in a bamboo recliner and lightly rocked himself, with drying squid and nori seaweed lying about him on the ground. The thick, briny smell of the sea filled Kaizong's nostrils.

When Uncle Chen had informed him that the head of the Chen clan, the real chairman of the extended family enterprise, wanted to see him, Kaizong had tried to imagine the man. But his visual imagination had been so poisoned by Hollywood that all he could conjure up were classic portrayals from movies about the mob, like Marlon Brando from *The Godfather* or Robert De Niro in *Once Upon a Time in America.*

He certainly did not picture this shriveled old man lounging around in his underwear and tank top like some neighborhood grandfather.

The ninety-two-year-old face was wrinkled like wax paper. His eyelids, half shut, trembled slightly, revealing the whites of his eyes. As though detecting a shift in the wind with his nose, he opened his eyes slowly, saw Kaizong standing in front of him, and smiled. The wrinkles on his face rearranged themselves into the corners of his eyes and the laugh lines at the corners of his mouth.

"Great-Uncle, how are you?"

"I'm well! You are that . . . that . . ."

"Kaizong."

"That's right! Kaizong. Excellent name. It's an allusion from *The Book of Filial Piety*, right? It means getting right to the point."

The old man struggled to get up. Kaizong rushed to steady the rocking recliner for him. It was said that one of Great-Uncle Chen's ancestors had obtained the rank of *jinshi jidi bangyan*—meaning not only had he passed the three-yearly examination at the Imperial court, a far rarer and more difficult achievement than passing the country, provincial, or national examinations, but he had been distinguished by being ranked second overall out of all the examinees. With such an illustrious and scholarly ancestor, it was no wonder that Great-Uncle Chen recognized the source for Kaizong's name right away.

"Why don't you help me up onto the roof? 'The setting sun is infinitely beautiful,' as the poets say; we should treasure each chance we get."

Kaizong supported the head of the clan as they ascended the stone staircase, open on one side, until they emerged onto the parapetless roof deck, ring-shaped like an unadorned stone bracelet lying between the mountain and the sea. Drying laundry and blankets, seafood dehydrating in the wind, and monocrystalline solar panels were arranged neatly in patches, giving a layered, orderly texture to the whole scene. The sun dove at the surface of the sea, and the light turned from white to gold, and then dimmed until it became a red fire that set the cottony clouds on the horizon aflame. The sea breeze caressed their faces, bringing with it a moist, salty freshness. Kaizong felt reinvigorated and waited for the elder to speak.

The old man's face sparkled in the setting sun like a piece of Taihu limestone, filled with the pores and wrinkles of eons. He gazed in the direction of the sea, and his sunken eyes seemed to conceal a strange light.

"I went to the temple yesterday and prayed for a divination slip." He handed a slip of red paper to Kaizong.

> Ksitigarbha Temple, Sexagenary Stems-and-Branches, Goddess Mazu's Oracle
>
> The fifty-eighth sign, Gui-Wei, ○○● ○●●, of the element of Wood, advantage Spring, suitable for the East.
>
> A snake's body desires to be a dragon;
>
> But fate seems to have other ideas.
>
> A long illness requires rest and relaxation;
>
> Many words are spoken, though few are wise.

Kaizong knew that the coastal inhabitants on both sides of the Taiwan Strait had the custom of praying to Mazu for safety on the sea, but he couldn't figure out what this obscure bit of oracular text had to do with him.

"Whose future does this slip speak of?"

"Good question." The old man did not turn around. "I prayed for it on behalf of Silicon Isle."

The answer wasn't at all what Kaizong had expected, and he understood right away the worries hinted at by the clan head's fortune. Whether he had really obtained it from Mazu, the poem clearly revealed the Chen clan's attitude toward the TerraGreen Recycling project. Of course, if the elder really intended to express his opinions via the will of the heavens, Kaizong could marshal no arguments against it.

"I've been alive for almost a century and have never left Silicon Isle. I've seen the rice paddies dry up and wither and our soil turn into poisoned wasteland; I've seen reef islands sunk with explosives, bays filled in to reclaim land, ports and bridges spring up faster than crops; I've seen warships bare their gray spines on the horizon while schools of fish retreat farther away and grow more sparse; I've heard the loudspeakers, the radio stations and TV stations broadcast an endless stream of songs of celebration, but folk operas about the suffering of the common people find few patrons and are dying out.

"Silicon Isle is sick with a deep and serious illness, but it is not a disease that can be cured by a simple, strong dose of harsh medicine. To the contrary, to speak in the language of folk medicine, such an attempt might well arouse a stronger, poisoned tongue of flame to attack the heart."

So selfish. Chen Kaizong's first response upon hearing the elder's soliloquy was disgust.

He knew very well how people were exploited and oppressed. This was a common theme throughout history: take any group of people—it didn't matter if they were of different races or compatriots—some always set themselves apart as a higher class, and, in the name of gods, the nation, or "progress," made laws and constructed rules that allowed them to dominate the lives of the other classes, to own their bodies as well as spirits.

Survival is sufficient justification. It was easy for Kaizong to convince himself when he was dealing with abstractions in textbooks, but when everything was real, living and breathing before his eyes, the matter was completely different.

In the last few weeks, he had immersed himself in the lives and labor of the waste workers. He saw the pallid, sickly complexions of the young women and their rough, spotted hands, the result of corrosive, harsh chemicals; he breathed in the odors that made him gag, tasted the nigh-inedible fare provided by the bosses that passed for food, and understood the unbelievably low wages offered to them. He thought of Mimi; thought of her guileless smile, and underneath, the particles of heavy metal stuck to the walls of her blood vessels; thought of her deformed olfactory cells and damaged immune system. She was like a self-regulating, maintenance-free machine, and like the other hundreds of millions in the high-quality labor force of this land, she would work day after day tirelessly until her death.

Kaizong's heart skipped a beat, and he couldn't explain why he was feeling this way. He saw that the elder had turned around to gaze at him in his entranced state. The elder smiled, and, almost carelessly, said, "I hear that you're close to one of the waste girls."

"Her name is Mimi." Kaizong corrected him deliberately.

"Of course. I'm just not used to referring to them by name."

"I think it's possible to get used to it over time." Tamping down his anger, Kaizong struggled to maintain his speech in the respectful register. He did not want to offend this powerful man.

"Ho ho, young people always think that the Great Wall could be built overnight."

"No, but it is very possible for it to collapse overnight."

"I guess we'll just have to wait and see. Don't you have a date with her tonight?"

Kaizong was taken aback, but the old man was no longer looking at him; instead, he stared into the distance.

Kaizong rapidly replayed the scenes of his time with Mimi: the dead dog whose body still spasmed; the sea full of glowing blue lights, the spirit of Tide Gazing Beach at night . . . he was trying to figure out where the clan head had implanted his spies. Abruptly, he realized that the sparkles coming out of the deep-sunken eyes of the old man were not reflections of the setting sun at all: the tiny blue dots flickered like the status lights on a wireless terminal gathering secrets from the ether.

Contrary to Scott's expectations, they *did* manage to catch his intruder.

The interrogation room was clean and brightly lit, unlike what he had imagined. The man had a young face with strong features, and one of his hands was cuffed to his chair. As Scott came into the room, the young man's eyes seemed to look up and to the right, as if matching Scott's face with some image in his head. He spoke in Cantonese-accented English. "We meet finally, Mr. Scott Brandle. I've been looking forward to this."

"Do you know me?"

"More than you can imagine."

"Oh, please elaborate."

"Let's not waste too much time on your identity, shall we? Exxon-Mobil, Rimbunan Hijau, the World Bank, TerraGreen Recycling, and the terrifying puppet master behind them—don't all of these changing names share the same last name: Greedy?" A smug grin filled the man's face.

"Good joke. But let me remind you, Greedy folks have long arms. You'd best get to the point before I smash my fist into your pretty face."

"You won't." The young man tilted his head at a corner of the ceiling. "They're watching us, and probably listening, as well. If I were you, I'd tread carefully."

Scott adjusted his chair awkwardly; the legs of the chair scraping across the floor made an unpleasant noise.

"Who *are* you? And what do you want?" He deliberately lowered his voice, as though unaware of the sensitivity of the monitoring equipment.

"It's not what *I* want, but what *we* want. We know about the tricks you used in Venezuela, Papua New Guinea, the Philippines, and West Africa—you come in as saviors to promote local economic development and provide jobs; nicely done, ha! We don't care about any of that; it's how the world functions. But we *do* care about your side gig, the sort of little cracks you make that can derail a roller coaster. Believe me, you don't want to get involved in this scandal; it will be dirtier than you can possibly imagine—even if your hands aren't exactly clean."

Scott said nothing. Clearly these people had obtained some intelligence that he was unaware of.

The task should have been simple. He came to Silicon Isle under the name of Scott Brandle, a high-level executive for the TerraGreen Recycling project. Using a series of familiar techniques—advanced environmental protection technology, projections for increased economic output, models for input-output ratios, promises for mid- and long-term social benefits and new jobs, sexual bribes, and so on—he was going to play his hand quickly and lure the local government to sign the agreement for jointly developing an industrial park for the recycling industry. TerraGreen Recycling would contribute the technology and some funds, and the Silicon Isle government would allocate the land, broker an accord among the local clans, integrate the existing waste-processing industrial resources, and supply the large amounts of cheap labor necessary later.

On the surface, it wasn't a bad deal; indeed, the balance seemed to be tilted slightly in favor of Silicon Isle as TerraGreen Recycling would agree to provide additional funds to clean up the heavily polluted water and soil.

In return, TerraGreen Recycling would have the right to purchase Silicon Isle's recycled renewable resources at a favorable price. This would solve, at a stroke, the biggest headache of the local government: a long-term, steady cash flow that could be used to repay the interest and principle on the loan from the bank and bring about a handsome yearly increase in GDP.

This was also why Director Lin Yiyu had changed his previous attitude and tried to conclude this deal despite the heavy pressure he faced. Unlike officials who passed through local assignments like a revolving door, he was born and bred in Silicon Isle. All of the Lin family's relations by blood and marriage were concentrated here, and he wanted to accomplish something of real benefit for the future generations of Silicon Isle and leave behind a good name. But reality was too harsh: he was squeezed between two panels of the same door—the clan and the government—and though he strove to wiggle through the narrow crack, he had ended up a homeless dog, pitiable and lost.

Of course, Scott understood that the deal was too perfect to be true. Only the powerless hooligans who lived in the streets fought with their knives out in the open; killers of real skill kept their weapons sheathed and achieved victory without blood staining their edges.

"I hear that suspects often die during interrogation here, and the official autopsies never show anything wrong." Scott kept his voice cold.

"I was prepared to die the moment I set foot on Silicon Isle. And I will not be the last." The young man met his gaze fearlessly.

"Why don't you just tell me what you want?" Scott was suddenly tired of this game. He had been in costume for too long, taken on too many characters, and he no longer remembered what he should be like when he wasn't playing a role.

"Let me make a phone call, and my boss will contact you directly. It's not clean here."

Clean. The word felt like some allergen to Scott and he laughed uproariously though the young man's searing gaze seemed to be trying to weld his lips shut. *There's nothing clean in this world.*

"We'll make it clean." Scott let the double entendre hang in the air, got up, and left the room. The camera in the corner of the ceiling continued to show a tiny figure, distorted through the lens to resemble a flattened cockroach whose dead legs slowly extended as the joints relaxed.

The setting sun coagulated into a bloodred bright glow on the horizon.

The elder's face was like a burning sheet of paper: the page, or what remained of it after the passage of so many years, curled in the leaping flames, turning to ash. Though his eyelids drooped, he saw through everything; though he spoke no words, he was louder than a clanging bronze bell.

Kaizong understood very well that the figure who stood before him was far more than an old man at the twilight of life. The sparkling lights that emitted from his eyes were clearly the result of the latest model of augmented-reality contact lenses, though Kaizong wasn't sure of the access level. In this restricted-bitrate zone, an old man so equipped was a terrifying figure, as though he could tear off his disguise and, in a flash, turn into a cold-blooded warrior.

But the elder smiled and shook his head. Softly, he said, "I know you two went to Tide Gazing Beach. That's not a good place."

Not a good place. Such an ordinary phrase made Kaizong's heart sink. "I've heard some rumors—"

"They're true," the old man interrupted. "It's called palirromancy."

It was impossible to see Tide Gazing Beach from where they were standing. Only the pointy apex of Tide Gazing Pavilion peeked out from behind the intervening roofs, arranged like stacks of turtle shells—easy to miss unless one sought it out. The sea gradually lost its crimson-gold glow as the sun continued to sink, first near the shore, then farther away, like melted lead cooling down and turning gray. The thin, undulating white lines on the surface appeared as patterns moving across an oscilloscope: jumping, vanishing, reappearing, like an endless musical score, a song of gravity lasting eons.

Kaizong listened as the elder emotionlessly described a piece of history not recorded in any book. Abruptly, he felt a chill along his spine. *It's just the wind,* he thought, *please, let it be just the wind.*

It was said that Tide Gazing Pavilion was built by Han Yu, a Vice Minister of Justice during the Tang Dynasty. Han Yu had argued against Emperor Xianzong's[13] plan to install the Buddha's finger bone in the palace, and, as a result, was banished from the court and demoted to

[13] Xianzong's reign (AD 805–820) was distinguished by his military campaigns against independent regional warlords to reunite the Tang Empire. Han Yu is considered one of the finest and most influential writers in the Chinese literary tradition, in both prose and poetry. He advocated a return to Classical literary styles and cultural orthodoxy for the empire and opposed Buddhist influences (somewhat analogous to the role played by Cato the Elder for the Roman Republic in resisting Hellenization).

the position of Prefect of Chaozhou. After a visit to Silicon Isle—which wasn't called Silicon Isle back then, of course—Han Yu had ordered the construction of the pavilion. Outside the pavilion, there had once stood a stone stele carved with Han Yu's calligraphy: "Those who observe the tides may know the world; those who hold on to beneficence and virtue may bring good fortune." Later, the stele fell into the sea in a tropical storm.

Some had argued that Han Yu's couplet was an expression of his resentment toward Emperor Xianzong, but this was the result of an only partial understanding of history. As a matter of fact, the two lines were aimed at an ancient custom of the natives of Silicon Isle: palirromancy.

Palirromancy was a technique of divination whose origins were lost in the mists of time. It was supposed to be the distillation of the wisdom accumulated by generations of Silicon Isle fishermen. Analogous to the principles of other methods of divination, palirromancy interpreted the positions, conditions, and trails of flotsam and jetsam washed ashore by the tides as signs of the future. However, while other methods of divination mostly relied on lifeless objects—branches, turtle shells, animal bones, sand piles, coins, bamboo rods—palirromancy relied on living things.

The ancient people of Silicon Isle believed that as living beings drowned in the tides, they linked to the spirit world and became extremely sensitive and receptive of messages from the future, turning into powerful tools for diviners to derive more precise visions of what was to come.

The unique lagoon formed by the shoal of Silicon Isle was the ideal location for palirromancy. The ancient inhabitants of Silicon Isle stood at the end of the tentacle and tossed the living sacrifice into the water and then waited on Tide Gazing Beach for the drowning creature to be tossed ashore. It was said that earlier, the beach had been artificially divided into twelve equal sections and marked with granite slabs carved with sigils to aid in the divination effort, but during the Cultural Revolution, all the markings had been destroyed.

"Then . . . the sacrifices they used . . ." Kaizong had trouble speaking and cleared his throat.

"Newborn calves and lambs, or dogs," the elder answered. "Most of the time, at least."

The sacrifice was bound with special ropes and knots so that the creature could not escape by swimming or treading water, but had plenty of room to struggle and thrash to prolong the drowning process. In death, their long, painful journey through the sea left their bodies twisted into hideous postures, as though they had suffered injuries in their dialogue with the spirit world: terrifying expressions, empty gazes, sodden souls.

If the sacrifice arrived onshore still alive, then its fate depended on the message it brought from the spirits. If the augury was auspicious, then people waited until the creature died and then buried it with the proper rites; on the other hand, if the augury was inauspicious, then people killed it by stoning and buried the carcass in some random desolate spot, leaving behind no marking to prevent the ill fortune from following any trails to the house of the soothsayer.

Kaizong knew very little about Vice Justice Minister Han Yu, but Great-Uncle Chen painted the verbal portrait of an extremist who was willing to risk his head to argue that the supposed finger bone of the Buddha should be "consigned to complete destruction via burning flames and surging waters so that the people will no longer be plagued by a false faith, and future generations may be freed from such danger." For such a staunch atheist to utter the words "those who observe the tides may know the world," which seemed to hint at a mild sort of admiration, was almost inconceivable.

Great-Uncle Chen explained that this was because Han Yu, whose political ambition had been thwarted, had asked the soothsayer to predict his own future and witnessed the palirromancy ceremony himself. A dog's limbs were bound, and then it was thrown into the sea, belly-up. An hour later, the carcass, its belly swollen, was tossed onto the beach in that same position; a second wave followed, lifted up the carcass, flipped it over, and left it with its snout in the sand.

The soothsayer interpreted the omen in the following manner: although it was impossible for Han Yu to overturn his fate during this cycle, he should maintain a low profile and wait for the next cycle, when he was certain to return to the capital in a position of great power. The augury was, overall, quite auspicious.

When Emperor Muzong, Xianzong's son and successor, acceded to the throne, he recalled Han Yu to the capital and promoted him to Dean of the Imperial Academy, and then Vice Minister of Defense and Vice Minister of Personnel. The pavilion and stele were gifts by Han Yu to thank the spirits for the good omens they gave him.

"How do you explain the second line in his couplet, then—'those who hold on to beneficence and virtue may bring good fortune'?" Kaizong wondered how the great scholar felt about the sacrifices. He had a hard time imagining Han Yu, the legendary hero who had chased crocodiles out of the rivers of Chaozhou,[14] as the original conservationist, protector of animals.

"Occasionally"—the old man's eyes began to flicker—"we also used humans for palirromancy."

---

[14] The story of Han Yu chasing away the crocodiles that plagued the inhabitants of Chaozhou is a complex mélange of folk legends and historical record. Han Yu himself composed a famous essay addressed to the crocodiles—still studied by Classical Chinese students as a fine example of his witty, unornamented style—that perhaps should be better read as political metaphor. Readers unfamiliar with the background may imagine this story as somewhat analogous to the legend of Saint Patrick banishing the snakes from Ireland.

"Hey, Fake Foreigner, now do you understand why the boatman didn't dare to land the sampan?" Mimi had asked, that night at Tide Gazing Beach.

They were in a mass graveyard. A few random wooden plaques stuck into the dark-colored soil indicated that bodies were buried in this plot of land. However, the plaques contained only the year of death; there was no year of birth or name. Scattered here and there were a few slips of ghost money and some bits of burnt incense and candles. In the pale light of the moon, the sight seemed especially ghastly. Mimi put her hands together, lowered her eyes, and muttered a prayer.

"These are . . ." Kaizong lowered his voice, as though afraid to disturb the nameless, homeless ghosts.

"They're anonymous bodies washed ashore by the tides; some were trying to smuggle themselves into Hong Kong; some were supposed to be women and children killed by the natives in their . . . ceremonies . . ."

Despite being a staunch atheist, Kaizong shuddered at this. However, he quickly calmed himself down: *This is surely nothing more than an urban legend made up by the migrant workers to smear the natives.*

"You dragged me all the way here in the middle of the night just for this?"

"Of course not. Look! Over there!" Mimi tilted her head, indicating an immense shadow in one corner of the graveyard.

"Wow." Kaizong stopped in front of the object, stunned by its size and eerie appearance.

He took out his ruggedized mobile phone and wiped off the condensation. The screen emitted a pale glow that illuminated this Buddhist-Daoist guardian of the graveyard—an almost three-meter-tall exoskeleton robot, a mecha. The alloy armor was covered by Daoist charms so that it was no longer possible to tell the armor's original paint color; from every protrusion in the armor hung strings of plastic or wooden Buddhist prayer beads that struck each other in the breeze like wind chimes; even the joints were covered with bright red ribbons representing wishes for good fortune.

Compared to the Su-35 fighters being auctioned on eBay, this mecha wasn't so impressive, nothing more than a toy abandoned by some impulsive, wealthy individual. The increasingly esoteric development of material sciences and manufacturing techniques made reverse engineering into a difficult and impractical art. Take the example of the mecha's electroactive artificial muscle fibers, which took the place of traditional hydraulic actuators: even if you figured out all the details about the fibers' structure and composition, you would have no way of replicating them. The era when it was possible to intercept and capture an enemy fighter and use it to significantly improve a nation's own aeronautical-engineering capabilities was long gone.

Kaizong was curious: *How did this mecha come to be here? And why does it look so strange?*

Mimi opened her eyes after her prayer. As if she had heard his unspoken questions, she hesitated for a moment, and then said, "It's because of Brother Wen."

Brother Wen had claimed the rare find as soon as it arrived in Silicon Isle. In his private laboratory shed, he managed to repair all visible signs of damage and reconnected the virus batteries to a source of power. Further exploration revealed two sets of controls for the mecha. The first was remote control. He tried to crack the communication protocols, but for some reason, the system failed to respond. Defeated, he turned to the other control system: force-sensing linkage. This required someone to climb into the cockpit of the mecha and pilot it by having the powered armor sense his movements and mirror them.

Of course he wouldn't take the risk himself. Instead, he chose Ah Rong, an orphan.

Skinny Ah Rong made a striking contrast against the bulky metal exoskeleton as he climbed into the cockpit, his face full of pure joy. He shifted his arms and legs around until the indicator lights lit up. Excited, Brother Wen shouted at him to start moving. Since the machine wasn't properly tuned to this specific pilot, the movements of the mecha were slow and clumsy, like an astronaut walking on the moon. Hundreds, even thousands, of times a second, the force sensors communicated their data to the central computer, which, after making the required calculations, transmitted signals to the electroactive muscle bundles, causing them to contract and making the mecha move. If delay intruded into any link in the process, the pilot would feel like he was moving through a viscous liquid, where motion fell significantly behind will.

Based on Mimi's description, Kaizong managed to get a pretty good picture of what had happened.

Ah-Rong-mecha's movements gradually became smooth and agile. Ah Rong also grew excited, wielding the robot's mechanical arms to crush the junk heap. He began to run, and the crowd of spectators ran along with him.

It was an unbelievable combination of strength and speed. Ah-Rong-mecha ran with Ah Rong's characteristic light, open stride, but each footfall smashed against the ground, rumbling dully. He ran with no destination or direction in mind, like a blinded Hercules in search of an outlet for his brute strength.

Brother Wen ran after him, breathing heavily. He shouted for Ah Rong to stop, realizing before anyone else that something was wrong.

Ah-Rong-mecha seemed to be trying to shake off something; he swung his arms and legs wildly, destroying the houses, trees, and cars that got in the way. The terrified crowd scattered, trying to get out of the way of this out-of-control metal monster. The beast, trailing a cloud of dust, debris, broken branches, and glass shards, left the territory of the Luo clan and headed for the no-man's-land of Tide Gazing Beach.

The waste children running ahead of the monster screamed with ignorant joy: *Ah Rong is on fire! Ah Rong is on fire!*

Indeed, puffs of black smoke emerged from the cockpit of the galloping exoskeleton, carrying the odor of burnt flesh. Only now did the crowd understand that Ah-Rong-mecha's goal was the sea.

But he didn't make it.

By the time Mimi rushed to the scene and shoved her way through the dense crowd, she saw Ah-Rong-mecha standing still next to the mass graveyard. The boy's scrawny body, charcoal black, was smoldering and smoking in the alloy armor like an overcooked piece of shriveled bacon. Uselessly, Brother Wen tried to put the fire out with armfuls of sand. Some wires short-circuited, and sparks flew everywhere. The spectators' expression showed horror with traces of satisfaction underneath, as though they were enjoying some dramatization of death. On Brother Wen's face, she saw a complicated expression, an amalgamation of regret, defeat, and perhaps a trace of sorrow.

Within three days, the tragedy had turned into another episode in the legends surrounding Tide Gazing Beach, and the orphan Ah Rong became, in the retelling, another example of the relentless logic of karma—his fate was surely the result of some sin committed in a previous life.

No one remembered the role played by Brother Wen.

Kaizong examined the burn marks left inside the cockpit: the seat was still caked with traces of the fat from the incinerated corpse, as well as silicate crystals left by the fire, stuck around the logo of Lockheed Martin. *Earlier short circuits in the electrical systems must have led to overheating*, he thought, remembering the scene from Xialong Village. He wanted to throw up.

"No one wants to touch junk associated with death." Mimi put her hands together again in a pose of prayer. "Everyone feels this area is filled with bad luck, and if anyone stumbled in here by mistake, they had to buy ghost money and incense to make offerings to this . . . deity. They all say that it had brought Ah Rong here for payback."

Mimi's tone was filled with uncertainty, as though she didn't quite believe what she was saying, but also dreaded the metal armor.

At first, Kaizong didn't understand the source of her dread; he even thought her superstition a bit funny. However, as they were leaving, he glanced back and seemed to see a cool, blue flash of light inside that infernal armor that had once smelted an innocent soul. When he tried to get a closer look, it turned out to be only the reflection of the lighthouse in the distance sweeping its beam across the desolate graveyard and pale white beach, carving an ephemeral trail across the surface of the sea, culminating in a bright point in the distance.

The sea at night was like a slumbering, black beast whose even, potent exhalations were infused with a hypnotic power. This was a place where few set foot. Years ago, the place had also been a mass graveyard for the anonymous corpses who had failed in their attempts to smuggle themselves into Hong Kong. Luo Jincheng gazed at the shore rising and falling through the window of the car, like some bone-white blank funereal scroll slowly unfurling under the light of the moon and the lighthouse. At the end of the scroll was an orange glow that brought some feeling of warmth to the chilly scene.

That was his destination, the place that people in private referred to as the "Hall of Charity and Piety." On Silicon Isle, the living didn't need charity, only the dead.

The girl turned out to be even younger than he had imagined. Her chest heaved violently, and the wounds from scraping against the ground had not yet stopped bleeding. Animal-like moans emitted from her gagged mouth, and her eyes were filled with terror; however, they revealed no confusion, as if she had long anticipated the arrival of this day.

Luo Jincheng indicated that they should untie her. After a few coughs, the dirty rag in her mouth fell onto the ground, soaked with her spit, like some hairball coughed up by a cat.

"Don't be afraid." He squatted down and smiled kindly at her. "I'll let you go as soon as you answer a few questions."

The fear on her face did not diminish one whit.

"Have you seen this boy?" Luo Jincheng held up his phone to show her the wallpaper.

Her pupils dilated and then dimmed immediately.

"Tell me, what did you do to him?" Luo Jincheng's tone was placid, and bystanders might even have thought they detected traces of pity.

The girl remained still for a few moments, and then began to shake her head convulsively.

Luo Jincheng looked up at the ceiling lamps and the warm yellow light they cast over everyone in the room, creating the comfortable, homey atmosphere one might see in a sitcom. Without their glinting metal instruments, perhaps the actors would look even more appropriate for the scene. He sighed.

"Why is that American always with you?"

A dreamlike expression flitted across the girl's face, as if she was asking herself the same question. After a while, she said her first line.

"He said he likes talking with me . . ."

Knifeboy and the two other thugs erupted into hysterical laughter. The howling was so loud that the hanging lamps seemed to sway.

Luo Jincheng turned back angrily, and the laugh track cut off. He shook his head and looked back at this waste girl, so fragile that she could snap in half at any moment. *I'm fucking wasting my time.* He stood up.

"Keep her here; bring her to me on the eighth day of the lunar month."

Luo Jincheng walked to the door and seemed to remember something. He turned around and, taking note of the unnamable excitement on the faces of these rascals who had followed him for so many years, he realized that he was looking at versions of himself from years ago. He raised his voice.

"I need her alive."

Kaizong ran in a panic; it was long past the hour he and Mimi had agreed on. An invisible hand seemed to be squeezing his stomach in time with his wildly beating heart, and a feeling composed of suffocation and nausea tumbled in his body with each stride. He couldn't push away the horrible scene in his imagination; he couldn't believe that such barbarism had been the custom in the land of his birth for thousands of years, that the blood in his veins bore such a savage heritage.

He had difficulty catching his breath, as though he himself were that suffering dog whose limbs had been tied and then tossed into the heaving waves, left there to struggle against death, surrounded by surging bubbles and blue-green patterns of light, and carried by an irresistible force to be dashed against the distant beach. The dog turned into a baby, a child born out of wedlock whose soft skin turned pale and wrinkled in the briny water like swollen maggots, spinning and tumbling in the vortices stirred up by the tides, and slowly, like dancing kelp, the baby unfurled into a young woman whose soft waist was seized and flexed by the hidden currents, whose body was forced into impossible poses like some stringless puppet, suffused with a fragile and vicious beauty.

Unchaste women and their bastard issue. The elder's words echoed in his mind like some spell. *They leave no trace in Silicon Isle, like the unofficial history I've been telling you.*

Then how can you know these things so well? As soon as he spoke, he regretted it.

Slowly, the corpse of the woman in his imagination spun around in the tide and the seaweed-like hair parted to reveal a bloodless face.

Mimi's face.

Finally, Kaizong was at Mimi's shed. He leaned over and grabbed his knees. Sweat poured down his back and he gulped for air, ignoring the odd looks the women waste workers cast his way. She wasn't at work, and she wasn't in her shack. Mimi was gone and no one knew where. Anxiety landed on Kaizong like a murder of crows. His whole body trembled as he had when he had seen the blue sparks flying out of the eyes of the leader of the Chen clan.

He would never be able to forget the expression on the elder's face as he revealed the answer to the riddle.

I am also an observer of the tides. The old man's face was utterly calm. His entire conversation with Kaizong had been laying the groundwork for this moment.

Or perhaps he had only intended to make Kaizong late for his date.

Kaizong stood in the dim, humid dusk, gazing at the empty end of the road, waiting for something that would never come, lost. The muscles on his face contracted and twisted, as if he was struggling to dismiss some idea, some thought that would not leave, like a buzzing fly. But the harder he tried, the more the premonition swelled and multiplied, like proliferating cancer cells that took up every inch of space in his mind.

He would never see Mimi again.

IRIDESCENT WAVE

For all tomorrow's parties.

—SBT (Silicon-Bio Technology) advertising slogan

PART TWO

IRIDESCENT
WAVE

7

Every fifteen seconds, a bright white beam shot through the only window, appearing and disappearing in a moment, temporarily bleaching the dim yellow light in the room. The shadows seemed to come to life and, panicked, dodge the beam with circular motions and climb up the moldy and cracked walls until they merged into dark obscurity.

The first time she saw the beam of light, Mimi had thought she was catching a glimpse of hope. Frenzied, she had thrown herself against the wall and cried out for help in a hoarse, blood-spittled voice. Then, the light had disappeared, and all was silence except for the sighing of the ocean.

By the time the beam of light appeared for the seventh time, Mimi's mouth was sealed by duct tape. No matter how much she struggled, her hair a mess, her eyes looking wild and crazed, in the end, all she managed to accomplish was to leave a depression in the smooth, silvery surface where her lips were. Her hands were taped behind her as well, the arms having been pulled back until her shoulder blades formed an obtuse angle. Tears and sweat mixed together on her face, stinging her eyes and soaking her collar. She felt pain all over her body but couldn't tell where the wounds were, as though innumerable ants were nibbling at the ends of her nerves, as though she was slowly being put to death through a thousand cuts.

The only parts of Mimi's body that remained free were her legs. Earlier, she had kicked hard at the crotch areas of the men, and even tried to run through the iron gates; they had easily picked her up and dragged her back to the corner on her knees like some stray cat.

The bright beam swept through for the fifteenth time. The men's faces were illuminated, and the glowing, colorful films applied to their shoulders seemed to dim in the strong light; she could see the hairs on their upper arms, the blood vessels under the skin of their elbow pits, and the bloodstained needle; their movements slowed in the steamy, humid air; sweat dripped from their faces, and the corners of their mouths cracked open, revealing waxy, yellow enamel.

Someone said something, and peals of laughter overwhelmed the sound of the surging tides and the humming from the refrigerator's compressor.

In despair, Mimi watched as Knifeboy's Adam's apple moved up and down, his breath quickening, his pupils dilating, his consciousness slackening. But the thing she feared most didn't come to pass. Knifeboy didn't undo his belt and remove his loose, baggy forest-green sweatpants. Instead, he put on an oddly shaped helmet and stood right in front of Mimi.

The helmet was connected by a cord to an augmented-sensing device shaped like a six-tentacled octopus. Skinhead and Scarface hauled it out of a tank filled with nutrient fluid and wrapped the dripping, pale gray, translucent tentacles around Mimi's body and limbs. The cold, slimy sensation brought out goose bumps all over her skin.

Knifeboy gestured for the other two to back away. He closed his eyes, as though to concentrate. After he gave a heavy sigh, the red light on top of the helmet lit up, signaling a successful connection.

Mimi had heard of devices like this. It was what Brother Wen had warned against, as he begged her to have restraint in her use of Halcyon Days. It would only lead to wanting more, he'd said, craving more, until you would do anything, pay any cost for the next hit.

In the pale light, the tentacles looked otherworldly, a tech of nightmares. The tentacles would create a shock of pain in one person and transform it into a shock of pleasure in another, Mimi had heard. For the person wearing the helmet, it was an experience richer, more encompassing, more addictive than that of any drug in the history of mankind.

The tentacles came alive and tightened abruptly around her, glowing crimson. The nanoelectrodes buried under the synthetic skin assaulted her pain nerves with fierce pulses, and an unspeakable agony covered every inch of her. A keening like that of a dying animal emitted from her throat, and tears rolled down her face. She looked pitifully at her torturer, her body convulsing as though suffering a seizure.

But the man ignored her. The world no longer mattered to him. The biofeedback signals gathered from Mimi's body were being continuously fed into his helmet through a high-speed cable, creating the formula for this new brand of ecstasy.

The forty-ninth beam of light pierced Mimi's body. Her spine arched so that her face was tilted as far back as possible, almost breaking her neck. She felt warm liquid flowing down her legs; she had wet herself. The indescribable pain blurred her vision, and countless sparkling lights seemed to shoot out of the edges of her field of vision toward the center. The entire world was distorted.

The shaft of white light slowed down, the intervals between its visits stretched longer. Mimi knew that this was only an illusion—the world had never changed one iota for her sake. Futilely, she counted: the light reappeared a hundred times, maybe a thousand, each wait longer than the last, interminable. Each shock from the tentacles caused the world in her eyes to shake, contract, fill with sparkling lights; she no longer felt pain, only numbness and a deep, abiding weariness.

Mimi didn't know what kind of emotion she was experiencing: anger, despair, sorrow, hatred—maybe it was all of these, but none seemed quite right. She couldn't pin that sensation down: it wasn't capable of being captured by language, and it shifted and changed with the passing of the beam of light, the tentacles' every movement, and the stimuli perceived by each of her pores. Familiar scenes flashed before her eyes:

the trees of her home village, her mother's tears, chili paste, the rise and fall of the tides on the beach, junk heaps, the swollen body of the chipped dog, the stench of burning plastic, the setting sun, the horizon undulating at night, the blue-green glow of the jellyfish, Brother Wen's strange prosthesis, moonlight, Kaizong in the moonlight, Kaizong coming to her rescue on the night of the Ghost Festival, Kaizong lying on the beach next to her gazing up at the stars . . .

These distant, unreal fragments of memory were chaotically stacked together as the tentacles shifted through different patterns of motion. Mimi felt the inside of her body burn; drops of sweat on her skin sizzled and boiled, turning into steam that clouded her view. Everything in the room was slightly and eerily distorted, like mirages in a desert, like a nightmare from which she could not awaken.

Knifeboy's two forgotten assistants excitedly discussed the newest attraction in Dongguan's red-light district: *made in Eastern Europe . . . highly modified lumbar suspension system . . . satisfy the most exotic tastes . . . prosthetic sphincter muscles with adjustable strength . . . foreign whores with electric motors . . .* Scarface laughed lecherously and his facial features seemed to twist and jiggle like jelly, the scar on his left cheek glowing with blood. They were like an inattentive audience treating the violent spectacle before them as an episode of some poorly made soap opera.

Mimi felt a jolt as, without warning, the tape over her mouth was ripped away; the searing pain was like having her skin cauterized with a branding iron. Before she could even refocus her eyes, she felt something closing around her throat, forcing her to open her mouth to suck in air. A slimy, hot object forced itself between her lips and began to press into the cavity between her tongue and palate. One of the tentacles was trying to enter her, to seek fresh nerves to torment.

Knifeboy moaned again, an inhuman noise.

Mimi visualized the connection between the squirming object in her mouth and Knifeboy. In a flash, she made up her mind and bit down, her jaws clenching like a triggered trap.

A scream of unbearable suffering.

Mimi stared at Knifeboy's convulsing face with hate-filled eyes. The veins on Knifeboy's forehead bulged as he stumbled forward, trying to pry the helmet from his head. Mimi clamped down even harder, and as the tentacle between her teeth writhed and contracted, Knifeboy screamed again. The two lackeys milled around, seemingly unsure of whether to first help remove the helmet or try and pry open Mimi's teeth. The white beam again swept through, illuminating by turn each person's frozen pose and expression like some still scene in a pantomime.

You fucking cunt! Knifeboy's howl finally broke apart the tableau vivant.

Out of the corner of her eyes Mimi saw a blue flash. Skinhead was coming at her with a taser, the arc of light between its electrodes flickering like the tongue of a black viper. Instinctively, she loosened her jaws and tried to get out of the way, but she was too late; a powerful force erupted in her head, and her vision exploded into millions of blue-purple daisies, spinning, tumbling, dancing with orange stripes, everything contracting and getting entangled, all the illusions stacking together and rushing through a tunnel, stalling, returning to the origin.

A cold, sparse, endless darkness.

The sea. Pale like the skin of a corpse, the sea stretched out until it touched the leaden gray sky. At first glance, the sea appeared as a block of solidified polyester plastic: there was no motion, no spray, no birds, only the horizon as still as death.

Mimi found half of her stuck in the dead sea. The water was up to her waist, not cold, not hot, like something that separated her from all sensory stimuli and made the bottom half of her body numb. She thought about turning around, and before she could even move her leg muscles, her face had already been turned 180 degrees. She saw the shore, equally pale, but glowing a rough, frosted, matte light, like sandpaper that had been glued around the edge of the sea; there was no sense of depth to it at all.

A figure appeared on shore. It wasn't moving—maybe he was lying on the beach? But no, Mimi could see the entirety of his body as though she were hovering over him and looking down—the perspective was all wrong.

Who is that? The face expanded in her view until she could almost distinguish the pores and the wrinkles under the eyes. Chen Kaizong was staring at the sky, mesmerized. His gaze pierced through Mimi's body and focused somewhere in the bottomless depths of space. A key seemed to turn inside Mimi and forcefully wound up the mainspring, causing her entire body to contract as though all her strength was compressed and curled up inside the minuscule space inside her heart, waiting for a moment of uncontrollable release.

A familiar anxiety swept across the tips of Mimi's nerves, and Kaizong shrank back to a small figure on the distant beach. She turned around and saw the same nightmare that had tormented her countless times: at the distant horizon where the sea and the sky met, a nacre-like glow and an oil-film iridescence came at her like some roiling storm, rapidly devouring the pale edge of the world.

She didn't know what it was; all of her senses told her: *flee!* But no matter how much she struggled to coordinate her muscle groups to shift her legs, the distance between her and the shore didn't close by even an inch.

Mimi opened her mouth—she wanted to cry out, to make that man who had once saved her look away from the starry sky and lower his gaze to her. Kaizong's figure shifted, suddenly close, suddenly far, like a shadow puppet cast by the flickering candle in the wind, illusory rather than real. What emerged from her mouth was no longer human speech, but piercing, metallic howls that were infused with the staccato tremors of her terror.

She didn't turn her head but she could see the scene behind her. The iridescent wave was like some mutant aerobic microorganism madly reproducing and spreading over the surface, radiating into countless complex glowing paths like Moses emerging from the Red Sea. The sea was a piece of dull silicon being etched with incomprehensible markings, meaningless patterns and symbols that came from either the ancient past or the distant future—and all the lines, breaks and gaps, bumps and dips had only one ultimate goal: her body.

Mimi screamed Kaizong's name, but her electronic howl seemed to dissipate rapidly in the air and could not budge the man. His face rose into the sky like a *moai* from Easter Island, and as Mimi was assaulted by waves of emotion, the face shifted between high-definition clarity and disintegration. She extended her hands desperately only to find her own skin reflecting the strange rainbow sheen.

The wave loomed behind her, solidifying into a complex masonry arch decorated with fractal patterns, an electronic instance of Baroque architecture. The depressions and sliding tracks on the components clearly informed Mimi that her long-suffering, fragile body was the indispensable keystone for the completion of this masterpiece.

She saw a face in the smooth metallic surface of the wave, a trembling, iridescent face that seemed to be hers but also different: the expression on the face didn't belong to her, didn't belong to any person she knew; it was an expression of peace surpassing understanding, like a mirror reflecting itself, impossible for anyone to extract the subtle meanings hidden within. The face seemed to represent only existence itself.

Mimi's face convulsed in fear, and that other face flickered into a smile, gradually transforming into the face of some Western woman. It looked familiar, but she couldn't remember where or in which black market digital mushroom she had seen her.

Far behind her, Kaizong flashed once more into her view and then disappeared. She opened her arms, and as if accepting her fate, allowed that Hydra-like wave to pour into herself, to devour her. She heard the high-frequency whine coming from her own bones, all her nerves resonating, shattering, bursting into countless spinning mandalas. Her retinas twinkled, and billions of colors burned through the last defenses of her sense of self. Mimi's nose was filled with a familiar scent—the smell of milk on her mother's body—she struggled to hang on to the memory of it, the way she had tried vainly each time to leave this nightmare.

This time, she succeeded.

The first drop of rain drilled through the endless darkness and splashed against Mimi's face.

Next, the raindrops began to tap-dance against her blue plastic shroud. The ice-cold rainwater flowed into her mouth, nose, eyes, and her respiratory system instinctively convulsed, coughing up a clot of blood and then taking in a deep gulp of long-denied air. Her chest heaved violently, like a pumping bellows. Chaos filled her consciousness, and her limbs remained limp. She hadn't yet discovered that she was lying in a half-meter-deep hole in the ground and around her was a mass graveyard where the headstones stood as broken teeth strewn along the ground, phosphorescing in the sweeping beam of the lighthouse.

"Brother Knife, she . . . she's still alive," a confused voice said.

Knifeboy squatted down next to the hole, and the strain on his crotch made him cry out in a low moan. He watched the face in the grave and grinned after a moment.

"It looks like the heavens want this dumb cunt to die slowly." He lifted his arms and a shovelful of dark soil flew into the grave, falling on top of the blue plastic tarp. More shovelfuls of soil followed, gradually muffling the crisp, cheerful cracking of the plastic.

The mud splashed onto the pale white face, like crows landing in a field of snow. Mimi's eyes blinked rapidly a couple of times, as if protesting noiselessly. The black, malodorous mud covered her beautiful forehead, followed the curvature of her face and covered the delicate bridge of her nose, and slowly flowed between her lips and teeth. She seemed to cough a few times, but only lightly—a sound as insignificant as the breaking of a single reed stalk in the torrential flood of this black rain.

The depression in the ground gradually filled and all traces of disturbance disappeared, as if nothing had ever happened here.

Am I dead?

Mimi knew that this was not a dream, but her consciousness seeped out of her ruined body and penetrated into the tiny cracks in the water-logged soil: it rose and rose like some soap bubble lifting off the end of the blowpipe, and lightly, leaving behind no trace, left the ground and hovered in midair.

She was familiar with this height, but she could no longer see her own body or feet. She gazed down at the patch of soil burying her body—not with her eyes, and without the weight of pain; she didn't understand how this could have happened, just like she couldn't understand her nightmares. The Mimi of yesterday had worked hard to sniff burning pieces of plastic for twenty-five yuan a day, for the hope of one day being able to care for her parents, but now, her violated body was lying underground and her soul was adrift in the night rain, no longer bothered by the raindrops penetrating her shapeless consciousness. She felt a chill, but it wasn't a sensation from her skin; rather, it was a hallucination created by the shapes of the raindrops and the trajectories left by their rapid fall.

Almost subconsciously, Mimi reached out to dig through the soil to save herself, but she had no hands.

The three men stood not far away, smoking. The red glows of their cigarettes dimmed and brightened, and the white smoke seemed fragile in the dense rain. They were discussing something in whispers, and from time to time they had to stop to relight the cigarettes put out by the rain. Their expressions were as at ease, as if they had just returned from fishing. In the distance, a column of light pierced the darkness of the sea, lengthened, and swept across the world: the glowing lines of rain wove a dense fabric in the air like top-quality black cashmere mixed with silver threads. The men's outlines were highlighted while their profiles remained in the shadows, and their familiar faces were twisted into expressions of laughter.

In a moment, all her memories returned to the core of her consciousness like a storm: the recurring sweeps of the beam of light and the lengthening intervals of waiting, the viscous, thick bodily fluids, humiliation, the strong fishy-sweet taste—anger expanded slowly like a vortex until it turned into fury. She rushed at the men, unconcerned about herself, and her consciousness expanded like a rubber sheet, resilient, bouncy, and stretched thin. She was almost at the man responsible for her violation—she was going to scratch out his eyes, break open his skull, chew up his brains, bite his cock in half and stuff it in his mouth. She was going to torture him in every way she could, even if she didn't know that much about torture.

Despair filled Mimi as she felt herself pass through the bodies of Knifeboy, Skinhead, and Scarface like a wind passing through the dense rain: there was no contact, no friction, no body heat, nothing at all except a growing sense of powerlessness.

Is this my soul?

Abruptly, she "saw" the familiar Tide Gazing Beach. The sea, twinkling in extreme slow motion, inserted itself into the beach at a slant, and the waves of the tide appeared as silver scars that multiplied and healed repeatedly. Mimi suddenly understood where she was: the forbidden ground, the mass grave for babies born out of wedlock and unchaste women—the black guardian from Lockheed Martin stood erect in the storm, and she wondered if she had violated the spirits in some way for such a fate to befall her.

In a second, she had leapt in front of that god of death, but she did not take up the habitual pose of kneeling prayer; instead, she had descended from the air at a diagonal—if she still had had a flesh-and-blood body, her post at this moment would resemble an Apsara portrayed in the Dunhuang murals: a celestial nymph with lifted legs, arched back, face uplifted to stare into the eyes of the great robot, the ribbons on her dress dancing behind her like roiling waves.

The empty cockpit resembled an abyss. Mimi stared into the darkness and detected a familiar scent—it wasn't the result of airborne molecules that could be picked up by the nose, but a kind of information-carrying trace left by Brother Wen. She felt some formless barrier between her consciousness and the robot extending endlessly in every direction, like the door of some safe that had been broken into and then left in place; all she needed was to give it a final push and a brand-new world would be revealed to her.

Mimi could not resist the temptation offered by the abyss, like the call of some ancient instinct; she had nothing left, not even life.

The tentacles of consciousness extended like flexible seaweed, wriggling into that wall, searching for cracks and the mechanism keeping the barrier in place. To Mimi's surprise, the process seemed completely natural and she didn't even need to direct her movements. In reality, she knew nothing about what she was doing—all she could remember was the vision of Brother Wen's fingers moving in a blur as he broke through encryption locks and altered the programming code as though he were possessed by some shaman's spirit in a mysterious ritual. In her eyes, Brother Wen had seemed a god from another world.

And now, she had accomplished what even a god couldn't accomplish.

The wall didn't open or collapse—it simply disappeared. Which was more ridiculous: a formless wall disappearing or a dead woman struggling for life? Mimi's consciousness was sucked into the abyss.

The churning sense of space led to intense vertigo. Peaks turned into chasms, and vice versa. Mimi struggled to adjust to the new sensory signals, like a soul embedded into a strange new body. She needed time to wait quietly for power to build up inside her, weak at first but then growing stable. A tremor appeared in her chest—unlike human heartbeats, the amplitude was low but the frequency high, like some violent beast disturbed in deep slumber giving off a light sneeze, sufficient to terrify anyone observing.

She convulsed, and convulsed again. The movement didn't come from any flesh, but the depths of her consciousness. The invisible cilia of electricity gently brushed across billions of neurons and agitated crystal blue ripples, which extended and spread along a complicated three-dimensional topology. Another powerful spasm. Some switch seemed to be connected and she could see: the sights of a world unlike anything she had ever seen.

The raindrops were almost still: glowing crystals numerous as grains of sand in the Ganges hung suspended in the night air. Confused, Mimi tried to blink, but she had no eyelids. As her exoskeleton trembled, the starlike lights vibrated in sync, demonstrating their reality. The sky was a pale green and the sea indigo: wherever she looked, the center of her visual field became bright and limpid, with strongly defined outlines and clear details; however, the view grew dimmer and fuzzier in a radiating pattern from the center, distorted as though seen through the rim of a lens. All she heard was silence, as though the special alloy in the shell absorbed and filtered out all sound.

The raindrops began to move slowly, like a train departing the platform. A sensation of weight came out of nowhere, and Mimi almost collapsed before she instinctively resisted and held herself up. She finally realized that she was no longer controlling a flesh-and-blood human body, but a body made of metal.

Mimi-mecha stood still—it was a strange feeling. She knew very well that her real body lay dead under the earth, but she shook off the water gathered in the depressions in the shoulder of her armor and listened to the buzzing of the electroactive artificial muscle fiber bundles contracting. She didn't breathe, wasn't anxious, and there was no emotion standing in the way of her ability to act. She understood exactly what she had to do.

Not too far away, three green-glowing human figures trembled in the darkness.

Mimi-mecha began to walk, each stride leaving a deep depression in the muddy, soft earth. The green sky began to flicker irregularly, and the raindrops seemed to accelerate, though they still fell slower than they did in the physical world. She was starting to understand that this was a visual hallucination, like the enhancement brought by digital mushrooms. Time had slowed down because her mind had sped up.

The black armor smashed through the matrix of rain, and as the wind brushed across its perfect surfaces—the result of supercomputer calculations—the result was a howling like the call of foxes or owls. Mimi-mecha was amazed by how fast this gigantic body could move. The three human figures soon swelled from being about the size of seashells to man-sized, and the three pale faces lit up in her visual field, their expressions a mixture of confusion and horror, their facial muscles not even finished with the task of twisting all the features into place.

Mimi-mecha extended her right arm and slammed it down at an angle. The cigarette dangling from the lips of Scarface, squatting on the right, broke; a sharp, clean, red line followed the direction of the old scar on his left cheek and traversed the rest of his face at an incline—and the top half of his head slid off; the shear extended across his right scapula and took away most of his right arm. Mimi saw bright, pastel-colored liquid spewing from that clean, perfect cut. She understood now that the brightness of the color represented heat.

The minty green was so warm it was almost the color of milk.

Almost simultaneously, her other iron hand clamped around Skinhead's skull and lifted him off the ground by his head. Skinhead struggled like a hooked catfish, and his kicking legs struck against the alloy armor in muffled, irregular beats. The wet spot in the crotch of his pants expanded rapidly. Mimi deliberately and slowly increased the pressure in the pincers, watching as the bald head slowly deformed and broke between her fingers, and more bright green-white liquid erupted from the crushed skull. She gazed at this process, entranced, until the broken corpse of the man fell to the ground, leaving only a mixture of bones, blood, and brain matter in Mimi-mecha's hand, glowing like poor-quality jade.

She had spent too much time on this game and almost forgotten her real goal. Knifeboy was now several hundred meters down the beach. The flames from the body film over his shoulders flickered and shook violently in the night, as if about to go out at any moment.

Mimi-mecha took two great leaps, but then collapsed into the sand on her knees. Her consciousness grew blurred and thin, and she couldn't gather enough strength to control the exoskeleton. Mimi realized that she wasn't a completely free soul, but was still tethered to that buried, dying body. As soon as her body truly died, her consciousness was going to dissipate.

She struggled up, turned around, and with heavy steps returned to the mass graveyard, where she sought her own grave.

Her field of vision changed: the ground was divided by glowing lines of light into a grid, and Mimi's gaze passed through the grid to see the bones, coffins, and grave goods buried with the bodies. She surveyed the bodies in strange poses: some were cats, more numerous were the dogs, and there was one grave where three bodies were packed together so that their limbs were entwined like some monster with six arms and three heads, a terrifying sight. She saw a tiny corpse curled up, an outsized head on top of an undeveloped body, a baby like a cicada larva sleeping in the darkness underground. All the muscle fibers in the robot contracted at once, as though shivering.

Mimi saw herself: a slender glowing shadow that was gradually dimming, stiff like some dead dog, lying quietly in one of the grid boxes, not much brighter than the other long-dead corpses.

She plunged her robot arms deep into the wet soil, shoved off armfuls of the black earth, and plunged them in again. Mimi dug so determinedly that she didn't seem to care if she might harm her body. She saw everything and kept her immense power under absolute mastery so that her movements could be controlled within the precision of the width of a single strand of hair. Gradually, the blue plastic was revealed in cracks in the soil, like a sea rising under the greenhouse effect gradually swallowing up land until only scattered black islands were left.

Mimi-mecha extended her arms and gently lifted the body out of the grave and more gently set it on the ground. The plastic shroud unrolled, revealing the clam-like pale flesh speckled with hints of green, appearing swollen in the rain. Mimi gazed at that familiar yet strange face, an unspeakably odd sensation in her mind—this was not like staring into a mirror. In the mirror, a person unconsciously adjusted her facial muscles and expression in the hope of achieving the best aesthetic effect, but right now, she was looking at a completely slack face with no trace of life.

The cold alloy fingers manipulated the young girl's body. Mimi didn't know how she could save herself. She saw that the light green in her chest area was gradually cooling to match the cold cyan in the surrounding region, indicating that her life was seeping out of her grasp. Mimi extended two thick metal fingers, placed them between the two small breasts, and began to rhythmically compress the center of her breastbone like they taught on TV. The soft human body convulsed under the mechanical force, but the position of the heart in the grid remained still, giving no sign of life.

Get up! Get up!

Mimi cried voicelessly in despair. She lost control of her own strength and she saw her chest sink as her metal fingers pushed her flesh body into an indentation in the soil. She watched as a mixture of blood, water, and mud spewed from her nose and mouth, and she seemed to see hope itself.

Her heart still did not come back to life.

I need electricity!

The thought set Mimi-mecha's nerve bundles aflame like lightning. Within thirty microseconds, the electroactive muscle bundles in her arms created a circuit and formed positive and negative terminals, with the current and voltage adjustable by contracting the muscle fiber bundles. She had no idea exactly how she was able to do this, just as a battle-hardened soldier could not tell whether his first reaction upon hearing the sound of a gunshot came from complex memories stored in his muscles or a command from his brain.

Crackle. Blue sparks flickered. The current flowed from the left side of the breastbone into the heart and then out of the right scapula.

In the darkness, that green, bud-like heart seemed to contract once.

She increased the current. *Crackle!* The whole body bounced off the ground and fell back, splashing mud everywhere.

The green bud contracted violently and then relaxed. Mimi felt some force pulling on her consciousness, trying to drag her out of the robotic exoskeleton shell—the force came from the naked girl on the ground.

Crackle. Another violent jolt. A feeling of nausea overwhelmed her. In a moment, Mimi seemed to be back in that cold, wet, scarred human body, but within tens of microseconds she was back in the hardened safety of her steel castle.

Crackle. Crackle. Crackle.

Mimi's consciousness oscillated rapidly between the robot and the human body, her vision flickering uncertainly. The heart was gradually recovering its regular rhythm, and the life force was growing stronger, but at the same time, she was losing her power to control the alloy armor. The limp joints were no longer able to support the weight of the shell, and she could feel the robot leaning over, collapsing under the influence of gravity.

Below the immense metal shell was the young girl in a coma.

Pain. Wetness. Trembling. Nausea. Extreme exhaustion. These uniquely human sensations filled the center of Mimi's consciousness with more frequency, and the last sight Mimi-mecha could see was herself falling unsteadily toward the fragile human body. She could almost see that pallid chest and the freshly recovered heart within—the body was going to be crushed into a meat pie by the multiton war toy.

No!

To her shock, Mimi heard her own voice drifting weakly in the storm. She opened her eyes with great difficulty: in front of her was the immense, hideous visage of the black killing machine. Rainwater flowed down, following the simple, clear channels in the armor, falling into the space between her lips. The robot extended its arms against the muddy ground just as it was about to crush Mimi's body and held its weight suspended above the young girl.

Between her and Death was the distance of a kiss.

Mimi struggled to move her pain-racked body, and inch by inch, crawled out from beneath the robot. The pouring rain pierced the endless night, drenching her, blurring her eyes. She was cold, trembling, and helplessly confused, her familiar body now heavy and disobedient to her will. The white beam of light appeared again, carelessly sweeping across the night sky, the surface of the sea, the beach, the graveyard, striking Mimi coldly and then departing noiselessly, leaving behind not a trace of warmth or compassion.

She recalled the nightmare she had been through, and vomited uncontrollably in the rain.

Luo Jincheng observed the trembling male figure curled up in the corner: the flames over his shoulders were dimmed; the stench of urine emanated from his body; trails of drool hung from the corners of his mouth; the wide-open eyes, laced with webs of blood, could not focus on anything—it was almost impossible to recognize him. Luo could not recall ever seeing Knifeboy so terrified and panicked. He had run away from home at nine and joined the street gangs with eyes full of hatred, and then Luo Jincheng had picked him out in a gang fight and turned him into a loyal dog of the Luo family.

The boy had been thin as a bean sprout, but he had wielded his bicycle chain like a silver snake in the crowd, with drops of blood splashing against his young face, twisted with rage—Luo could never forget the expression on that face, as if he yearned to destroy the entire world.

Knifeboy was a bastard, others had told Luo. His mother had been seduced by a migrant worker, who disappeared as soon as the boy was born. The mother's relatives all advised her to get rid of the baby, but she insisted on bringing up her son. Under the contemptuous stares and whispered disapproval of everyone around him, the boy had grown up to have a pair of narrow eyes whose gaze was sharp as knives—*just like that no-good migrant,* everyone who had seen his father said.

Later, his mother had married a local man, and the stepfather had waited until the mother was away before tossing Knifeboy into the chicken coop and the dog house, forcing him to fight the chickens and dogs for scraps of food and covering himself with shit. Then the man had told his mother: *Dirty and low blood flows in his veins—look at how much he enjoys the filth of animals!* His mother had then held Knifeboy all night, sobbing, telling him, "You can't stay here anymore. I can't protect you from suffering." Not a single tear dropped from Knifeboy's beautiful eyes.

After Knifeboy ran away from home, his mother never looked for him, even though he lived only a few streets away—so close that, as the saying went, when he pissed, his mother couldn't have missed the stench. He passed by his mother, stepfather, and half brother in the streets multiple times, but they never recognized him. He developed quickly: his frame and muscles strengthened by frequent fights, his hair cut in a wild style and dyed strange colors, his beard wispy, soft, and bluish. He always kept his eyes lowered as he passed his family, afraid that they might look into his eyes and know who he was.

His half brother disappeared mysteriously when he turned four. They searched everywhere but could find no trace of him; rumor had it that the boy had been kidnapped by outsiders and sold into Northwestern China. His stepfather howled and cried for most of a month and seemed to age a decade in a few weeks. Even Knifeboy felt some compassion.

Should have left him alive, he thought. *Maybe even left them some sign.* But it was too late.

Vengeance was a biological instinct deeply rooted in his constitution. When he had killed the child, he had stared at that much younger face, which bore some resemblance to his own, and acted without hesitation.

He hated himself, just as he bore a deep hatred for the world. Luo Jincheng understood this very well: it was the key for why Knifeboy was so useful. But now, the Knifeboy before him was like a castrated dog who had lost all will to fight; he squeezed his legs tightly together and mumbled fragments of nonsense.

Ghost. There's a ghost.

The murders were indeed exceedingly strange. At the scene, they found the mutilated corpses as well as an abandoned exoskeleton lean-ing against the ground whose batteries had been exhausted. There were numerous trails of footprints: on the beach, in the mud, bare, heavy, not made by human feet.

Luo Jincheng concealed all information about the murders. Even though he had been in the business of intimidation and violence for de-cades and his imagination was as rich as his experience, he couldn't puzzle out the sequence of events. The bloody maze before him lacked a critical clue, a key to unlock the mystery: that feeble waste girl.

From a variety of sources, he found out about Knifeboy's dark habits, his reliance on violent, virtual devices to feel stimulation of any kind: Luo Jincheng guessed that this had something to do with Knifeboy's harsh childhood, but he had never asked Knifeboy about it, as though it was some kind of awkward secret shared by a father and his son.

Mimi was a victim as well as a witness, perhaps even a suspect in hiding.

The date for the "oil fire" ritual designated by the *lohsingpua* was ap-proaching, and his son was still in a coma, shrinking and weakening daily like the husk of a drying piece of apple. Things were not going as planned. Luo Jincheng felt uneasy: he needed the blessing and reassur-ance of the spirits.

Is our deal still in place?

He clasped two crescent-shaped wooden cups together overhead, closed his eyes, and prayed before tossing the cups to the ground. The two cups cracked apart and both came to rest with the curved side fac-ing down. Laughing cups indicated that the spirits did not care about this matter, and had dismissed it with a smile. Luo Jincheng refused to give up and tried the augury three more times, but each time ended with laughing cups.

Brother Wen—Li Wen—sat in his simple shack full of strange smells and listened to the rain pitter-pattering against the corrugated iron roof.

All sorts of broken prostheses lay scattered around the shed, and augmented artificial muscles of various thicknesses and metal tools hung on the walls. The entire room seemed like a bloodless abattoir, and he was the butcher.

Before him squatted a few young waste men whose dull gray composite fabric clothes were wet from the rain. They all wore augmented-reality glasses whose wires came together and plugged into the delicate black box in Li Wen's hand. They seemed eager to ask questions, but Li Wen's slow and methodical rhythm held them in check.

"Brother Wen, was it you who found Mimi? Where?"

Li Wen nodded and then shook his head. ". . . at the entrance to the village. She had walked there by herself."

"How is she? Let's cut the balls off all those bastards! None of them will ever have children!"

"She's in the hospital, still in a coma. The police are guarding her. We can't get in, but the Luo clan won't dare to try anything either."

"Fuck that shit! We put our lives on the line to make them rich, and they do this to our girls? What kind of world is this?"

"Brother Wen, let's burn down the Luo clan mansion and kill every Luo and feed them to the dogs!"

All the other young men seconded the suggestion.

"Try using your brains for a second!" The veins in Li Wen's temples jumped, and his expression was one of great suffering. In that moment, a familiar face flashed in front of his eyes: his little sister. That face overlaid Mimi's pale, violated face, and the two seemed utterly similar, whether as a result of an actual resemblance of features or the shared expression of despair. He hadn't been able to protect his sister. When the same thing was happening again to someone he cared for, the pain was nigh unbearable.

"Why do you assume it's done by somebody from the Luo clan?" Brother Wen asked them. "Who witnessed it? Who got a picture? If you just attack without proof like a bunch of rabid dogs, how are you any different from them?"

He forced down the fiery rage threatening to erupt out of his chest.

The anger was trying to turn him into a beast, incinerating reason to ashes until he committed some horror that could not be undone. But he could not give in. He needed time to analyze, to think. For Mimi's sake, he had to make sure every move he made from now on would lead a step closer to true victory.

The young men went quiet. After a while, they timidly asked Brother Wen what they should do.

"If they adhere to their usual pattern, they're going to monitor our communications. I'm sure they'll activate all the panoptical smart CCTV cameras at all the street corners and watch everything the waste people do, including analyzing the video feeds to read our lips. Even though Silicon Isle is a restricted-bitrate zone, they definitely have some dedicated data lines for this.

"But I've written a program that works like a controlled virus. When activated, as long as two pairs of glasses are less than half a meter apart, it can crack the sharing settings on the other pair and replicate itself over along with a designated segment of captured video. For the next few days, we can use our eyes instead of our mouths and ears to communicate. You can take videos of yourself talking in the mirror and then spread the videos around, or pass on any unusual scenes you manage to capture. Do you understand?"

The young men pondered this for a while and turned to Li Wen with eyes full of awe, as though he were some god sitting high above. Li Wen tried to stop their worshipful gazes with a clumsy explanation: "I'm the source for almost all the augmented-reality glasses in this town. It's no big deal to make the key to open locks I installed myself."

"So what should we do now?"

"Look at me." Li Wen turned the face of one of the waste men toward himself. "Let's test this out.

"This is a war, a war between *us* and *them*. Mimi is one of us. She is our family, our sister, our child. And we must protect each other like we protect our land, air, and water." An unnatural, bitter smile appeared on Li Wen's serious face, mixed with a trace of guilt as though he were the real assailant. "The Luo clan wants Mimi. They have their smart monitoring net, but we have our human spies. If they dare try to harm her again, you guys must cast the view to everyone. We'll get justice from the natives of Silicon Isle through honorable and legitimate ways, the justice that belongs to each one of us."

The young man who was staring at Li Wen unplugged his glasses from the box in Li Wen's hands, looked thoughtful for a minute until the green light at the upper right corner of the lens lit up, and turned to one of his companions. The two nodded at each other in a ritual greeting full of meaning, and as their foreheads leaned toward each other, another green light lit up like a firefly eager to mate.

Looks like I have to get this done myself.

Luo Jincheng gazed at the misty, rain-drenched scene outside the car window. His spies reported that Mimi was in the ICU of the Silicon Isle Central Hospital. She was in a coma and only Chen Kaizong was with her, the American and Director Lin Yiyu having just departed. Only a few guards left behind by Director Lin were posted outside the ward. *This is our best chance to act,* the voice on the other end of the phone call had urged.

Drops of rain on the glass, buffeted by the wind, rolled about, attracted each other, coalesced into flickering streams that traced out complicated patterns against the blurred background, then broke apart, disintegrated, and returned to separate, glistening drops.

Like people's fates, Luo whispered to himself.

You think fate is in your own hands; but in reality, fate isn't controlled by anyone. It follows its own path.

Everything he did was perhaps preordained by fate, like the narrow paths followed by the droplets of water under the influence of the wind, the tremors experienced by the car, the tiny motes of dust stuck to the surface of the glass, and countless unknown other forces. A younger Luo Jincheng would have called those forces a person's natural-born talents, vision, diligence, or luck—but he now knew that all these were important but also unimportant. A person was situated in the grand picture that was the world, immense and unpredictable; all that he could know of the world was fragmentary and limited, like a blind man trying to know the elephant by touch—and this picture was constantly and rapidly expanding.

The car stopped in front of the hospital. A few of his underlings walked ahead of him, with him following close behind. They had deliberately dressed plainly, hoping to be mistaken as patients or visiting family, but their mechanical, regular gait and their alert postures exposed them. Others quickly got out of their way, their faces full of apprehension.

The guards at the door of the ICU noticed the unfriendly newcomers and tried to call for backup, but in a minute they were immobilized and forced to kneel in a corner. An unsheathed knife glinted coldly in front of their eyes: the threat silent but powerfully oppressive.

Luo Jincheng nodded, pushed the door open, and walked into the ward by himself. Kaizong looked up, revealing an exhausted face filled with alarm and suspicion.

"Who are you?"

"Luo Jincheng."

The young man paused, as if searching for the name in his memory. His brows suddenly knit into an expression of fury.

"What are you doing here? You're not wanted."

Luo Jincheng shook his head carelessly. He walked closer to the bed to get a better look at the patient, but Kaizong blocked his way.

"Get out of here! Now!" He growled quietly like some cornered beast.

"Young man, you need to watch your manners." Luo Jincheng retrieved a pack of high-quality blue-packaged Zhongnanhai cigarettes, picked one out, tapped it, and held it between his lips. "Don't listen to those wagging tongues. I never laid a finger on your girlfriend." He pointed at the woman on the bed, plugged full of tubes and electrodes. "She *is* your girlfriend, right?"

Before Luo Jincheng could retrieve his lighter, Kaizong grabbed the cigarette out of his lips and tossed it onto the ground, grinding it into the floor with his shoe.

"You will pay for this!" Fire seemed to shoot out of Kaizong's eyes and he clenched his fists, shaking uncontrollably as though two forces were struggling for dominance in his body. In the end, he did not swing his fist but spat on the ground—half a month ago, Kaizong would have been disgusted by such behavior.

"I'm sure I will. But before then, I'd like Mimi to help me."

Kaizong glanced at the emergency call button next to the bed; his mobile phone was there, as well.

Luo waved a finger, indicating that Kaizong should not behave rashly. "I have a few men waiting for me outside, but I came in here by myself. This is a gesture of goodwill, do you understand?"

Kaizong took a deep breath, as if weighing the entire situation. "What do you want from Mimi?"

"You are asking questions! Now, that's a good start." Luo took out his phone and tapped the screen a few times before handing it over to Kaizong. "Recognize this?"

It was the photograph of Mimi sitting in front of the junk heap with the prosthetic limb, looking thoughtful. The photograph had given Kaizong his first impression of Mimi, and he resisted the impulse to turn and stare at that scarred face with tightly shut eyes, now mostly hidden behind the oxygen mask.

"The picture was taken by my son, Luo Zixin." Luo's tone became gentle and slow, full of worry. "After that, he caught some strange disease and fell into a coma. The doctors can't help him."

"And you think Mimi *can*?" Kaizong's voice dripped with sarcasm.

"We need to hold a ritual." Luo seemed a bit embarrassed. Choosing each word carefully, he revealed the ridiculous plan. "It's the 'oil fire' ceremony. The *lohsingpua* will exorcise the misfortune from my son through Mimi."

Kaizong was stunned; he stood still as if trying to devote every bit of brainpower to understand the words. Then he began to laugh hysterically. The tense atmosphere in the room seemed to transform into joy, and a few faces looked in at the window at the unusual sound.

"You're very funny, Boss Luo, really funny." Abruptly, Kaizong cut off his laughter and broke the illusion of good cheer. "Do you think that you can risk the lives of others just so you can try to save your son through some ignorant witchcraft?"

"When I was your age, I held the same contempt for superstition." Luo Jincheng nodded to show understanding. Then he returned to his habitual commanding tone. "When you're older, you'll have seen so much that you can't help but start to believe certain things. Why don't you keep going?"

Suspiciously, Kaizong flipped through some more pictures in the phone's album. After a few pictures of pots of flowers and seascapes, his breath caught and his pupils contracted. The phone shook in his trembling hands.

"You're looking at my men. They disobeyed my orders and, on their own initiative, did some bad things to Mimi. They've paid the price." Luo Jincheng paused for a moment, staring at Kaizong. "But I didn't do this to them."

Slowly, the horrible images of the broken corpses slid across the phone screen and were replaced by the picture of the robot whose dark metallic frame was limned in gold in the dawn light. The robot was leaning at a sharp angle, pushing itself up with its arms plunged into the earth; in the ground directly under its chest was a person-sized depression whose outline seemed familiar.

"I don't understand . . ." Kaizong's brows were knit in a deep frown. The information before his eyes wove into a complex net, but there was a missing piece in the middle, a dark hole.

"Lin Yiyu is a sly dog: unless the meat is fat and juicy, he wouldn't extend his paws." Luo Jincheng carefully observed Kaizong's reactions. "Ah. I guess your boss didn't tell you the whole truth either. He's also looking for Mimi through the government. The Lin clan must be getting something out of this."

"But why?"

"That is also why I'm here. The answer to all the riddles is in this girl." Luo gazed at the figure of Mimi in the hospital bed and added in a whisper, "Maybe even my son's salvation."

Kaizong walked next to the bed, and his gentle, sorrowful gaze fell against the bruises, scrapes, and red scars on Mimi's pallid skin, followed the lines and tubes of various colors onto the dark green surface of the monitor screen with its steady waveforms. He bit his lip and pain distorted his face; a column of air seemed to swell in his throat but was forcefully pushed back down. He hung his head and for a moment, gave the illusion of being a prince about to kiss the slumbering princess, but he remained frozen in his pose.

"You won't benefit by taking her away now." Kaizong spoke slowly. "Don't you understand? The war has already started."

Luo Jincheng stood under the soft light. His face was dark and his jaw tightened. His arms were crossed and his shoulders hunched, as though distressed by Kaizong's words.

Lin Yiyu and Scott Brandle sat next to each other in the backseat of the car, each staring in silence at the blurry, rain-drenched scene outside the car. The slate-gray streets of Silicon Isle slowly slid past the two sides of the car like a Postimpressionist painting done in bold strokes.

Scott's phone rang. He glanced at it and pressed the Reject button. It rang again.

Director Lin looked at him and made a gesture that meant *please*. Scott rejected the call again and gave Lin an overly formal smile. Director Lin muttered something in the Silicon Isle topolect.

"You don't need to be so polite, Director Lin. I know you understand English."

". . . Only a little. Um . . . the temporary interpreter? He here soon. Chen Kaizong, he busy . . ."

"You're far too humble, Director Lin. You don't need an interpreter at all. I've seen your résumé—you were one of the top students on Silicon Isle back in your day." Scott continued to smile.

"But *you* need an interpreter, Mr. Brandle." The habitual, submissive expression disappeared from Director Lin's face, and his tone was cold and his English smooth.

"So you've decided to stop calling me 'Mr. Scott'? Sorry to be blunt, but you were overacting."

"On Silicon Isle, acting is sometimes necessary for survival. If you want to do business here, you have to play by our rules."

"I totally understand. But I don't understand whose side you are really on. Remember, you can't possibly please everyone—"

"Especially not Americans." Director Lin's eyes glinted with a hint of slyness. "You think I'm a two-faced bastard who's just a mouthpiece for the government as well as the big clans, ignoring the interests of the people of Silicon Isle. Let me ask you this: have you ever thought about the fact that they are like our parents? Without our parents, we're nothing."

Scott lifted his eyebrows, as if recalling something particularly interesting.

"Let me tell you a story," Scott said. "When I was little, I once ran into my parents' bedroom and saw them lying on the bed, naked. There was nothing beautiful about those two nude bodies—I was filled with shock and shame. In the end, I pretended that I saw nothing and quietly tiptoed my way out of the room. But if I were to encounter such a scene now, I would perhaps choose to cover them with a blanket. I love my parents, the same as you."

"I don't think this is at all an appropriate comparison. There are two sides to every issue: you choose to see only one side."

"For instance?" Scott laughed contemptuously. "Are you going to start in on yin-yang and the philosophy of tai chi next?"

"For instance." Director Lin took a deep breath, as though struggling to suppress his impatience and anxiety. "TerraGreen Recycling always treats the three clans as obstacles, instead of applying the principle of divide and conquer and allying with some to check the others; TerraGreen Recycling always wants the government to issue forceful directives, ignorant of the fact that experience has taught the government to be careful and hesitant; TerraGreen Recycling always wants to appeal to the people of Silicon Isle with environmental protection and productivity gains, but you don't seem to understand that robots are even more efficient and environmentally friendly. The natives are concerned about what will happen to the excess laborers and whether they'll turn into a roving, destabilizing force. Also, you keep on bringing up Minister of Ecology and Environment Guo Qidao—"

"Oh?" Scott sat up straight.

"It appears that your databases aren't all-powerful. The young man who tried to steal the data from your computer is a member of an extremist environmental organization called Coltsfoot Blossom. The founder of the organization, Guo Qide, is Minister Guo Qidao's twin brother . . . So, I urge you to not jump to conclusions on anything. We Chinese say that you must strategize from the board before your move."

Scott looked thoughtful and made no reply.

Abruptly, Director Lin's tone became wheedling. He was so used to switching with ease between his various personality masks that it was sometimes hard for his audience to catch up.

"As for me, all you have to do is trust one thing: on all of Silicon Isle, there's no one who stands closer to you than I—"

An insistent ring from his phone interrupted his confession. He glanced at Scott and took the call. In a second, his face transformed. He told the driver to turn around immediately and dialed another number on his phone.

"Someone broke into the ICU—" His words hung in the air like the rain-drenched black garbage bags dangling from power lines.

They call us "the waste people." Waste is dirty, inferior, lowly, useless, but omnipresent. They produce waste every day; they can't live without the waste people.

They think we are confined to the shacks, the wastewater pools, the incinerators, the abandoned fields—they are wrong. We are also in the security rooms of their hotels, the kitchens of their restaurants, the medical supply sterilization rooms of their hospitals. The clean water they drink, the cars they drive, the escorts working in their nightclubs, even their babysitters—anywhere where they don't want to get dirty, the waste people struggle there to make a living. Do they really think they can avoid us?

When they seized Mimi, we saw but said nothing. We've grown used to their displays of power, to being treated as trash, to being humiliated, violated, to being discarded after they're done with us, to disappearing without any noise. We can even imagine everything that was done to this girl, all the tortures, the beatings, the burning with cigarettes, the drowning, the cuts, the rapes, the electric shocks, the live burial.

We just pray that we won't be the next one to suffer such a fate.

But then, she returned alive. On a rainy night, naked, scarred, covered in blood, she numbly walked through the villages and streets full of waste people, like a zombie—but she was a reminder to every witness that they were also only the walking dead of the future. She was like an oracle bringing us a message from the spirits: a person lives not just for the fact of existence itself.

The war has begun.

Back in the hospital.

"It's very well written." Luo Jincheng's praise was sincere. "Did you write this?"

"It's an underground pamphlet," said Kaizong, shaking his head.

"I guessed that it wasn't you." Luo smiled as the face of Li Wen flashed before his eyes. "Americans have no need to wade into this muddy water."

"They are allowing the natives to see this on purpose."

"This won't go anywhere. Trust me, I know the Chinese better than you do."

"I'm Chinese also. Conflicts and pressure have been simmering and building up for ages, needing only a spark. If you take Mimi away at this critical juncture, you'll be pouring oil on the fire."

Luo had to admit that Kaizong had a point.

"Then what do you suggest?" He had changed his mind. Originally, he had planned to break into the hospital ward and take the girl away by force. But now, his gut told him that such a course of action was impracticable.

"Disclose the truth; punish the ones responsible severely; establish clear rules." Kaizong seemed to have been prepared.

"Ha, you're still thinking like an American." Luo grinned coldly. Kaizong was advocating changing the rules of the game and reshuffling the cards. TerraGreen Recycling would then be able to take advantage of the situation and seize the initiative. "The truth is in a coma on this bed; the ones responsible are already dead. As for clear rules? There has always been only one rule: the law of the jungle and survival of the fittest."

Before Kaizong could answer, an alarm ripped apart the silence of the hospital and howled without cease.

"Boss!" The goons he had left outside the door called for him anxiously. Luo rushed out of the ward and saw that policemen armed with automatic weapons filled the hallway about ten meters away. He raised his hands and slowly stepped between the two sides in the tense standoff.

"This is just a misunderstanding." He gave a friendly smile and twisted his head to indicate that his underlings should drop their knives. They fell crisply against the tiled floor.

The captain in charge of the policemen seemed to recognize Luo Jincheng. He gave an order and all the guns swung as one to point at the ground. The captain also smiled and stepped forward, enthusiastically shaking hands with Luo Jincheng, who a second ago had been the leader of the suspects. The situation changed so rapidly that Chen Kaizong was utterly stunned.

"Boss Luo, what happened here? We received a report that some violent criminals had broken into the hospital to take hostages. Director Lin is personally involved. He's going to be here in a minute."

Luo's face spasmed uncomfortably. He was not yet ready to directly confront the Lin clan. "You know how rash young people can be. It's just a small conflict. We'll leave immediately."

"Um . . . that might put me in a difficult position." The police captain put on an embarrassed look. "I've got to take a few of these people in for a report. Please help me out?"

"Of course! We'll cooperate fully." Luo Jincheng nodded and a few of his minions obediently stepped forward and allowed themselves to be cuffed with high-strength plastic and left with the police. Luo Jincheng nodded at Chen Kaizong, who was still in the ICU, as if saying farewell, and also, *I'll be back*.

He took only three steps before he seemed to hear someone call his name. He stopped and turned to look at the stunned Chen Kaizong, standing next to the hospital bed.

It wasn't sound, at least not any sound that human ears could detect. It came through the floor underneath his feet, an unsettling tremor like the foehn wind in the Alps spilling out of the ICU. His chest seemed to be compressed by some great pressure, and he had difficulty catching his breath. His heart leapt wildly as though some hand were reaching inside his body to stir the organs about, casually mixing up their positions. The veins above his temples stood out and he felt countless steel nails being driven into his skull. Nausea, fear, dizziness overwhelmed him, and he collapsed to the ground on his knees, dry-heaving violently.

The world seemed to tremble before his eyes. The edges of everything grew blurry and gave off a rainbowlike sheen. He realized that it was his own eyeballs that were shaking uncontrollably, but the vibrations were not in synchrony with the tremors of the reflection in the glass window before him. The small angle of polarization in the window gave the reflected sky and clouds in the window some sense of depth, and the frequency of the tremors accelerated. A black bird flew through the image in the mirror, and the glass exploded outward from the ICU, as though broken by the passing bird, and pearl-like fragments spewed into the sky before scattering all over the floor.

Luo Jincheng saw a growing pool of blood on the ground—the source was his own mouth and nose. Out of the corners of his eyes, he saw that the policemen were struggling painfully in strange poses. Their figures became blurry and slow, like wild ghosts and wandering souls.

He realized that he was going to die like this: a pointless, absurd, cruel death, like his disappeared cousin and his family in the Philippines, like his son trapped in a coma. His clan seemed to be entwined with some evil force that endowed them with wealth, power, and opportunity, but also cursed their genes, a Faustian deal.

I guess this is karma working out in the present life. Images of the men he had killed and the evil deeds he had done flashed through Luo Jincheng's mind like a train passing through a tunnel, and the still images painted on the walls came to life in the rapid flashes—the jerky, stop-motion animation replayed his turbulent life, and the train rushed toward the distant but bright and warm exit, the farther shore.

See you in the next life. He silently bid his farewell to the world.

The quaking abruptly ceased, and everything returned to normal. His consciousness landed back in the solid, real world.

Luo Jincheng lifted his head and forced his eyes to focus. He looked through the broken windows and the open door and saw Kaizong, unharmed, half kneeling at the head of the bed, looking to be in a trance. Between him and Luo, the medical equipment in the room stood like a line of guards; they pulled the wires still attached to Mimi and the power cords plugged into the wall as taut as the cables on a suspension bridge. The soft screen on the multifunction monitor was broken, and the long-suffering waveforms slid across the broken glass, lost among the white noise. The panel over the respirator and the defibrillator swayed a few times under momentum, came loose, and tumbled to the ground.

". . . it's an infrasonic attack . . . damn it . . ." Some screamed; others moaned.

"Backup requested! Backup requested!" Piercing feedback came out of the walkie-talkies and seemed to stab right through Luo Jincheng's pain-racked skull.

The figures of the injured policemen gradually solidified and their outlines came into focus: some were comatose; some had blood coming out of their noses and ears; some, still panicking, were looking for places to hide; some were trying to get help—the whole scene resembled some illogical farce.

Luo Jincheng brushed off the glass fragments in his hair and over his body and wiped away the blood on his face; swaying unsteadily, he got up and reentered the ward as the LED-lit ICU sign above the door fell and dangled from its wire, the green light flickering. He was going to confirm an almost absurd guess.

He stopped before the defensive barrier formed by the medical equipment, as if afraid that these lifeless machines could awaken at any moment and leap at him, jaws open. However, nothing happened; they stood still, flashing their broken lights and emitting the irregular whirrs associated with malfunction. Kaizong had been standing in a location that seemed to have been spared the effects of the standing wave and he was unharmed, but he appeared overwhelmed by the events of the last few minutes. Apparently unsure what to do, his expression was wooden, although he'd unconsciously positioned himself to shield Mimi's supine body in the hospital bed.

"It's her," Luo Jincheng said.

Kaizong stared at him, his body frozen in place but fear creeping into his face. His terror wasn't just due to the ambivalent declaration by Luo, but also because of the immense space behind those words for imagination to roam. Logic and intuition warred for dominance in his mind. He opened his mouth, but no words came out.

Luo Jincheng took a tentative step forward, followed by another. Nothing happened. Just as he was about to penetrate the line of medical equipment, there were a few crisp cracks, and all the tubes and wires attached to Mimi's body and the mask on her face snapped off and, propelled by the elastic energy, swung at Luo like multiple whips, whipping through the air loudly.

Luo was prepared and ducked out of the way. The wires, tubes, and mask fell harmlessly to the floor like limp tentacles. He looked at Kaizong, a complex expression on his face, but he dared not come any closer to the bed.

Abruptly, Kaizong leapt up as if shocked and retreated some distance away from the bed.

The young woman's body, which a moment ago had been as still as a corpse, trembled slightly. Chen Kaizong and Luo Jincheng, a pair who a minute ago had been mortal enemies, now shared the same expression: a mixture of terror, suspicion, and hope. It was possible that at this moment, they had reached some subtle understanding: the waste girl who was once called Mimi had long surpassed their, and perhaps even all humankind's, ken or imagination.

Mimi's pale and scarred face convulsed and the right corner of her mouth lifted, like a mysterious and dangerous smile that, ripple-like, disappeared momentarily. Her eyes trembled under their lids, as if at any moment she might open her eyes to gaze upon this cruel and incomprehensible world. Kaizong waited, his hands balled into fists, the palms sweaty. The trembling continued for tens of seconds, or maybe a few minutes, but for these two men in the room, it seemed to last an eternity.

The trembling stopped, and the translucent lids rested over the eyeballs like pink petals. Kaizong and Luo Jincheng let out a held breath almost at the same moment.

Three seconds later, the trembling started again.

9

Scott ducked out of the taxi, pulled the zipper on his North Face waterproof jacket all the way up, and tugged down the brim of his hat to hide his attention-grabbing Caucasian face. He quickly strode onto the early morning wharf, avoided the vendors hawking the daily catch and their accompanying fishy stench, and searched for something among the dense, shuttling schools of fishing boats and sampans.

He located his target in a moment: an old speedboat that had just docked to unload. The boat's paint was patchy, revealing mottled rust, like the body of some aging great white that had survived numerous fights. The boatman was shouting at the longshoremen in topolect, and the empty hull was riding high in the water, swaying gently in the surf over the trash-strewn surface.

Scott jumped onto the ship, thudding against the deck. The boatman stared at him angrily; but just as he was about to let Scott have a piece of his mind, he choked back his curses at the sight of the bundle of cash thrust under his nose.

"Do you have enough fuel?" Scott asked in his broken Mandarin. He had to repeat himself a few times before the boatman got used to his strange accent.

"Where do you want to go?"

"Out to the sea. Just roam about a bit." Scott put on a carefree expression. He looked around casually; no one was paying attention to them.

"I can't go too far. I've got to get home for breakfast." The boatman turned on the engine, and the deafening roar was accompanied by torrents of white foam thrown up at the stern.

The speedboat left the busy harbor and headed for the open sea, dragging behind it a fading white trail.

The temperature, which had been close to forty degrees Celsius a few days ago, had dropped precipitously due to the tropical squall. Carried on the cold sea breeze, droplets struck Scott's bared face and it was hard to tell whether they were from the rain or sea spray. Looking at the GPS on his phone, Scott struggled to direct the boatman to adjust his course with gestures. Land had disappeared from the view, and only occasional reef islands stuck out of the ocean like dog's teeth.

"Any farther and we won't have enough fuel to get back." The boatman seemed to regret his decision. He slowed down the boat, tense and alert against the foreigner at his back.

"Over there." Scott glanced down at the map on the phone and pointed to the empty sea before them. The boatman muttered something in the local topolect and reluctantly guided the boat over.

"No more." The engine noise ebbed and then shut off. The boat glided forward a bit under its momentum and then heaved up and down between the sky and the sea.

The boatman stared at Scott with a guarded expression, as if ready to pick up the crowbar on the deck at any moment, even though the foreigner was at least a head taller.

Scott grinned at him. He patted his pockets but couldn't find any cigarettes to offer as a friendly gesture. He shrugged and spread his hands, hoping to calm the man. *It's time.* He squinted and surveyed the sea, but the surface remained awkwardly empty.

The boatman with the rough, dark skin seemed to have reached the end of his patience—at any moment now he was going to chase Scott off the boat with the iron bar and head back for the safety of the harbor. The soft sound of another engine came from behind them: a light double-decked passenger and cargo diesel boat was coming at them from a distance, its waterline painted an outdated green. They couldn't see anyone on board.

Scott grinned at the boatman again to demonstrate his trustworthiness.

The diesel boat stopped next to the speedboat, and the surging wake made the deck under their feet sway more violently. The side of the cabin slid open and a Southeast Asian face appeared. "Mr. Scott Brandle?" he asked in heavily accented English.

"That's me." Scott held out his hand, hoping for a handshake or, better yet, being pulled over to the bigger boat.

He got handed a satellite phone instead.

"I don't understand." Annoyance showed on Scott's face. "Where's your boss?"

"Phone." The man illustrated his answer with a mimed gesture.

"I don't think so." Scott forced a smile. "This is not how you do business in good faith. I have to see your boss, do you understand? Otherwise, the deal is off!"

"Phone." The man smiled back. "You . . . look . . . she."

The space shuttle-shaped satellite phone rang in Scott's hand, a rather unusual series of Jamaican-style electronic beeps. Only now did Scott realize that he was holding a video phone. Helpless, he looked around, took a deep breath, and pressed the Accept key.

"I do apologize for meeting you under such circumstances. This is the only method that would guarantee security, both yours and mine. The commercial satellite channel is heavily encrypted, and my boat has the equipment to produce interference waves—anyone trying to listen in or record will only get white noise."

On the screen appeared an Asian woman about thirty-five years of age. She spoke in fluent British-accented English and her hairstyle was short, efficient, complementing her copper-toned skin. She seemed used to such meetings: her expression was confident, calm, and she held Scott's gaze steadily.

"I'm very happy to make your acquaintance, Mr. Scott Brandle." The woman inclined her head in a respectful greeting suggestive of a Japanese geisha. "I'm Sug-Yi Chiu Ho, commander-in-chief for this operation."

Scott nodded. He got right to the point. "Ms. Chiu Ho, a man under your command tried to steal confidential business information from my computer. Was that pursuant to your orders?"

Surprise flitted across Sug-Yi's face, but she quickly adjusted and answered without guile: "Indeed. I take full responsibility for that. However, I'd like to ask you to reserve judgment until you've heard the whole story."

"I'm all ears."

"Two months ago, we—that is, Coltsfoot Blossom—received an internal intelligence report that cargo containers from New Jersey bound for Silicon Isle by way of Kwai Tsing were adulterated with prosthesis waste infected with highly dangerous viruses, believed to be part of SBT's spring recycling program. Through the IoT RFID tags, we tracked the movement of the containers, hoping to intercept the shipment before the ship entered the wharves at Kwai Tsing and reveal the truth to the world.

"However, due to an accident, we were forced to break off the operation. *Long Prosperity*'s cargo, after unloading, was distributed to various locations in the Chinese interior, and we could no longer track them. However, we have reason to believe that the virus-infected waste is in Silicon Isle right now.

"You, Mr. Brandle, are our reason."

Scott raised his eyebrows and gave no immediate reaction. The young man in the interrogation room had been clear that Coltsfoot Blossom had somehow managed to figure out his real identity. "Scott Brandle" was nothing more than one of his many pseudonyms. His profession was often given the sensational moniker of "economic hit man." He didn't care much for the media's scaremongering and exaggerations, but he couldn't deny that killing was often a professional necessity.

Salvation requires sacrifices—always has.

He had convinced himself with this article of faith. He played the roles of energy expert, high-level financial analyst, environmental researcher, or infrastructure engineer, and, employed by giant chaebols or famous multinational conglomerates, he wandered the vast interiors of third-world countries like a hungry hunter. From the rain forests of the Amazon to the prairies of Mozambique, from the hellish slums of southern India to the resource-abundant waters of Southeast Asia, he and men like him painted lovely futures for local governments: double-digit economic growth and numerous jobs plus what the governments cared about the most—social stability. They brought the local populations industrial parks, power plants, clean water, and airports, bought their trust with pretenses, until they crowded into the factories and began to slave away like robots stuck with repetitive, mechanical tasks, toiling long hours in exchange for wages lower than what their parents had been able to earn.

It's how the world functions. Scott recalled the truth spoken by that young man, his hand cuffed to the chair in the interrogation room.

Economic hit men tossed out sweet lures like advanced technology, easy credit, and favorable purchasing terms, and, in the name of "progress" and "joint development," enticed the local governments to sign agreements that required them to construct massive engineering projects, take up heavy debt, and then offer up precious, irreplaceable resources like oil fields, minerals, and the genes of endangered animals.

The hit men walked away with their fee, the officials counted their bribes, and the people were left with the job of paying off the debt, as well as a polluted and ruined homeland.

"I fail to see the connection," Scott said innocently.

"Perhaps you should consider a change in career to acting." Sug-Yi gave a kind a smile meant to disarm. "Scott—may I call you Scott?—among the shareholders of both TerraGreen Recycling and SBT, there is an institution called the Arashio Foundation, of which no public information is available."

Scott said nothing.

"It is also a shareholder of all your previous employers." Sug-Yi tossed out this tidbit carelessly. A bargaining chip.

"Is this an attempt at blackmail?" Scott couldn't help himself.

"Consider this an offer to help you wash away the blood on your hands."

"Thanks, but I prefer soap."

"Scott, this is your last chance. Silicon Isle might turn into a second Ahmedabad: do you really want to see such a tragedy repeated?"

"That *was* an accident." For a moment, Scott lost control of his voice. It grew shrill.

"One hundred and twenty-eight dead, and more than six hundred lost some or all mobility. This is what you call an 'accident'? Can you look those children in the eyes?"

"I was there—" Scott lowered his voice. Nancy's pale face in the water drifted before his eyes. He seemed to give up. "Tell me, what do you really want?"

"Evidence! Solid evidence that can bring down SBT! We want to know how they're transporting toxic prosthesis waste to developing countries and how they're covering it up."

"Ms. Chiu Ho, you're asking me to risk my neck to help you environmental extremists to satisfy your sense of moral superiority."

The woman grinned as if anticipating his question. "We can offer you more. Remember how the stock market reacted after the truth about Enron got out?"

"You're going to short SBT?" Scott did a quick calculation in his head: these people might make billions if they timed it right. "I've always thought of you as pure idealists."

"Coltsfoot Blossom is best for results-driven idealists." Sug-Yi's reply came as precisely as an automated phone answering service.

"Fine. Tell me what is this thing you're so interested in." Finally, Scott had a chance to ask the question that had plagued him.

The smile disappeared from Sug-Yi's face on the screen. She seemed to be figuring out just where to start.

"Have you heard of Project Waste Tide?"

In the weak dawn light, Kaizong saw white figures flashing behind the distant windows of the ICU. He dashed over, thinking that they were medical personnel waiting for him.

A quarter of an hour ago, he had received an urgent call from the hospital that Mimi was awake. Without telling anyone, without even stopping to brush his teeth or wash his face, Kaizong had jumped into a cab to rush to the side of the woman who was never far from his thoughts. The radio in the cab played the familiar leitmotif of Tchaikovsky's *1812 Overture* to announce the hour. Now, at 6:01, Beijing time, the passionate melody, sped up by half a beat, circled around his mind like a breaking news alert.

The air was filled with the fragrance of magnolia. Commingled with the smell of disinfectant, the effect was one of sweetness betrayed by a hint of anxiety.

Kaizong didn't bother waiting for the elevator but dashed up the stairs to the third floor, pausing for a moment in front of the ICU to calm himself down. He opened the door.

The room was unlit, and the bed empty. He was about to press the call button for the nurse when he noticed a still figure in front of the window, her back to him. The dim morning light limned a familiar outline.

"Mimi?" Kaizong asked tentatively. Unease crept into his heart.

The young woman remained still. Some seconds later, the body film on the back of her neck began to glow with a golden *mi*. Seen through the thin fabric of her hospital gown, the lit-up character appeared steady and strong. She turned around, a smile on her face, and the line dividing light from shadow slowly swept across her face until the smile was completely within the shadows.

"Kaizong, you're here." Her voice was still crisp and tender, as though nothing had happened.

He stood, amazed for a moment, before acknowledging the greeting. He flicked on the overhead lights and approached her, examining her smiling face carefully. Her wounds had healed remarkably well, and only a few faint scars remained on her forehead.

"What? Don't you recognize me anymore?"

"No . . . Do you feel well?" Kaizong reached out to hug Mimi around the shoulder out of habit before remembering that he was not in America, and his hand stopped awkwardly midair.

Abruptly, Mimi seized his hand and cradled it in her own palms, her movements as determined and precise as if governed by some prewritten program.

"As well as coming back to life from death."

Kaizong was stunned. Electrical shocks seemed to fire off all over his body, and he couldn't answer at all.

Mimi's expression turned to one of uncertainty, and then, after a moment, understanding. She let go of Kaizong's hand, lowered her head, and softly said, "I heard that you took care of me this entire time. Without you, perhaps I'd be dead long ago."

Kaizong relaxed. He took up Mimi's hand. "Don't be silly. Director Lin agreed to send guards to be with you twenty-four seven. You won't be in danger anymore."

"Danger?"

"It's all in the past now. If I could have put you somewhere safe back then—" He stopped, biting his bottom lip. He felt like an idiot. His babbling made no sense, had no meaning.

A trace of almost unnoticeable hesitation flashed across Mimi's eyes. "What really happened? I . . . I can't seem to remember any of it . . ."

"The doctor said you need time to fully recover." The image of Mimi's smile on Tide Gazing Beach flashed before Kaizong's eyes, and he felt thousands of needles stabbing into his heart. He forced himself to keep the rage off his face. "Why don't you rest for a bit? I'll go get the doctor and see if you need to remain in the hospital for observation or if you could go home."

"Go home?" Mimi's face was all confusion.

Kaizong was at a loss for words. Mimi's home was thousands of kilometers away, unattainable. In their talks, she shared with him that she had no sense of attachment or belonging to any corner of Silicon Isle. A place without memories could not be called home. Kaizong understood that feeling very well.

"Your real home." Kaizong tried to comfort Mimi with a warm smile.

He turned and was about to leave before he heard the humming behind him: it was the familiar melody from the *1812 Overture* excerpted by the radio station. Kaizong's face shifted in an instant, as though the music had been stolen from his thoughts and then implanted into the girlish vocal chords, as ethereal as porcelain. Mimi stared at him, her face impassive and her lips slightly parted, like a woman-shaped music box. The precise notes drifted from between her lips, and even the sped-up beat was imitated exactly. The short musical phrase repeated over and over, without any emotion, and then abruptly stopped.

Goose bumps erupted on the skin at the back of Kaizong's neck. He suppressed the impulse to examine her closer and fled from the ICU, fled from the girl he had once saved.

Back at the hotel, waves of nausea assaulted Scott. Some of it was no doubt due to the swaying ride over the sea, but the rest came from a strong sense of having been duped.

He tried to connect through the secure chat program, but "Hirofumi Otogawa" never answered. Belatedly, he realized that it was two in the morning back on the American East Coast. *That fucking liar!* Scott struck the keys angrily and attempted to release some of his anger on a porn site, but the browser kept on showing him "451 Forbidden"—the HTTP error indicating that the website was unavailable due to local law, a reference to Bradbury's novel.

In this restricted-bitrate zone, they won't even permit you the comfort of self-abuse.

Scott couldn't even laugh. He had imagined that his job in Silicon Isle would be cleaner, as least compared to the dirty deeds he had done in

Southeast Asia, Southern India, and Western Africa. He was wrong, so very wrong.

The secret was rare earth metals, nonrenewable resources more precious than gold. They were like the witch's magical dust in fairy tales: a small amount was enough to greatly improve the tactical value of ordinary materials and bring about astounding leaps in military technology, allowing the possessor to hold on to an overwhelming advantage on the modern battlefield.

The Art of War. Scott thought about that Chinese classic taught at West Point. *It's now* The Art of Killing. He clearly recalled the videos shown to TerraGreen Recycling personnel at the internal briefing.

During the Cold War, the Soviet Union's Papa-class, Alfa-class, Mike-class, and Sierra-class submarines flitted through the strategic choke points of the world's oceans like ghosts, reaching speeds of up to forty knots and diving to depths of four hundred to six hundred meters. American torpedoes, in comparison, were as slow as crawling turtles. The USSR had achieved this by leveraging the rare earth element rhenium, which significantly strengthened the titanium alloys that allowed the construction of fast-cruising, deep-diving hunter-killer submarines.

Through the smoke and fog of the Gulf War, America's M1A1 Abrams tanks, equipped with laser range finders enhanced by yttrium that could "see" as far as four thousand meters, thoroughly dominated the Iraqi T-72-derived tanks whose range finders were limited to below two thousand meters. The Abrams could aim, lock, and fire on the enemy long before the possibility of return fire and blow the opponent to smithereens. Similarly, night-vision goggles containing lanthanum allowed American soldiers to see as clearly at night as during the day and confidently kill enemies with precision.

However, almost half of the world's reserves of rare earth resources were concentrated in China, and China was responsible for over 95 percent of global production. Starting in 2007, the Chinese government imposed a strict quota system to greatly reduce the total amount of rare earths exported, causing global prices to skyrocket. "The Chinese Century!" Western media exclaimed in alarm. The developed nations had grown used to cheap rare earths, and, as such an age receded into the past, their strategic technology advantage, achieved and maintained with great effort, was going to fade into nonexistence. The world faced the prospect of a redistribution of power.

Scott held himself back from the verge of an emotional breakdown. He initiated his VPN software and waited until it negotiated an encrypted tunnel to an overseas server so that his packets could be sent, encrypted and unmolested, out of China before being redirected to his ultimate target—an Eastern European website featuring hard-core pornography. Although the speed of connection was slow, at least he was free of the Great Firewall.

This is the eighth trick in the Thirty-Six Stratagems: "passage under cover of darkness."

Just like the path chosen by TerraGreen Recycling.

TerraGreen Recycling had developed the technology for recycling rare earth elements in consumer e-waste. More than 80 percent of the rare earths used in chips, batteries, displays, and similar electronics could be extracted and reused. However, the pollution generated by the process far exceeded EPA standards, and the processor would be required to pay into a trust fund to pay for anticipated environmental harms. Furthermore, adding to the already sky-high labor costs, American law required the employer to purchase expensive insurance for the workers and to reserve risk-mitigation funds in anticipation of outbreaks of work-related diseases decades down the road.

In other words, it wasn't worth it.

This was the problem with democracy: by the time the congressmen finally understood the seriousness of the threat and proposed their bills, by the time interest groups were finally done with their squabbling and compromised on a joint industrial policy, the United States of America would probably have fallen to the status of a third-rate country, perhaps even a mere satellite of the Greater China Economic Sphere. The dissolution of the European Union was an object lesson, and no one in the

West could forget the sight of the red field and golden stars of China's flag waving over the beaches of Ibiza after its purchase by a Chinese group in 2022.

Thus, TerraGreen Recycling had to devise a creative outsourcing strategy within the framework of existing laws. Under the banner of "Green Economy," TerraGreen Recycling would transfer waste and pollution overseas, to the vast lands of the developing nations. TerraGreen Recycling would help them construct industrial parks and production lines and enjoy their endless, cheap labor, and, pursuant to the contract, be given priority access to purchase the valuable rare earths produced at a substantial discount.

Scott remembered that the last page of the internal report contained a large equilateral triangle whose vertices were colorful circles filled with bold, giant letters: "**WIN-WIN-WIN**."

The government wants economic development: we give them GDP growth.

The people want to eat: we give them jobs.

We want cheap rare earths: all the costs have been carefully calculated.

Scott had felt some unease. He had been haunted by nightmares after the accidental release of toxic gases in Ahmedabad: under the green miasma, bloated bodies were strewn all over the ground, their eyes cloudy due to the deformation of the crystalline lens. To reduce costs, he had chosen to use gas valves supplied by local manufacturers during the bidding process; they had quoted lower prices and offered higher kickbacks.

Those gray eyes would blink as though thousands of raw, unprocessed freshwater pearls were flickering simultaneously, and he would scream and wake up with his body covered in cold sweat. The psychiatrists couldn't save him, only Jesus could.

But he was about to step onto another godless land, to commit an act of blasphemy.

Scott had felt that he had to do something. He had convinced the board of directors to allocate some of the investment specifically for local environmental remediation as a "gesture of goodwill"—even though according to the standards set by the EPA, the conditions after remediation weren't going to be much better than hell.

In this world, there are many forms of cleanliness, many forms of fairness, and many forms of happiness. All we can do is to choose from among them, or to have our choices be made for us. Scott tried to comfort himself. *I can only do what I can.*

But now, Coltsfoot Blossom was hinting at him that Silicon Isle was going to once again stain his hands with blood.

The data from the porn site came back to him via the encrypted tunnel of the VPN server. A writhing Ukrainian model appeared on his screen, her flesh draped in brightly colored scraps. She teased and danced, using every trick at her disposal to entice visitors to click on the button for the paid channel, to satisfy their virtual but primitive desires. You could even design the exact face and figure of the object of desire: he or she could be your boss, neighbor, teacher, student, a cashier at the local fast-food restaurant, a fading starlet, a criminal, a politician, a passerby, pet, husband, wife . . . or even yourself.

Scott found himself anxious and unaroused. The cursor wandered over the page aimlessly while the virtual model responded to the movements of the arrow with exaggerated moans and mechanical movements. He suddenly realized what he should be doing, and flicked over to a search engine, inputting "Waste Tide." After 0.13 seconds, more than 5,100 hits came back.

He clicked on the link for "Project Waste Tide," certain that the VPN service was capable of retrieving the censored page. The trace route showed that the linked video was stored on a server in low Earth orbit, about four kilometers from the surface. The server, named Anarchy. Cloud, was set up to avoid the censoring organs of various governments. The VPN server took twice as long as usual to download the page, and the empty frame gradually filled in, bit by bit, like a dot-matrix printer filling up a desolate wasteland of information.

10

"What in the world happened to Mimi?" Kaizong pressed the doctor.

That wasn't Mimi, or at least not the Mimi he had known. It was more like something that deliberately imitated Mimi's gestures and patterns of speech. *Something inhuman.* He shuddered.

Mimi had never called him "Kaizong"; instead, she had always said "Fake Foreigner."

"The situation is a bit complicated—" The doctor hesitated and then brought up some three-dimensional scans on the display. "I've never seen such a . . . brain map."

He manipulated the display. "This is a typical BEAM image—oh, that's 'brain electrical activity mapping.'" A darkly colored brain hung in virtual space, and the animation showed various horizontal cross sections as irregular blotches or stripes of color appeared and disappeared, indicating shifting activity levels in various regions of the brain. "And this is Mimi's."

Kaizong gaped at the magnified, flickering image.

If a typical BEAM image could be described as a brush-painting landscape done in the broad strokes of *xieyi* style, Mimi's brain resembled a realist painting done in the *gongbi* style one might expect at the height of the Tang Dynasty, full of meticulous, fine details. As the animation flipped through the cross sections, the patterns built up into a complex, magnificent palace. The various colored regions were finely crafted components joined together by mortise and tenon, but endowed with dynamic ebb and flow. The whole scene resembled a carnival full of gaudy-hued costumes parading through a giant city, but order also emerged at the macro level, displaying a harmonious sense of beauty.

"How did she get to be this way?"

"Good question. Based on some biochemical indicators, we think a virus had invaded her brain—as a matter of fact, the infection had occurred in waves, with the last instance about a month ago. The virus could perhaps explain some aspects of this rare organic disease, but it is not the only cause. We also discovered this in her brain."

Another brain map appeared. It was translucent and the folds and creases were only faintly visible. Kaizong thought some fog seemed to shroud parts of the image and made it impossible to see clearly—perhaps a result of the resolution of the display.

"This is the ACC—the anterior cingulate cortex, behind your forehead." The doctor zoomed in on a region, much as one would use Google Earth to descend through the cloud cover and zoom in on some country, city, and street, evoking the perspective of God. "It's an important area responsible for cognition, behavior, emotion, learning reinforcement, and registering pain. You're looking at it under one million times magnification."

The layer of fog gradually cleared as though some nebula in space drew near and resolved into individual stars, each giving off a metallic glint and suspended in a vast universe made of neurons and extracellular matrix.

"These metal particles have diameters ranging from one to two-point-five microns, smaller than individual neurons. Normally, harmful particles like this will become trapped in the lungs as the result of respiration, leading to pneumonitis and pulmonary fibrosis, even damaging the specific immune system. In this case, however, they were able to cross the blood-brain barrier and enter the cerebral cortex. I have no idea how that happened."

Kaizong stared at the computer-simulated, dark blue jungle of axons, in which the metal particles hovered like silent monoliths out of *2001: A Space Odyssey,* forming an endless matrix that extended to the end of the universe. Through his mind flashed the images of Mimi abjectly sniffing at the burnt plastic; Xialong Village's hellish, thick, sticky, dirty air; junked electronic toys; abandoned fields; burning trash; children smiling like blossoms in the toxic soil.

God comes with leaden feet, but strikes with iron hands, he thought. History's retribution was always imbued with uncertainty: sometimes vengeance was visited upon an entire race, but occasionally, it could be as precise as a bolt of lightning striking a single dead tree in the middle of a wasteland, setting it alight like a blazing torch at night, illuminating the inky sky.

Mimi was the unlucky girl singled out from billions, touched by history.

"Is her life in danger?" Kaizong asked anxiously.

"I really don't know. Nothing in my experience is even remotely similar. The metal particles embedded in her cerebral cortex form a complex lattice that seems to be working synergistically with her neural network—don't ask me how. Mimi's head shows signs of injury from electric shock, so maybe that provided some kind of activation energy. All I know is that modern neurosurgical techniques are incapable of implanting the particles with such precision, and we certainly don't know how to extract the structure.

"It's as if her brain has been turned into a minefield. You'll never know when an impulse may come off some nerve ending"—the doctor snapped his fingers, looking solemn—"and trigger a chain reaction."

Kaizong kept quiet. He had been harboring the hope that after this episode, he might finally be able to protect Mimi from further threats. Deep in his heart, he had always attributed Mimi's tragedy to his own tardiness to their date. He had replayed that day compulsively in his mind countless times—what if time could flow backward, what if he had ended his talk with the head of the Chen clan earlier, what if he had arrived at Mimi's shack on time . . . perhaps everything would have turned out differently.

But he knew that history never had room for what-ifs.

Kaizong couldn't deny that, at some level, he had imagined himself as a kind of emissary returning home, bearing treasures from a distant land. As soon as he opened his treasure chest, all the problems of Silicon Isle would be gone in a puff of smoke. Only now did he understand how wrong he had been. He couldn't save Silicon Isle, couldn't save Mimi, and he especially couldn't save himself. His laughable sense of superiority had been pulverized by hard reality: the faster he ran, the farther his original goal receded.

"If Mimi had gone to the periodic screenings, perhaps we could have found this earlier . . ." The doctor's tone was full of regret.

"She wasn't working for the Chen clan before; she belonged to the Luo clan."

A face floated before Kaizong's eyes, a smooth, pale, bloated face full of malice and deceit, like some dead tissue floating in a jar of formaldehyde. Luo Jincheng.

The doctor's face shifted. *Ah, that explains it.*

The website was clearly not some authorized production—it more closely resembled a wiki built up by obsessive fans. Text, pictures, chronologies, and videos were strewn about randomly, with little attention to organization. Scott browsed through the pages quickly—many of the articles made wild leaps of logic and were composed in the tone of the conspiracy theorists that he was familiar with, the products of brains filled with pathologically twisted imaginings about human history.

Though the site hadn't been updated in a while, Scott managed to find what he was looking for.

A fifteen-minute-long summary video.

The opening section was an excerpt from a black-and-white documentary: a warship burning over the sea, then the gray flaming wreckage gradually sinking beneath the surface. Text on the screen read:

On March 3, 1943, an American B-25C Mitchell bomber, nicknamed "Chatter Box," damaged the rudder of the Imperial Japanese Navy destroyer *Arashio*, which caused the destroyer to collide with another ship. The destroyer ultimately sank about 55 nautical miles southeast of Finschhafen, New Guinea. The ship's 176 survivors were all rescued, except the captain, Lieutenant Commander Hideo Kuboki.

A photograph of Kuboki in military uniform appeared onscreen. Then the scene shifted to a laboratory on some school campus. An elegant East Asian woman concentrated on her instruments while conversing mutely with the cameraman.

After the Japanese defeat, Kuboki's fiancée, Seisen Suzuki, left for the United States to pursue graduate studies and eventually became an American citizen. She received her Ph.D. in Biochemistry from Columbia University, and in 1952, under the direction of the U.S. military, initiated and led the top secret Project Waste Tide. The name is a nod toward the ship on which her fiancé had died.

Scott finally learned the origin of the mysterious foundation among TerraGreen Recycling's shareholders.

The next segment of the video was marked as "U.S. Military, Top Secret." The view seemed to be from a fixed camera, and the flashing numbers in the bottom right indicated that the video had been sped up multiples of tens of times. The background was the interior of a sealed room; the lens faced a one-way glass window in the opposite wall, which reflected the wall under the camera, chillingly blank.

Between 1955 and 1972, Project Waste Tide performed experiments in Maryland on human subjects drawn from inmates on death row and serving life sentences. The goal was to research hallucinogenic weapons capable of mass deployment so that victories may be won on the battlefield without having to fire a shot. The researchers conducted trials with multiple natural and synthetic drugs, and finally settled on 3-quinuclidinyl benzilate, or QNB, which can be absorbed through the skin or respiratory system in aerosol form.

A prisoner was led into the room and sat down in front of the one-way observation window. The video played at several times normal speed, and the prisoner's figure shook as if seized by uncontrollable convulsions. He couldn't remain still—the empty room seemed to contain invisible monsters that disturbed his mind and threatened his safety. He screamed noiselessly and rammed his head against the walls, tore out his hair, rolled on the floor, and rent his clothes into shreds. Waves of white noise rolled across the camera image, distorting the view.

Abruptly, the video slowed down to normal speed. The naked man stood facing the camera and caressed his face with his hands. Without warning, he dug out his eyeballs with his fingers, as calmly as one might pull out the rubber plug in the bathtub drain. The eyeballs, trailing blood vessels and nerve bundles, fell from his palms, and dark liquid spilled out of his empty sockets. He sat down, relieved, and collapsed to the ground softly as if his spine had been abruptly extracted.

QNB functions as a competitive inhibitor of acetylcholine (ACh), a neurotransmitter that increases responsiveness to sensory stimuli and plays an important role in learning memory, spatial working memory, attention, muscle contraction, exploratory behavior, and other cognitive functions. QNB acts on the muscarinic receptors found in the synapses of smooth muscles, exocrine glands, autonomic ganglia, the cerebrum, and other parts, effectively lowering the concentration of ACh reaching receptors and leading to dilated pupils, lowered heart rate, flushed skin, and other symptoms. In severe cases, the effects include coma, ataxia, loss of spatial and time sense, memory impairment, inability to distinguish reality from illusions, irrational fears, and uncontrolled semi-autonomic behaviors such as undressing, talking to oneself, picking, scratching, and other similar actions.

The video went through a series of jump cuts: a crowd dancing bizarrely in a square; a primitive tribe conducting a mysterious ceremony in the jungle; young men and women at a wild party; a military parade with goose-stepping soldiers . . . The selection of footage differed in palette and quality, and, accompanied by retro German electronica, had a powerful effect on the viewer's mood. Scott wasn't sure what the scenes were intended to show. Many times he thought he had caught glimpses of genocide and cannibalism, perhaps just individual frames: crimson red, shaking, firelight. He felt a growing unease.

More astonishingly, QNB could cause multiple subjects to fall under the sway of a shared hallucinatory experience. For instance, two subjects might pass an invisible cigarette back and forth or even play a game of tennis with invisible rackets and an invisible ball. When the number of affected people rose above a certain threshold, a spontaneous mass religious experience might be triggered. Sometimes these invoked existing deities—Jehovah, Allah, Shakyamuni—but sometimes entirely new gods were created. The results often led to panic and disaster.

War began: the green trails of shells and bullets above a desert seen through night-vision goggles; mechanized troops shuttling through the ruins of a city; the face of a soldier full of exhaustion and despair; some politician gesticulating through a righteous speech; bombers skimming over their targets; an exploding armored personnel carrier; a collapsing building; bodies being blown apart; children playing and running through streets strewn with corpses—turning into survivors with missing limbs a second later. None of this was new to Scott.

> The American defeat in Vietnam and the heavy losses indirectly led to the introduction of QNB as a military tool after 1975. It helped the United States win numerous regional wars and greatly reduced American casualties: Afghanistan, the Persian Gulf, Sarajevo, Ethiopia . . . Internal classified documents indicate that the military viewed QNB as a nonlethal chemical weapon with no long-term negative effects, and continued to assure the civilian leadership that such use was consistent with the public image of an America "fighting for peace."
>
> The truth, of course, was otherwise.

A middle-aged man appeared onscreen. His face was blurred out and his voice altered to disguise his identity. The subtitle indicated that he was an American sergeant, a veteran of one of the Gulf Wars. Due to damage to his gas mask, he had breathed in a substantial amount of QNB. He had been discharged more than ten years ago and now worked in the logistics industry.

> Interviewer [off camera]: How did you feel when it happened?
>
> Man: . . . I don't remember [shaking his head slowly]. I'm sorry, I can't recall clearly . . . It was terrible. [silence] I'm really sorry. I don't want to relive it.
>
> Interviewer: According to an internal report, you believe that your hallucination was connected with the hallucination experienced by the enemy?
>
> Man: [confused] . . . I can't be certain. I couldn't understand what I was seeing. All I felt was terror, rage, anger directed

at my brothers, as though they . . . they were the truly evil side. I even wanted to kill them, all of them.

Interviewer: Did you?

Man: No! Of course not! Never . . . [uncertain again] Maybe while I was dreaming.

The other men in his unit reported him for erratic behavior and he was forcefully taken away from the front and sent to a hospital for psychiatric evaluation followed by medical discharge.

Interviewer: Do you feel free from the effects?

Man: [silence, heavy breathing] . . . I still suffer nightmares, sometimes. The doctors tell me it's PTSD . . . but I know it's not. Have you read anything by Lovecraft? Cthulhu? My dreams are like that. [quickened breathing, louder] Darkness, chaos, filth—it's as if something wants to rip you apart in your brain. Look, I'm not talking about physical suffering; I'm not. You wake up and see the boundless sky full of stars outside your window: that's the opening in its iris. It's staring at me all the time. Do you know how that feels? Do you fucking know?

[The camera zooms in: the arteries in his neck are pulsing wildly. Fade to black.]

Three weeks after this interview, David M. Friedman (Sgt. USA) was found dead in his apartment, having shot himself through the mouth. He was 38.

Scott had to pause the video until his gut settled down. The short video contained far more information than he had anticipated.

Mimi was gone. The ICU was empty.

Kaizong hounded the guards at the door like a madman but all he got were shrugs and ambivalent answers. He rushed down the stairs, his chest tight, an uneasy premonition overtaking him, just as it had the day of their missed date: if he lost Mimi again, it would be forever. There was no trace of her in front of the hospital. Early-rising patients and their visitors walked about, their pallor glowing brightly in the dawn light.

In despair, Kaizong searched desperately through his mind for any information that might help him get in touch with Mimi. He regretted following the fundamentalist faith of his parents and not having access to prosthetic implants for augmented reality. Then he saw Mimi devouring her breakfast in the cafeteria on the ground floor. She wasn't alone; a man sat across from her, his back to Kaizong's gaze.

That powerful frame was so familiar to Kaizong that his heart began to beat wildly; the cruel grin on Luo Jincheng's face flashed before his eyes.

He went up to their table and stood between Mimi and Luo. Placing his hands on the table, he leaned down and glared at Luo, making sure that the man knew he no longer cared about the consequences.

"Kaizong! Why don't you sit down and have some breakfast, too? I mentioned that I was hungry, and Uncle Luo here offered to take me to breakfast." Mimi stared at him innocently. Bits of rice were stuck to the corners of her mouth and moved up and down as she chewed.

"Uncle Luo, thank you. I think you might want to say goodbye if you're finished. Mimi needs her rest." Kaizong struggled to keep his tone even.

"No need to be so polite! We're all friends." Luo Jincheng smiled. "Mimi has agreed to come and visit Him-ri with me after eating. Today is a propitious day; good luck for everything."

Kaizong looked at Mimi, surprised. She picked up a fried dough stick with her chopsticks casually—the locals called them "ghosts-in-oil."

"Unless the doctor releases her or she wants to leave, Mimi isn't going anywhere."

"Young man, you should come with us. There will be other people there you already know." Luo Jincheng glanced around and lifted his chin slightly, indicating to Kaizong that he should not act rashly. Kaizong noticed that a few other men were sitting in the far corner of the cafeteria—although they looked like regular customers, they glanced over at Mimi's table from time to time with considering expressions, as though coveting the fried dough sticks, soy milk, and porridge with salted vegetables.

Luo gestured for Kaizong to sit and switched to the Silicon Isle topolect. "You're just like your father: stubborn, perverse, don't know what's good for you."

Kaizong suppressed his anger and displeasure and sat down slowly.

"Back when your father and I were both young men—not much older than you, in fact—I called him Elder Brother Xianzhe. He had ambition and wanted to build Silicon Isle into a major cargo port in eastern Guangdong Province. But that required money, a great deal of money, as well as time." Luo Jincheng half lifted his face, and his gaze seemed to penetrate history's layers of curtains, ending on the distant past. "The government couldn't wait that long. They wanted results, tangible, visible results that could move the GDP so that they could write up a pretty report and get promotions and make money. Silicon Isle chose a different path, and that's how we ended up here."

Kaizong was about to object when Luo silenced him with another look. "Don't jump to conclusions so quickly, youngster. History is the way it is because it follows certain patterns, otherwise you and I would not be conversing here today. I have to say that your father saw further than most and he's daring and bold. He gave up the easy riches he could have made and left the country, arriving in America as a stranger with nothing to his name. His struggles gave you the good environment you grew up in. You can say that I'm selfish, that I'm complicit in injustice—I don't care. My belief is simple: an animal has to be strong enough to prevent its offspring from being hunted or enslaved; it's the same with mankind.

"And so, your father and I are the same; we differ only in the way we express our love."

If he hadn't witnessed too many examples of the Luo clan's abuse of the waste people, Chen Kaizong would have been ready to applaud and cheer this heartfelt speech. He thought of his own father, of the memories in fading color of the years they spent wandering, trying to survive in a foreign land—and he experienced a biological revulsion, like a conditioned reflex.

He could never associate that kind of drifting, uprooted life with a father's love, no matter what the logic.

He couldn't understand why his father had decided on that course of action, not even after so many years. Rationally, he could cite all kinds of hard evidence to justify his father's choice, but emotionally, he could never accept it. For a man to take those who depended on him and depart from the land of his birth, to leave behind the foundation of their culture and existence in search of the feeling of security elsewhere— that was something that occurred only in historical times of famine or war, not in a so-called time of prosperity and peace.

Mimi found some chili paste and mixed it with her rice porridge: a vortex of red and white, barbed intensity the companion of mild delicacy, a mixture that awakened the taste buds. Kaizong looked at Mimi and seemed to finally understand the subtle contours of his own feelings for her: they were more than an ordinary couple, a man and a woman; in fact, they were like a pair of prisoners in sympathy, captives of this land that did not belong to them; they were strangers in Silicon Isle, and yet, they could not deny the complex web of feelings that tied them to the place.

"Uncle Luo, I'm full." Mimi looked up, her tongue flicking over the corner of her mouth to pick up the stray grains of rice. The *mi* character behind her neck never stopped glowing.

Luo Jincheng stood up, and Kaizong followed suit. The two stared at each other, not saying a word. Mimi looked up at them, her face peaceful.

"Can I trust you?" Kaizong finally said, helplessly. He put his hand on Luo's shoulder—he knew how rude such a gesture was, but he couldn't help it. "Can you promise you won't hurt her?"

Carefully, Luo took Kaizong's hand off of his shoulder, held it in his own hand, and shook it forcefully twice.

"There's a folk saying among the people of Silicon Isle: *lodaitaocug-cui, danzêgbhuno.*[15] *When Big Luo says 'one,' it will never be 'two.'*" His smile held traces of pride as well as embarrassment. "I am Big Luo."

Once again, Seisen Suzuki appeared on the screen before Scott. It was decades later, and though her hair was graying and her face no longer smooth, she still displayed her uncommon elegance and graceful temperament. She appeared in various forums: companies, human rights organizations, international NGOs, governmental bodies. She waved her arms, shouting as though defending something, but few were in the audience. Her figure appeared lonely and aged, like a willow shriveling and dying in the winds of time.

As a result of Dr. Suzuki's incessant lobbying, in 1997, QNB was formally listed in the Chemical Weapons Convention. She dedicated the latter years of her life to researching cures for the long-term consequences of QNB and invented an experimental treatment involving gene-modified viruses to repair the muscarinic receptors in the brains of victims. However, due to lack of funding and necessary technology, the treatment could not advance to the clinical trial stage.

Dr. Suzuki was never married. Due to the constraints of military security protocol, she never revealed the total number of victims suffering diseases related to QNB exposure.

[15] With full tone marks: *lo⁷dai⁷tao⁵cug⁴cui³, dan⁵zêg⁸bhu⁷no⁶*.

The scene shifted to a blurred, pale yellow; the lens soon focused, revealing the detailed patterns in the wallpaper. An old woman dressed in white sat in front of the camera, her posture easy and elegant, imbued with a highly controlled, precise beauty. Taped to the inside of her right arm was the white curve of an auto-injector, from which a green LED flashed. The numbers at the bottom of the screen indicated that it was March 3, 2003.

She nodded and smiled at the camera, the wrinkles on her face sketching out its soft curves.

She spoke in English.

"I am Seisen Suzuki, the inventor of QNB, and a sinner.

"Sixty years ago today, my fiancé, Hideo Kuboki, died in a sea battle. His tragic death forced me into making a wrong choice: I believed that I could, on my own, stop the terrors of war. As you all know, I came to the United States, obtained my doctorate, joined the military, and invented QNB. They told me that thousands upon thousands of soldiers were alive because of my invention, and had the chance to return from the battlefield to be reunited with their loved ones.

"They were telling the truth, but they were also lying.

"QNB caused irreversible physiological changes to the brain's nerve-ending receptors. The survivors would spend the rest of their lives in an inescapable web of delirium, terror, and hallucination. I have tried to remedy my error, but it is too late. I confess my sins and apologize to all the victims.

"I must also confess my sins and apologize to all the experimental subjects who were injured or died during the research process. You had already paid the price for your crimes, and did not deserve the torture I inflicted upon you. It matters not that my intent in committing evil was to do good—evil is evil; or perhaps the evil in my heart that sought vengeance had disguised itself as good, resulting in all this. I honestly don't know . . . please, all I can say is I'm sorry."

The old woman bowed her head deeply; the loose folds of skin at the back of her neck were stretched taut, like the membrane under a bird's wings.

"Today is the anniversary of my fiancé's death, and it is also the day of my atonement. I hope my death, though insignificant, will tell everyone that war destroys not only flesh, but also the soul. May all our souls rest in peace."

She smiled once more and pressed the button on the auto-injector. The green light flashed faster, turned yellow, then red, and finally went out.

Seisen Suzuki took a long breath and closed her eyes, as though savoring the chemicals flowing into her veins. The expression on that face, carved by the vicissitudes of life, changed rapidly as though each wrinkle was relaxing. Abruptly, her eyes flew open and she gazed at some spot above the camera, her face aglow with the joy of meeting a dear friend after long separation. Softly, she spoke in Japanese: *"Kuboki-kun, hibari yori sora ni yasurō tōge ka na."*

My dear Kuboki, resting here atop the ridge, down below, the song of soaring skylarks.[16]

---

[16] The haiku Suzuki quotes was composed by Matsuo Bashō in 1688 at the age of forty-five. It describes a scene on the road that passes from Hoso-toge/Tonomine (in Nara) through the Ryumon mountain range. English translation by Amy C. Franks © 2014, used with permission.

She closed her eyes again, as if asleep, the heaving motions of her body gradually slowing down until they ceased, some formless thing having departed from her aged shell. Suzuki was like a puppet whose strings had been cut, collapsing slowly under the influence of gravity. Her noble head bowed, and then her whole body sank into the chair.

Seisen Suzuki died at 83. Project Waste Tide was then quietly shut down and all related documents sealed away. The ownership of the three-hundred-plus patents she had been granted is a mystery, and an unknown number of victims suffering the aftereffects of QNB are still scattered around the world, struggling with daily life.

Scott sat still in his room, unable to dismiss the poignant scene of Suzuki's death. He could not have imagined that Project Waste Tide had shrouded such shocking secrets. A complex set of emotions warred within him: respect for this scientist, sinner, and ordinary woman who had waited alone for more than sixty years for her fiancé, but even more so, he felt pity, for this woman had shouldered too much of the responsibilities and guilt that did not belong to her.

Am I not the same? The idea flashed through his mind, and he chuckled. Even his pity turned out to be nothing more than a part of his self-protection mechanism.

Numerous nodes of complex data surfaced like reef islands in the sea, forming a confusing maze. Scott lifted his hands and, like a conductor facing a symphony orchestra, traced out graceful arcs in the air. His hands shifted through a dazzling array of gestures, which the high-precision sensors caught and translated into digital signals that acted on the corresponding information nodes: moving, magnifying, folding, unfolding, revealing details, building connections . . . A flashing web gradually took shape, a network of irregular topology that exuded the beauty of a twisted rationality.

The corners of Scott's mouth curved up in a hint of a smile; he had some ideas on how to solve this riddle.

Gently, he spun his index finger and brought the information node named "Mimi" to the center of the network and marked it with a golden question mark.

11

She suspected that she was trapped in a shell named "Mimi," but she didn't know the reasons for her confinement.

It was like that distant nightmare: she bored into the body of a steel giant and turned into the giant itself—waving her metallic glinting arms, ripping apart barriers made of frigid rain and wind, running, leaping, hunting . . . killing. She knew it wasn't real. She hoped it wasn't real.

However, right now Mimi was experiencing the hallucination of being a guest in her own body. Since the moment she recovered her consciousness, this sensation had only grown stronger. Even worse, she couldn't control this flesh body as effectively as she had controlled the robot. The anxiety surfaced time and again, seizing her autonomic nervous system and heart and shaking them about; but then, a euphoric peace of unknown origin would be secreted from a certain part of her brain and calm her anxiety, making her feel she was on cloud nine. At other times, her heart palpitated and unease gripped her, while needles pricked at some phantom limb as if trying to prevent her from thinking of some idea or taking some action.

It was as though this body was trying to tame the soul incarcerated within it.

She remembered standing next to the window, after waking up in the hospital, and watching as Kaizong hurried out of the taxi. She had wanted to wave at him, to shout at him, to use every means at her disposal to let him see that she was standing right here. She'd wanted to give the fake foreigner a hug—something she had never done and wouldn't have even dreamed of doing. *You are nothing but a WASTE GIRL.* The label had been branded in her heart more securely than the film applied to the back of her neck, impossible to erase. All of her actions and choices had been circumscribed by that label, an invisible line that she had not dared to cross.

She had stood there, unmoving, until Kaizong appeared in the doorway behind her.

Then she'd heard an impossible conversation being carried on. Inconceivable words drifted out of Mimi's lips and disappeared. She'd seen Mimi grip Kaizong's hand, let go, and then his hands had seized hers. She was certain that she had gone insane.

This body had achieved what she had dreamed of but never managed to act out, even if it was such an insignificant gesture. But every gesture from this body seemed to be aimed at controlling Kaizong, which made Mimi anxious. She had never so clearly felt the difference between genders when it came to receiving and decoding information, and it was a difference that could be exploited. Shame and satisfaction filled her mind almost simultaneously, like red hot sauce stirred into white rice porridge.

She'd heard music, the music that played in her mind. Like a tune from a wound-up music box, the tune repeated itself endlessly. The high-spirited melody was so familiar, and, mixed with the twisted horn blares and the drumbeats that struck the ends of her nerves, brought about a singular pleasure.

Even more terrifyingly, she'd known where the music came from. In a flash, a kind of logical integration capability she had never mastered assembled all the fragments into a path of clues and displayed it before her.

The cheap sound systems in the taxis could not distinguish between bass and midrange tones, and so they were only tolerable to the listener when playing music with simple parts, high-pitched tones, and little reliance on harmony. The Silicon Isle traffic station had adjusted to the need and broadcast a large number of *shanzhai* songs processed to display such characteristics, thus becoming the cabbies' standard station on the job—just another excruciating local quirk. However, every hour, on the hour, all the local stations had to rebroadcast the city central station's time announcement, which involved a segment of two commercials set against the background of a piece of classical music. The traffic station, in order to save time, decided to compress the segment, thus causing it to sound half a beat faster than the original.

Just like the *1812 Overture* coming out of Mimi's lips.

She had felt afraid of herself—a profound sensation of terror that seeped into her marrow. Kaizong had taken her to places in taxis; she had, from her shack, listened to the standard time announcement music play on various stations countless times; and she might have, during random dinner conversations, heard Brother Wen mention these kinds of technical details, which only a geek would care about. But she had never imagined that her mind possessed such power to organize scattered bits of information and weave them, like silk strands extracted from disparate cocoons, into a coherent picture.

She couldn't understand the meaning of this new awareness; all she could see was the shock and terror on Kaizong's face. A wave of sorrow chilled her heart.

She had discovered that she *felt* this world differently. She didn't know how to describe it precisely, but it was like someone who, after jumping out of a deep well and seeing the open sky and earth for the first time, gained rich multiple perspectives and finely layered emotions. Even when she thought about everything that had happened on Tide Gazing Beach, pure hatred and disgust were now replaced with a grander, more complex emotion. She seemed to understand why Knifeboy had done what he had done, and his ultimate fate. She even pitied him.

The Luo clan turned their ancestral hall into the site for the ceremony: washed stone walls, red bricks, clay tiles. The shrine held a golden statue of the Buddha from Chiang Mai in Thailand at the top, and the tablets of generations of Luo clan ancestors were arranged in rows below. Electric candles flickered amid twisting columns of incense smoke. Luo Zixin's bed had been moved to the middle of the hall. His pallid, puny body lay still, stuck full of tubes and wires, and his eyes were tightly shut, revealing no sign of life; if not for the slow beats from the cardiograph, one might have thought this was a drowned corpse.

The idea for conducting the ritual here was to take advantage of the power of the ancestors and the Buddha to suppress evil spirits, but all who were present in the hall shivered as though standing in an ice cellar. Surrounded by the uncanny atmosphere, they felt a prickling sensation on their backs.

Kaizong saw Director Lin Yiyu come into the hall and finally understood what Luo Jincheng had meant by people Kaizong "already knew" as well as how the security at the hospital had been so easily breached. Director Lin nodded at him but didn't come closer. His expression was even grimmer than Luo Jincheng's, as though it were his own son who was in a coma.

Mimi sat calmly to the side, waiting for the show to start.

Kaizong refocused his attention on her: her habitual timidity tinged with anxiety was gone, replaced by a calmness that seemed to come from deep inside, the confidence of someone fully in control of the situation. He didn't believe it was an act: the glowing *mi* at the back of her neck was the surest proof. Something had *changed* inside Mimi. *Is it the metal particles?* Kaizong grew apprehensive again. He didn't know how to face this brand-new Mimi; he even felt a trace of fear.

Her face looked different from before. There was no longer a mark on her bottom lip from her nervous biting, and her brows seemed arched higher. *What kind of soul is hidden under that face?*

The *lohsingpua* appeared right on time in a sleeveless, multicolored dress, the wrinkles on her face smoothed over with a thick layer of red makeup and her facial features painted to resemble an angry spirit. She had Mimi sit about three feet from the crown of Luo Zixin's head, so that Mimi was the midpoint of a straight line from the child to the golden Buddha. Then she stuck a piece of green film with the character for "edict"—*chi*—onto Zixin's and Mimi's foreheads, just like the one on her own.

She lit a candle and sprinkled the spicy, pungent holy water made of wormwood, calamus, and garlic around the ancestral hall, muttering all the while and praying for goodwill from the spirits. When she was done, she returned to Zixin's bed and accepted an oil-filled porcelain bowl from her assistant. After chanting more incantations, she lit the bowl on fire, and orange flames indicating incomplete combustion rose from her hands, dancing uneasily.

She began to circle Zixin's bed in a clockwise direction; her gait was slow and jerky, following some inaudible drumbeat. In a low voice, she muttered verses of Buddhist scripture, interspersed from time to time with loud howls like chill winds passing through a pine forest in deep night. Everyone in the hall felt goose bumps on their backs.

Kaizong's heart was tugged into his throat, where it clenched with every step the *lohsingpua* took, terrified that she might trip and spill the scalding, burning bowl of oil onto Mimi. He didn't believe in these superstitious rites and didn't really think that Luo Zixin would wake up from his coma as a result of the performance or that Mimi was going to die in the boy's place; however, there were aspects of the spectacle he was witnessing that he couldn't explain: for instance, how could the witch hold the bowl, whose surface temperature was surely now in the triple digits, with her bare hands?

Mimi showed no hint of surprise or fear; she simply watched the *lohsingpua* with a curious expression. Her face brightened and dimmed by turns as the woman with the bowl of flames circled around her, the light reflecting from her eyes in peculiar patterns.

The few VIPs present gasped. The *chi* in the film applied to Zixin's forehead flickered to life; almost simultaneously, the film on Mimi's and the *lohsingpua*'s foreheads also lit up.

The witch moved faster. Like a busy worker bee, she traced out a complex figure-eight pattern around Zixin's bed and Mimi, shifting her direction constantly. The fire flared in her hands, and her howls seemed to echo and dash around the hall. The three *chi* characters on their foreheads winked in synchrony, speeding up in rhythm, but Zixin's cardiogram continued to be as steady and calm as before.

The audience held their breaths, waiting for the climactic moment. As soon as Mimi screamed with fright, the witch would smash the bowl against the ground and shriek at the top of her lungs, completing the "substitution" phase of the ritual. However, someone wasn't following the script: Mimi didn't even shift from her sitting pose, while the witch was already having trouble catching her breath. Sweat had carved multiple trails in her makeup, like bloody tears.

Kaizong watched the farce with growing interest, wondering how it was going to end.

Another collective gasp. The film over Mimi's forehead began to flicker at a different frequency, no longer in sync with the other two. Her placid expression had also changed; she knit her brows, deep in thought, or perhaps struggling against some invisible force. She stared at some spot in the air as her eyelids quivered, a familiar quivering that made Kaizong's heart palpitate.

The film over Zixin's forehead syncopated and departed from the flickering rhythm of the film over the *lohsingpua*'s forehead. Gradually, its rhythm approached Mimi's. Some invisible hand seemed to be adjusting and coordinating the three lights. Right now, Mimi and the comatose boy were tuned to the same channel. A look of incredulity appeared on Luo Jincheng's face, mixed with a trace of anxious hope.

Slight perturbations appeared in the recurrent waveform on the cardiogram, as though a pebble had been tossed into the pond. Ripples spread, shifting the positions of peaks and valleys, stretching and shrinking the amplitudes.

The witch's feet staggered, and the flickering tongues of flames almost licked her wrists. Kaizong was about to go up and stop her when a hand gripped him by the shoulder, gently but forcefully restraining him. Director Lin Yiyu shook his head at him. *Wait. It will soon resolve.*

The flickering of the green light over the *lohsingpua*'s forehead lost its own beat and began to approach the rhythm of the other two, searching for a new unity. She appeared weak, not even in control of her own howls. Her expression became even more hideous, a mixture of terror and exhaustion. Her eyes rested on Luo Jincheng's glum face; she knew she couldn't stop; she understood the price of failure.

But even the smile on the golden Buddha couldn't save her.

The inevitable stumble came. The *lohsingpua* fell to the ground on her face. The fire-spewing porcelain bowl hung suspended in the air for a moment, tumbled upside down, and plummeted onto her body. The bright yellow flames, following the path of the flowing liquid, covered her body, turning her multicolored dress into a coat of flames. The assistant screamed and tried to help her out of the dress, desperately beating at her in an effort to put out the fire. Wretched wailing, accompanied by pungent smoke, filled the hall, mixing with the flames of the votive candles.

The porcelain bowl rolled on the ground and came to a stop at Kaizong's feet. Director Lin rushed forward, squatted down, and carefully tested the surface with the back of a finger. He looked up at Kaizong and silently mouthed a word: "Charlatan."

Kaizong quirked his brow and turned his gaze back to the boy in the bed. Luo Jincheng was already at the bedside, gazing at his son intently, completely oblivious to the two clowns rolling around on the ground next to him, screaming and trying to put out the fire. Luo Zixin's cardiogram settled into a new steady rhythm. The *chi* characters on his and Mimi's foreheads slowed down their blinking and dimmed until the green lights went out.

Mimi gently ripped the film off her forehead, her face tired.

Everyone took a few steps forward but dared not press up too closely against Luo Jincheng. The audience waited about a meter away from Zixin's bed and watched as the boy's eyelids began to quiver, as though he was entering a REM sleep cycle.

"Him-ri, Him-ri . . ." Luo Jincheng called to his son in the local topolect, love suffusing his gaze.

Kaizong had to admit some measure of admiration for how quickly Luo Jincheng managed to shift his expressions and emotional states. He thought back to Luo's soliloquy earlier on the nature of a father's love, and was reminded of his own faraway father. Perhaps Luo was right.

The quivering stopped. After some time, Zixin's eyes fluttered open, revealing pure, light brown irises.

"Him-ri!" Something wet glistened in Luo Jincheng's eyes.

The boy looked uncertainly around him, taking everything in. He seemed to struggle to recall where when who he was how . . . and who this man was looking at him with tearful eyes.

". . . *Baba*?" he offered tentatively.

Luo Jincheng remained still, utterly amazed. Everyone present had heard him clearly; though the tones were only slightly different, the change was unmistakable. This boy of Silicon Isle, after being in a coma for months, was speaking Modern Standard Mandarin instead of his native topolect.

Kaizong looked over and caught a flitting smile at the corners of Mimi's eyes.

Mimi was learning to compromise with this body. She started by overcoming her anxiety.

When Luo Jincheng's face had first appeared in the doorway of the ICU, she had been like a wild hare scenting a hunter, and the urge to run had been nearly impossible to suppress. But she didn't. Mimi's body held her in place. The golden film on the back of her neck dimmed only for a moment before brightening again. The horrible wave of memories seemed to be dammed outside her consciousness, and all that was left was the sensation of their uneasy pounding against the barrier. She was amazed by the ease with which she performed her role: her breathing was steady and her facial muscles relaxed. With blank eyes she conveyed to Luo Jincheng this simple message: *I remember nothing.*

And Luo Jincheng had believed her.

The control lasted until she set foot in the Luo clan ancestral hall and sat down by Luo Zixin's bed. She recalled that distant, unreal past: the prosthesis that had pricked her, the boy taking a photo in secret, the cold blood. Everything had started then.

Mimi was filled with regret. Her mother had always taught her to be kind because whatever we did, the heavens were watching. After coming to Silicon Isle, she had begun to doubt her mother's teaching. Humiliation and harm were inflicted on the innocent around her every day; even if the heavens possessed billions of eyes, most of them seemed to be averted from the reality of this world.

Mimi became a pragmatic animist, believing that spirits lived in everything. As long as she prayed faithfully and provided the required sacrifices, she would be protected. This was how the waste people could survive in this living hell. There were incense burners everywhere outside the waste-processing sheds, which the faithful fed with plastic scraps; combined with polyimide films charged with magical symbols and incantations, the censers glowed in the night like will-o'-the-wisps warning passersby to stay away from forbidden places.

Could this boy also be a sacrificial offering for some spirit? Who will benefit from his sacrifice? Mimi watched the shuttling figure of the *lohsingpua* palming the bowl of burning oil, doubt creeping into her heart.

Green flashes like raindrops appeared before her eyes, and Zixin's and the witch's foreheads lit up. One still, one moving, the two lights were like a star and a roving planet in a universe that did not distinguish between magic and technology. She understood that the lights had nothing to do with her; most likely, they were the result of remote manipulation by the *lohsingpua* or her assistant. The boy's condition wasn't affected substantively.

Like some switch being flipped, she sensed a subtle transformation in Mimi's body. The hairs on her skin stood up and her vision brightened; an uncontrollable tremor began somewhere deep in her brain and ended at the skin of her brow, where it spread, ripple-like. In a flash, she understood what her body intended, even though she couldn't say how she had come to such understanding. An invisible bridge across consciousnesses had been constructed through the sensors in the body films applied to her and Zixin's foreheads and radio waves: she was at one end, and Luo Zixin was at the other.

She knew what she had to do. She had to awaken this boy to repair the harm from her earlier mistake. No matter what kind of violence his father had inflicted on Mimi, the boy was innocent. When Brother Wen had harmed the boy, Mimi had not stopped him, and that made her responsible. In Mimi's eyes, the world should have revolved around such simple, clear rules. It was people, convoluted people, who added complexity to it, made it hard to understand.

But things were not as simple as she anticipated.

The meningitis caused by the viral infection had inhibited the boy's consciousness. The neural receptors, blocked by proteins manufactured by the virus, couldn't conduct the bioelectrical signals of thought. But that wasn't the most important problem. The blocking mechanism had already decayed due to preprogrammed regulation of protein expression and should no longer affect neural impulses of ordinary strength. She couldn't understand the meaning behind this piece of data, but Mimi's body seemed to understand the implications intuitively. Her consciousness jumped across the springboard of her body film's radio transmitter and reached into the boy's brain like a tentacle sweeping through regions of the cortex, seeking a deeper cause.

It was language.

To her surprise, Mimi discovered that the virus's consciousness-inhibiting protein functioned like a safety mechanism. Similar to the fuse in a circuit, it was designed to activate when the energy load of neural transmissions exceeded a certain threshold, shutting off the connection to protect the neurons from being burnt out. However, for some reason, Luo Zixin's blocking mechanism had been set with an extremely low safety threshold such that as soon as he began to think with the Silicon Isle topolect, the fuses tripped and the neurotransmission circuits shut down.

The Silicon Isle topolect was an ancient language containing eight tones with exceedingly complex tone sandhi rules. Its informational entropy thus far exceeded that of Modern Standard Mandarin with its simple four tones. This was the root cause of the boy's coma.

She was not at all prepared for what happened next. Abruptly, Mimi's mental tentacle hardened and reached into the boy's Broca's area, located in the inferior frontal gyrus of the left hemisphere, which was responsible for speech production and control. Like a precise laser scalpel, the tentacle manipulated this most refined and complex artifact as though the wielder were in possession of billions of years of practice and experience.

Sweat beaded at her brow, moistening her hairline. Once again she was astounded by the powers her body seemed to possess without her knowledge, but this time, she hoped for a good conclusion.

The tentacle softened, contracted, and jumped back into her body through the film. Almost casually, as it retracted, it also touched the consciousness of the *lohsingpua*.

A *fraud*. Mimi understood everything in an instant. Brother Wen's mysterious helmet had accidentally planted the embryo of change in her mind, and Luo Jincheng and Knifeboy had hatched the embryo from its shell with violence, but it was this old woman who, by insisting on pulling Mimi into the clumsy con of an "oil-fire cleansing," had connected all the triggers and brought to life the full form of the monster in her mind.

The witch had created today's Mimi.

A fleeting thought, and it was done. Mimi watched as the bowl of flames floated up, turned, tumbled, and bloomed against the body of that middle-aged woman awkwardly sprawled along the ground. *A little gift from me to you. A gesture of respect.* The corners of her mouth lifted into a blameless smile.

The scene descended into pandemonium. People rushed around, some trying to put out the fire, others watching to see what would happen next; Luo Jincheng knelt at the bed calling the name of his darling child; Director Lin and Chen Kaizong whispered to the side.

Slowly, in response to his father's cries, the boy opened his eyes. Out of kindness, Mimi had not modified his Wernicke's area, responsible for understanding language, so that he could still understand the Silicon Isle topolect. However, for the rest of his life, he would only be able to speak in Mandarin with its four sparse tones, like the outsider waste people that his father so despised.

He said ba^4ba, instead of the tone-shifted ba^7ba^5 of Silicon Isle. Luo Jincheng was instantly transfixed.

Kaizong's worried gaze swept to her face. With some effort, she suppressed the impulse to laugh aloud even though she thought this a very appropriate joke.

A water-carrying rickshaw was parked outside the gate of the Luo clan mansion, waiting for servants to unload the bottled water onto handcarts. The middle-aged waste man driving the rickshaw looked particularly anxious, muttering incessantly while the augmented-reality glasses he wore flashed their green light. Finally, all the purified water had been unloaded, and the rickshaw cart rose slightly. The driver turned right around and returned at a mad dash the way he had come, not even bothering to wait for the Luo servants who called out in surprise, asking if he wanted his money.

He glanced back a few times; no one was chasing him. Gradually, he slowed down, and merged into the crowded traffic of Silicon Isle Town.

"Uncle He, what's wrong with you?" a few waste people greeted him. "You are acting like you've seen a ghost."

There was no hint of a smile on his sweat-drenched face as Uncle He stopped the rickshaw and gestured for one of the waste people to approach. Still sitting astride the rickshaw, he leaned over as if attempting to bump foreheads with the other man. Soon, the glasses worn by the other man lit up with a green light as well. Uncle He didn't linger but started the engine again and rode on, spreading the video he had captured about ten minutes earlier.

The video showed a black car speeding into the Luo mansion grounds.

Even from this distance, it was still possible to distinguish the figures climbing out of the car. A girl was supported by others and helped into the mansion. The loose white clothing she wore didn't seem to be a fashion statement but more resembled a hospital gown.

Uncle He was certain that the girl was Mimi. He had to let Li Wen know this news right away.

The sun slowly climbed up to mid-sky and turned scorching. Uncle He felt himself enveloped by a sticky, thick cloud of steam that made progress difficult. Countless varieties of noise and stench assaulted him from every direction, and he found the smatterings of speech he heard incomprehensible. Many pairs of eyes swept past his vision: the eyes of waste people, natives, and others he couldn't tell. He saw the waste people meeting in the road, inclining their heads at each other like nineteenth-century European gentlemen while the Silicon Isle natives around them cast suspicious side glances. The way the despised waste people greeted each other appeared incomprehensible and insufferable to the natives, who thought of themselves as superior.

Uncle He kept the rickshaw steady and smoothly traversed the busy, crowded market, maintaining the appearance of normalcy for the sake of the monitoring closed-circuit television cameras. Still, in the end he couldn't hold back a sweaty grin as his chest convulsed with laughter.

There were two Mimis, she had gradually come to accept this fact, and she named them "Mimi 0" and "Mimi 1."

Mimi 0 was the waste girl from the distant home village: cautious, guarded against everyone, oversensitive yet full of curiosity, pitying a malfunctioning chipped dog, liking a Silicon Isle boy with an ambiguous identity—but so lacking in self-confidence that she kept him at arm's length. She would forever remember that night when the bioluminescent jellyfish had spun like a nebula, when the surface of the sea had glistened with silver light like billions of fish scales, when Kaizong had lain next to her on the beach to gaze up at the stars, and a feeling that she could not name or describe had caused her heart to skip a beat and the world to waver, making her dazed and dazzled.

She was Mimi 0.

Mimi 1, on the other hand, was a presence that she could not summarize at all. On that long, dark, rain-drenched night, it had come to possess this body like a ghost and become its master. It seemed to be omniscient and omnipotent. Though the two of them shared this body, Mimi 0 was like a hitchhiking passenger who knew nothing about the thoughts of Mimi 1 and certainly could not interfere with them. She saw everything Mimi 1 wanted her to see, and she struggled to follow the inhumanly complex and profound streams of consciousness, learning, understanding, being uplifted. Mimi 0 was terrified of Mimi 1 but also worshiped her, prostrate before a machinelike, incomparably precise, controlling power. She even sensed a beauty that she had never experienced in her life, like standing at the peak of a towering mountain and gazing down upon the magnificence of all Life. Her legs turned to jelly and she trembled uncontrollably, the pressure in her bladder growing, and yet, she was unable to resist the allure of the desire to find out the truth.

In her mind, Mimi 1's face was always overlaid on top of the face of a Western woman, like a ghost image. She yearned to know who she was, but she was also worried that the introduction of a third person wouldn't make the situation any simpler.

At this moment, however, Mimi 0 and Mimi 1 shared a rare consensus: exhaustion. Waking the boy had consumed too much energy, and they both needed nourishment. Mimi was starving.

But the farce was still not over.

Luo Jincheng screamed at the medical staff on site, who scrambled to examine the boy; the *lohsingpua*, her dress full of holes from the fire that revealed the rolls of fat at her waist, tried to sneak away with her assistant, but the Luo clan's guards seized them and made them kneel in a corner to await Boss Luo's decision; Director Lin Yiyu was on the phone while he surveyed the room, reporting on the situation to his interlocutor with a glum, unchanging expression; Chen Kaizong's face appeared in her field of vision: he was kneeling next to her, his expression distressed, apparently asking her some question.

All the noises had mixed together and knit into a textureless wall that buzzed and pressed against her auditory nerves. It was as if her blood sugar level had lowered past some threshold, causing some sensory channels to shut down to avoid giving her vertigo. Mimi tried to read Kaizong's lips, but she couldn't; her concentration seemed to slip away from cracks in her consciousness and scatter onto the ground, merging into the dust.

Someone else broke into the hall, and white light expanded from the open doorway like a sphere that gradually faded. The newcomer was shouting something repeatedly at the top of his lungs, and everyone in the room stopped, turning to look at him. He repeated himself so many times that the syllables of each iteration stacked on top of each other, reinforcing each other in Mimi's mind. Gradually, clear words emerged from the murk; she finally understood.

"The waste people are coming!" he was shouting. "The waste people are coming!"

The fear that flooded the faces of the Silicon Isle natives confused Mimi. In the world she was familiar with, such terror belonged only to the waste people, especially when they faced one of the natives. She had seen countless waste people kneeling on the ground, begging for mercy; strong, weak, old, young, dirty, helpless—they knelt before the Silicon Isle natives because they had dirtied his clothing, unintentionally stared at him for too long, touched her child, brushed against his car, or even for no reason at all, simply because they were waste people.

She could never forget the expressions in the eyes of those who knelt, like thorns of frozen fire that stabbed into her heart. She understood that if any one of them hadn't done so, perhaps the next day he or she would have turned into a rotting corpse by the side of the street like Good Dog. She also couldn't forget the expressions in the eyes of the Silicon Isle natives: they stood, heads slightly lifted, as if they belonged to a completely different species whose birthright was to gaze down upon these people like animals, upon these people who were no different from themselves whether by genes or culture.

But now, the natives were afraid. What was frightening them?

Everyone headed for the exit. With Chen Kaizong's support, Mimi also followed. Her pupils contracted as her eyes gradually adjusted to the bright light. She saw the source of the terror.

Outside the Luo mansion, facing the guards and the chipped dogs across the iron gates, more than a hundred waste people stood in a dark mass. They stood in the glaring sun, their expressions impossible to see, faces and bodies contaminated with dark stains—the toxic dust and fumes from incinerating plastic and acid-washing metal. They sacrificed their health and lives in exchange for insignificant scraps to fill their bellies and distant dreams, built up the extravagant prosperity of Silicon Isle, and yet they were seen as only slaves, bugs, disposable trash. They were forced to watch it all with numbed gazes.

It had been too long. The ice in their eyes began to melt in the sunlight, turning into searing flames.

Mimi saw Brother Wen standing in the middle of the crowd. There were no banners, no slogans; only silence. But when they saw Mimi appear with the Silicon Isle natives, holding her arms, an invisible force seemed to spread among the crowd: the sound of muscles tensing was like the sighing of a breeze across a field of wheat, wafting up the flavor of boiling adrenaline.

Director Lin Yiyu shouted angrily into his phone.

Mimi felt her own consciousness parting like flowing sand into two separate streams: Mimi 0, overexhausted, was lost in a chaotic confusion; Mimi 1, on the other hand, understood that the waste people had come for her and knew also how to stir up or dissipate this oncoming war. She had to make a choice.

She stopped, shook off Kaizong's hands. She looked at his once-confident face, now filled with uncertainty and hesitation, and smiled. Slowly but resolutely, she walked forward by herself. The sun was blazing hot and she felt weak, as if each step sank into soft mud that gave her no purchase. The iron gates rumbled and carefully opened a crack.

The crowd outside slipped in and out of focus. She thought of herself as sitting inside a tiny boat that drifted over the sea at night, and the gentle waves lifted her up and then set her down.

She stood before the narrow opening, almost able to smell the sweet tang of rust on the iron grille. Mimi turned and saw that Kaizong had hesitantly followed her. He lifted up a hand, as though in farewell but also like a soldier readying himself for the final assault.

She had reached her limit, though. Whatever strength had been holding her up drained away, and she collapsed toward the ground.

The crowd cried out in surprise.

But she did not strike the hard ground. Kaizong leapt forward and, at the last moment, managed to catch Mimi's body and pulled her into his embrace.

The move was the final straw for the crowd gathered outside the iron gates. Their tolerance had finally been breached, and a bestial bellow erupted from their chests as they rushed at the half-open gate with their unarmed bodies, clanging and dinging as flesh struck metal. The surprised guards tried to shut the gate, but it was too late. The chipped dogs barked violently and leapt toward the flood of waste people pouring through the gate.

Mimi looked up at Kaizong's blurry silhouette against the white light, felt his solid, warm embrace, and couldn't understand if this was the result of her own actions or the outcome of Mimi 1's careful planning. She only heard a deep vibration through the air like the infrasonic waves before a tidal wave struck shore; it stirred her innards and made her uneasy.

She saw a dark shadow heading for Kaizong's head—the motion was slowed down like a scene captured by a high-speed camera; a muffled explosion whose sound lingered in the air; Kaizong's arms loosened and his head jerked backward, tracing out a bloody arc through the air. She wanted to scream, wanted to get up, but her body, like a stringless puppet, would not obey.

Warm liquid fell against Mimi's face, filled with the scent of rust. She was beginning to be certain that she was nothing more than a pawn to be sacrificed in some Great Game.

12

Luo Jincheng sat in a rosewood sofa chair while Lin Yiyu remained standing. Before them was a huge, solid mahogany desk. The man behind the desk sat with the back of his chair toward them, revealing only a balding head with a few wisps of hair. The man stared at the gigantic aquarium built into the wall, entranced. Some soft but large creature crept slowly against the bright, colorful background.

He seemed to have forgotten about the two visitors behind him, anxiously awaiting his instructions.

"Mayor Weng . . ." Lin Yiyu couldn't hold back any longer, but then he faltered.

Luo Jincheng cast Lin a contemptuous glance. "If we don't do something quickly, I'm afraid we're going to face even bigger trouble."

The man behind the leather chair back remained silent. Just as the patience of the two visitors was about to collapse completely, a slow but forceful reply came.

"Bigger trouble? Why don't you tell me what trouble could be bigger or more serious than kidnapping a teenage girl and causing hundreds of migratory workers to assemble and clash violently with the police? Ah, you think because the strike is harming the Luo clan's business, the town is supposed to foot the bill?"

Luo Jincheng had no answer. He could almost sense Lin Yiyu next to him chuckling silently in schadenfreude.

"But Director Lin, you kept the truth from me, and I think we have to also assign you some blame for this mess, no?" The corners of Director Lin's mouth convulsed, as if he had been slapped in the face. "Deploying the police without proper authorization is one of those things that could turn out to be nothing or a big deal. You're lucky that no one died. However, I'm interested in how you intend to appease the Americans."

"Absolutely! I've already invited the most prominent ophthalmologists from the provincial capital, and they're sparing no effort at treating the patient. The waste people responsible for the crime have already been apprehended."

An eerie peal of derisive laughter erupted from behind the chair back.

"My dear Director Lin, you're competent and skilled at maneuvering around officialdom, but I think you've got to become a little more politically aware. Others may be able to get away with using words like 'waste people,' but you can't. Don't you understand?"

"Yes, yes . . ." Beads of sweat covered Lin Yiyu's forehead. Luo Jincheng had to use every ounce of willpower to not laugh out loud.

"The bidding for this project has drawn enormous attention," Mayor Weng continued. "The provincial capital sent word that Silicon Isle is to be a trial for Sino-American cooperation, a point of focus. Boss Luo, it's fine if you're not on board to help, but you can't mess this up for me. Of the three clans, right now you are the least cooperative and cause the most problems. Why don't I get up so you can sit down in the mayor's chair and do whatever you like? Would that make you happy?"

"Come on, Mayor Weng, don't talk that way. All I wanted was for the Americans to pay a bit more. Like you, I'm working for the benefit of Silicon Isle." Luo Jincheng's words appeared conciliatory, but there was an edge to his tone.

"Pay a bit more? Aha, he paid with an eye! Is that enough for you? Say, Director Lin, you've been standing all this time. How about we find you a seat? Or are you worried that you'll tremble so much that you'll fall out of the chair?"

"I'm good. I'm good with standing. I get to see farther if I stand." Lin Yiyu deliberately glanced at Luo Jincheng.

"See farther? Pshaw. I think you might be looking, but you aren't *seeing*. Look over there."

The two followed Mayor Weng's finger and gazed at the glass aquarium, uncertain what game the mayor was playing.

The aquarium appeared unremarkable at first glance, but it was said that the sand, soil, coral, and plants inside had all been carefully transplanted from their original natural environment. The water quality, trace elements, acidity, illumination, temperature, artificial waves . . . everything was technologically manipulated to replicate the real ocean environment. However, fish were not the main actors in the scene; the ruler of this miniature world was an octopus with a half-meter-long mantle, a common species in the sea around Silicon Isle. At this moment, the cephalopod was lazily hanging on to the side of the aquarium with its twenty-four hundred suckers. From time to time, it curled and waved one of its arms, waiting for the next feeding.

Luo Jincheng saw the mayor's hand lift up and press the buttons on a white remote control.

The background of the aquarium instantly turned from the cerulean sea bottom to a field of molten lava, flashing a terrifying crimson. Almost simultaneously, Luo Jincheng noticed the octopus transform from head to toe to a matching shade of red, as though the octopus had had too much to drink. The skin of the octopus even imitated the bubbling lava in the background with multiple bright yellow circles that surfaced briefly before disappearing.

Another press of the buttons on the remote, and the molten lava turned to desert. The octopus's skin turned to a brownish yellow, sandy in texture, complete with faint traces left in the sand by hot passing breezes.

The desert shifted to a tropical jungle, and the octopus's green this time appeared a bit dull and uneven, matching the background only imperfectly. The mayor explained that this was due to the effects of the astaxanthin in the octopus's body.

The jungle transformed into an intense, ever-changing, animated scene where splashes and whirls of color entwined and wove together chaotically, like some madman's improvised doodle. The octopus struggled to keep up with the changes but could only capture portions of the picture from time to time. The rate of color changes in the octopus's skin was clearly slowing down.

The chaotic background disappeared and was replaced by a mirror.

The octopus seemed frightened. Instead of its earlier, leisurely pose, it now held on to the glass wall with only three arms and raised the other five arms high like banners proclaiming its sovereignty. Its twin in the mirror engaged in a similar display. The surface of both octopuses began to flash. Inside the chromatophores, the source of the animal's coloration, elastic sacs filled with various pigments expanded and contracted. Collectively, like the pixel arrays on a display or a spinning kaleidoscope, the chromatophores formed into an endless series of colorful images.

Luo Jincheng stared at the scene in wonder and began to understand why the mayor seemed so mesmerized by it.

The transformations continued without cease.

The mayor pressed the remote one more time and everything returned to the tranquil azure scene at the start. The octopus lazily came to rest between the gravel and sand, merging into the bottom.

"To us, this little critter appears as one of the most alien animals on Earth. It has three hearts, two memory systems, and its body is covered with ultrasensitive chemical and tactile sensors." The mayor lectured like a genuine octopus expert. "But from a certain perspective, it is also extremely similar to us.

"Sensitive to its environment, it constantly changes itself, disguises itself, and could even be confused by itself into a deadly cycle. Once, I waited patiently to see if an octopus in front of a mirror would eventually settle down to a stable pattern; I ended up with a dead octopus. And this was how I came to understand that stability was the same as death."

The leather chair finally spun around and revealed the face of the occupant. Mayor Weng looked utterly at peace, even a bit bored in his eyes.

"Director Lin advocates imposing a temporary curfew; Boss Luo suggests shutting off the communication channels of all the migrant workers. Both of these paths might lead to the same result. Even if we manage to suppress the smaller incidents, much bigger trouble isn't going to be far off."

Luo Jincheng and Lin Yiyu stared at each other helplessly. They understood that it was pointless to expect a real answer from Mayor Weng today, and they had no choice but to retreat, defeated. Just as they were about to leave the office, they heard the mayor's earnest farewell.

"I hope you haven't forgotten how Silicon Isle became a restricted-bitrate zone."

Luo Jincheng bit his bottom lip and clenched his jaw, having apparently come to a decision.

Scott Brandle called his temporary interpreter at five minutes past midnight and claimed to want to take a stroll through the night markets because he was hungry. He could tell that the man on the other end of the line was suppressing his displeasure as he replied that he needed to consult Director Lin first. Five minutes later, Scott's phone rang, and the interpreter's tone was much improved. He even solicitously offered to take Scott to one of the most-frequented food hawker lanes in Silicon Isle.

Since Kaizong was still in the hospital under observation, Scott had to accept the temporary arrangements made by Director Lin. The new interpreter was a young man named Xin Yu. He hadn't even graduated from college yet and was home on summer break when he was drafted for this duty. His accent was terrible and he sometimes used the wrong expressions, but his understanding of Silicon Isle's current situation far exceeded Kaizong's.

Xin Yu's typical excuse for every mistranslation was that "the Silicon

Isle topolect is among the most ancient and unique of extant Chinese topolects. There are many words that I don't even know how to translate into Modern Standard Mandarin, let alone English."

Scott usually shrugged his shoulders and said, "I wasn't hoping for much anyway"; and then he would laugh and clap the young man with the wounded look on the shoulders.

Though it was after midnight, the hawker lane was brightly lit and busy with customers. All kinds of flavors and smells wove through the air, stirring the appetites of visitors. Scott acted like a real tourist and followed Xin Yu to every stall, inquiring after the ingredients, methods of preparation, and cultural backstories of the local delicacies. Many of the dishes were far more complex and subtle than he had imagined. Of course, considering that he came from a young country that had been founded only about 250 years ago, it was understandable that his own culinary culture had progressed but a few steps beyond tossing the meat over an open fire after skinning the kill.

From time to time, Scott stopped and pretended to be admiring some scene while stealing glances behind him. He noticed a diminutive man who had been following them from the hotel like a shadow, maintaining the distance of about ten meters. Ever since Scott's return from his brief sortie to the open sea, he had been finding more spies around himself, watching his every move. However, he couldn't tell who had sent this particular snoop.

They were at a fishmonger's, a waterless aquarium spilling over with the smells of the bounty of the sea. Grouper heads as big as the torso of a child hung in the air along with grouper sections, and sea creatures of various shapes and colors were spread out over the crushed ice in the display cases. Japanese scad, *ure* eels, red crucian carp, flathead mullets, fishes called *angmagling* and *dêggianhe,* Japanese blue crabs, *gohoi* crabs, *moham* clams, Chinese razor clams, *hianglo* conchs, geoducks, squids, cuttlefish, sand prawns, mantis shrimp[17] . . .

Scott was stunned by the string of names—Xin Yu was pretty sure

---

[17] With full tone marks: *uʹre⁷, ang⁷mag⁸ling⁵, dêg⁴gian²he⁵, goʹhoi⁸, mo⁷hamʹ, hiang⁸lo⁵*.

many of them had no English equivalents—and the glistening scales, shells, membranes, carapaces . . . He was especially interested in a plate of greenish-black crustaceans. By appearance, they had probably come out of the sea but seconds ago, clearly not cooked or processed in any way, but the hawker encouraged him to have a taste. Xin Yu pinched open the mantis shrimp's shell and revealed the kernel of translucent flesh, handing it over to Scott.

Scott flared his nostrils but couldn't detect any odd scent. Carefully, he tore off a strip and placed it in his mouth: a waxy, glutinous texture accompanied by a fresh sweetness awakened his taste buds.

Scott had tried the best sashimi in Akasaka District, Tokyo, where they took the tuna fresh from Tokyo Harbor, and sliced from the jaw. Each fish had yielded only two slices of the precious flesh, decorated with snowflake-like patterns of fat and steeped in the concentrated fragrance of fish oil. The taste had been unforgettable.

But it was nothing like this. Not at all.

His surprised, joyous expression moved Xin Yu, who hurried to explain that this delicacy was made by marinating fresh mantis shrimp in a sauce made of salt, cooking wine, diluted soy sauce, garlic, hot peppers, coriander, and other spices for ten to twelve hours. Afterward, the shrimp was chilled to between minus 15 and 20 degrees Celsius so that the shrimp muscles could contract and give it that crisp mouthfeel.

Scott tore off another, bigger strip to savor the taste. Xin Yu added, with some regret, that due to the polluted seawater and the increased incidence of esophageal cancer, the government had warned the townspeople many times not to consume raw seafood. Scott choked and began to cough violently, red-faced and teary-eyed.

With a smile, Xin Yu gently patted his back. "Don't worry. One bite won't kill you."

Scott figured out that the young man was getting him back, and laughed. He gracefully declined the hawker's offer of a taste of dried pufferfish and went with Xin Yu into a beef restaurant.

"The people of Silicon Isle are such gourmets." Scott glanced back and saw that the spy had taken a seat at the noodle shop across the way. "When you're away at college, you must miss the food here a lot."

"Absolutely. No matter where the natives of Silicon Isle go, they always remember the taste of home. Once, I was the guide for an old overseas Chinese tourist who had left Silicon Isle several decades ago. We went to that snack shop over there and he just inhaled four bowls of dry noodles within minutes. He didn't say anything afterward, but his face was wet with tears." Xin Yu waved his chopsticks through the air, clearly moved by the memory.

"Are you planning on coming back after graduation?"

". . . I don't know." The energy that had animated Xin Yu seemed to vanish in an instant. "My parents want me to find some way to emigrate overseas. They tell me that the environment out there is better, and I'd have more of a future . . . you understand. Silicon Isle is a restricted-bitrate zone."

"That's what everyone says." Scott smiled and casually looked back, and his gaze met the spy's before he moved his eyes away quickly. "Maybe I can help you with a recommendation letter or something. You know that TerraGreen Recycling is a big multinational."

"I know! One of the Global 500! I'd be really grateful, Mr. Brandle."

"Don't mention it. Oh, I wondered if you could do me a favor."

"Just say the word."

"Can you go to this address and get me some takeout? An order of sea urchin would be great." Scott showed him the address on his phone. "Then we'll meet up at the end of the lane, near the archway."

"No problem. But—" Xin Yu paused thoughtfully and went on. "I heard that heavy metals tend to concentrate in sea urchin. Don't eat too much."

As a young man, Luo Jincheng had been obsessed with owning things. Whatever he fancied—toys, cars, money, land, women, or power—he would pay any price and do anything to acquire. He attributed this desire to the deprivations of his childhood, and as he grew older, he dressed it up as the motivating source of his own success.

Gradually, however, he had come to discover that mere possession wasn't enough to maximize the value of capital. Making capital flow and circulate was the key to true prosperity in the information age.

Luo Jincheng built up an effective intelligence network to gather the latest information on major ports, various channel buyers, and the price fluctuations in international raw-materials markets, which gave him the bargaining power to stay atop the e-waste trade and to buy low and sell high. He still remembered the old days, when trading had been done without the aid of complete information. The supplier typically opened the shipping container and only allowed the buyer a glance to estimate a price, and the crafty ones would handpick the most valuable pieces of e-waste and leave them at the top, disguising the cheap trash of little value underneath.

It was like gambling at one of the street peddlers who sold geodes. Before cracking open the rock, no one knew whether the inside was filled with delicate, crystalline jade or mere crude stone. A single choice could make a man a millionaire overnight or push him into bankruptcy. The e-waste business wasn't quite as risky, but a major player like Luo Jincheng would still pray to the Buddha and make offerings before each big trade, hoping that the shipping containers would bring him fortune.

Once he mastered the flow of information, he could determine the value of a shipping container of e-waste based on publicly available information such as the ship's course and ports, the cargo manifest, the container number, the loading time, the consignment details at departure, and so forth. Then he could, based on the anticipated processing time, predict the market price at the time when he'd be ready to sell and thus come to the negotiating table well armed. This guiding principle guaranteed that the Luo clan squeezed better than average profits out of every deal. As a result, his reputation grew and the name of Boss Luo spread far and wide.

This was also why such a complex mixture of feelings had assaulted him when Li Wen had threatened the three clans with his notebook slammed onto the table. The young man's patterns of thinking and charisma reminded him of a younger version of himself. If Li Wen weren't a waste man, Luo would have considered having him as a partner, and who knew what they could have achieved together. Alas, none of these hypotheticals would ever come to pass due to a tiny, but unalterable, fact.

Luo Jincheng wondered: *How can a man with such gifts and talents spend his time among the waste people and toil away in lowly trades that have no hope of real success?*

He soon forgot the question, which was perhaps unanswerable. However, he did take note of the fact that Li Wen was among the first new migratory workers to join the waste people after Silicon Isle was punished by the government and designated a restricted-bitrate zone. Compared to previous waves of workers, the new arrivals were getting slightly better wages because many of the migratory workers had left after the imposition of restricted bitrate, leading to a temporary spike in demand.

Indeed, not only were migratory workers leaving in droves, even some families who had been in Silicon Isle for generations were emigrating. In this age when the speed of information determined everything, restricted bitrate meant that there was no value, no opportunity, no future. Who would want their children to live in a place with no future, even if it was the home to which they were bound by history and blood?

As for the incident that resulted in Silicon Isle's restricted-bitrate status, the government never presented an official explanation. Many rumors circulated, some of them as thrilling and implausible as the plots of Hollywood films. Due to his special relationship with the government, however, Luo Jincheng was able to gather fragments of knowledge over meals and drinks with officials, which he managed to piece together into an approximation of the truth.

The incident began with a young woman who had been lured to Silicon Isle with false promises—later, the government would declare that she had run away from home of her own free will.

Such episodes were not exactly rare. In the economically developed regions along China's southeastern coast, one could find many such "runaways" who found out the truth of their situation only after they were stuck. They were paid a pittance for their labor while they harbored dreams of someday making enough to return home in respectable circumstances. Living on the margins of the prosperity that did not belong to them, they toiled day after day in the most mechanical, repetitive, and trivial assembly line work.

The young woman wrote home a few times, and her letters indicated that she was working in Silicon Isle, her life was good, and her family should not worry about her. But then, all communications ceased. The family burned with anxiety, but they were poor peasants in southwest China, thousands of kilometers from the coast. They had to resort to contacting the police in Silicon Isle via the internet, asking for their help in searching for the girl. The conclusion, as one might imagine, was a perfunctory "exact location unknown."

The young woman had an elder brother who was at college in one of China's biggest cities. It was said that due to the family's poverty, the parents could only pick one of the pair of siblings to send to college. The brother was smart and got good grades, and the family's hopes for success were all pinned on him, but he planned to give up the opportunity for his sister. In his view, a boy was like a bull who always had the possibility, however remote, of plowing out a field for himself based on talent, effort, and luck; but a girl was like a pearl oyster who had to face the tumultuous ocean with her bare flesh. He wanted to do what he could to protect his baby sister.

Just as he was about to give up on taking the college entrance examination, the sister made a more extreme choice.

She ran away from home, leaving behind only a letter. She was close to her brother and understood the sacrifice he planned to make. She declared that unless he managed high enough marks in the examination to get into his dream school, he would never see her again. This letter later on became a powerful piece of proof in the official explanation that she was merely a common runaway.

The brother knew how stubborn his only sister was, and he had to suppress his anxiety and focus on the exam. He managed to do exceptionally well and was accepted by one of the elite schools. He swore that he would spend the rest of his life to pay his sister back and take care of her. However, just as he was about done with four years of diligent coursework and ready to start the job search to dig for his first bucket of gold, his sister stopped communicating, seemingly vanished.

"Exact location unknown" struck him in the chest like an icepick. He refused to trust anyone and pledged that he would find her with his own methods. He knew the art of crafting code, of shaping symbols to carry out his will without forbearance.

Almost unnoticed, a certain computer virus with directed propagation began to spread among IP addresses in Silicon Isle, infecting more and more machines and taking over web terminals frequented by the waste people. It showed no symptoms other than filtering all the information passing through the infected terminals with a special algorithm that looked for certain words and phrases and semantic patterns. When matches were found, it tossed off a packet to a secret address. The target address was dynamically disguised in clever ways, and if one were to try to trace the packet to find the ultimate destination, the task would be as difficult as trying to ascertain the ballistic trails of bullets fired from a roller coaster based on the timing of the shots alone.

With great patience, the brother finally obtained an encrypted video being passed around the underground discussion forums of Silicon Isle.

It was a recording from a live feed. Against the dim background, two men's faces were blurred out, leaving behind only their semi-naked bodies and the tools they held in their hands. A third man's voice spoke from offscreen. All their voices had been processed to obscure identifying characteristics, though it was obvious that they spoke in the Silicon Isle topolect. The video was recorded through a pair of augmented-reality glasses, and showed the typical characteristics of first-person-POV recordings: shaky, unfocused, but with a strong sense of *I-am-there*.

A body was curled up against the foot of a wall like a bundle of rags, emitting from time to time inhuman moans. Strangely, an augmented-reality helmet set to sleep mode was still on her head, the yellow light dimming and brightening slowly, like breathing.

The two men in view conversed, snickering and tittering now and then. With the help of translation software, the brother found out that they had been sent by their boss to deal with this piece of "trash." The woman, a migrant with no local attachments, had become addicted to digital mushrooms and lost the ability to work. As such, she would have appeared to government inspectors as an "unsanitary spot" marring the boss's record. The two men also revealed that her vestibular system had been damaged irreversibly, and she wouldn't have survived much longer. They were putting her out of her misery.

The cameraman—the wearer of the augmented-reality glasses— ducked down and struck the floor with some hard object, producing a series of crisp knocks. He also tapped his tongue against the roof of his mouth, making *tsk* noises the way one would to attract the attention of a cat. The "trash" suddenly let out a ragged breath, sat up, crawled rapidly toward the camera, grabbed the object out of the hand of the cameraman, and stuck it into a slot in her helmet. The light turned from yellow to green, flashing rapidly as the data finished transferring. The woman kept her face lowered as reptilian screeches emerged from her throat, as though a monstrous thirst for a particular kind of neural stimulation had devoured all her human dignity.

You can make her do anything if you promise her this, said the cameraman, who had been silent until then.

The eyepieces of the woman's helmet lit up, glowing eerily in the dark. She began to sing, the tune bringing to mind the style of some regional folk opera. Her high-pitched voice swerved around sharply, like a cold snake writhing in the night, and even her limbs began to twist and shake mechanically as she danced to her singing.

What a show! We get a night at the opera! The two men guffawed and danced, mocking her with their exaggerated imitation.

Abruptly, the woman's voice became rough and piercing. As though she had gone mad, she rushed at one of the men, bringing him down and locking her arms about his thighs. The other two were so stunned that for a moment they did nothing as their companion screamed for help. In the end, the cameraman picked up a shovel and struck the woman a hard blow on her head. She fell.

I guess she didn't enjoy my mushroom too much.

The man approached the motionless body, leaned down, pried off her helmet, and turned her face to the camera.

How fervently the brother hoped that the video would cut off at that point so that the victim's face would never be revealed, so that he could maintain a shred of false hope. But he forced himself to continue to watch, to endure the long sequence of camera shake, the lighting so dim that he felt dizzy. The view abruptly shifted to a close-up of the woman's face: her eyes half open, pupils unevenly dilated, weakly gasping for air. A dark liquid seeped from her temples down her face like two streams of concentrated tears.

It was his sister.

Hand me a garbage bag, said the cameraman. *Time to take her out.*

He shut off the monitor and, in the dark, lit a cigarette with trembling hands. He took two quick drags and tossed the cigarette, grinding it into the ground with his foot. He was silent for the rest of the night, and only as dawn arrived did he figure out that his extraordinary rage arose not only from the violence he had witnessed, but also from the way the violence had been displayed. The attacker had used technology to present the scene in first-person POV so that anyone watching the video became a source of violence along with him and was forced to experience the perpetrator's pleasure in the attack. The brother had to suppress the powerful, biological disgust he felt for himself, as though he had murdered his sister.

Of course, much of this story occurred only in the imagination of the storytellers. In reality, the brother had passed the video on to the police, hoping that they could follow its clues and find his sister, even just her corpse. But the police chose another path: they erased all traces of the video from the Web and sealed off all channels of information. Like ostriches sticking their heads into the sand, they pretended that nothing had happened.

This was how they preferred to deal with any crisis.

The brother sank into utter despair, his rage stretched thin and torn into shapeless fragments of data by the thousands of kilometers in distance. He finally understood that the source of the tragedy was an invisible, intangible wall, a barrier that divided one people with the same blood and ancestors into two moieties, marking some as high and some as base, endowing some with privilege and others with suffering.

He would strike back.

The virus, now with its parameters adjusted, swept across the data terminals of Silicon Isle. Like a swarm of hungry locusts, it chewed up every bit of data it touched, filtering for nuggets of information. The results, after layers of routing, were directed at the major news outlets. And some of the information involved the secret documents describing the Silicon Isle government's bidding process for major engineering projects. Like lit matches dropped one by one into a weak fire, slowly and with great effort, the flames cooked the frogs in the pot.

In the wake of the media frenzy over the exposed government scandals, the case of the missing girl lost its attraction. The audience's interest waned and shifted; new scandals and new celebrities showed up one after another, consuming attention that was as sparse and precious as virtue.

However, upper levels in the machinery of officialdom were enraged by the leaks coming out of Silicon Isle—not because of the corruption and fraud, but because the media exposure had discredited the image of the local government, and that impacted the chances of promotion for the officials supposedly supervising them.

The supervisory officials finally decided that Silicon Isle had to pay a price for its lax data security. From the high-bitrate designation of a coastal, developed region, Silicon Isle was stripped of two levels of access and trapped in the kind of low bitrate usually found only in backward regions in China's interior. There would be no more augmented reality, no more enterprise-level cloud services, and certainly no more benefits from the special government policies designed only for Special Data Zones.

In a corner of the digital map of the world, the light of Silicon Isle went out.

Many who had lost much of their wealth as a result of this rezoning offered a bounty for the identity of the author of the virus, swearing that they could cut off his hands and blind his eyes or even remove his head and attach it to a life-support machine so that he could spend the rest of his life in a living hell, but they never succeeded. The brother of the vanished girl was like the serpent Ouroboros, whose head swallowed the tail until it had consumed itself and disappeared from the physical/digital world without leaving behind any trace.

Every time Luo Jincheng thought about the conclusion of the story, he tried to imagine what that talented young man, if he were still alive, would be doing now. Would he still be searching for his sister's killer, sparing no effort? Or would he have already given up on all hope for life and turned to the permanent embrace of death? *Revenge is a dish best served cold.* He shivered, as though that pair of eyes burning with the fire of vengeance were right behind him.

No, it wasn't my fault.

He tried to comfort himself. During those years, all the clans were engaged in similar activities, selling illegal digital mushrooms to the waste people in order to maintain the clans' control over them. If some addicts, lacking in self-control, overdosed and lost the ability to work, then it was necessary to clean up the mess to avoid getting the clans in trouble. To be sure, every clan had its own way of dealing with the issue: deporting the disabled out of Silicon Isle was one way, and making them disappear was another.

Protecting their young was an instinct all animals were born with, even though the beneficiary of his protection at that time was only a wild pup who had followed him for many years. Today, this damnable dog had once again choked on the same bone, and the troubling waves he had set in motion remained surging and whirling beneath the surface, in the lightless depths, brewing for another furious storm.

He decided that this time, he would sacrifice this dog, whose name was Knifeboy.

———

The puny man with the gloomy face watched as Scott and Xin Yu parted from each other. After hesitating for a moment, he decided to follow Scott.

It was two in the morning, and the crowd in the hawker lane grew sparse, but the LED signs of the stalls and restaurants continued to shine and blink, bright as ever. Scott picked up his pace and the lights around him swayed and drifted in his vision, leaving long afterimage trails. A thousand enticing aromas found their way into his nose, the product of organic molecules strange to his body, stimulating his nerves with a trace of alarm.

If only the people of Silicon Isle spent just a fraction of the brainpower they devote to food on environmental protection, Scott thought with some regret. The snoop was now closer, and Scott could hear his hurried footfalls behind. An automatic body film booth flashing with fluorescent colors appeared next to the street, devoid of customers. An idea popped into his head, and he ducked in, closing the door lightly behind him.

The space within the booth was narrow and stuffy. Scott had to bend his neck and stoop down to make his large frame fit within the small volume. The virtual model on the screen gave him a mechanical smile and began to explain the season's latest patterns and how to use the machine. Against the wall was a flexible, silicone disk attached to a segmented, omnidirectional arm, used for applying one-time inductive body films. Scott inserted some coins, selected a garish, heart-shaped pattern, and adjusted the branding temperature to the maximum.

This temperature setting is suitable only for applying films to hard surfaces. The virtual model accompanied the warning with an incessant stream of "uh-oh"s.

He waited, holding his breath.

Three minutes passed. There was no sign of movement beyond the booth door. Just as Scott's patience was about to run out, he saw a curious hand slowly pull the door open. The fish was biting.

Scott grabbed that hand and dragged the man into the booth in one motion, pulling the door closed behind him. As the astonished spy's face was crushed against Scott's powerful chest muscles, he kept mumbling apologies in English and tried to open the door and back out of this tiny, crowded world of two. Scott lifted his knee to the man's waist and pressed him against the wall while his left hand choked the man around the throat, and his right hand grabbed the spy's right hand, which was reaching under his clothes for some weapon.

"Who do you work for?" Scott squeezed his left hand until the man's eyes bulged and the veins on his forehead stood out and his face turned red.

"Sorry! Sorry!" the man repeated like a broken record.

"Talk!" Scott kicked him in the back of the legs, and the man fell to his knees, his head crushed against the display screen by Scott's hand. The vivid fluorescent light danced against his face. Scott pulled over the heated silicone disk until it was but inches away from the man's cheeks, the heart-shaped pattern in the middle making a sizzling noise. Feeling the heat, the man looked terrified as beads of sweat rolled down his face. He no longer repeated his bad English, but instead began to patter in the Silicon Isle topolect.

"Your name!" Even Scott found the heat from the silicone disk nearly unbearable and his shirt was soaked through with sweat.

The man struggled fiercely with every ounce of his strength, and the disk kissed his left cheek, making a noise one normally associated with dropping food into a deep fryer. Scott smelled the familiar aroma of burnt meat, and an unbelievably high-pitched scream came out of the man's mouth, which degenerated into a wailing interrupted by quick gasps, as though he had turned into a hyperventilating chipped dog exposed to the scorching sun.

The disk came off with a crisp, kiss-like pop. The man slid to the ground weakly and curled up at the bottom of the tiny, two-square-meter booth. On his left cheek was a giant, pink-glowing, branded heart.

Scott searched the man and found a knife and an old mobile phone.

For good measure, he gave him a hard kick in the chest. The man moaned once but made no other move. Scott ducked out of the booth and tossed the knife into the bushes, tucked the phone away, adjusted his wet clothes, and headed for the rendezvous spot.

"What in the world happened to you, Mr. Brandle? You're sweating so much." Xin Yu had been waiting for a while. "Here you go: your sea urchin."

Scott accepted the small, chilled box and wiped the sweat from his forehead. "I haven't worked out in a while, so I decided to go for a jog."

"Jogging? In Silicon Isle? With this weather?" Xin Yu looked unconvinced. "I guess this is what they call a cultural divide."

Connecting . . . connection established . . . encryption active.

HIROFUMI OTOGAWA: Clean?

CHANG FENGSHA: Yes.

HIROFUMI OTOGAWA: How's progress?

CHANG FENGSHA: Kaizong's operation went well, and he's recovering. The incident has turned into an unexpected bargaining chip for us.

HIROFUMI OTOGAWA: I'm not sure I like where this is going.

CHANG FENGSHA: Ha! Don't worry. I guarantee the contract will be signed before I die.

HIROFUMI OTOGAWA: If you discover any hidden risks, please communicate them to me immediately.

CHANG FENGSHA: Well, since you mention it . . . there is something.

HIROFUMI OTOGAWA: ?

CHANG FENGSHA: SBT-VBPII32503439. I've researched all the product serial numbers for SBT, including research proto-types, and I've found no trace of this number. It obviously isn't just some "minor accident," as you put it. It wasn't even designed for humans. Right now, it's like a ticking bomb. I don't know when it's going to go off, and I don't know what kind of effect it's going to have on the Silicon Isle project.

HIROFUMI OTOGAWA: . . .

CHANG FENGSHA: I understand that when an economic hit man is carrying out an associated task of convenience assigned by the Arashio Foundation, he has no right to be given all the information. However, I have no duty to undertake the associated risks either. I want this provision written into the contract. If you continue to maintain silence, I'm going to find someone willing to talk.

HIROFUMI OTOGAWA: . . . This is a very long story.

CHANG FENGSHA: Well, it's the start of a long night in Sili-con Isle. I promise you I'll stay awake for the whole thing.

13

The inky color of night hadn't yet been bleached away, and the street-lights remained lit, sketching out the contours of the shoreline. There were puddles of water on the ground, perhaps the remains of a shower during the night, faintly reflecting the indigo sky. On the horizon was a faint golden red line, smoldering, spreading, building up to a fiery dawn that would soon cover the eastern sky like a burning curtain. The trees stood dead still in the shadows, their branches drooping. This was going to be another windless, blistering summer day.

Scott lay in bed in his clothes and watched as his window gradually brightened. He knew that he needed sleep—or at least his heart needed the rest—but he wasn't sleepy at all. Under his threats, his contact back in the PST time zone, "Hirofumi Otogawa," had revealed part of the puzzle for him, but the answers had only led to more questions. His restless mind was like a sandbox game in which he scratched out complicated mazes, wiped them away without a trace, and sketched new replacements without end.

Scott felt that his nervous system was trapped in a feedback loop. He decided to get out and walk about.

As he passed the hotel's luxury display cases, something caught his eye: a limited-edition 2015 Ducati Monster 1000 EVO Diesel.

Unlike other motorcycles of the same model, this Diesel-Ducati collaboration eschewed the traditional ostentatious polished metal exterior for a combination of matte green and carbon black that coated everything from the engine cover to the exhaust pipe, from the wheels to the axles, making the whole resemble a giant beetle about to take flight.

Scott felt a part of his brain light up. He had been repressed for too long in this restricted-bitrate zone; the turtle-like network speed and the bogged-down progress of the project made it hard for him to breathe. He suddenly understood what he needed: speed. The careless sensation of hurtling along like a lightning bolt, even if it meant placing a man's fragile flesh and bones on the edge of a knife. A powerful desire, almost suffocating in its urgency, drove him, and he yearned to press his skin and flesh against this cold metal monster, as it trembled, growled, and bolted away, never to stop.

Ten minutes later, once again invoking the all-powerful name of Director Lin Yiyu, he managed to obtain the key, goggles, helmet, and a free gas card.

Gingerly, the young man in charge of the rental emphasized various precautions. Scott brushed him away. *When I rode across America on my bike, you were still but a sperm in your daddy's balls.*

The air-cooled L-Twin-cylinder engine rumbled, delivering a steady stream of 100 horsepower; the maximum engine displacement of 1078 cc surged out of the twin carbon-black exhaust pipes stacked on one side like the snorting of an angry bull. Scott leaned forward and straddled the bike, savoring the delightful sensation brought about by its precisely engineered ergonomic design. He adjusted the goggles and helmet, and lightly twisted the throttle, and flew off along the deserted street on the back of this giant beetle.

It was still early, before the arrival of the trucks carrying e-waste; the inhabitants of Silicon Isle were still in slumber, with an occasional drunk lying by the side of the road, a puddle of pink vomit before him still warm from his body. Street-cleaning trucks playing retro eight-bit electronic music slowly swept the road while fishing boats heading out to sea tooted their whistles, like ancient beasts of legend moaning in the fog. Inch by inch, light chased away the darkness, and the sun finally rose.

Like a gust of wind, Scott swept past all of this. The scenery stretched and distorted in his vision, blurring like the wild strokes of Postimpressionists. He had to keep himself from howling, and all sound was tossed behind with the streaming air, fading rapidly. He shifted and sensed the higher torque from a lower gear, as though the mechanical beast between his legs had melded with his body so that no matter what the road conditions, the machine would sensitively and appropriately translate his intent into motion.

Fusing Man with machine. The idea surfaced in Scott's mind, unbidden. Just like the shocking tale he had heard a few hours ago.

The mysterious prosthesis with the serial number SBT-VBPII32503439 was intended to replace the back of the skull between the coronal suture and the lambdoid suture, including parts of the parietal and occipital bones. It wasn't designed for the human skull, however. The prominent ridge in the middle was meant to replicate the sagittal crest present in the skulls of gorillas, chimpanzees, and orangutans.

After Project Waste Tide was shut down, the military transferred more than three hundred related patents to newly founded commercial companies in various fields, among them the core technologies of SBT and TerraGreen Recycling.

But Project Waste Tide never truly stopped. Hidden and decentralized, it had infiltrated all areas of human technology, changing the trajectory of the world's progress. After several rounds of financing, spin-offs, and mergers and acquisitions, the military background of the Arashio Foundation that held stock in the various companies had become obscured, but multiple top-secret research projects continued to be run out of the public eye.

One of these projects was the experimental treatment advocated by Dr. Suzuki in her later years for using gene-modified viruses to repair the muscarinic receptors damaged by QNB, but the research goals had changed completely. The virus known as the "Suzuki variant," further modified to target other neural structures, evolved into multiple new varieties with amazing commercial value.

One of them was perhaps the ultimate weapon against brain aging.

There are about 100 billion neurons in the human brain, each of which connects to up to a thousand other neurons through synapses. Through neurotransmitters, the neurons communicate with each other and perform functions such as information sharing, coordinated action, memory formation, and so on. Synaptic damage and aging lead to neurological disorders, memory loss, autism, Alzheimer's, and other neurodegenerative diseases. Such damage is often irreversible, like time's arrow.

However, one variety of the new virus could, working in conjunction with synaptic connection strengthening HDAC inhibitors, form new connections from aged axons. This was a key step in humankind's quest for eternal life, though the premise was that we must be willing to give up our fragile, aging-prone mammalian shells.

A nondescript, silver, domestically manufactured Volvo appeared in the rearview mirror. It flashed its headlamps, indicating that Scott should pull over. He frowned, tired of this endless game of cat and mouse. The throttle of the Ducati roared, and the bike leapt forward and agilely turned onto a side lane.

Whether out of anger or the thrill of the chase, Scott's heartbeat became irregular. He stopped gunning the engine and reduced his speed, waiting for the pacemaker to do its job.

Another variety of the new virus had revolutionized the battery industry.

Scientists found the genetic codons that enabled animal cells to aggregate metal atoms and introduced trace amounts of the single-strand DNA into the virus, where it caused specific molecules to form on the surface of the virus, capable of selectively adhering to metal atoms and particles. Complexes formed in this manner via adhesion were effective battery anodes and ideal conductors.

The virus battery technology was transformational at every level: designers could precisely adjust the DNA injected into the virus to produce electrodes made of different metals; batteries could be made by mixing the corresponding components at room temperature, thus avoiding the risks associated with the high temperatures required for traditional battery manufacturing; and, most key of all, the electrodes made in this manner could span the scale from nanometers to ten centimeters, which meant that batteries no longer had to be bulky, cumbersome devices, but could be embedded into anything one might imagine.

Like the thumbnail-sized virus-enhanced battery inside Scott's chest, which had saved his life multiple times.

The motorcycle roared onto a road next to the beach. The slightly salty sea breeze struck Scott's face, and he greedily gulped down the rare fresh air. Over the ocean, long rows of unbroken swells glowed golden, gilded by the surging sun. Large, irregularly shaped clouds, dragging long trails behind them like tens of thousands of bronze horses leaping out of the sea, joyfully galloped toward the empyrean with ringing hoofbeats against reef islands peeking out of the foam and spray.

A new day had begun in the world.

Chen Kaizong watched himself in the mirror. He closed his left eye, opened it, then closed his right eye. Something didn't feel right.

The operation was a success. His damaged right eye had been completely removed and replaced with SBT's latest electronic model, the Cyclops VII. The color of the iris had been carefully adjusted so that there was almost no discernible difference between the left and right eyes—other than the fact that the new eye appeared brighter because it was so perfect and limpid that it lacked the spots and faint blood vessels left by the passage of time.

I've turned into a cyborg after all. Kaizong became emotional as he imagined facing his parents and having to explain this. Maybe saying nothing was the better choice. He thought of the article of faith that his mother often recited, especially when, as they watched the news, the first-person-POV footage made her dizzy.

Man is meant to look at the world through his own eyes. Any attempt to perceive the world through a perspective that transcends the self is a transgression against God.

The artificial retina worked very well. While he had been asleep, the doctors had "installed" the user manual for the prosthetic eye into his visual cortex via fMRI. Afterward, the "sleep spindles" in his EEG showed that the information had already been transferred from the hippocampus to the cortex for permanent storage, much as one might save the data from a USB stick onto the hard drive. The technique for using the right eye and interpreting its data became part of Chen Kaizong's permanent skill repertoire, much as riding a bicycle, swimming, or speaking English.

For All Tomorrow's Parties. 全为明日派对。

Each time Kaizong paid conscious attention to the workings of his right eye, the advertising slogan drifted through his mind in both English and Chinese. Maybe it was a reminder installed as part of the user manual, like a symbol of confidence. The manufacturer was making a pledge to the customer: *Don't worry. SBT provides a three-year warranty, whether you obtained one of our eyes, hearts, muscles, or some other prosthesis.*

But in the world he had come from, the replacement cycle for prosthetic body parts was far shorter. Indeed, the media coined the semiserious term "body fast-moving consumer goods" (FMCG) to describe them. SBT's technology had turned the trade in prostheses into a business like mobile apps, sneakers, fashion, and online games: anyone could find, in a market full of choices, something that met their needs, was affordable, and provided good after-purchase services. Moreover, the black market was full of jailbreaking tools that could add unauthorized fun to prostheses.

At parties, people no longer showed off their new gadgets, jewelry, or hairstyles, but prosthetic cochleas that improved the sense of balance, artificial muscles with augmented contraction characteristics, prosthetic limbs that obeyed mental directions, or updated firmware that enhanced sensory organs.

SBT developed a revolutionary substance for mediating between the biological and the electronic worlds. Extracted from the gladii of squids, this modified chitosan complex could convert the biological ion flow that carried brain signals into electric currents that could be deciphered by machines, thereby seamlessly forming a feedback loop between the nervous system and the prosthesis. The invention had expanded the definition of the boundary of the body beyond imagination.

Chen Kaizong once watched his roommate Ted swap limbs with other people at a weekend party so that they could experience the wild bash through each other's senses. Kaizong had been stunned like some Texas farm boy setting foot in Times Square for the first time, not sure even where to look. For him, drinking was drinking, doing drugs was doing drugs, and casual sex was casual sex: he had never imagined that there could be big differences between individuals' sensitivity thresholds and sensory receptors.

Ted, barely able to stand straight, held on to his new girlfriend and explained that it was like holding a red-hot lead ball against your forehead and sticking a creamy, cold, gelatinous tentacle through every orifice in your head and flicking it back and forth. *Yeah, the difference is that huge.*

Kaizong shook his head, unable to comprehend.

He became an outsider. Standing apart from fashion, he hid among the dusty library stacks and conversed across time with philosophers and wise men who had been dead for hundreds or thousands of years until he finished his obscure thesis—read by him and his advisor and no one else. This was the only way for him to feel safe, to shield himself from the crazy world around him. He was terrified that he might start to dance to the industrial breakbeat and join in this bacchanalia dedicated to the senses until he was lost in the depths of the flesh.

One night, Ted knocked on his door. A strange expression on his face, he asked, *Caesar, I need your help.*

Kaizong closed the book he was reading and listened to his roommate recount the story in a hoarse voice.

Ted's girlfriend Rebecca had been in the middle of a vacation in Ecuador when an accidental fire killed her as well as the friends who were traveling with her. Little of their bodies remained except a pile of fire-resistant prostheses. Ted and Rebecca had gotten together after a summer party, and one of the ways they liked to please each other was to frequently update their prostheses to maintain a sense of freshness. That was also the source of the problem.

Due to the severity of the fire, DNA identification was ineffective; the prostheses were so damaged that no data could be recovered. The coroner, faced with a pile of intricate polymer composites, had no choice but to pack everything into one box and ship it back to the United States. Rebecca's grief-stricken parents, like other American parents of children that age, were limited in the knowledge of their daughter's life to the extent of a weekly phone call and had no way to know what she had done to her body. They hoped that Ted could help them identify the parts that belonged to their daughter so that they could bury her. May God help guide her lost soul.

Unfortunately, as Ted faced four pairs of eyes, five half-melted silicone breasts, one right hand and two left legs, his mind was a blank. Rebecca went through prostheses so quickly that he could not remember the small differences between various editions.

However, Ted finally recalled a conversation between Kaizong and Rebecca the last time they all saw each other.

Your right eye is very special, Kaizong had said to her. *The Chinese have an expression for it:* míng móu shàn lài.

What does it mean? Rebecca asked, a smile lifting the corners of her mouth.

It means that your eye is so limpid that it seems able to speak. Kaizong blushed.

Listen to you! Ted punched Kaizong playfully in the arm. *Who knew you could be so smooth?* Ted turned and gazed at Rebecca lovingly. *How come this eye is so quiet toward me?*

It's new. It'll warm up to you soon enough. Rebecca lifted her face for a kiss.

Ted now gazed at Kaizong with sunken eyes. He was scruffy, unkempt, disheveled. Holding on to Kaizong's arms, he begged, *Please. Please help me find the eye that could speak.*

But . . . Awkwardly, Kaizong tried to explain. *That was when Rebecca was still alive . . .*

You're Chinese! You told me the Chinese don't believe in God anyway. What difference does it make whether she's alive or dead? Ted shouted.

And so Kaizong walked into a morgue for the first time. The stainless-steel drawer was open, revealing plastic bags filled with oddly shaped prosthetic organs and limbs. The attendant took out one of the bags: like fresh transgenic lemons found at supermarkets, the contents were an unnatural, frosted white. Eight prosthetic eyes that had belonged to the dead.

Suppressing nausea, Kaizong carefully examined each one. The layer of clear polymer film around each eye had half melted, loosely enclosing the delicate mechanisms within like a ball of multiflavored ice cream someone had taken a bite from. They had once all been embedded into beautiful faces, and one of them had even given Kaizong an enchanting smile.

But now they all looked equally ugly, devoid of life.

Kaizong turned around and was about to admit defeat, but the despair in Ted's eyes stopped him. He hesitated for a moment and picked out two eyes at random and nodded.

The two electronic prosthetic eyes were placed inside an elaborately carved cremation urn. The priest read from the Gospel while Rebecca's loved ones sobbed and crossed themselves. The electronic hymns began to play, and sunlight, refracted through the stained-glass windows, fell against the picture of Rebecca's perfect face, the product of many operations.

Kaizong finally accepted the fact that for the fashionable new generation living in the developed West, prostheses were no longer merely aids for the handicapped or even decorations or components of the body, to be exchanged and upgraded at will; rather, prostheses had already become a part of the definition of human life: they were the repositories for our joys, sorrows, terrors, and passions, our class, our social status, our memories.

Your prostheses are *you.*

Luo Jincheng was in need of a slow archer.

The waste people were planning something; he could feel it but knew nothing about the details. They demanded that Luo Jincheng produce the men responsible for the attempted murder of Mimi; otherwise, they'd refuse to return to work. Luo understood that the demand was but a cover for something far more painful.

In the Web of the unrestricted-bitrate world, even an ordinary person had access to various tools to track down fleeting targets. Take the analogy of a hunt: a hunter armed with bow and arrows looking for prey in the forest could choose to upgrade his weapon to a high-precision automatic rifle augmented with a night-vision scope, infrared detectors, or a sonar positioning system; he could also choose to ride in a bipedal exoskeleton armor instead of being on foot to increase mobility; he could also use a shotgun and lure the target into moving, thereby exposing itself for the killing shot.

But Silicon Isle was a restricted-bitrate zone. That meant everything was slowed down. Any data stream that exceeded the threshold rate would set off alarms and draw the attention of the public security agency. The hunter might think himself a praying mantis after a cicada, but a far more powerful hunter, a siskin, was watching him. Here, only bows and arrows were safe to use as weapons. However, this didn't even touch upon the real difficulties. Imagine if the speed of light were reduced a hundred million times: by the time the image of the prey three meters away struck your retina, activating the nerve impulses that would result in vision, the information was already a full second out of date. Even if your prey were subject to the same laws and had to move slowly, the effectiveness of any positioning system you might call upon would be diminished geometrically. Hunting in such a world was not much better than a blind man looking for a needle that had fallen into the sea.

The professional slow archer came into existence in response to the difficulty of tracking data in a restricted-bitrate zone. Like most bounty hunters, they handled jobs that were risky, of dubious legality, and could not be dealt with through official channels. This was the chief competitive advantage of the slow archer.

The slow archers described the secret of their success as "spreading the net by slow arrows." Conceptually, this was analogous to shooting tens of thousands of arrows simultaneously in every direction, but the arrows were connected to each other by invisible links of information. Through the gaps between the trees of this restricted-bitrate forest, the arrows passed slowly, so slowly that they were almost standing still, until they wove an airtight web with their dense trails. All the hunter had to do then was to wait until the prey ran into the web. One touch was enough: all the linked arrows nearby would concentrate on the spot and slowly, but forcefully, tear the prey apart and nail it to the tree.

Metaphors provided visual clarity: shadows flashing through the woods like the wavering lines produced by high-speed schlieren photography; dust and falling leaves disturbed by the flight of the arrows, twirling, tumbling, twinkling in the sunlight; the mixture of the somber scent of humus in the soil and the fragrance of flowers, fruits, and green leaves, stimulating the most sensitive olfactory receptors; even the expectation of the warm liquid spewing from wounds in the prey and its salty, rusty tang.

None of this, of course, existed in the digital world. In their place were highly abstract algorithms and programs that turned the complicated, messy real world into a set of mathematical models and topological spaces. Like a real spiderweb, the web would be deformed by any insect that got caught in it, and the rate at which such deformation progressed exceeded the rate at which information might be transmitted under the restricted-bitrate regulations. In this world, the shortest path between two points was no longer a straight line. Although the technique seemed to defy human intuition and logic, it had proven to be effective.

Just like the upgraded version of the computer virus that had resulted in the bitrate lockdown that ruined Silicon Isle.

Luo Jincheng walked into a hardware store with the name Zhenchang. Inside, it was as dark as the inside of a coal mine. After his eyes had adjusted to the dimness, he was stunned by the rows of preindustrial implements hanging on the walls. The inefficient tools of another age glinted with a metallic light, the culmination of hundreds or even thousands of hours of manual labor and technique, exuding a primitive but sturdy beauty. Each tool was handmade and thus endowed with a unique shape, including blemishes, as though imbued with fragments of the maker's soul. This was a quality that the perfect molds of modern mass production could not match.

Luo took down a strangely shaped short machete. A tiger-face insignia was engraved on the hilt, near the throat of the scabbard. The blade itself reflected a matte light, rough and cold.

"A fine weapon," exclaimed Luo. "Except it's a bit too fast."

"Too fast?" The young store attendant wasn't sure he had heard correctly. "Do you mean it's too sharp? Are you interested in decorative blades without a cutting edge, perhaps?"

"I want something *slower*."

The young man looked thoughtful for a moment. "How slow exactly?"

"As slow as the water in Dual Tides Reflecting the Moon."

"Follow me." The young man stepped aside to reveal an even darker passageway, indicating that Luo should enter.

Luo Jincheng felt that at first he was ascending, and then descending. Several times, he was worried that his head was going to bump into a wall, but the passage was far more spacious than he imagined, though the humid, hot air was difficult to bear. After walking for a while, they saw light in the distance, filled with watery mist. It was a door, and the powerful chill of air-conditioning seeped through the cracks.

"Elder Brother Tiger, someone's looking for you." The young man brought Luo Jincheng through the door and then respectfully backed out.

This might have been the dirtiest and messiest room Luo Jincheng had ever seen in his life, barely better than the waste people's scrap-storage sheds, filled with buzzing flies. Countless coils of wire lay on the floor like intestines, and the wires climbed onto various pieces of machinery so that there was almost no room to stand. A set of high-powered air conditioners droned, spewing white mist and cooling the computers on floor-to-ceiling racks, where green lights flickered and the ceaseless humming of all the machines called to mind a busy beehive.

"Hard Tiger," a slow archer of some renown, hunched over a tiny desk in the corner, draped in a black hoodie. The multiple hi-def displays in front of him were divided into numerous subscreens, some showing scrolling numbers, some flashing through webpages, some compiling code, and a few exhibiting nude bodies trembling and moaning.

The man was absorbed by a bowl of hot *kway teow* rice noodles with meatballs, slurping and chewing loudly. Luo Jincheng stood behind him, waiting patiently.

Finally, Hard Tiger lifted his head and let out a satisfied burp. "To what do I owe the pleasure of Boss Luo's company?"

In the corner of one of the screens, Luo Jincheng saw the live feed from the closed-circuit cameras in the hardware store, as well as the data retrieved by the computer based on recognizing his face.

"Brother Hard Tiger's eyes are indeed as keen as the legends about them. Since you're no doubt well informed concerning recent events, I won't waste your time. I'd like you to keep an eye on the digital activities of a few individuals for me."

"A few? Surely Boss Luo is being modest! I think the waste people under your control number at least in the four digits." Hard Tiger turned around, revealing a sleep-deprived, scruffy face under the hood. "Even the strikers alone are in the hundreds."

"These are details—"

"The price depends on details."

"Are you worried that I won't be good for it?"

"I'm worried that no one would dare to collect a debt from you."

"Fine, I'll pay half up front." Luo Jincheng's eyes roamed unpleasantly as he estimated the damage. "The other half will be paid when you finish."

"You'll pay seventy percent up front. Moreover, Boss Luo"—Hard Tiger smiled confidently; in the Silicon Isle topolect, his nickname, Ngên Houn[18], meant "absolutely, certainly"—"I need you to agree to something."

"I'm listening."

"I'd like you to move the shopping lane you're planning one street over to the east. I don't want to move, and my neighbors don't want to relocate to the new district either, where we'd be next to the waste people. This street is an insignificant piece of your portfolio; you'd hardly miss it, but as long as Silicon Isle is stuck in a restricted-bitrate zone, you'll need a slow archer."

Luo Jincheng quirked an eyebrow and felt a stab of pain in the palm of his hand—he had, without realizing it, been holding on to the machete with the tiger insignia. He unsheathed the machete, and the blade reflected Hard Tiger's shocked, twisted expression. In a single, swift motion, he swung the weapon at Hard Tiger, and just as the edge was about to come into contact with flesh, his wrist twisted and the machete stabbed into the desk forcefully, spilling wood splinters everywhere.

"Deal," Luo Jincheng answered with an easy smile, as though he had just convinced himself.

Taking advantage of the darkening twilight, Li Wen returned to the village with dozens of waste people who had been released for "having committed only minor offenses." So many had been involved in the mass incident that the limited Silicon Isle police force was overwhelmed, and prolonged detention and formal charges for everyone were out of the question. Besides, they really hadn't done that much; so, after their roles

[18] With full tone marks: *Ngên⁷ Houn²*.

were recorded in their permanent digital records, they were let go with only a verbal warning. The unlucky soul who had wounded Chen Kaizong, on the other hand, had been beaten to within an inch of his life and was in prison, awaiting trial.

"You really know how to pick your target," the officer entering records into the computer had joked with them. "Of all the people there, you managed to injure the only American and thus escalated a civil dispute into an international incident."

"How could a kidnapping resulting in such severe injuries be dismissed as a 'civil dispute'?" asked Li Wen. "Mimi is barely an adult!"

"We're investigating." The officer shifted to bureaucratese. "We will endeavor to make a full and complete report."

"We don't want a report! We want justice!"

"If you keep this up, I'm happy to invite you to wait for justice in these cells."

Li Wen clenched his teeth and said no more. He sorted out his thoughts: as soon as he was free, he would order his most trusted lieutenants to carry out his plan. The scene of Mimi's collapse at the Luo mansion replayed in his mind constantly, interrupting his brooding like a cold claw climbing down from his spinal column, grabbing hold of his innards and shaking them about. He knew that it was a manifestation of his guilt.

Finally, he was back at his own shack: dim, dirty, smelly, messy, but it put him at peace. Home, sweet home.

"Listen, your job is to modify the decision logic programming for all the chipped dogs. As soon as anyone from the Luo clan approaches, make them bark." The film on the chest of the young man Li Wen was addressing lit up with the purple character for "war," and he jogged away from the shack to carry out his instructions.

"You, over there, take a few people and bring back the mecha from Tide Gazing Beach."

"You, head over to the territories of the Chen and Lin clans and assess the situation; tell our brothers there to be ready for new orders."

Like a general who has finished issuing orders, Li Wen sighed. Almost immediately, however, something he had been most worried about pulled his nerves taut again.

"Where's Mimi? Take me to her immediately."

Since the hospital's security personnel could no longer be trusted, the unconscious Mimi had been brought to the home of a back-alley doctor who had dedicated himself to helping the waste people. Although the conditions were primitive, the place did have all the necessary medical equipment. Dr. Jin—that's what everyone called him—attached the diagnostic terminals to Mimi's body and frowned at the chaotic numbers and figures dancing across the monitors. Her blood sugar level was dropping precipitously and was now lower than the critical threshold necessary to provide sufficient energy for regular cardiopulmonary functions.

"She's . . . hungry," Dr. Jin proclaimed his diagnosis.

This was only the first step, of course. Further analysis showed that 83 percent of Mimi's energy was being consumed by her brain activities. Such brain metabolic levels were unheard of in any mammal, or any creature on Earth with a brain. Similarly, no regular food-intake methods could sustain such astonishing levels of energy consumption.

However, every back-alley doctor had his own secret cures.

Dr. Jin attached an auto-injector to the inside of Mimi's elbow; then, he retrieved six bright red sealed vials from a hidden storage area in the semibasement.

"These are all I have left: high-energy fructose mixtures reserved for military use. Each dose is capable of maintaining a supply of ATP for twelve hours. The Special Forces rely on this to remain alert for hours without the need to eat or sleep. However, once these vials are used up, you'll have to find your own solutions."

Thus, by the time Li Wen saw Mimi, she no longer looked exhausted; in fact, she looked overenergized. The corners of Mimi's mouth were slightly lifted and her eyes wide open, gazing at Li Wen curiously as though she had no memory of anything that had passed. After searching in her brain for a while, she calmly pronounced Li Wen's full name—instead of the familiar "Brother Wen."

"Mimi? Is it really you?" Li Wen blurted out, and immediately regretted the rash question.

"Who else?" Mimi rewarded him with her familiar smile.

Li Wen tried to get rid of the strange suspicion floating at the back of his mind. *Of course. Who else could she be?* A powerful joy replaced the anxiety that had been plaguing him, and relief flooded through his body. He turned on the recording feature of his augmented-reality glasses, and a green light came on.

"Say hi! We should spread this good news to our people."

Mimi appeared in his vision, but for some reason, her image began to blur, flicker, as though some invisible outside light source were illuminating her from infinitely far away: warm, serene, and resplendent. Although he was looking at her straight on, Li Wen had the impression that Mimi had grown much taller and acquired an awe-inducing aura that made it impossible to stare at her. A barely audible chant seemed to hover over the scene, and he couldn't tell if it was the result of synesthesia caused by what he was seeing or if there really was enhanced audio from some decoded stream. Mimi's smile seemed to possess a kind of magic that made his heart swell and feel moved without knowing why— he even felt the impulse to cry. For a moment, he almost thought he saw someone else: the mysterious face of a Western woman was superimposed over Mimi's. He thought he had seen that face before.

Li Wen tried to rationally analyze the situation, but his efforts were crushed by the whirling, colorful halos emanating from Mimi's figure. All that was left in his heart was a pure sense of worshipful devotion, colored by a trace of fear.

"I'm back," the revived goddess declared to the world.

The revelation spread among the waste people like a nuclear chain reaction.

14

For some reason, Scott could not drive the story from his mind.

Since the FDA strictly regulated clinical trials conducted in the United States, many high-risk drug trials had been moved to developing countries: Iaşi, Romania; New Delhi, India; Mégrine, Tunisia; Santiago del Estero, Argentina—in these corruption-ridden, mismanaged regions of the world, hundreds, even thousands, volunteered to be trial subjects for pennies. Most of the money went to the hospitals, the doctors, and the recruiters of the trial subjects, while the pharmaceutical companies obtained the data they needed to secure FDA approval and then made billions with the new drugs.

Many of the subjects were underage and had to lie to be in the trials. Poverty meant that they couldn't afford expensive modern medical care, and their bodies were thus highly sensitive to the active ingredients of trial drugs—like pristine laboratory mice. For their troubles, they received a few wrinkled dollar bills, a free breakfast, unknown side effects, the risk of a lengthy incubation period, and a high probability of dying from complications.

This was the price of progress: winners take all.

However, SBT wouldn't take this particular path for outsourcing. Their project, having to do with the brain-machine interface, required too much secrecy and involved too many risks. SBT managed to find another safe haven: chimpanzees, who share 99.4 percent of their genes with humans and whose intelligence levels are comparable to children five to seven years old.

The SBT engineers surgically replaced parts of the skulls of the test subjects with prostheses to make it easy to stimulate the brain with various electric signals and observe the reactions and changes in neuronal clusters in specific regions of the brain. This was a semi-invasive procedure that avoided the damage that could be caused by probes and guaranteed the precision and strength of the stimuli.

The engineers devised a set of reward/punishment mechanisms akin to Skinner boxes. Based on accumulated experimental data, they built a simple mapping model for motor nerves so that the chimpanzees could, after sufficient training, mentally direct robot arms to grasp food out of the reach of their physical limbs. Experimenters could also input specific signals to stimulate the fear or reward regions in the chimpanzee brain to direct the animals' movements and accomplish simple tasks.

Some genius on the team installed virus batteries in the prosthetic skull, and the result was a warm-blooded, furry, remote-controlled female chimpanzee. The engineers voted to name her "Eva" in memory of a female robot from an old animated film.

Eva demonstrated unusual learning abilities. She could even solve a game of the Tower of Hanoi on her own without any hints. A star of the experimental team, she received special treatment not given to the other chimpanzees: her own room, an unlimited daily supply of tropical fruits, and her favorite, Korean *gulbi,* the salted and dried yellow croaker. Some even bought her ballet shoes until management put a stop to the escalating silliness.

A bold proposal was put forward to inject Eva with drugs that would enhance the strength of her synaptic connections to increase her intelligence. No one seriously objected, because the project team had already spent a great deal of money while they were still far from achieving the goal of a working prototype for the brain-machine interface.

Unexpectedly, the "enlightened" Eva regressed in all her test scores.

The chimp seemed anxious, frightened, depressed. Surveillance recordings showed that when Eva was alone, she would manipulate her lips and nose in various ways while blowing air out in an attempt to cause the soft tissues to vibrate. The researchers concluded that she was trying to imitate the human ability to make sounds by modulating the air expelled from the lungs. She was trying to talk like people.

Ultimately, Eva failed. Millions of years of evolution could not be bridged in a single night.

The experimenters designed a special touch keyboard for her and taught her some simple concepts via a combination of electrical stimulation and pattern recognition: "banana," "person," "happy," "afraid," "eat," and so forth. But they encountered great difficulties when teaching Eva to distinguish "Eva" from "other chimps." Eva just couldn't seem to separate herself from the other members of her species. The linguists tried to teach her the concept of self, but she responded with anger, howls, and a terror that she showed by covering her eyes with her hands.

Finally, Eva expressed her wish using a long, long sentence. Her dark eyes full of layered sorrow like the folds of an agate, she pursed her soft lips repeatedly and caressed her belly. Eva was lonely. Eva wanted to return to the other chimps, even though she was no longer the original Eva.

The experimental team threw a big going-home party for Eva. They dressed Eva in a custom-made evening gown, presented her with a cake, had her blow out the candles, and treated her just like a real human being. Then they helped her undress and took her to the large enclosure where the other chimpanzees were housed.

The humans did not understand the looks in the eyes of the other chimpanzees in that moment. They waited outside the enclosure, expecting to see some warm reunion scene out of a soap opera. Stupid human chauvinists.

Almost simultaneously, all the chimpanzees curled up in the corners of the enclosure leapt at Eva as if they had gone mad. Howling, they bit her with their canines. Hatred and rage spilled out of their eyes, as if an alien soul were hiding in the chimpanzee body in front of them, deceiving them like a skilled charlatan. But now, now they were going to reveal the truth about her.

The stupefied experimenters finally recovered from their shock, retrieved tasers and tranquilizer guns, and dispersed the out-of-control chimpanzees with great effort. What remained of Eva was only a mangled corpse. Eva's sorrowful, bleeding eyes stared lifelessly up at the ceiling, and her expression was one of utter puzzlement. Her prosthetic skull had been pried open, showing the pink brain underneath, already half eaten.

The prosthesis lay next to the body like an exquisite bowl with a milk-white pool of brain matter at the bottom, bearing silent testimony to another failure of civilization.

It was sealed and kept in frozen storage as a piece of evidence. Serial number: SBT-VBPII32503439.

Kaizong couldn't help wanting to compare the differences between the worlds seen through his two eyes.

Alternately covering one eye or the other with his hand, he slowly swept his gaze across the room. The pure white sheets on the bed glowed softly; the beige wall next to the beige curtains demonstrated minute gradations of hue and fine textures; the composite table and chairs were accurately represented in perspective; each small object on the table cast a blurry shadow, sketching out its spatial position in a manner indistinguishable from normal vision. If he had to find something to complain about, it was that when he moved his right eye too quickly, objects remained unusually clear instead of blurring slightly as he was used to.

The user manual explained that this was because the prosthetic eye's moving-image processing algorithms still needed to be improved; the customer was urged to wait for the next patch.

Focused by a highly integrated, complex optical system, the light of the world landed on a flexible polyimide-based artificial retina whose area was only sixteen square millimeters and whose thickness was only one hundred microns. Specialized chips then converted the light into coded pulses emitted by millions of nanometer-scale microelectrodes. The signals traveled through the retinal ganglia, the optic tract, and the lateral geniculate complex to finally end up inside the primary visual cortex, where they were interpreted as vision.

The prosthetic eye allowed the user to recover 99.95 percent of normal vision; indeed, it replaced the most exquisite, most mysterious product of billions of years of evolution—the eye—and might even have improved on it in some ways.

A layer of capillaries covers the human retina; light has to pass through the blood vessels and nerves to reach the light-sensitive rods and cones. The shadows of the blood vessels reduce the quality of the light, and the optic nerve head is the cause for the anatomical blind spot. Our eyes must constantly jitter in saccadic movements to scan the visual field so that the brain can synthesize the faulty images, eliminate the shadows, and combine them into a whole picture.

These structural flaws add to the brain's processing load and make our eyes especially fragile—any bleeding or bruising would result in shadows that affect vision. More seriously, the photoreceptor layer is only loosely attached to the retinal pigment epithelium, so that even slight trauma may cause retinal detachment, leading to permanent loss of vision.

The prosthetic eye, on the other hand, could completely remedy all these flaws with technical advances.

If you are only using one prosthetic eye, we will simulate the flaws of the unimproved human eye algorithmically to maintain balance between the two eyes, said the user manual.

Kaizong pushed open the door and stepped onto the balcony. The sun was too bright. He squinted his left eye while his right eye had already reacted by sharply constricting the aperture, softening his view of the scene. He hadn't just changed one eye; the entire world had changed.

I need time to adjust to this. Kaizong felt a growing sense of unease.

From the balcony he could see a beautiful garden with trees, winding paths, pavilions, an artificial lake, and rock formations. Many patients accompanied by their visitors were strolling through the garden to regain strength.

A little boy dressed in a hospital gown was running through the flower garden, followed by a few older kids in some kind of game. Kaizong tried to focus on the object moving rapidly at their feet. Theoretically, the prosthetic eye's focal range could exceed the human eye's ten times over, but the default factory setting was equal to regular vision. Customers all over the world loved to install augmented-reality software in prosthetic eyes to enhance their functions, although in restricted-bitrate zones, the data delay could impede vision. This meant that the preinstalled network module in Kaizong's Cyclops VII was practically useless.

The object at the children's feet was a ball, but not a common ball. The ball seemed to move on its own, tracing out a patternless path while flashing in different colors. Each time the ball changed its color, they tried to kick it using different techniques to alter its path, and then erupted into cheers or shouts of frustration. Kaizong was not familiar with this new game at all.

The little boy was undoubtedly the best player. His gait was swift and agile, like that of a gazelle leaping across the prairie. He seemed to casually land each time at the precise spot where he could easily extend his foot before everyone else to tap the ball lightly, causing it to change color. It was as if he were manipulating the ball with his hands rather than feet.

The game was over. The others lifted the boy up to celebrate his victory. The legs of his pants rolled up, revealing two silvery-gray structures incongruously planted in his sneakers, skinless, muscleless, glinting coldly in the sun. The other kids gazed at his prosthetic limbs with envy and touched them gingerly, as if coveting some Christmas present. They yearned to possess limbs like these someday, even if they had to give up their flesh-and-blood limbs in exchange.

Strangely, ever since Kaizong's surgery, the scene with the witch and Mimi replayed in his dreams repeatedly. Everything he had once believed in—science, logic, philosophical materialism—had crumbled in this farce. He could no longer tell which parts were mere fraudulent stage magic and which parts real. At the same time, his growing uncertainty was accompanied by a developing sense of empathy with the people of Silicon Isle: they belonged here. This sea, this air, this patch of land formed everything they believed in. They lived in accordance with their faith, no different from anyone else in the world.

Kaizong did not hate the waste person who had blinded him in the right eye; to the contrary, he felt ashamed of his old prejudices. The moral principles or faith of the waste people were no less worthy than those held by the intellectual elites of Boston University and were no farther from civilization. Their choices were in fact closer to the essence of life, an essence that had not changed in the hundreds of thousands of years of human evolution.

Kaizong looked up at the distant sea. Its surface was like a sheet of paper being wrinkled constantly. Thin, long waves appeared like tears, flickering like bits of mica; a page turned over, then another page, disappearing at the edge of the sandy beach. Clouds roiled in the sky, slowly swallowing the light from the sun. The world was no longer the world held on to by his father's generation, and God was no longer the God they believed in. People now worshiped power far more than honesty, kindness, virtue. He wasn't sure which was closer to truth.

He knew only that he was closer to Mimi, at least a little.

Scott forced his thoughts back to the present. The Ducati roared as it advanced through the bright sunlight. He felt sorrow for Eva, who could find no home, no world where she belonged, and for himself.

He had grown used to calling across oceans at midnight after much hesitation so that he could exchange a few meaningless words of greeting with Susan, his ex-wife, and then try to converse with his daughter. Tracy was popular at school; busy with parties, busy with dates, busy with rehearsals for her rock musical, *Orange Blood*. After a perfunctory "Love you, Daddy," she would hang up before Scott could reply, leaving him alone in the silent darkness.

Home had already become a distant and abstract concept, in both space and time.

You can't blame them; you really can't.

From the day Scott had stubbornly tucked that old photograph into his wallet, he knew that the shadow would always follow him, perhaps until the day he died. But the consequences were still unanticipated. That shadow devoured the love, hope, and courage in his heart, and then spread to his wife and daughter and everyone around him like cancer.

Tracy told him, *I don't want you to always think of me as a three-year-old.*

Susan told him, *You're no longer the man I knew. You're like a bottomless pit; no matter how much patience and care we give you, your heart remains dark. I'm sorry, but I can't live a life like that.*

If Nancy were still alive, she would be about Mimi's age now. Ever since he had met the waste girl in the ICU, Scott couldn't help being reminded of his own daughter.

He knew that Mimi was the last person to come in contact with that particular prosthesis. Based on what he had heard from Director Lin, Scott was virtually certain that the virus was already having an effect inside Mimi, and the effects far exceeded his imagination. It almost seemed as if the Suzuki variant was endowed with a strong survival instinct that drove it to adapt constantly to the needs of humans, to transform itself to gain the opportunity for the lineage to continue. It was a survival strategy based on rapid mutations.

No one could predict Mimi's future. However, like Eva, she could no longer go home.

Scott's intuition told him that the secret hidden within this young woman was thousands of times more valuable than the Silicon Isle recycling project. He could even see the paths leading to the goal overlaid on top of the scene in front of him like augmented-reality plans. He would take advantage of Kaizong's sentimental, unseasoned love and construct a lie that would bring Mimi away from Silicon Isle and into the international market, where her potential value could be fully exploited. When absolutely necessary, he would open the box of take-out sea urchin supplied by Coltsfoot Blossom, which contained his trick of last resort.

Is this what you really want? Scott asked himself.

No. I want to save her. I won't harm her, I won't.

Scott told himself again and again that the medical examinations showed that Mimi's brain was a minefield that could threaten her life at any moment. The techniques available in Silicon Isle, even the whole of China, were insufficient to save her. She needed the best custom medical team the world had to offer, but such treatment demanded a commensurate price.

Everything was as it should be.

Scott knew very well why he had to manufacture hypocritical excuses to dress up his actions so that they didn't seem so mercenary, despicable, even evil. He had to save himself, had to release what remained of his life from the grip of that dark shadow.

He believed that the ray of light was Mimi.

However, one final piece of the puzzle worried him.

Hirofumi Otogawa had told him that the sealed, refrigerated prosthesis had been identified by the automatic systems as a piece of medical waste and then sorted and packed into the waste shipped to Silicon Isle by computerized processing. In other words, no person needed to take responsibility for this accident. It was an error. The SBT security department was investigating whether similar accidents had occurred in the past. Improper disposal of prostheses infected with highly dangerous viruses would be a huge scandal, and the mass media would chase after the truth like drug-sniffing dogs who have scented cocaine.

An unanticipated error, Scott pondered. *An error that might crash SBT's stock and make Coltsfoot Blossom into a household name. And I'm the patch for the system error.*

But what if it wasn't an error at all?

The sun baked the road. Scott was soaked in sweat, and the Ducati cooked his thighs. He wanted to return to the hotel and take a shower. He increased the throttle, and the motorcycle followed the curve of the shore to the last exit. The Volvo he had shaken off was waiting for him.

260 // CHEN QIUFAN

Enraged, he turned the throttle to maximum and swept past the Volvo like a lightning bolt. In that half a second, he caught a clear glimpse of the driver's face in the rearview mirror: a heart-shaped branding scar on his cheek. Instantly, Scott understood. The road he was on was hemmed in by steep slopes. He had nowhere to go.

His speed approached 120 kph. As he climbed over a hill, the light Ducati became airborne for a moment before dropping back onto the road. The Volvo was right on his tail and tried to pass him a few times, though Scott managed to stay ahead of him with some nimble maneuvers. Like a bird trying to capture a darting insect, the two shadows, one gray, one black, skimmed along the road one right after the other. The roar of the engines reverberated through the fields, and alarmed birds took flight.

The Volvo seemed to lose patience and began to press against the Ducati. A dull, solid *thump;* the two vehicles were one for a moment before separating, like a forceful, flitting goodbye kiss.

Another *thud,* much heavier this time.

Scott cursed and struggled to keep the bike upright. However, this contest between the motorcycle and the car was like a fight between a flyweight and a heavyweight, and Scott was doomed to lose. A piercing, grinding noise came from the right side of the Ducati as it was pressed toward the sharp, jagged rock wall on the side of the road.

Scott braked hard. The front wheel screamed against the ground and activated the ABS. The slim, graceful Ducati managed to squeeze between the narrow gap between the Volvo and the cliff, unharmed. Scott could almost feel the rough surface of the rocks barely scraping over his skin. He battled to keep the Ducati upright, but overcompensated and tumbled to the ground.

The Volvo also screeched to a stop. The driver didn't get out, however, as if he was trying to confirm something. After Scott finally climbed to his feet and straightened the bike, the Volvo flashed its taillights twice, like a contemptuous grin, and sped away as though everything that had happened were but a meaningless game of tag.

Scott checked himself and found only a few scrapes. He got onto the Ducati, whose engine now sounded like the hacking coughs of a tuberculosis patient. Scott raised his head like a knight who has vanquished the windmill and slowly cruised toward the hotel.

A ludicrous scene was playing out at the negotiating table.

While the representatives of the three clans were in heated argument against Mayor Weng, the three clans also disagreed with each other. Lin Yiyu tried to interrupt multiple times, begging the three clans to forget the past and try to all take a step back for Silicon Isle's future, but Luo Jincheng shouted him down, leaving him embarrassed and annoyed. Chen Xianyun seemed to contradict Luo Jincheng on every point, but spoke ambivalently on critical points. Only the Lin clan representative seemed interested in making a deal, and it was possible that they had already come to some secret understanding with the government. Scott sat to the side, looking dazed, as he waited for Kaizong's translation. However, Kaizong's expression was wooden and he paid no attention to the scene, as though his spirit was wandering elsewhere.

"What are they talking about?" Scott asked Kaizong. He had reached the limit of his patience.

Kaizong seemed to have been awakened from a dream, and replied in a sleepy voice, "You know: investment ratios, disposition of excess labor, land use planning, preferential policies . . . everything having to do with money."

"Have they discussed the technology? Or all the benefits that will accrue to Silicon Isle because of the project? Their children and their children's children will no longer have to breathe this shitty air or truck in drinkable water from far away." Scott looked puzzled.

Kaizong turned to his boss and spoke in an almost chilly tone. "They don't care, sir."

Scott fell heavily against the back of his leather chair, looking thoughtful. "I'm finally beginning to understand why the Chinese are called the cleverest people, but not the most intelligent or wisest. Oh, I'm sorry, Caesar, if you are offended."

"Not at all, Scott. I agree with you. Even if they sign this agreement, as long as these people run Silicon Isle, nothing will change."

"We'll see." Scott patted Kaizong on the shoulder a few times.

The edge-enhancement algorithm for the prosthetic eye appeared still in need of improvement. It was supposed to imitate the lateral-inhibition functionality in the ommatidia of the compound eyes of horseshoe crabs. When Kaizong focused his gaze on one of the speakers, for example, the resolution of objects around the speaker would be decreased to enhance the clarity of the focus subject. However, the abrupt way the enhancement kicked in felt unnatural and made it hard for him to look about the room.

In the end, Kaizong chose to leave his gaze on the giant mural that formed the backdrop to the conference room. The lacquer painting had been donated by an ethnic Chinese businessman living in Vietnam. Against a vivid black background, thin lines of gold, silver, lead, and tin sketched out the entirety of Silicon Isle, and then bits of nacre from the shells of marbled turban, abalone, and pearl oysters were added to form a mosaic. The workmanship was exquisite. Kaizong thought the scene looked familiar, but it took a while before he realized that it was the perspective of viewing the moonlit isle from the sea outside Tide Gazing Pavilion. In a flash, memories overwhelmed him like a flood and left his heart in turbulent confusion. Only a few weeks had passed since then, but that episode felt like it was from another era.

That clear, joyous face lit by the moon magnified in his mind. He missed her, missed her so much that it hurt. The pain was inside, like a needle trailing a long thread weaving between his organs until everything was tied up in knots and a single tug made everything ache.

Kaizong couldn't say clearly how he felt about Mimi. Admiration? Curiosity? Commiseration? Protectiveness? Fear? Or maybe a combination of all of these? No, it was a deeper, more complex emotion that couldn't be expressed in words, but one that could be felt through the visual signals transmitted by his prosthetic eye.

Some kind of broken, incomplete love?

All he knew was that he wanted to see her. Whether she was still Mimi or had already transformed into another kind of being.

However, the strike by the waste people had not only ruined Kaizong's right eye but also led to the total collapse of the fragile peace that had held between the natives of Silicon Isle and the waste people.

The streets outside were strewn with long yellow police tape marking the edge of the town, and police sentries patrolled the line twenty-four hours a day. Waste workers not native to Silicon Isle who tried to enter the town had to present electronic authorization from their employer. Silicon Isle was under red alert. Fear, like the intermittent black rain, drenched the heart of every native. On the other side of the police tape, there was only silence and the ceaseless barking of chipped dogs echoing over the empty waste-processing spaces. Other than the twice-daily scheduled caravan that brought them food and water, there was no other contact with the waste people and no one knew what they were planning.

It was like the powerful supertyphoon that was about to make landfall within twenty-four hours. By international convention, though incongruous with its violent nature, the typhoon was named Wutip, meaning "butterfly" in Cantonese.

Kaizong understood the silent prayer behind the worried faces of the locals: *I haven't harmed the waste people; I shouldn't have to worry about their vengeance.* However, as long as they lived here, no one could claim to be fully innocent. Everyone had benefited in some manner by exploiting the blood and sweat of the waste people, even if it was just an insignificant bit of convenience. Everyone had, at one time or another, looked at the waste people with contempt or disgust, or insulted them with a careless or hurtful word. Everyone had had the thought, even if only momentarily, that the waste people were born low and that they were fated to live in the company of trash, destined to be filthy until their deaths.

He that is without sin among you, let him first cast a stone at her.

Chen Kaizong thought about the country that he called home now. In that society that prided itself on being the very model of freedom, democracy, and equality, prejudice and discrimination had to take on more subtle and hypocritical forms. Invitations to clubs and parties were sent to prosthetic eyes to be read by retinal scanners; those who couldn't afford to implant enhanced enzymes couldn't buy special foods and beverages at supermarkets; those with genetic flaws might not even be able to obtain birth permits; the one percent could extend their lives by swapping out the components of their bodies endlessly, achieving a de facto perpetual monopoly on society's wealth.

Kaizong shook his head lightly, not even noticing that he had sighed.

"Are you thinking about her?" Scott asked.

"Who? What?"

"That young woman, Mimi."

Kaizong remained silent.

"You've changed a lot since coming here," Scott said.

Kaizong shrugged.

"At first, you acted like a hero. Or at least pretended to be a hero. But now, you're like a deserter."

"I can't do anything; I can't save anyone." Kaizong's voice trembled and his eyes moistened. "I can't even see her anymore."

"When I was in the army, my drill sergeant told us, *Never act like a Hollywood hero. A real hero knows the difference between an order, a mission, and life itself, and will prioritize them correctly at key moments.*"

"The doctors tell me that she could die at any moment, and they don't have the necessary medical expertise to treat her here." Kaizong struggled to keep his voice calm. "But she belongs to the Luo clan, and so Luo Jincheng will use her as a bargaining chip."

"I understand. I think this is a key moment for you."

"I *don't* understand."

"It's very simple. If you think this recycling project is more important, then we need to forget everything else and focus on making a deal."

Scott paused for a moment. "On the other hand, if you think Mimi's life is more important, then we need to negotiate with Luo Jincheng until we can find her and take her away. Fuck the project."

"Are you testing me?" Kaizong's face was full of suspicion.

"No. Look at them." Scott gestured at the negotiating representatives. "What do they care about?"

"Money. Power." Kaizong thought for a moment, and then added, "Maybe women . . . and their children."

Scott grinned, revealing his perfect white teeth. "See, you *do* understand them. People are always paying too much for the wrong things, and I once made the same kind of mistake. I want you to think it over carefully before giving me an answer."

Kaizong's chair scraped against the floor. He shifted awkwardly to disguise his unease. The arguing voices of bureaucrats and merchants to the side seemed to soften and become more pleasing; their figures blurred and, like shadows or puppets, they mechanically repeated the same sentences. The immense lacquer mural behind them, in contrast, grew clearer and came into focus. The rare nacred shells twinkled like moonlit eyes, embellishing the picture of an ever-changing Silicon Isle buffeted by the waves of progress.

He was once a man who habitually avoided decisions and who comforted himself by claiming that the only logical choice was giving in to the invisible forces and patterns of history. Now, however, his eyes turned from hesitation to resolve. The decision was no longer difficult.

Kaizong slapped his hand down on Scott's shoulder. He had never acted so familiarly with his boss, so unguarded. Scott's wounds, still not fully healed, exploded with spasms of pain. He winced.

"Thank you."

Kaizong's eyes once again glowed with hope, and there was a trace more gratitude in his right eye than his left.

PART THREE

FURIOUS STORM

. . . you see perfection in imperfection itself. And that is how we should learn to love the world.

—Slavoj Žižek, *Examined Life*

15

The rain began at dusk and didn't seem to ever want to stop.

The bright yellow police tape trembled in the wind, whistling intermittently. Raindrops dense as schools of fish traced diagonal lines in the warm, hazy cones of light cast by the streetlights. A change of the guard at the sentry post: salutes, water dripping from the black rubber raincoat, flowing into the rain boots, pooling at the feet. The new sentry shivered, blew out a mouthful of white mist that quickly dissipated in the wind. Though it was high summer in Silicon Isle, right now it felt as chilly as a damp cellar in winter.

On the other side of the line marked by the police tape, everything remained quiet. Occasionally, a few dogs rhythmically barked at each other in the dusk, hinting at some distant, empty space. The shack villages of the waste people resembled a mass graveyard where the black structures were corpses strewn about without order in the tall grass. Faint light emitted from the seams of windows and doors like the orifices of the corpses, as though they were silently howling in their death throes. Their last breaths trembled in the wind and rain, at risk of extinguishing at any moment.

"I heard that they're planning on cutting the water and food rations in half tomorrow." Illuminated by the dim light, Li Wen stared at the dark, cold night outside. The rain struck the cheap corrugated iron roof, crackling like kernels popping in a kettle. "They are almost at the end of their rope."

"We're going to stay a step ahead of them," Mimi said lightly as she inserted another vial of red liquid into the self-injector attached to the inside of her elbow. For the next twelve hours, it would steadily inject the high-energy fructose mixture into her veins, ensuring that her hyper-metabolic brain could obtain enough ATP to continue to function normally. She had to pay a cost for this benefit: rapid shallow breathing, high body temperature, emotional instability. It wasn't too different a feeling from falling in love.

This was the last vial in her possession.

"Everyone's ready." Li Wen heard the chipped dog inside the shack give a low snarl. He had cracked the software running on the chipped dogs, and, with Mimi's help, transformed them into communication tools. When necessary, they could also become weapons.

"Have you recharged the spirit of Tide Gazing Beach?" Mimi asked.

"It's ready and waiting for you in the shed. How did you manage to crack the wireless communication protocols?"

"The same way you open a lock with a key."

This was the source of Li Wen's unease. He understood the principle, but he couldn't figure out the path she took to achieve the results. Mimi was no longer the ignorant waste girl he had once known, or maybe she had never been. The Mimi in front of him now was like a veteran weathered and tested by many wars whose strategies and plots were too deep for him to guess.

"Are you sure about this?" Li Wen watched, concerned, as Mimi put on the augmented-reality glasses and activated the tiny attachment next to her ear. A blue LED started to glow. "Your luck is going to run out one day."

Mimi smiled and said nothing.

When she was still Mimi 0, Brother Wen had often showed off his skills to her. Using a modified radio and cracking software, he had demonstrated how he could circumvent the bitrate-restricting firewall briefly and connect the augmented-reality glasses to the high-speed network outside so that the wearer got to enjoy the pleasure of freely observing the world. The cheap equipment had cost a fortune on the Silicon Isle black market, and not everyone dared to make use of it.

You've got to be very, very careful, Brother Wen had warned Mimi. *Don't register on any site; don't make any comments; don't leave any traces. As soon as you see the red light go on, disconnect immediately. That means the net guardian spiders have detected some kind of vibration in their webs, and will be tracing the strands to be on you in a moment. Once they lock on to you, you'll never escape. The spiders will pierce your body with their fangs and inject the poison that will paralyze your nerves and dissolve your muscles, and then they'll slowly tear you apart, chew you up, and digest you in acid.*

Circumventing the bitrate restrictions was a major crime. No one would even notice your disappearance.

Yet now, she was going to bring a whole crowd with her in an attempt to break through the firewall. This was like a group jumping off the top of a skyscraper, equipped with only a single parachute.

The blue-purple glow from the LED lit up Mimi's face. Her features seemed to drift in space, mysterious and perfect.

Li Wen was mesmerized by her, and then he became angry at himself for the reaction. He knew that the worshipful sensation was nothing more than an artificial suggestion implanted in his mind that was intended to infect every waste person via the video virus. He understood that he had to pay a price for this mad game. He recalled how the old Mimi had often partook of digital mushrooms while plugged into the high-bitrate network, and her expression had been distant and confused, as though the act of browsing for information was but a compensatory behavior her brain engaged in to prevent her sense of self from collapsing into an abyss.

Or maybe that wasn't even Mimi, but some other personality in her subconscious trying to study the world through Mimi's flesh?

Li Wen shuddered as though a column of ants were marching across the back of his neck, slowly climbing onto the back of his skull. He secretly activated the pattern-recognition function in his glasses and waited, like a frog waiting for a passing fly, for that strange Western face to flicker into existence.

It appeared suddenly, and once again overlaid Mimi's face like a veil of light for an instant before fading away.

Got it!

The computer soon returned the search results to Li Wen's glasses, but that only deepened the mystery. The face belonged to Hedy Lamarr, the Hollywood star who had invented the frequency-hopping communication technique that would become the foundation for CDMA digital wireless networks later. A woman who excelled with both beauty and brains.

He finally recalled the strange digital drug called HEMK Ekstase. The initials of Lamarr's birth name, Hedwig Eva Maria Kiesler, were HEMK, and *Ekstase* was a sensual 1933 Czech film in which an eighteen-year-old Lamarr made her debut.

Why would this prodigy who has been dead for decades appear in Mimi's brain?

"Give me some music," Mimi said.

The young woman endowed with a virtual personality by Li Wen reclined in her chair like Manet's Olympia. In that moment, Li Wen realized why he was willing to risk everything for her like a reprogrammed chipped dog. In her current state, Mimi was a cyber goddess, capable of transcending all layers of the net, of the world even, and she had hooked him on every level, too. There was nothing he wouldn't do to help Mimi.

"Something with a kick."

The tall figure of Scott stood before the iron gates. The broad, black umbrella shielded his face from the monitoring cameras; the black rain fell endlessly and streamed from the edge of the umbrella into an indistinct blur. The spotlights came on, and warm steam rose in their rays as they focused on the umbrella from different directions, collecting into a bright spot. Some hidden speaker emitted a series of stiff commands in a language Scott was unfamiliar with. He shifted the umbrella slightly so that his pale, non-Chinese face showed in the beams of the spotlights, and the rain drenched his shoes.

The iron gates screeched painfully as the two panels slowly slid apart. The chipped dogs inside the compound began to bark furiously.

Scott slid in sideways, recalling the first time he had dealt with one of the fierce creatures. That afternoon at Xialong Village seemed so long ago.

Luo Jincheng greeted him at the front door of the mansion with a smile that Scott had first seen grinning smugly up at him from the manila folders of his TerraGreen research files. Next to Luo Jincheng stood a few muscular young men whose expressions assured Scott of their familiarity with violence.

"Mr. Brandle! What an honor! I guess at least one good thing can be attributed to this typhoon if it has brought you. Where might your able assistant be?"

"I know that you're comfortable with English and a savvy businessman. There are some discussions where it's best to keep the number of participants down."

After the two sat down inside, Luo Jincheng gestured for his minions to leave them. Then Luo busied himself at the eight-immortal table. He lit the brazier, boiled the water, unpacked the tea leaves, uncovered the pot, loaded the tea leaves, poured the water, cleaned the cups . . . After a complicated series of steps that resembled an artistic performance, a pot of tea was ready. Luo Jincheng arranged three tiny Yixing clay teacups about the size of walnuts in a tight triangle. Then, as Scott watched, mouth agape, Luo poured the first infusion into the three cups as he moved the stream evenly over them, and then poured the tea away. The mellow fragrance of the tea filled Scott's nostrils and seemed to seep into every alveolus in his lungs.

Luo Jincheng then refilled the pot with fresh water—timing it so that the water had just started to boil and the bubbles resembled fish eyes—and once again moved the pouring spout over the three cups so that they were filled evenly, without any one of them receiving an infusion more concentrated than any other. By the time the cups were about 70 percent filled, Luo paused, and then carefully dipped the spout over the cups in turn, as though dabbing paint, until the cups were fully filled. Finally finished, Luo presented a cup with both hands to Scott.

"Mr. Brandle, please have a taste of our top-quality Phoenix *baiye dancong*, a variety of oolong." Luo Jincheng looked serene and self-composed, as though he had just completed a tai chi session.

"I see why *ganghu* tea is so highly regarded." Scott held the exquisite cup and admired it. The liquid inside appeared golden and translucent, exuding a complex fragrance in which the dominant flavor of tea was further embellished with traces of Osmanthus, jasmine, and honey.

"The tea leaves are collected from Wu Dong peak, in Phoenix County, at an altitude above one thousand meters. There, the tea bushes are steeped in fog and cloud, from which they absorb the essence of nature. The *dancong* part of the name refers to the fact that each tea bush gives off a different aroma, and each must be treated distinctly and processed with care."

Scott expressed his admiration as he sipped the tea slowly. The floral, mellow flavor filled his mouth, and, as he swallowed, his tongue seemed to detect an aftertaste of sweetness. He could not imagine the subtlety of the flavor being replicated through a modern industrialized production line. Luo Jincheng smiled and indicated that he should feel free to enjoy another cup.

"Here in Silicon Isle, we always prepare three cups, even when two or four are sitting down to have tea. The extra cup goes to the guest, or the host does without—the principle is to always think of the other side first. It's the same when we do business." Luo Jincheng picked up the last remaining cup, closed his eyes, and savored the tea.

"I suppose it's the same principle we use: look for a win-win solution." Scott acted as if he had just been enlightened.

"So, what has brought you to my humble abode today, Mr. Brandle? I'm all ears."

"A business proposal in which we both emerge as winners."

"Oh?" Luo opened his eyes and gazed at the storm raging outside. "Permit me to be frank, then. I'm guessing you're here to ask for that waste girl, am I right?"

Scott said nothing. This old fox was even craftier than he had imagined.

"Although she's only a waste girl, she still belongs to the Luo clan. She's a bit like one of the tea bushes on Wu Dong peak—although she has some innate talent, the process of plucking, fermenting, baking, and rolling will determine the final market value. I have a duty to act in the best interests of the young people under my charge, don't you agree?"

Scott almost laughed out loud. For this criminal mastermind to suddenly launch into a speech about his sense of responsibility, as if all that Mimi had suffered had nothing to do with him, was really too much. The Chinese, no matter how he thought he had finally figured them out, constantly surprised him. This was a people modeled on the classical yin-yang symbol: they somehow managed to harmonize opposites and unified the best and worst qualities without appearing to be bothered by the contradictions.

"I don't think you need to worry about the price. I work for Terra-Green Recycling, not some no-name startup."

"What price are you planning on offering, then?" The sly old fox could no longer suppress his excited tail.

"As you know, the formal signing ceremony for the project isn't until next week. Anything is possible before then." Scott put down his cup and showed Luo his professional, ambivalent smile.

"I was under the impression that we're done with dividing the cake at the negotiating table."

"Well, you might still get a bigger slice."

"How much bigger?"

"If you successfully facilitate Mimi's departure with us, you will receive three more percentage points than the original agreement."

"I don't think either of the other clans would be willing to give up any of their share."

"Wealth Recycle would."

Luo Jincheng looked thoughtful. After a while, he gazed at Scott serenely and said, "Is that girl really worth that much? What if I decide that I want to keep her?"

"Then you'll be escalating this into a political incident—an outcome that no one wants, trust me. Also, I'll take her away from you in the end, no matter what." Scott's tone was now firm and cold.

As far as Luo Jincheng could see, Mimi was the start of all his misfortunes, but certainly not the end. He personally witnessed the young woman's extraordinary skills during the "oil fire" ritual. She had seemed to be possessed by some spirit, and though she had awakened his son, she had also left him with a permanent condition that would make him into a laughingstock. He knew very well that he had no hope of truly controlling this young woman, regardless of his application of violence, money, or raw authority. She was beyond what he could comprehend. He really was very happy with Scott's proposal, but his habitual curiosity made him want to probe for Scott's bottom line.

"I will think about it." Luo Jincheng refilled the three cups and invited Scott to help himself.

"I will expect your answer tomorrow." Scott drained his cup.

One of Luo's minions rushed into the room and handed a mobile phone to Luo. Luo glanced at it and stood up. "My sincere apologies," he said. "Something has come up that requires my immediate attention."

"Of course. Thank you for your hospitality." Scott got up to leave, but then seemed to remember something. He turned back, retrieved a phone from his pocket, and deposited it on the eight-immortal table.

"Would you please return this to its rightful owner and pass on my regrets for his . . . 'lovely' face?" He smiled, turned, and left in the company of Luo's bodyguards. At the door of the mansion, he opened the umbrella, and stepped resolutely into the pouring rain.

Luo Jincheng stared at his departing figure, and his face spasmed a few times. He held the mobile up to his ear, and Hard Tiger's voice, disguised by software, emerged from the earpiece.

"Boss Luo, there's something you should see."

Kaizong's raincoat flapped behind him in the gale like the wings of a giant bat, flickering uncertainly at the edge of the cone of illumination cast by the streetlight.

The rain came heavier now, the drops accelerated by the wind striking his bare face painfully like bullets. His right eye had been preset to be more sensitive than regular eyes in dim light, and the brain was forced to combine the images from both eyes and achieve some compromise. However, when the rain forced him to close one eye or another, the world would dim or brighten. He regretted not wearing goggles, but the waste people would not have such equipment, either.

He stumbled closer to the sentry. The guard held up a hand to stop him; Kaizong showed him the electronic ID card, and the reader held in the guard's hand beeped. The suspicious guard compared the photograph on the ID with his face. Forcing himself to be calm, Kaizong brushed the wet hair stuck to his forehead aside to reveal his features. The guard waved him by, and Kaizong let out a held breath. He knew that heading the other way across the border—coming into Silicon Isle Town—would be much harder.

The night wind's chill mercilessly pierced the raincoat and made him shiver. Kaizong struggled along the muddy path, where shallow and deep puddles reflected the faint light like an uneven mirror and pointed his way. Vague childhood memories floated through his mind. Silicon Isle was often assaulted by typhoons, and the terrain of the town made it prone to flooding. Thus, Kaizong and his childhood friends had often floated in wooden buckets and paddled themselves through the muddy water with their hands as they splashed each other in water fights. This was perhaps one of his few surviving happy memories of Silicon Isle.

Typhoons visited Silicon Isle like some yearly festival—sometimes more than once a year, if they felt generous. The people, farmers by tradition, gradually gave up their fight with nature and abandoned the fields, turning to trade, fishing, waste recycling. They called the shift a sign of progress, but Kaizong wasn't so sure.

Under the faint illumination of distant lights, Kaizong found his way to the village of the waste people. Hundreds of simple, rough shacks similar in appearance surrounded him, and he didn't know where to start. The simplest thing would be to do what he had always done and walk straight in to look for Mimi, but the times were no longer normal. Pamphlets full of inflaming exhortations had spread to every corner of Silicon Isle, and, as a native, Kaizong might not meet a good reception here if he revealed himself.

Another cause for his uncertainty was Mimi's current intentions.

He had to find Mimi and convince her to leave Silicon Isle with him so that they could fly across the Pacific Ocean and allow a group of American specialists to open up her skull and diffuse the ticking bomb inside. This sounded like a story more preposterous than local folk legends. Would she believe him?

And a bigger question still: did she even need Kaizong to rescue her?

Due to the heavy rain, all the chipped dogs had been kept inside, and the rain and wind made their sensitive noses useless. Kaizong was glad that he didn't have to repeat his boss's feat of subduing snarling dogs with his bare hands. Quietly, he crept close to one of the shacks and peered in from the edge of a window.

A strange waste man lay half naked on the bed, the augmented-reality glasses on his head flashing a blue light.

Kaizong ducked down and clumsily waddled his way to the next shack like a beached whale. Inside, he saw two women covered with complicated jewelry made from junked electronic components. Their augmented-reality glasses were flashing in sync. He left again, and witnessed similar scenes in the other shacks he spied on. Kaizong began to realize that this wasn't a coincidence.

He found a narrow gap between two shacks and squeezed himself in. The rain-drenched garbage emitted a stench that made him gag. The walls on both sides were the color of rust mixed with lichen and covered by graffiti featuring male and female sexual organs. Everything was covered with a layer of sticky filth. Kaizong held his breath and carefully poked his head up from between two windows so close together that they almost couldn't be opened at the same time. As expected, the inhabitants of both shacks were lying in bed with augmented-reality glasses on, and the flashing blue lights on their glasses were in sync, as though they were members of the audience in some silent, still concert.

Kaizong was reminded of the eerie scene of Mimi at the "oil fire" ritual.

The flashing lights weren't the only things in sync; the expressions on the waste people were also highly coordinated: sometimes tense, sometimes amazed, sometimes smiling . . . it was as if countless invisible strings had been let down from a giant hand and extended into each shack on this dirty patch of land, controlling the facial muscles of every waste person. In Kaizong's experience, only fundamentalist religious ceremonies in which all participants were caught up in the same emotional fervor could achieve such results. A chill wind seemed to penetrate the back of his collar, and all the hairs on Kaizong's back stood on their ends.

"Who's there?" a voice shouted from behind him.

He turned around, scrambling for some explanation, but lost his footing in the wet mud and tumbled into a puddle. The rotting stench of the earth filled his mouth and nose, and he was soaked through. Kaizong gagged a few times, spat out the mud in his mouth, but before he could even get up, something cold was held at his throat.

It was a blade shaped like the spine of a fish, glinting coldly in the wind and rain. Kaizong was stunned to see that the blade emerged from a sheath in the marble-like muscles of the arm—it was a part of his assailant's body. What little illumination there was came from behind the person, leaving the face hidden in darkness. All he could hear was the crisp cracks of rain striking the attacker's body.

"You don't belong here." The voice was female. "You're going to die."

16

A net that divided space and time. Luo Jincheng stared at the projection on the wall of his own living room, deep in thought.

Hard Tiger, still in his lair, was sending him the real-time image data through a dedicated fiber-optic cable.

Although the real-time dynamic stream had been greatly compressed after processing by sparse matrices and Fourier transforms, it still showed delays, jumps, and breaks under restricted bitrate. Against a dark background, dots of light like the stars of the Milky Way sketched an irregular surface floating in three-dimensional space. Like Indra's net, which was made up of billions of sparkling jewels at each vertex reflecting the infinite connectedness of the universe, the lights here described the ups and downs and the twists and folds of space. Each light flashed with a different color and intensity, which indicated the type of data and velocity of flow. At this zoomed-out scale, however, the differences were not apparent to the eye.

The light cast by the network fell against Luo Jincheng, and he appeared as a ghostly dark presence at the edge of the galaxy, as though this world were missing a piece.

Hard Tiger's low, deep voice emerged from the phone speaker as he held forth on what Luo was seeing, caring not one whit for how incomprehensible the stream of jargon sounded to his audience.

"I can't see a damned thing . . ." Luo Jincheng muttered.

A small rectangular region was marked out in the galaxy and the view zoomed in on it. Luo Jincheng felt as though he were riding on a spaceship rocketing into a strange new sea of stars. Hundreds of lights burned around him like stars, surrounded by dense, flickering streams of data. A few of the stars were emphasized as their brightness was turned up while the rest faded into the dim background.

"The slow arrow system detected some unusual movements. Take a look at these dots: they suddenly became very active, but haven't come close to the warning threshold."

"Can you find their exact location?" Luo Jincheng asked.

"The positions and distances in this network are extrapolated based on IPv6 addresses. Even with redirects and concealing proxies, we can still trace them back to their physical locations. Of course, that's not the end of the problem . . ."

The view zoomed out and returned to the galaxy as a whole. A few hundred stars in the galaxy now brightened, showing that they were flickering in sync. Their positions seemed random and patternless.

"This is like taking hundreds of stars in the galaxy, millions of light-years apart, and having them emit super powerful flares so that the light and energy released by all of them would reach the same observer at the same time. The span of times that must be coordinated is so wide that it's comparable to the range from microseconds to centuries. This is an extremely sophisticated frequency-hopping camouflaging technique. I don't think the waste people even possess the equipment to achieve it."

That American again, Luo Jincheng thought. "Do you have any other methods?"

"No problem is harder than Hard Tiger." The slow archer's voice revealed barely suppressed excitement. "In my system, every data vertex reflects, in real time, the shifting parameters at every other vertex. This is the key to overcoming the bitrate restrictions. I have already filtered out the hundreds of vertices that are flickering in sync; one of them must be the center, the core. I just need more data. Give me some time."

Luo Jincheng turned so that his face was hidden against the galaxy of information and his expression unreadable. He walked next to the eight-immortal table and picked up the mobile left behind by Scott Brandle, glancing at the time.

"You've got twenty minutes."

"Twenty minutes?"

Scott was sitting in the car, listening to Kaizong's replacement, a local young man named Xin Yu who was providing a simultaneous translation of the words transmitted by the bug embedded in the mobile.

"I really don't understand what they're talking about." Xin Yu rubbed his ears, red with embarrassment. He had felt lost and struggled mightily with the complicated jargon. "I'm sorry."

"Don't worry about it." Scott turned on the wipers, and a fan-shaped region of clarity was scraped out of the curtain of water on the windshield. The Luo mansion was not far from here, standing like a gloomy castle in the storm. "Do you mind waiting a bit longer?"

"I'd like you to let me out, actually." Xin Yu grinned. "To be honest, I haven't seen such a fierce typhoon since they built the Shantou Bay Bridge. I've heard the elders say that the floods used to be so bad that even cars would be washed away."

"What does the bridge have to do with typhoons?" Scott's heart wasn't really in the conversation; he was focused on detecting signs of activity in the mansion.

"The bridge changed the feng shui, of course. To connect Silicon Isle and Shantou, the bridge has to span Phoenix Island. It's said that the phoenix's wings are held down by the bridge's piers, and it can't fly anymore. Thus, powerful typhoons always make landfall some other place and don't assault this region directly anymore. As you can imagine, some also claim that the bridge changed the fortunes of Shantou and Silicon Isle, which is why both places have been in decline."

"Interesting . . ." What Scott really wanted to say was, *You Chinese are skilled at making up chains of cause and effect between things that have nothing to do with each other, but you never try to see if your own faults are at the root of your problems.*

Luo Jincheng had blamed his son's illness on Mimi; Mimi explained her own misfortunes by resorting to spirits; Kaizong simplified everything as the inevitable trends of history. This shallow habit of thought seemed to be embedded deep in their genes, and generation after generation, the tendency reinforced itself until it became a dominant characteristic of the culture of this people. Scott wasn't interested in judging it, but he did find the phenomenon intriguing.

Based on the intercepted snippets of conversation, it was obvious that the waste people were planning something. Luo Jincheng's patience was also close to the breaking point. At this crucial juncture, Scott could only wait for an opportunity to act. He hoped that everything would progress smoothly along the lines he had designed, but the game was full of unknowns, and any minor deviation might upset the entire scenario.

Scott couldn't get through to Kaizong's phone no matter how many times he tried; he really despised these devices designed for communication under restricted bitrate.

"Scott," Xin Yu said, frowning. "They're talking again."

"Tell me what they're saying."

"Okay—" A piercing noise coming out of the earpiece made Xin Yu shudder and he pulled the earpiece out, staring at Scott in shock.

"They know!"

The knife stopped at his throat as soon as Kaizong had blurted out Mimi's name.

"Who *are* you? What are you doing here?" The woman's tone was rough, and she didn't show any signs of being willing to move the knife away.

Muddy water streamed down his hair, and Kaizong tasted a bitter, fishy tang in his mouth. He squinted, trying to prevent water from getting into his eyes. But he dared not make any sudden movements with his hands, and was forced to sputter. ". . . save . . . save Mimi . . . she's . . . danger . . ."

The woman burst out into loud laughter, as if Kaizong had just told a hilarious joke.

"I think you need to save yourself first, dumbass."

Kaizong forced himself to be calm. He knew that if he told the truth, he might receive even rougher treatment. The raindrops struck dense, interfering ripples in the muddy puddles. *Think, damn it. Think like a waste person.*

He noticed a deep rut in the mud extending into the distance, as though some heavy object had been dragged into the village of shacks. He recalled the photograph of the mecha kneeling on the beach he had seen on Luo Jincheng's mobile phone, and realization struck him.

"You've moved the spirit of Tide Gazing Beach." He looked up at the woman, brooking no denial. "This spirit is angry, very angry! Do you remember those thugs from the Luo clan killed by the spirit? That was only a start."

The fish-bone-shaped knife retracted like some docile pet into the sheath formed by the woman's arm muscles. She lifted Kaizong out of the puddle with a single hand and tossed him aside like a bag of garbage.

"If you are lying to me," she said, "I'll cut your balls off and feed them to the dogs." However, at least some part of her murderous tone had been replaced by awe.

Kaizong stumbled through the mud behind the powerful woman. He tried the phone in his waterlogged pocket, but it was now as unresponsive as a rock. The squall raged, and from time to time, the woman stopped to dodge the swarms of silvery butterflies flitting through the air—thin fragments of metal with edges as sharp as razors.

"She's in there." The woman pointed to a shack and shouted. The gale made it hard to hear her. "But you can't go in right now."

"Why not?" Kaizong screamed back to be heard.

"Because I said so."

Abruptly, Kaizong dashed forward, ducking out of the woman's grasping hand, and headed for the shack. He slipped and skidded over the mud, soft and disgusting. He had just caught a glimpse of the blue flashes coming from inside the shack when he felt a heavy blow on his back and tumbled to the ground. His arms and legs were then immediately secured in a professional wrestling hold, and he felt waves of pain and heard ominous cracks coming from his dislocating joints.

"I told you to not fucking move!" The woman grabbed him by the left leg and dragged the powerless Kaizong into a temporary shed filled with junked prostheses. She pulled a rubber dildo out of the pile and, with astounding arm strength, stretched it into a rope, which she used to tie Kaizong's hands securely to a water pipe.

"You better learn your lesson. Next time, I'll use your own dick." The woman cackled and walked into Mimi's shack.

Kaizong was angry but also wanted to laugh at the absurdity of the situation. The deformed rubber penis dug into the skin over his wrists, and no matter how much he struggled, he couldn't get out of his binds. The wind grew stronger, and the dislodged prostheses struck him despite his efforts to dodge out of the way. He was lucky they were mostly made of silicone. Then he heard the screeching of metal, and a crack opened in the corrugated iron roof over his head. The tear opened up as the wind twisted and rolled the iron like a sheet of paper.

Damn! If the shed collapsed, all the weight of the structure would instantly land on him. Even if he didn't die from being crushed, he might end up suffocating. Kaizong struggled even more fervently against the pipe, hoping to shift his body at least into a safer position to preserve his life. But the pipe didn't move one whit.

Kaizong bit into the rubber dildo-rope and put all his strength into his jaws. He hoped that he could bite through the composite material, whose hardness measured 90A on the Shore scale, but he couldn't even leave any tooth marks on the faux cock. *This may be the most awkward moment of my entire life,* Kaizong thought. *And now my life is about to be over.*

A few more piercing shrieks of metal sundering, and Kaizong watched as the corrugated roof rose and disappeared into the night air like some magic carpet. The entire structure of the shed jolted and emitted a slow but sharp howl of deformation. It was about to lose its balance, disintegrate, and turn into a pile of rubble. And Kaizong was going to be buried alive with thousands of dirty pieces of prostheses like some avant-garde installation art piece by Damien Hirst—except for the fact that no one was going to pay millions of pounds to buy his corpse.

The metallic scream abruptly stopped, and everything sank into silence.

Kaizong squeezed his eyes shut and prayed, hoping that God would forgive him for his tardy piety.

"Stand Up," the last track on The Prodigy's fifth studio album, *Invaders Must Die,* roared through Mimi's ears. However, she didn't know this. Her vision trembled slightly in sync with the powerful electronica beats and the passionate melody. She was riding a herd of stampeding wild horses.

Hundreds of waste people were connected to Mimi through their augmented-reality glasses, sharing her vision. Glimpses of countless ceilings flitted through Mimi's vision, differing in brightness, angle, color; she valiantly pushed aside these interfering, useless bits of data and attempted to direct the high-speed data stream to flow to every terminal in sync with the beats of the music. It was like the comb and roller of a music box, where the bumps on the roller rang the various tines of the comb to transmit information at different frequencies, which were then reassembled by the decoding mechanism at the receiving terminal into a complete piece of music. This was Li Wen's proudest accomplishment.

We can only get to the closest server in Shantou, he had said.

That's good enough, Mimi had answered.

Mimi 0 could feel the scattered, confused crowd of consciousnesses behind her back; she was going to lead them on a fantastic journey. She still could not understand how her other self was capable of accomplishing this—it was like some hidden instinct within her, like cellular mitosis, like plant phototaxis, like animals searching for food, mating, reproducing. The only progress she had made was to grow used to the conversation between the two Mimis, like the precursor to completely split personalities.

Let there be light, Mimi 0 thought.

She saw them. Hundreds of thousands of dynamic images loomed in front of her eyes, data so complex that the human brain was incapable of processing them. She felt dizzy, nauseated, lost.

Welcome to the "Compound Eyes" system of Shantou, which connected hundreds of thousands of cameras and image-recognition artificial intelligence. Twenty-four hours a day, seven days a week, the system kept under surveillance the city's every street, every corner, every expression on every person, searching for signs of crime or acts of terrorism and protecting the lives and properties of the inhabitants. Mimi was now an invader in its heart. She was looking for something special.

Soon, she realized that her search technique was inefficient, like looking for a needle in a haystack. Mimi 1 reorganized the logic for presenting the video feeds and re-created all of Shantou from a first-person point of view based on the geography of the streets and the locations of the cameras. Unlike regular human vision, this was a view where each perspective was all-encompassing, panoramic. It was like Correggio's dome fresco, *Assumption of the Virgin,* at the Cathedral of Parma, where everything around the observer appeared in a vortex of concentric rings, with the vanishing point of the perspective the apex of the dome. As the observer moved closer, more details were revealed at the center of the vortex without end.

Imagine the world as a strange apple. The depressions at both poles are deformed and deepened until they connect, turning it into a doughnut.

The skin of the apple, meanwhile, remains intact and can slide up and down the "hole" of the doughnut like an endless treadmill. The observer is situated somewhere in the hole, and what he sees is the ring-shaped world endlessly unfolding.

More fantastically, as the observer moves toward any point in the wall of the doughnut, the point would automatically open up, expand and surround the observer in a new doughnut-view. A perfect, self-organizing, fractal structure.

Hundreds of passengers wriggled under Mimi's wings, getting impatient.

Mimi moved. Rationally, she knew that her body was still imprisoned in that tiny corrugated-iron shack quaking in the storm and that her consciousness was only about a dozen kilometers away, wandering inside the dull metal boxes of a data center. However, the images swirling around her gave her the illusion of having transformed into a winged angel gliding over this concrete and steel jungle. Her virtual body swept over streets, passed through houses, shops, bridges, parks, elevators, trains and buses, and glanced quickly into countless lit windows, not overlooking any spot.

It was dusk, but the city was already awakening into a sparkling tapestry.

In the rain, the traffic crawled through the city's main arteries and capillaric side streets like gleaming blood. Hundreds of thousands of equally anxious and numb faces hid behind the windshields, cleared by the unceasing sway of wipers that polished the wet glow of neon against glass. The self-driving cars were stuck between cars driven by those who refused to trust computers, and horns blared as the decibel counters on noise monitors rose and rose. Many glanced in the rearview mirror with a crooked set in the mouth that indicated ill intentions.

Three hundred thousand windows automatically lit up; the smart sensors understood the moods of the men and women coming home and automatically adjusted the temperature, the color of the lighting, the channels showing on the TV or the music playing through the sound systems; five thousand restaurants received automatically generated take-out orders; the health-monitoring systems synced up with the body films, and, based on dozens of parameters such as body temperature, heart rate, caloric intake/consumption, and galvanic skin response, made suggested plans for the next day's activities. Exhausted face after exhausted face.

The offices in the skyscrapers were lit bright as day. The giant eye zoomed in and observed a hundred thousand faces staring at computer monitors through closed-circuit cameras; their tension, anxiety, anticipation, confusion, satisfaction, suspicion, jealousy, anger refreshed rapidly while their glasses reflected the data jumping across their screens. Their looks were empty but deep, without thought of the relationship between their lives and values, yearning for change but also afraid of it. They gazed at their screens the way they gazed at each other, and they hated their screens the way they hated each other. They all possessed the same bored, apathetic face.

A young teacher spoke to a wall of screens filled with the faces of anxious parents, explaining her concerns regarding their children's obsessive immersion in virtual reality. As soon as the call was over, she rushed to put on her own VR rig.

A boy who wished to win the school's Maker Faire sneakily approached his father's favorite German shepherd with a neural-modification harness.

A naked man logged into an encrypted channel, where an albino alligator with skin covered in tactile sensors wrestled a mechanical octopus in a swamp; the electrical signals from the alligator's skin were transformed into sexual stimuli injected directly into the man's cortex. Fifteen thousand co-fetishists were logged into the same channel.

On an open plaza, a group of retired women danced in sync to inaudible music. They were dancing with customized augmented-reality partners, and in their minds they were again as fleet-footed and nimble as they had been decades ago.

In a luxurious apartment, a man sat stiffly on his bed, impassively observing the exaggerated expressions and stale routine of a comedian on TV. He stared at his own face on the giant screen, sobbed noiselessly, and lifted a gun.

A flock of birds rose into the evening air, dissipated like a column of black smoke, and then gathered back together, forming a series of irregular shapes against the indigo sky. Occasionally, the beam of a searchlight swept through, and the black smoke transformed into a flickering patch of silvery gravel. The cameras went through a series of quick cuts and the focal distance was set to maximum in an attempt to follow the flight of one particular bird. All the birds looked like the same bird, following the direction of the flock, imitating the posture of companions nearby; no one dropped out; no one set out on its own; in the jungle, this meant food and safety.

She browsed through the cameras rapidly and patched the disparate images into a smooth, dynamic vision. Like a diving bird, she swooped past a glass wall hundreds of meters tall, and in the mirror was the strange, deformed reflection of the city with its flashing neon lights that engraved the mental patterns of consumerism into the retinas of all viewers, drifting and changing with their shifting gazes.

She saw everything, except herself.

Mimi saw even more: the lonesome, the gamblers, the addicted, the innocent . . . hiding in brightly lit or dark corners of the city, worth millions or penniless, enjoying the convenient life brought about by technology, pursuing stimuli and information loads unprecedented in the history of the human race. They were not happy, however; whatever the reason, it seemed that the capacity for joy had degenerated, had been cut off like an appendix, and yet the yearning for happiness persisted stubbornly like wisdom teeth.

Mimi felt a wave of pity for them, civilization's favorite children.

She found what she was looking for, a very-small-aperture terminal mobile satellite communications link installed on top of a van that was showing its age. The signs on the van indicated that the equipment belonged to some privately owned TV station. Mimi couldn't get into the network from the cameras, however; she had to make a real move.

We're running out of time. Let's go have some fun! She seemed to hear Mimi 1's exhortation to the flock of confused, excited tourists.

Don't be rash! Mimi 0 warned Mimi 1.

Why not? Mimi 1 smiled at her.

She cut off the video feed to conserve bandwidth and leapt into the void of the network; soon, she found the location of the satellite van, but the network on the vehicle wasn't hooked up to the VSAT system. Possible plans surfaced in Mimi's mind one after another, but none of them survived her rigorous analysis.

A gentle reminder: we have about three minutes and twenty-five seconds before the slow arrows catch up to us; only two minutes and thirty seconds before the spiders are alerted, Mimi 1 whispered into her ear.

Shut up! If you think you know better, why don't you take over? Mimi 0 said angrily.

It's very simple. Mimi 1 grabbed the wheel from her. *Let go.*

It was as if a speeding tour bus suddenly lost control and ran into a transparent wall. Mimi felt crushed between two immense forces and she couldn't breathe. The tourists who had been sitting behind her bounced toward the windshield like bullets, but there was no glass to hold them back. All the consciousnesses riding along with her were suddenly let loose, and, like hundreds of feral horses still dragging their reins, dashed in every direction before being tripped up by the weight of the bus. They commingled, conversed rapidly, and reached a compromise, coalescing into a unified force.

In a flash, Mimi knew their goal; alarm churned her stomach, but it was too late to stop them.

The tourists invaded the security system of the prison just outside the borders of Shantou proper. Using the cracking tools supplied by Mimi 1, they broke through all the digital locks for the cells and locked the prison guards in their offices. It took a few seconds before the prisoners understood what had happened, and, taking advantage of the incredible opportunity, they rushed out of their cells and emerged from the prison gate, heading for freedom in the rain.

Why did you do that? Mimi 0 raged at Mimi 1.

Wait and see. Mimi 1 gestured for her to return to the satellite van.

Within 2.37 seconds, Shantou's "Compound Eyes" system detected the unusual activity at the prison and raised a level 2 alert that mobilized the entire city's police force. The TV station that owned the van got wind of the news and ordered the crew to rush to the site for footage of the breaking news. Rapid response was the secret of their victory over the state-owned TV station. The green light for the VSAT system lit up, and the system began searching for and locking on to the satellite signal.

See? Mimi 1 made a joking bow. *After you.*

Mimi 0 ignored her and invaded the VSAT system, trying to redirect the antenna to point at a secret LOSS, or low-orbit server station.

There's too much terrestrial interference. We can't get a steady signal. The C-band used by the VSAT system overlapped in part with the frequencies for terrestrial microwave trunk lines, while the Ku-band, which had higher frequencies, was severely impeded by rain fade. Add to this the rapid progress of the van over uneven terrain, and the uplink signal just couldn't lock on to the server station.

I guess it's up to us again. Mimi 1's tone was teasing, as though she had been prepared for this. Once again, she was about to incite the out-of-control waste people, but this time Mimi 0 stopped her.

No . . . Her words trailed off weakly.

You know that we don't have much time. Mimi 1 shook her head. *We really have no other choice.*

The reveling tourists now behaved like an exploding piece of fireworks in reverse, gradually gathering at the center from their scattered state. The chaotic noises of their thoughts spontaneously harmonized into a rhythm, into a shout, and, like a powerful laser beam, struck the traffic-control-center systems. Signal lights across the city blinked wildly, and terrified drivers tried to dodge out of the way as cars collided and rolled over in an endless series of dull thuds. The spiked blares of horns were as dense as bramble on the noise monitors; columns of smoke unfurled into the sky; firelight flickered everywhere. Panicked passengers emerged from their disabled vehicles holding on to wounded limbs, dragging trails of blood across the road. Sobs, screams, explosions, breaking glass, and the unceasing rain wove into a complex tapestry of atonal music infused with intense pathos.

The satellite van stopped by a pileup involving dozens of cars. The cameraman excitedly jumped out of the cab with the HD camera over his shoulder to capture the scene for the breaking-news broadcast. Rubberneckers gathered to record the sight with their augmented-reality glasses and uploaded the clips to social media before even re-membering to help survivors. This was the second piece of hot news occurring within one minute, and as ripples spread over the network, the accidents took some of the attention away from the jailbreak.

I hope you didn't kill anyone, Mimi 0 said coldly.

I didn't. Mimi 1's tone was serene. *They did.*

The VSAT system finally connected with the low-orbit server station called Anarchy.Cloud. After confirming the link, Mimi, along with several hundred culprits responsible for the tragedies that had just swept the city, shot four hundred kilometers above the surface of the Earth through a carbon-fiber prism sector antenna. Here, the air was sparse, hot, filled with ions and free electrons, and for a few milliseconds, Mimi experienced the sweet illusion of being back in her real home.

"Time's up." Luo Jincheng's tone brooked no disagreement. "I'm going to find her even if it means I have to raze the entire village."

"Three minutes! No, just two!" Hard Tiger's voice trembled. "My rep-utation is on the line!"

Luo Jincheng said nothing as he stared at the remnants of the mobile phone, which he had crushed to pieces with his heel. Among the scat-tered components was a tiny bug, about the size of a bean sprout. *That pale-skinned swindler!* He no longer believed any promises made by

Scott Brandle. He had to find and hold on to the bargaining chip named Mimi. The dishonesty of the American enraged him; in addition to what should have been his by right, Luo was going to squeeze Brandle for even more concessions as compensation.

The bright dots in Hard Tiger's projection extinguished one by one until the few remaining stars were so sparse that they seemed to outline some imaginary object and form a new constellation, a constellation representing deceit, betrayal, and duplicity. But he couldn't tell what it really was.

"Bring me Knifeboy," Luo Jincheng whispered to one of his flunkies. "And gather everyone under my command."

War had never lacked sacrifices.

An almost naked Knifeboy entered the room crawling on all fours. One end of a thick iron chain was attached to his nose ring, and one of Luo's goons held the other end. The underling scolded Knifeboy and kicked him in the ribs. The muscles on Knifeboy's back bulged and a murderous glint shone from his eyes as drool hung from the corners of his mouth. The underling cursed and backed off, pulling the chain taut. A pain-racked Knifeboy lifted his face and breathed heavily.

"Why isn't he dressed?" Luo Jincheng was displeased.

"Whatever we put on him, he tears off and chews it up in his mouth. He's really like some rabid dog."

"Give me the leash." Luo grabbed the chain and caressed Knifeboy's scarred face, pity showing in his eyes. The fierce beast instantaneously turned into a tame sheep and curled up at the foot of Luo Jincheng, rubbing his neck against the legs of Luo's pants and whimpering at his master. It was as though his yearning for normal human emotional bonds, long suppressed, could only be expressed in this sick, twisted manner.

"Good doggie, good doggie. Daddy is going to feed you now." Luo Jincheng scratched Knifeboy behind the ears and watched with a complicated facial expression as the young man squinted his eyes with pleasure.

Luo Jincheng turned back to Hard Tiger's display. Only a single bright spot remained, flickering at the center of the universe. Before Hard

Tiger had a chance to zoom in to display the relevant details, the entire wall went out. There were no more stars, no more galaxy. In the darkness, only Hard Tiger's dry, hoarse voice echoed in the empty room. A faint, reddish spot hovered in the air, an afterimage.

"Boss Luo . . . all of Silicon Isle has been cut off the network."

```
Welcome to Anarchy.Cloud.

We provide information storage and remote computing ser-
vices from low orbit server stations. Our operating entity
belongs to no nation, political party, or corporation. As
far as practicable, we endeavor to help you circumvent laws
like the American PATRIOT Act and the supplements to the
European Union's Article 29 of the Data Protection Direc-
tive, which are designed to invade data privacy in the name
of antiterrorism.

We are a group of amateur wireless enthusiasts from
around the globe with a simple faith in pure libertarian-
ism. ☺ We hope our services can help you, during your brief
corporeal existence, to evade authority, resist control,
and embrace freedom, equality, and love. XOXO.
```

The message was automated. Here, four hundred kilometers above the surface of the planet, there were no cameras, no microphones, and no sensors. Everything that was not strictly necessary to the operation of a server farm in space had been stripped away in order to reduce mass and the accompanying costs.

I demand an artificial response. Mimi 1 issued the instruction. There was no answer.

What the hell are we doing here? Mimi 0 could no longer hold back.

```
I demand an artificial response. Only Nixon can go to
China. I repeat: Only Nixon can go to China.
```

296 // CHEN QIUFAN

What? Mimi 0 couldn't believe her virtual ears. Even more unbelievably, Anarchy.Cloud responded.

ANARCHY.CLOUD: Wow, looks like we got ourselves an old hand here. You better have a good reason for waking me up in the middle of the night, China girl.

MIMI: We need an independent network to link my friends and me together. It has to be fast!

ANARCHY.CLOUD: Oho, looks like you're in a heap of trouble. In another thirty seconds, the net guardian spiders will be on you; there's also a skilled archer on your tail; Typhoon Wutip is about to make landfall at your physical location, and the wind velocity near the eye is projected to reach 55 meters per second . . .

MIMI: The only thing you need to tell me is can you do it or not.

ANARCHY.CLOUD: Listen, baby, you lack the necessary equipment. What you are asking for is a fucking reverse intrusion. We've never tried anything like that . . . well, maybe once, but I can't guarantee anything . . . More important, what can you give us?

MIMI: The model of Hedy Lamarr's consciousness. I know you, or at least one of you, has a special hobby in collecting the consciousness models of celebrities.

ANARCHY.CLOUD: . . . Are you serious? I've never heard of anybody uploading her.

MIMI: She died on January 19, 2000, and her brain was immediately frozen. A couple of decades later, it was thawed out by NeuroPattern, Inc., who did the neural mapping.

ANARCHY.CLOUD: You sound pretty confident of your information.

MIMI: Think about it: she was the prettiest and smartest woman in the history of the human race. She was the inventor of CDMA, sharp, sensual, and she lived a life of endless adventure and glamour. With her, you can . . . do many things.

She knew she was attempting to control her opponent's reptilian brain. Though a bit of a dirty trick, it was effective.

ANARCHY.CLOUD: Hmm . . . One more question: how do we know you have her?

MIMI: That's easy. She was encrypted and disguised as a digital mushroom, which I downloaded and ingested. Thus . . . right now she's a part of me.

ANARCHY.CLOUD: Ah, that explains why you're so skilled with the frequency-hopping technique.

MIMI: Do we have a deaaaaaaaaaaaaaaa . . .

The cut-off data stream echoed in Mimi's mind. Her consciousness came into focus, and she saw again the cold, damp corrugated iron shack filled with the odor of mold. The storm had grown louder and fiercer, and the roof swayed from side to side. Li Wen came closer, his expression one of concern. His lips opened and closed, as though trying to tell her something important. Mimi got up and vertigo struck her as she collapsed into Li Wen's arms.

Since her awakening, Mimi had never experienced such a strong sense of uncertainty. She was tense, as though she was once again that insignificant waste girl of the past. The golden glow of the *mi* character on the back of her neck faded, and adrenaline filled her bloodstream.

She knew that the typhoon was about to strike.

17

"Don't move!"

Kaizong opened his eyes and saw the woman swinging the fish-bone-shaped knife at him. He tensed and reflexively squeezed his eyes shut. Abruptly, the binds around his wrist fell away. The rubber dildo had been sliced apart cleanly, the cut as smooth as a mirror.

Before he could offer a word of gratitude, the woman had dragged him out of the shed. Behind him came the sound of the steel frame collapsing, and all sorts of prostheses spilled in every direction from the impact of the falling roof, like a spontaneously exploding prosthetic monster.

Kaizong knelt in the mud as the rain drenched him. He trembled, partly from terror and partly from the cold. With quivering, pale lips, he finally managed to squeeze out a "Thank you."

"You're lucky. Mimi said she wanted to see you. If I had come another second later, you'd really be no different from that rubber dick." The woman laughed lasciviously and extended a powerful hand to him. "I'm Dao Lan."

The cold wind came through cracks in the corrugated-iron walls and scurried around the shack. Still, under the dim yellow light, the room felt much warmer than the outside. However, when Mimi saw Kaizong in his wet, dirty clothes, she didn't show any signs of intimacy. Instead, she simply walked up and examined him.

"How did you get yourself looking so filthy?"

"The rain was . . . really heavy," said Kaizong.

Mimi glanced at Dao Lan, who stood to the side, looking a bit embarrassed.

Kaizong continued. "You are not looking very healthy yourself."

"My energy consumption is . . . really heavy." Mimi tapped the self-injector attached to the inside of her elbow. "I'll be fine once the drip catches up. What are you doing here?"

"I want you to leave here, with me." Kaizong grabbed her cold hands, but the hands slid out of his grasp like slippery fish.

"I can't leave, at least not now." Mimi shook her head and avoided Kaizong's heated gaze. "The people here need me. They're in danger."

"*You're* in danger, don't you understand?" Kaizong turned away from the others and whispered, "The doctor told me that the blood vessels in your brain could rupture at any moment. Scott promised me that he'd bring you to America and find the best doctors for you."

Mimi didn't show any sign of fear or hesitancy, as he had feared. She simply gave him a light smile.

"My life hasn't been mine since that rainy night when I offered it to that spirit."

The waste people around her put their hands together in a gesture of prayer.

"If that is so"—Kaizong spat the words out from between his teeth—"then why did the spirit make us meet?" Now his body trembled from equal parts rage and cold.

Mimi's eyes softened. She wiped away the mud on Kaizong's face and rested her hands on his shoulders.

"Maybe this was all part of the spirit's plan, to bring you to me. Look at you: You're no longer the same as the old you. You're not an American, not a man of Silicon Isle, and not a waste person. You're one of us. You should fight with us."

Everyone in the room put their hands on Kaizong's shoulders.

Kaizong was speechless. He gazed at the girl in front of him, the most complicated, contradictory person in the world, exuding an incomprehensible draw that made everyone around her obey her, even look at her with an irrational devotion. He had once been moved by her pure ignorance, but now, he was the ignorant one. Under that frail exterior and gentle voice, was there a hidden demon skilled at pretense and acting who was waiting for the opportunity to tear off her mask and reveal herself?

Even more inexplicably, he found himself unfazed by this risk. His heart beat faster and his veins bulged. It was a fatal sensuality based on the attraction of the unknown.

"All right, I'll stay." *If she's not leaving,* Kaizong decided, *I'll just have to stay by her side.* He knew he couldn't protect her. But he wanted that feeling, not only to be part of Mimi's incomprehensible plan, not only to recover that sense of belonging that he had long not felt, but most of all, to feel the indescribable vitality this young woman brought with her, which made him feel *alive.* He was staying for himself, not for anyone else. A few loud barks drifted into the room, mixed with the sounds of the storm. The chipped dogs in the shack all started barking furiously at once in response.

"They're here." Gentleness disappeared from Mimi. She clenched her fists like a fierce warrior, and rage shot from her eyes.

The lackey running next to Luo Jincheng struggled stubbornly with the umbrella. Over and over, the raging wind turned the umbrella inside out. Finally, Luo had had enough of the farce and shouted at the young man to let go. The black umbrella rose into the air, spinning and tumbling like some giant bat, and vanished in the darkness.

Their cars became stuck in the mud not long after they entered Nansha Village. Holding on to the leash for Knifeboy, Luo Jincheng led about twenty of his most trusted thugs on foot to brave the fury of Typhoon Wutip and look for the final bright spot in Hard Tiger's projection. He could have commanded many more, but the sudden network cutoff made it impossible for him to get in touch with them. Luo was unhappy with the situation, but there was nothing he could do.

They broke into every shack along the way, cursing, smashing, threatening, bashing—just to find that waste girl.

The chipped dogs barked at them madly, an intermittent beat in the storm caused by the beating of a butterfly's wings, like the drumroll before a big performance.

Luo Jincheng raised his hand, indicating that everyone should gather around him. There was no need to comb through every shack. The woman they were looking for was standing in front of him. She appeared so tiny in the dark rain that it seemed a gust of wind could break her or blow her away. At first, the waste people from nearby shacks watched warily, but gradually, they emerged from their homes and stood behind Mimi. Their faces were resolute with anger, and the electronic accessories on their bodies glowed only faintly due to short circuits from the rain. Like statues, they stared at Luo and his men, the recycled prostheses on their bodies glinting with a crude light. They were like a long-dormant volcano that possessed great energy, just waiting for the moment of eruption.

"Please don't misunderstand. We're not here to cause trouble." Luo Jincheng wiped away the rain on his face to reveal a generous smile. "We're here to apologize."

A brief, confused murmur rippled through the ranks of the waste people. The expression on Mimi's face, however, didn't change. Kaizong stood right next to her, glaring at Luo.

The rattling of an iron chain. With a powerful kick, Luo sent the naked, wet Knifeboy sprawling in the mud between the two sides. Confused, he looked around, and pitifully crawled back to his master for comfort. But Luo kicked him even more forcefully in the ribs, and with a scream, he tumbled a few meters back and curled up on the ground.

"This is the culprit who abused Mimi. I'm giving him to you to do as you like."

No one knew what Luo Jincheng was really planning.

"But I also have a request." Luo Jincheng looked around at the crowd of waste people. "On the night that Knifeboy committed his crime, two of my men died horribly on Tide Gazing Beach. All the evidence indicates that there was only one other person there at the scene."

Like a gentleman, Luo bowed to Mimi, and lifted his left arm in a gesture of *please.*

"Mimi, can you tell me, and tell everyone present, who was the killer?"

Kaizong felt Mimi's body tense, and her expression changed by just a trace.

"And if that's impossible, perhaps Mimi could come with me to the police to help with the investigation?"

"Absolutely not!" Kaizong stepped forward and shielded Mimi from Luo. All the waste people shook off the rain, and anger returned to their faces. They had all seen or heard too many similar stories of "cooperation" with the police, and all of them ended tragically.

"What a hero!" Luo Jincheng applauded sarcastically. "A Silicon Isle native who speaks for the waste people! An American willing to sacrifice an eye to protect the Chinese! Chen Kaizong, I truly admire your loyalty to TerraGreen Recycling. Would you be so kind as to reveal how much you and your boss are getting as your fee for this deal so that you would go to so much trouble to ensure that Mimi is brought to the United States?"

"I don't know what you're talking about," Kaizong said. "I don't categorize people the way you do. All men and women are created equal."

"I'm sure that's what the Americans had in mind when they treated the rest of the world as their private landfill."

"You'll reap what you sow." Kaizong glared at Luo. "It's just a matter of sooner or later."

Luo Jincheng smiled and swept his hand decisively. "Since negotiation has failed, I have no choice but to resort to violence. Remember, everyone, I want Mimi alive, and I don't want the American harmed—well, not too much."

Body films of various colors lit up on Luo's thugs. Beneath the skin-tight, waterproof Lycra shirts wrapped around their bulging augmented muscles, the glowing patterns appeared as sigils climbing up their limbs and bodies. The metal electronic accessories on their hands and arms flashed and made crisp dings in the wind as they banged them against each other. The pack of thugs grinned wolfishly, and leisurely advanced against the waste people.

Kaizong grabbed Mimi and dragged her to safety behind the crowd. He could feel her struggling to get away, but he held on. No matter how much power this girl had once demonstrated, she had not yet recovered from the exertions of the trip to Shantou, leaving her in the body of a mere mortal. She needed powerful protection, but there was no super-hero here.

The secondhand prostheses of the waste people were clearly no match for the quality equipment worn by Luo's thugs. Dao Lan rushed forward, her fish-bone blade raised, but the thugs grabbed her arms and legs and one of the phosphorescent men forcefully detached the fish-bone blade from her arm and stabbed it into her chest. Blood spurted and mixed with the rain, soaking her agonized face.

Dull thuds of body striking body filled the night air. Luo's thugs adjusted their augmented muscles to the maximum enhancement setting, and the prostheses bulged disproportionately on their bodies, like cosmetic surgery gone wrong. They tore into the ranks of the waste people, breaking limbs and tearing off prostheses. In the tumult, the wounded waste people went limp like garbage bags with holes punctured in them, and cloudy white viscera dripped out. Tossed carelessly aside by Luo's henchmen, some of the waste people were impaled on sharp protrusions, some had their necks wrung, and still others tried to keep the innards from spilling out of their torn bodies as they howled desperately at the impassive sky, their screams soon overwhelmed by the roaring wind.

The noble victors displayed their artificially enhanced shells and stepped over the bodies of the lowly vanquished, gradually closing in on their ultimate prey, the waste girl named Mimi. As the raging rainstorm washed away the blood on the ground, the crimson streams coalesced and flowed toward the sea. The furious wind shook all things rooted to the ground, vowing to break them, shred them, scatter them to the sky, until these products of civilization, boastful of their refinement and ruggedness, had turned into smithereens sunken into the earth, where they would twinkle silently and wait for the next cycle of life.

The faces of the thugs no longer held any pride or dignity, no meaning, no goal, not even enjoyment; all that was left was the mechanical, repetitive act of killing.

There would be no winners in this game.

Mimi tried to reach the exoskeleton robot hiding in the shed with her consciousness, a repeat of the miracle that she had accomplished on that other rainy night long ago. But she couldn't.

Perhaps it was because the fructose mixture hadn't been able to replenish the ATP she had consumed in the draining trip to Shantou; perhaps it was because the screams from behind distracted her; but there was an explanation that Mimi was most reluctant to admit and that was also most likely to be true: she could call upon the power to leap across space, to enter the remote-control system of the battle armor without the aid of any wireless communication, and to become Mimi-mecha, only when she was on the verge of death.

It was just like the sacrificial beings who struggled painfully against death in palirromancy: the closer they were to death, the closer they were to the spirits.

She shielded herself from the inference of the outside world. The dying cries instantly became faint and distant, as though a thick wall had come down between her and them. Once again, Mimi focused all her energy, as though searching for a candle light in the endless night. Her face was pallid; her skin was clammy; and the muscles over her body spasmed. She had failed again.

Mimi. She seemed to hear some voice caressing her ear out of the rain.

Mimi. The cry seemed closer. She let down her shield.

Mimi—the bellowed name was like a thunderclap at her back that extended into a low, deep, continuous rumbling. Shocked, Mimi turned around and saw Kaizong shouting her name in extreme slow motion, his facial muscles twisting and deforming like a semisolid. Behind him, blood-covered Luo clan thugs were leaping and running in similar slow motion. The phosphorescent patterns on their bodies left glowing trails through the air, like a solidified flood rolling toward her.

Kaizong tried to stop them with his body, but a deformed, bulging arm swept at him, and he rose into the air, floated over the crowd, and fell toward a mountain of e-waste. The mountain collapsed and buried him underneath.

The beasts did not pause but headed straight for Mimi. She could almost smell the stench spewing out of their mouths.

The augmented-reality glasses on her face lit up.

Mimi's consciousness gushed forth like the flood from a burst dam. All her imprisoned and repressed energy was released at once, and the pleasure of freedom filled all time and space. She knew that Anarchy. Cloud had succeeded. *We have a deal.* She smiled, and within milliseconds connected to the steel god of war of Tide Gazing Beach.

It's time.

With a loud explosion, Mimi-mecha broke out of the shed. Twisted metal fragments flew in every direction, and a few sliced through the limbs of the slow-moving phosphorescent men, suspended in air, and stuck into the ground. Mimi was still unused to the weight of this massive skeleton, and momentum carried her into a few of the thugs, trampling them. She lost her balance and fell slowly like a toppled tree at another thug lying on the ground, paralyzed with terror. Mimi tried to hold herself up with her steel arms, but ended up crushing half of the man's skull and an arm.

The wolfish horde were stunned by this abrupt new invader in their midst. Yet their murderous rage could not be quelled. They tried to surround the steel hulk of Mimi-mecha in an attempt to discover and ex-

ploit a weakness. In their limited experience, such a gargantuan robot
had to be slow and clumsy.

They were wrong.

Mimi-mecha extended the supersonic blades hidden in her arms.
Vibrating at the rate of forty thousand times per second, the blades cut
through molecular links with practically no resistance while simultaneously cauterizing the wounds with intense heat. They were truly
weapons that killed without spilling blood. She danced gracefully, like
some spinning lathe whirling to the syncopated rhythms of jazz. The
raindrops turned into steam as they struck the blades, and anyone who
tried to approach her would leave with an unforgettable memento—
clean, smooth, bloodless stumps as smooth as mirrors, with a faint aroma
from charred meat.

Very soon, SBT had more than a dozen new consumers for their prostheses.

She looked around. Among the fleeing figures, she did not see Luo
Jincheng. But she noticed another gift: Knifeboy holed up in a dark corner. Mimi-mecha leapt to him and lifted the chain attached to his nose
ring. She enjoyed the faint crackle from breaking cartilage as well as the
animal-like screams. Terror had deformed Knifeboy's face beyond recognition, and tears and mucus spilled everywhere. He struggled to get
away, but dared not apply too much strength. Finally, he lost control of
his sphincter, and dark excrement slowly flowed down his thighs.

Mimi, disgusted, raised her right arm. She was going to cleave him
in half down the middle the way a butcher might dress a pig carcass.

Don't kill him, Mimi 1 said.

Why not? Mimi 0 retorted angrily. With a jolt, she realized how close
she had come to becoming the other Mimi subconsciously, like an octopus changing its color endlessly to match its image in the mirror.

Save him for someone who wants to kill him even more than you do.

Mimi-mecha dropped Knifeboy like a bag of trash, wrapped the iron
chain around his neck twice, and tied it to the water pipe. She departed
from the steel shell and left this spirit in front of Knifeboy. Like the

Buddha's hand that had pressed down on the Monkey King, this inanimate guardian would guarantee that Knifeboy would not dare to escape.

Around her, everything was in ruins. The typhoon had conspired with the evil in men's hearts to complete a sacrificial rite. Except that the spirit the greedy men had summoned was an uncontrollable force that was going to destroy them.

Mimi went to help a wounded man who had lost his limbs. The painful sight activated her mirror neurons, and she empathized with him. Pain and desperation pressed against her consciousness and made it hard for her to breathe. Trembling, she connected to the network and reached out to the other waste people, calling for help.

She searched through the trash heap for Kaizong, tossing junk every which way as though she had gone mad. She found him, finally, lying on the ground. His wounds appeared fairly light, and after repeated, gentle calls from Mimi, he slowly opened his eyes. Weeping with joy, the iron grip over her emotions imposed by her other personality momentarily shattering, Mimi held Kaizong's muddy face and sealed his mouth with a deep kiss.

Kaizong felt a wave of dizziness and gazed up at the deep sky. Faint purple-red lights flickered behind the clouds like in a dream. He still couldn't quite believe all that had happened and all that was still happening; perhaps it was all a hallucination forcefully inserted into his consciousness by another power.

Scott straddled the Ducati and gazed at the storm-blurred Nansha Village in the distance.

Through his night-vision glasses, the cold raindrops appeared even darker than night. The wind drove the dark, slanted lines slowly across the sky, while the seams of the shacks in the village leaked heat, limning them with bright white outlines. A brutal fight was over, and the rain washed away the residual heat of blood and lost limbs, which cooled and darkened until they melded into the surroundings, dead.

It's not time yet. Scott congratulated himself on having had the foresight to not drive a car here. He watched as the clumsy metal boxes floated in the water, where they were impelled by rolling waves into spinning eddies; some were sunken into the quagmire the muddy roads had turned into; still others were trapped under tree trunks and branches broken by the typhoon. The nimble giant beetle he rode, however, could navigate through the flooded terrain with ease, stopping on a dime, turning in place, squeezing through narrow road segments, dodging tumbling utility poles, and dashing up steep inclines under full throttle.

He saw a dog paddling madly in the water.

The terrain of Silicon Isle resembled the irregular caldera of an extinct volcano, though with a far gentler slope. At this moment, Scott was at the highest point on the rim. Away from the center, the land sloped down to the e-waste-processing zone, extending all the way to the sea. Toward the center was the depression in which most of the inhabitants of Silicon Isle Town lived.

The ancient builders of Silicon Isle had constructed an elaborate system of drainage ditches to prevent flooding, a common problem in the region's monsoon-driven subtropical maritime climate. Taking advantage of gravity, the system of terraced ditches overcame the adverse conditions of nature. However, after hundreds of years, the world had been transformed by civilization far beyond the imagination of the ancients: the soil had grown poisoned, salinized, and desertified; and the ditches had collapsed, become clogged, or been repurposed for acid baths. The overflowing rainwater could no longer be smoothly diverted. Like trapped beasts, the surging currents threatened to devour and destroy everything.

Not even feng shui can save you now.

Scott watched as the water level rose in Silicon Isle Town. Many awakened from their slumber and discovered that the flood was already in their homes: beds were submerged; wires sparkled as they short-circuited; the network was cut off and there was no way to call for help; the terrified cries of babies interwove with the barking of dogs;

waterlogged houses collapsed under the buffeting gales, crashing into the flood. Outside, the cold rain continued without any sign of letting up.

Some never even got the chance to wake up.

Like a statue, Scott stood transfixed in place. The faint beam of the lighthouse swept by, chiseling his sharp features with light and shadows. Subconsciously, he reached into his waterproof pack to search for the two gifts from Coltsfoot Blossom and only felt a sense of relief as his fingers touched the hard material. A pale blue tongue of flame leapt up from the apex of the tallest building in Silicon Isle, and the light from the dissipating arc lit up a struggling figure not too far away from Scott.

St. Elmo's fire. Scott focused on the figure and smirked coldly. It was Luo Jincheng.

Scott took note of all the available routes. He wasn't going to make the same stupid mistake that Luo Jincheng was making now. Like some dog who had had enough of terror, Luo was irrationally aiming straight for home.

Scott, who was standing at the highest vantage point, saw that the road Luo was on would soon run into the most turbulent of waters.

18

"It's flooding!"

Mimi sat on the ground, leaning against the side of the bed. Next to her was the equally weak, half-kneeling Kaizong, who squeezed her cold, shivering hands. From the earpieces of the augmented-reality glasses came a cacophony of conversation carried by the temporary waste-people satellite network built by Anarchy.Cloud.

"This is divine justice!" "Absolutely. I hope they all drown." "Let's go watch them die." ". . . watch them die . . ." ". . . watch . . . die . . ." ". . . die . . ." ". . . . . ."

The noisy talk, filled with increasing anger, beat against her eardrums. The voices overlaid each other, interfered with each other, and mixed into a violent piece of rumbling atonal music. Suddenly, a girl's voice broke in like a silver needle striking ground, and all the other voices became silent.

"But the ambulances won't be able to get here either," the girl said.

The minority, who had held their tongues earlier, now cautiously voiced their opinions.

"All the police have been diverted to Shantou to chase down the escaped prisoners and to rescue car-accident victims."

"We are responsible."

No one spoke. No one wanted to admit to being a murderer, even if only indirectly.

"This is a natural disaster that no one could have predicted. We're not at fault."

"If we just stand by and watch them die, how is it any different from killing them?"

"The difference is whether there's blood on your hands, you idiot!"

"The blood has already stained your name and soaked into your soul. Your children will be disgraced as the progeny of murderers."

"Our children will suffer no matter what. Don't forget, we're waste people."

"But we can't view ourselves as waste people! We're human beings. People! No different from them."

"Shut the fuck up! If you want to go die yourself, no one's stopping you. But spare me your fucking moral lectures."

"Have you forgotten how the Luo clan tried to kill us? And you want to go rescue these animals, these scum?"

"Listen to yourself! That's what I call real waste. You can't even tell the difference between the Luo clan and Silicon Isle."

Mimi's face was bloodless. The unceasing demands of her excessive energy consumption had forced her to the edge of total collapse. The self-injector forced the last few drops of fructose into her veins. She didn't even have the energy to raise her voice.

"Stop." She whispered softly. "All of you, shut up."

All the sharp, crude, hesitant voices vanished.

"Do you remember what it was like in Shantou? No one argued; no one doubted. All of you made a decision together in the briefest of moments and chose a single direction for the collective. I don't know if that choice was right or wrong, but I think all of you had accepted that decision and its consequences . . ."

Are you sure about this? Mimi 0 asked. Sepia scenes flashed through her mind: the disdainful looks from Silicon Isle natives; the waste people timorously kneeling at their feet; the abuse by Knifeboy; the cruel, cold face of Luo Jincheng. She shuddered, and a physiological disgust dissolved into her blood along with the chemicals. It was beyond rage.

Unless you have a better solution, Mimi 1 replied. *I know you don't want to save them.*

If you give the order, they will save them. They worship you like a goddess, Mimi 0 spat out. *All those brothers and sisters who have bled and died to protect my life—their limbs and bodies are still lying out there in the mud and the rain and the wind like a pile of trash. I haven't even had a chance to record their names. And yet, here we're already discussing whether to save the families of the murderers.*

That is not my style. Mimi 1 chuckled coldly. Mimi 0's scalp tightened. *Don't forget, a goddess always has two faces.*

What is the point of all this? You killed them, and now you want to save them? Mimi 0's emotions grew more turbulent, consuming even more energy. The edges of her vision began to deform, blur, and faint pink cracks appeared.

It's not me, my dear; it's them. Mimi 1 seemed to shake her head, or perhaps the world swayed before her eyes. *If you stand at a high enough vantage point, you'll see that I'm not only saving the Silicon Isle natives, but also the waste people.*

"Now, let's choose."

A gray circle appeared in Mimi's vision, and two pie-slice shapes, one red and one blue, appeared in the circle. Both slices gradually grew in area. It was hard to tell which was bigger. Finally, the two slices, now each a semicircle, touched. The dividing line trembled as though the two sides were engaged in a vicious fight. As everyone waited for the final decision, the blue half jumped slightly and ate away a thin wedge of the red portion.

"We'll save them," Mimi announced. A cheer went up in her ears, mixed with some scattered complaints. Yet, she could distinctly hear that the complainers were also relieved and let out a held breath. Now, any further excuses would be stumbling blocks for the collective, and all plans and acts would be highly efficient. This was the decision of all.

The waste people organized themselves. Pieces of low-density silicone rubber waste were tied together into rescue rafts; bundles of plastic fiber were twisted into safety cables; translucent, impermeable artificial skin and LED bulbs were turned into emergency lights. The waste people divided into groups and followed the main thoroughfares of Silicon Isle Town to search for trapped survivors, directing them to places of refuge or high points, away from the turbulent eddies and undercurrents, and keeping in constant contact with them through augmented-reality glasses. They also hoped to find an open path so that the hospital's ambulances could get to Nansha Village, where dozens of severely wounded waste people needed medical attention.

Only Li Wen remained where he was, his face stiff as iron. His hatred for the Silicon Isle natives was so deep that a simple vote could not change his mind.

"Brother Wen," Mimi called to him. "I know there's something in your heart that will not let you go.

"But we're not only saving lives; we're also going to open the eyes of the souls of the Silicon Isle natives. If we allow ourselves to be filled with hatred, then they've won. We have to show them that we're not polluting waste or parasitic animals. We're human, the same as them. We laugh, we cry, we pity, we sympathize. We can even risk our lives to rescue them. We must extend our hand and see how the Silicon Isle natives respond."

The corners of Li Wen's mouth spasmed, as though he was struggling to hold his emotions in check. He croaked, "They killed my sister."

"I know. I've always known." Mimi put her hand on the trembling shoulders of the man. "You saved a copy of that video in your glasses. You hid it in the deepest part of the root directory and encrypted it so that you wouldn't have to be reminded of it—"

"But I haven't been able to forget it for even a second." Li Wen's lips trembled violently, and tears spilled from his eyes.

"Shhh, shhhh." Mimi cradled his head and caressed him as though comforting a baby. She put her lips next to Li Wen's ear and whispered, "I understand. I know everything. It's too late for your sister. But you still have a chance to ensure that no one else's sister or children will suffer the same fate. If you can accomplish that, do you think you'll finally feel free?"

Li Wen lifted his tear-filled eyes and stared at Mimi, unwilling to look away for even a second.

"Go find the mecha. It's guarding the answer you seek," said Mimi. "You can now control it directly."

Kaizong watched Mimi muttering into the empty air. Although he couldn't see what she was seeing or hear what she was hearing, based on snippets he heard from her, he could deduce how things were going. Kaizong's feelings were mixed. He wasn't sure if he should be pleased by this hint of a dawn of reconciliation or be pained by its late arrival and the heavy price that had been paid.

He watched as Li Wen let go and sobbed, and then watched as Mimi prayed softly like the Virgin Mary and put the augmented-reality glasses on Li Wen. He could see the images in the glasses faintly reflected on Li Wen's face. Gradually, Li Wen's body stiffened, as though he had seen the face of Medusa and been turned to stone.

Mimi whispered into Li Wen's ear again. Li got up and rushed out of the door into the falling rain.

"What did he see?" Kaizong asked. "What made him so mad?"

Mimi, who had recovered a bit of color, looked at Kaizong and lightly brushed her fingers over his right eye. He closed the eye instinctively, enjoying the gentle, loving touch.

"You'll see," Mimi said softly, "with the best eye."

A harsh white light exploded in front of Kaizong's right eye, soon radiating into colorful rays. The colors were so rich and varied that they exceeded the sum of all his previous visual experiences. The colorful rays seemed to emerge from some infinitely distant point at the center of his visual field and shot at him, causing him to experience the vertigo associated with high-speed flight. In another moment, the rays stopped, reversed direction, and gathered at the center, where they formed into a cone of light whose tip was pointed straight at his eye, as if intending to stab into his pupil until infinity had been embedded in his skull.

The world in Kaizong's eye expanded at an unbelievable rate. Everything was going to retreat into the distance, was going to be millions of light-years away. His consciousness condensed into a tiny speck of interstellar dust drifting in boundless space-time. A feeling of grandeur exceeding the experiences of all known life held him. It was so sacred, so sublime, but without the slightest hint of oppression or fear; it was like returning to some warm source, the womb that preceded the eons, the origin of the universe. A deity that he had never worshiped.

He wanted to cry, but he could not. Every inch of his skin seemed to have been freed from the control of the autonomous nervous system and trembled continuously.

The light cone dissolved, and the colorful rays shrank into dots that, like fog or sand, struck his artificial retina, inciting billions of dense, tiny, rainbow-hued ripples. The dots of light did not stop. They traversed his optic nerves and attempted to pierce into his cortex. Kaizong felt spasms of slight pain, like the experience of ejaculation, accompanied by a pleasure that could not be denied. Subconsciously, he wanted to cover his eye with his hand to evade this sense of shame that was the product of civilization.

"What do you see?" Mimi asked, smiling. She tentatively held his hand.

"I see . . ." His chest heaved. "It is like . . ." He struggled to find the words but finally gave up the futile effort. With eyes puffy and swollen from crying, he gazed at Mimi. "I think I understand."

The preinstalled network module on the Cyclops VII activated. He connected to the network shared by the waste people.

"Welcome, welcome!" The voices seemed to come from his ear and brain at the same time, both far away and nearby. It was as though the sensitivity of his visual cortex had been enhanced significantly, leading to synesthetic effects. "You're now one of us."

Kaizong saw Silicon Isle under the typhoon's assault, an unfamiliar sight: the streets had turned into zigzagging channels for the surging floodwater; cars floated like little boats, spinning in the water, bumping into each other, and drifting with the swift flow; houses poked their black roofs over the surface like reefs, and slowly disintegrated, broke apart, collapsed into the water; the trees that remained standing showed only their crowns, and naked children held on to the branches tightly, their fearful eyes sparkling like some species of tropical bat; the powerful wind seemed to make the entire world tremble; between the flashes of the emergency lights, debris of all kinds swept by like frightened birds dropping out of the sky.

All of this was accompanied by singing voices like a boys' choir. In the dark night, the plaintive sound was like a dull knife that scraped over the nerves inch by inch. He knew it was an auditory hallucination.

He saw a hand reach out to grab one of the branches and steady the raft; more hands reached out to help the children on the trees come down onto safety.

A trace of warmth came into the singing.

Tires attached to ropes were tossed to those struggling in the water. Some jumped into the water and swam for the old men and women who were about to be pulled under by the currents. Some removed the debris that clogged the openings of the drainage system. Shorted wires sparkled overhead while body films flashed in the surging torrents, marking possible undercurrents and whirlpools. The rafts tirelessly patrolled back and forth, carrying trapped refugees to more solidly constructed schools and public buildings.

Gradually, the expressions of the Silicon Isle natives turned from fear, apprehension, and suspicion to gratitude.

Thank you, they said.

Thank you, all of you, even more said.

The voices of the choir rose in great harmony, bright and clear, like a crystal tree reaching up toward the sky.

A familiar figure appeared in one of the perspectives Kaizong was looking through: a plump, middle-aged man in the water was holding desperately onto a branch with one hand to avoid being swept away by the flood. But a closer examination showed that his hand was some distance from the branch. The view zoomed in, and Kaizong saw that a strand of Buddhist prayer beads was wrapped around his wrist with the other end hooked to the pliable branch. The slender rope precariously resisted the combined force of the swelling current and his body weight.

The view shifted to the man's face: wet, pale, a few thin strands of hair messily stuck to his forehead, an expression of exertion. Luo Jincheng.

Again and again, he struggled to gain his footing in the raging current, but each time, his legs were swept out from under him, and he fell back into the water. He desperately gazed at the strand of prayer beads, slowly sliding off the branch, and muttered a prayer that could not be heard.

Save him or no? Kaizong wasn't sure if he was asking the others or himself. An answer soon presented itself.

The people whose perspective Kaizong looked through took some time to come to a decision, but ultimately, the raft approached Luo Jincheng. Due to the terrain, the current was more rapid here than elsewhere, and the raft struggled to hold steady a few feet from the man in the water. A hand extended to Boss Luo, once the master of Silicon Isle, but now hanging on to a strand of wooden beads for dear life.

Kaizong smiled at the virtual space.

Luo stared at the hand extended by a waste person. A complex series of expressions flashed across his face, as though this simple gesture was the most difficult decision of his life.

He lowered his eyes, shook his head, and finally lifted his left hand out of the water. Almost simultaneously, the strand of ebony prayer beads broke apart. Having lost his only support, Luo Jincheng was dunked into the water headfirst, and the fierce torrents swallowed him like a herd of wild beasts. Soon, not even a single trace of him was left on the surface.

Kaizong felt Mimi's hand tighten in his, her fingernails digging into her palm. The pain seemed a reflection of the complex mix of emotions that she could not express. His mind wandered for a moment, and his eyes left the shared image transmitted over the wireless link to seize upon the tall figure flashing across the window. The man dashed into the shack with a swiftness that seemed unbelievable.

It was his boss, the TerraGreen Recycling project manager: Scott Brandle.

Li Wen ran through the gale. His slender frame swayed to dodge the debris carried on the wind. Fire burned in his eyes.

Mimi had retrieved the video that he had sealed away. Those disgusting colors and the rhythmically bouncing perspective reappeared. Mimi froze the video and zoomed in on the anguished face of the girl, and then advanced the video frame by frame. Li Wen's heart bled as he stared at that face, the cherished face that was never far from his thoughts and that he could not bear to look at now for even a second. Mimi stopped on a certain frame, which didn't seem to look very different from the others. Then she zoomed in even further until the girl's dark irises filled the view, two abysses of despair that devoured all light. Software converted the image from color to grayscale, the jagged edges automatically smoothed by subsequent passes. A few pixels glowed with a faint red like a wound, and gradually brightened.

Li Wen finally saw clearly the image reflected in the eyes of his dead little sister: a deep red flame. Rage instantly petrified his body.

He could not forgive himself for having passed by that man countless times; he had even helped him, solved his problems, adjusted his body film with the flame design. After Knifeboy had abused Mimi the same way, he had focused on how to exploit the incident as a bargaining chip. But he had never imagined that his desire for vengeance had already been ground down and turned to numbness as a result of the meticulous plotting that occupied him day after day.

Finally, he saw the black battle armor standing in the wind like a tombstone. At its feet was a creeping figure like a groveling dog.

Countless times, Li Wen had rehearsed in his imagination how he would kill his enemy. He imagined cutting off the man's penis and testicles and stuffing them into his mouth, breaking all his limbs, poking out his eyes, piercing his eardrums, cutting off his tongue, destroying all his senses and hooking him up to a life-support system so that he would live out the rest of his life in an interminable abyss of darkness, silence, and pain.

He had been waiting for this day so long; yet, now that it was here, he was seized with an unprecedented panic. He had never killed a man, at least not with his own hands. Li Wen deliberately slowed down. He looked around. No one was in sight; only the ruins swept by the wind and rain. He wanted to find an appropriate weapon.

A rusty crowbar. He swung it a few times, leaving a few trails in the mud. The splatter covered him like blood.

Fuck you! He cursed at himself silently. *That is the scum who killed your sister, you fucking coward.*

He swung the crowbar a couple more times through the air, took a deep breath, and advanced on Knifeboy.

Knifeboy was on the ground on all fours. The chain around his neck was taut, yet his body was extended even farther, as if trying to escape from something. Li Wen poked at his back with the crowbar. There was no reaction. He flipped Knifeboy over, and what he saw made him stumble backward, almost falling over.

The chain was tightly wound around Knifeboy's neck, which was now a purplish red. His face was a dark green. His eyes were wide open while his tongue stuck out of his mouth and drooped down to his chest. Between his legs was a mixture of excrement and ejaculate, like a man executed by hanging. Compression of the carotid and vertebral arteries had caused his brain to die from insufficient blood supply, and the liquid in his body had spilled out when the smooth muscles in his lower body lost tension.

Li Wen tossed away the crowbar. Standing before the corpse, he felt empty. The wind abruptly stopped, as did the rain, leaving an unexpected quiet. He stared up at the sky, at a loss, and an opening appeared in the thick cloud cover like a deep well, through which the infinitely clear light of the stars shone. He drank in the sight of the stars hungrily, as if seeking to understand the mystery of the universe.

That eye gazed back at him.

Li Wen shuddered. Some force seemed to have poured into his body through the medium of starlight and filled the entire universe. There was no more hatred, no more anger, only a deep sense of awe. He closed his eyes and felt that power with all his heart. In his mind, his sister's face was superimposed over the starry sky, twinkling. She finally smiled, as she used to. Li Wen could no longer hold back the scalding tears that rolled down his face, as if the deep freeze in his heart had finally thawed and given him complete release.

After the eye of the storm, an even fiercer storm awaited him.

"Why are you here, Scott?"

"To take you away from here."

"Now?" Kaizong hesitated. "But Mimi is really weak right now. She might not . . ."

"Let me take a look." Scott approached Mimi with his right hand hanging at the waist. He extended his left hand to feel for Mimi's carotid artery. Mimi lifted her blurry eyes to give him a glance, and her fawn-like expression made Scott's heart clench. But he didn't hesitate as his right hand shot out, held an injector—one of the gifts from Coltsfoot Blossom—against Mimi's neck, and pressed the trigger.

"What are you doing?" Kaizong knocked the injector out of Scott's hands.

A terrified Mimi stared at Scott and struggled to get up, but in another second, her head drooped and she fell onto the bed like a boneless octopus.

"Don't worry. It's just a tranquilizer. For safety."

"Get the hell away from her!" Kaizong shoved him out of the way. "I can't believe Luo Jincheng was telling the truth, you greedy bastard."

"I'm sorry, Kaizong." Scott did look regretful. "The world is far more complicated than you understand. I hope that someday I'll have a chance to explain myself to you."

"Explain now! Otherwise you're not leaving this room with her."

Scott lowered his head, apparently giving Kaizong's suggestion serious consideration. He sighed lightly. Then, like a lightning strike, he crouched and swept one of his legs at Kaizong's lower body. Kaizong fell and Scott leapt up to straddle him, clamping a powerful hand around his throat. No matter how Kaizong struggled, Scott's iron grip remained fast like a robotic arm.

Kaizong's face turned red, and gurgling croaks came from deep in his throat. Strength seemed to leave his limbs, and his flailing arms gently slapped against Scott like soft tentacles, and then slipped onto the ground.

Finally, he stopped moving. His eyes looked like a pair of freshwater pearls that had been covered by a layer of condensation.

Scott let go of Kaizong's neck. Avoiding Kaizong's sightless gaze, he again apologized. Picking up the unresisting body of Mimi, he stepped out of the shack and draped her over the seat of the Ducati in front of himself. He started the motorcycle, and the wheels left a deep wound in the mud that extended into the unknown future.

19

This is a dream, Mimi told herself. *None of this is real.*

But what dream could match the insanity of what she was seeing?

She saw herself walking toward the sea. The water parted, opening a path down the middle, and she walked into the canyon between the two gargantuan walls made of seawater, each a few hundred meters tall, pinching the sky into a narrow slit. The color of each wall grew darker toward the bottom, turning from baby blue to a dark green that was almost black. The canyon extended into infinity, and shifting luminescent patterns swept by her as though she were in some high-speed tunnel. The farther she walked, the more surprised she became. The central canyon wasn't the only path; numerous narrow side branches dotted the walls, zigzagging into the darkness, perhaps concealing unknown terrors. Mimi dared not tarry and passed by with only the briefest of glances.

The canyon seemed to have no end—until she saw the figure of herself leisurely coming from the other direction, as though she were walking into a mirror.

But she knew it wasn't a mirror.

The two Mimis stared at each other, their expressions stiff, as though both were trying to anticipate the other's next move. Finally, one of them grinned slyly.

"Must we continue to play this silly imitation game?" she said. "I guess we've proven that our mirror neurons haven't been completely suppressed."

Mimi finally could be sure that the girl she faced was Mimi 1, and she herself, of course, was Mimi 0.

"You could have stopped him!" Mimi accused.

"I'm sorry, darling. I was very weak at the time. Also . . . I was distracted by your little boyfriend."

"Shut up!"

"He used a military-grade tranquilizer. It got through the blood-brain barrier too quickly. I only had time to break off a small set of synaptic connections to preserve the core of your consciousness before your frail human body decided to give up."

"Can you do anything else? What does this foreigner want with me?"

"I've already sped up the metabolism in your brain, hoping to bring more regions back online. But you know that you're already low on the supply of ATP. We're playing with your life." Mimi 1 looked worried. "Luckily, he wants *me*, so your life should be safe. Your abduction by Scott has already been shared with our brothers and sisters through the augmented-reality glasses, and hopefully there's still time."

"O Mistress, would you like a display of humble gratitude from me, your lucky, surviving parasite?" Sarcasm dripped from Mimi 0's voice.

"You're wrong, precious. You, me, even the entire human race—we're all parasites." Mimi 1 was unflustered. "Besides, surviving isn't necessarily better than a clean death. Do you remember those chimpanzees? If we fell into their hands, our fates would be thousands of times worse."

The bloody scenes flashed before Mimi 0's eyes. The pain made her close her eyes and wrap her arms about her head.

"What *are* you?" She squeezed out the question that had been plaguing her all this time.

"A nuclear explosion that has been slowed down a million times; a by-product of billions of years of convergent evolution; your second personality and life insurance; the free will that emerges from quantum decoherence. I'm accidental; I'm inevitable. I'm a new error. I'm the master and the slave. I'm the huntress and the prey." The other Mimi laughed, a sound colder than ice. "I'm only a beginning."

An indescribable shock made it impossible for Mimi 0 to answer. All those abstract, abstruse ideas seemed at this moment like echoes in her soul, things she already knew and understood. All she had needed was a tiny spark, and then, enlightenment.

"There's something else I haven't been able to figure out." Mimi 0 frowned with puzzlement.

"Oh?"

"Why did you go through so much trouble to get to Anarchy.Cloud? Just so you could construct the communication link between the waste people and trigger the cutoff of Silicon Isle from the network? That doesn't make sense."

A glint appeared in Mimi 1's eyes.

In an instant, Mimi 0 realized the answer. That model of Hedy Lamarr's consciousness uploaded to Anarchy.Cloud. Was that really all it was? "A persona backup? Did you hide a copy of yourself inside— 'passage under cover of darkness'?"

"Very good. You've indeed grown clever." Mimi 1 smiled. "I have a question as well. When Luo Jincheng was swept away by the flood, you experienced pain. Why?"

"He's evil. But he's still a person, a human being like me. When I was little, my mother often told me, a person should—"

"Humans are always exaggerating the effects of culture," Mimi 1 interrupted. "Pity, sympathy, shame, fairness . . . morality. These things have long been engraved in your posterior cingulate cortex, your frontal gyrus and superior temporal sulcus, and the dorsolateral and ventromedial regions of your prefrontal cortex, perhaps even long before the origin of the human species. These neural patterns allowed you to empathize with the pain and fear of other individuals. In the long process of evolution, this physiological foundation helped the human species to overcome or suppress various instincts of primates—selfishness, incestuous sexual desires, brutal competition, and so on—by substituting the bonds of clan identity and cooperation in place of conflict, elevating group harmony above individual sexual desire, instituting morality over force. This was how the human race survived and thrived as a species.

"But modern technology has damaged this foundation. Technology addicts indulging in overdoses of dopamine have destroyed their synaptic connections and become ill with moral failings. In one experiment, the test subjects had to choose between saving a ship full of passengers by tossing a heavily wounded individual overboard, or doing nothing. All those with damaged moral-emotive brain regions chose to kill in order to save, while the normal subjects chose to do nothing. The diseased think of life as some zero-sum game in which there must be winners and losers, even at the expense of the interests of others, including their lives. This is a planetwide plague.

"The Silicon Isle natives, the waste people, you, all of you are suffering from this disease. I chose this path to cure you so that the game may continue."

Mimi 0 knew that this wasn't the entire truth, but before she could ask more questions, a low rumbling roar came from the depths of the sea, filling their ears like whale song. Mimi 0 watched the rippling lights in the sea walls with trepidation; they seemed about to collapse at any moment and devour everything.

"What's happening?"

"The good news is that your consciousness is reawakening," Mimi 1 shouted at her. "The not-so-good news is that we've got to get out of here."

"How do we leave?" Mimi 0 shouted back at the top of her lungs.

"Hold on tight!" Mimi 1 grabbed her by the hand and flew up toward the top of the sea wall.

Filled with terror, Mimi 0 watched as the towering walls of water gradually closed up beneath her. The lofty sea mountains collided, resulting in giant waves hundreds of meters tall. She suddenly realized that the canyon she had been walking through was the gap between the two hemispheres of a brain, and those zigzagging branches were the complicated, dense folds and creases of the cortex. The brain-sea gradually turned from solid to liquid, and the luminous patterns sped up, illuminating the boundless, raging ocean of information.

The sky was filled with dark lines that expanded outward from the center of the visual field; light scattered from them in iridescence.

"We're being transported at a high speed. The conducting particles in your brain cause these visual artifacts as they move through the Earth's magnetic field." Mimi 1 paused in her explanation, and then added, "We have to return to the surface of consciousness immediately. I've heard the call."

Kaizong bounced up like a reanimated jumping corpse. After a long, painful scream, air refilled his lungs. He hacked and coughed violently until his stomach turned and thick strings of drool dripped from his mouth onto the ground. He saw that he was lying in the mud outside, and in front of him loomed the hideous face of the exoskeleton. Rain continued to fall from the gray dawn sky.

"I rushed over as soon as I saw what happened through the view shared by your glasses." Li Wen appeared from behind the giant robot, his expression looking unsettled. "I got here too late for Mimi, but at least I can help you."

Kaizong struggled to stand up on his unsteady legs and almost fell again; Li Wen hurried over and helped support him.

"We've got to catch them. Scott wants to bring Mimi out of the country." Kaizong gasped for breath. "Do you know how to track them?"

"The fastest way to cross the border from Silicon Isle is to head for the sea. I can hack into the dispatch center of the Shantou Maritime Bureau. All ships departing the port must transmit their positioning signals through the data hub in the dispatch center to dock with the satellites. I don't think your boss would try to navigate blindly. In this weather, that would be tantamount to suicide."

"How long would it take you to get in there?"

"If we're lucky . . ." Li Wen hesitated. "Maybe twenty minutes."

"We don't have twenty minutes!" Kaizong was almost screaming.

The two looked helplessly in different directions, like two homeless dogs.

"Damn! Can't believe I almost forgot." Li Wen's eyes lit up. "Mimi's body film! I installed an RF transmitter in there."

Kaizong was taken aback, and then his gaze grew chilly. "You're telling me . . . you've been tracking Mimi's position all along?"

"Theoretically, yes . . ." Li Wen avoided Kaizong's gaze and added guiltily, "I've always thought of her as a sister . . . I wanted to protect her . . ."

"Your sister? Is this really how you protect your sister?" Kaizong pressed up against Li Wen, and sparks seemed to shoot out of his eyes. He raised his fists, but stopped himself in time and forced them down. "So, you knew all along what was happening? You watched Luo Jincheng abduct her, watched Knifeboy abuse her, watched her almost die?"

"That night, I followed her to Tide Gazing Beach. But I was too late." Li Wen kept his eyes on the ground, and his voice was almost inaudibly soft. "I wanted to record . . . what was happening so I could blackmail the Luo clan. But I couldn't get a steady signal due to interference. I ran to save her; I really did. But I never could get a lock on her position. I trusted too much in my own plot, never anticipating they could be so cruel. I felt as though I had sent my own sister to her death . . . I couldn't bear losing her again. What happened after that was like a dream. I found Mimi and carried her back . . ."

"So in the end, you were an accessory to Knifeboy's crimes."

Li Wen shuddered, remembering the video of his sister. His legs turned to rubber and he fell to his knees. He muttered repeatedly, "This is my punishment . . . my punishment . . ."

"Remember your sister. Remember how those people treated her." Kaizong's face was stony as he sat on the ground, not caring as the rain soaked him. "Then remember Mimi. Let's hope we're not too late this time."

The corners of Li Wen's mouth spasmed a few times. He said nothing as he put on his augmented-reality glasses and his hands began to dance through the air. He shared the tracking view with Kaizong's right eye. A map of Silicon Isle and the surrounding sea appeared; a golden dot left the wharf and rapidly headed for the open sea.

"They really are headed for international waters. We have no ships. How are we going to catch them?" Li Wen looked dejected.

"What's that?" Kaizong highlighted a silvery curve across the bay between Shantou and Silicon Isle, a line that the course of the golden dot must cross.

"That's the Shantou Bay Bridge!" Li Wen quickly calculated the time to intercept. "You're right. We still have a chance!"

"But we don't have a car. How are we going to get to the bridge in time?" Kaizong looked around at the ruined landscape: pools of water, wreckage, and debris pockmarked the land and made it difficult to traverse the terrain.

"We have something much better than a car." Li Wen grinned as his fingers danced through the air. This was Mimi's gift to him, a completely open interface for controlling the mecha, more operator-friendly even than the OEM version. The hulk of the exoskeleton clanged and clattered. The top of the robot folded forward while the legs retracted to reveal caterpillar tracks. Soon, the robot had transformed into something that resembled an armored personnel carrier. With a dexterous leap, he got into the cockpit, and then extended one of the robot arms to lift Kaizong onto the shoulder.

"Hold on tight. This thing moves faster than it looks." Li Wen stuck his head out of the cockpit and shouted, "Try to get through to Mimi. We're going to need her help."

Kaizong glared at him. It was possible that he might never be able to forgive Li Wen. However, right now, Mimi's life was in danger and his heart had little room left for anger. He needed all the help he could get.

The black armored vehicle roared, and with a clanging, grinding clamor, shot through the darkness toward the brightening eastern sky, as pale as the belly of a fish.

———————

Scott held on to the rudder tensely. The windshield wiper wasn't working too well, and it looked like someone was pouring buckets of water directly onto the glass. Everything was a blur. The eye of Typhoon Wutip had just passed Silicon Isle and was now over this part of the sea. It would eventually make landfall at Shantou and degenerate into a tropical storm. This was the main reason why Scott couldn't switch to automatic navigation.

He twisted around to glance at Mimi. She was secured to the chair by the seat belt. Her face was bloodless and she showed no signs of waking up any time soon. The light fiberglass speedboat was being violently jolted by the wind and the waves, and anyone who was still conscious would be experiencing dizziness, vomiting, and even sympathetic nervous disorders. In this sense at least, Mimi was a lucky passenger.

Everything is going to be resolved, Scott thought. He had simulated and run through every scenario in his head, coming up with the perfect response for every development. Yet the situation had ultimately deteriorated to the point where he could not retreat in perfect safety. How could a perfect sequence of deductions have led to the wrong answer? He couldn't understand it. Maybe this was what the Silicon Isle natives meant by fate.

Luo Jincheng was no longer his untrustworthy ally, and Chen Kaizong was no longer his faithful subordinate. TerraGreen Recycling, SBT, and even the Arashio Foundation were no longer safe harbors. He needed a greater stage to properly make use of the amazing discovery hidden in this tiny boat. *Human history is about to end:* he had already drafted the public statement in his mind. The Coltsfoot Blossom ship waiting in international waters would be the first springboard on the path to a brand-new chapter.

Nancy. The face of his dead daughter refused to leave him. Scott felt depressed, as though everything he had done was but a futile attempt at evading guilt that would ultimately end in emptiness. He shook his head forcefully, knowing that this was but an excuse his conscience had concocted to maintain a consistent personality.

This is also the best choice for Mimi, he emphasized to himself repeatedly. *We have the best doctors, the best equipment, and the best environment. I haven't lied. We once had committed atrocities, but that was history, the impossible choices forced upon us by war. This is the twenty-first century, a golden age. There's no more need to apply barbaric, cruel, bloody methods to experimental subjects. Moreover, in her body, in her brain, is concealed the future for the entire human race. We'll give her a happy life, very happy.*

But what if she's not an error? Scott's heart skipped a beat. His pathological imagination began to run wild.

What if she's a new creation? God had created humankind in His own image. Humankind explored the mysteries of the world, invented theories, devised science and technology. Humans wanted to create something even closer to their creator, to make science imitate life, evolving endlessly to approach the apex of the pyramid. Humans would then entrust their future to technology and become its parasites, no longer progressing forward.

Some undetectable force, endowed with intentions not yet known to humankind, had disguised all the seamless links as an impossible accident. Perhaps similar accidents were occurring every day in every remote corner of this planet, giving birth to thousands of prototypes like Mimi. Life was a giant black box, and just when you thought it had reached a dead end, it would always find a new way out and continue its upward winding progression.

A new kind of life that crossed the boundary between biology and machinery. Human history was about to end.

But who is her creator? Scott shuddered as though a pair of eyes were staring at his back. He turned around at once, but all he saw was Mimi, still asleep.

The boat bounced violently in the gale. Scott had to slow down lest it capsize. The smartest thing to do right now would be to wait for the typhoon to pass and then speed across the calm sea. But he was afraid to see what further surprises he would encounter if he waited around. He had to leave.

A thin, silvery arc appeared in the dim sky, spanning the ocean. While the boat bounced up and down, it remained rock steady. As the distance closed, Scott recognized it as an artificial structure. Giant supporting piers, like the legs of elephants, loomed out of the rain and mist.

The cold wind scraped Kaizong's face like knives. Objects at the edge of his vision blurred and swept quickly by to be left behind. Silicon Isle in the wake of the typhoon resembled an apocalyptic scene, as if a toddler in the throes of a tantrum had destroyed a collection of carefully sculpted sandcastles, leaving behind nothing but meaningless chaos.

Immense, translucent creatures appeared on his right. They swooped over the ruins, howling with sorrow. Kaizong couldn't identify the creatures, chimera-like guardians of this dark forest full of pain.

Kaizong couldn't understand the meaning of their appearance, the result of some virtual animal programming. He didn't even know how to turn off this function. His eye seemed transformed, brand-new, a gift from Mimi. He became even more worried.

Tirelessly, he called for Mimi through the waste-people network. But it was as though he was tossing pebbles into a bottomless chasm, and he heard no responding splash.

The robot in its APC form navigated the uneven terrain nimbly, avoiding fallen trees and powering through deep puddles. It bounced and jolted, but never slowed down. The eastern sky became more translucent, as though the cloud cover was dissipating. A light pink fire burned behind a curtain the color of condensed milk, as though it might extinguish at any moment, or burst out of its shell.

The silver-gray bridge appeared in the distance.

Kaizong was certain that Mimi was there, just ahead of them. He repeated her name passionately, as though pounding his fist against a tightly shut door, but no one answered.

The robot roared onto the empty bridge and accelerated. Their end of the bridge was now clear, but the other end was still shrouded in gray mist and rain.

"She's coming!" Li Wen shouted from the cockpit.

Kaizong gazed over at the hazy sea, trying to discern what he was looking for. A white curve slowly extended across the dark surface of the sea and was about to cross under the bridge several hundred meters ahead of where they were.

"We're not going to make it!" Li Wen said.

Kaizong set his right eye to maximum zoom and tried to find Mimi in the cabin of the tumbling boat, as though seeing her might help him connect with her consciousness. He saw that familiar figure flicker in and out of existence, dissolving into millions of chaotic particles one minute and coalescing into order the next like some illustration of Schrödinger's cat.

He recalled the secret history of palirromancy told by the Chen clan head: living beings struggling in the sea, straddling the border between life and death. *Those who observe the tides may know the world.* All he wanted was to *see* Mimi's face.

Mimi! Bridge! Kaizong made a last, desperate attempt. He knew that if they didn't stop Scott at this spot, there was no more hope of rescuing Mimi, because the speedboat was about to reach international waters.

Mimi! Stop the boat!

He seemed to sense something. He turned to look at the other end of the bridge, where the thick cloud cover revealed an opening. The rising golden sun spread its light over the ocean like a sparkling carpet full of exquisite wrinkles. He saw a bottlenose dolphin, long thought extinct, leap out of the water in a perfect curve, its back glistening with mysterious golden light. The beauty of the sight was breathtaking.

He knew it wasn't real. The dolphin disappeared, as did the golden light. He didn't know what the hallucination meant.

Kaizong finally turned back at Li Wen's insistent cries. He saw the white curve of the speedboat's trail slicing across the sea, about to enter the giant white arch formed by the piers of the bridge.

20

The wheel in Scott's hand suddenly turned as stiff and heavy as barnacle-encrusted reef. Shocked, he watched lights flash over the instrument panel as the autopilot cut in. The boat nimbly changed direction and headed straight for one of the piers without reducing speed.

The immense, rigid structure expanded and loomed before the boat, pressing down upon Scott. He muttered a few meaningless words and subconsciously crossed his arms before his head. The speedboat struck the pier head-on in a soul-shattering metallic collision. The twisted bow, deflected by the pier, rose into the air. The boat's ascent slowed, stopped; it rolled over in the air and then tumbled back into the water, making a giant splash. The capsized boat bobbed in the water like a dead pufferfish.

Scott recovered as the roaring around him subsided. The instinctive protective posture at the last minute had saved his life, but he paid a price with two arms lacerated by glass shards and a dislocated right shoulder. The boat was still afloat but taking on water. His dazed eyes discovered that the girl, the treasure of the human race, was still secured to her seat with the safety belt. Her head was now pointing down and submerged in water.

Despite the pain, he swam over, lifted Mimi's head out of the water, and released the safety belt. The still-unconscious girl slid into the sea and her weight dragged Scott down.

"No! You can't die! You can't die here!" Scott screamed as Nancy's floating, pale face flashed before his eyes. He placed Mimi over his knees and pressed her back to squeeze out the water in her trachea. Then he flipped her over, and, pinching her nose shut, began to give her mouth-to-mouth.

"Don't die! Don't . . ." he begged, his voice cracking. He dragged over a broken table, placed Mimi over the rigid surface, and, crossing the fingers of his hands, began to compress her chest. Her chest slowly rose after each compression, but there was no heartbeat.

"Don't do this to me, goddamn it . . ." Scott was now sobbing uncontrollably. He slammed a fist against the back of the other hand, and the dull thuds transferred the force into Mimi's chest. "I'm begging you . . ."

He stopped abruptly. He seemed to hear the rumbling of underground currents.

Mimi convulsed and vomited a torrent of seawater. Then she hacked and coughed violently. Her chest began to rise and fall gently, and a bit of color returned to her pallid face.

Scott's expression was a complex mixture of joy and fear. He knew that it was time to bring out his last trick.

"Fuck! Fuck!" Li Wen swore nonstop as the robot braked to a hard stop and crashed into the metal guardrails of the bridge, leaving a deep depression.

"She heard me. She heard me!" Kaizong jumped off the robot and, together with Li Wen, poked his head over the edge of the bridge. The giant pier went straight down to the sea, a terror-inducing sight. The white belly of the speedboat bobbed not too far away, and there were no signs of survivors in the surrounding waters.

"We have to go down and save her." Kaizong turned to Li Wen, who looked frightened.

"I have acrophobia. Every time I look down from a high place, it feels like ants are chewing my balls. I . . . I can't do this."

"Useless!" Kaizong spat, and once again gazed at the sea, his heart clenching. His right eye went to work, calculating the distance, the wind speed, and the terminal velocity as a human body struck the water. A red warning light blinked. "It's too high to jump. The impact would kill me. But if we can be lower by about ten, no, eight meters, that might work."

Li Wen frowned as he pondered the problem; then his eyes lit up. "Buddy, I can't dive with you, but I do have an idea."

Kaizong held on to the iron fist of the robot as he dangled over the water in the cold wind. He forced himself to not look down. The moist, chilly air felt like a layer of ice against his skin, inducing goose bumps. The metal fist detached from the arm and descended slowly at the end of a steel cable, until Kaizong was a bit closer to the surface of the sea.

"More!" Kaizong shouted, enduring the vertigo.

The cable clanged against the gears and came to a stop abruptly.

"That's as far as the cable will go!" Li Wen shouted down.

"It's not far enough! We need just a bit more." Kaizong tightened his grip on the robot fist. Spinning and swaying with the wind, he swallowed hard, trying to reduce the tension somehow.

"Hold on really tight!"

The iron fist jolted hard and dropped. Kaizong instinctively squeezed his eyes shut and locked his arms about the fist. Li Wen had made the robot lie down flat on the bridge, poking over the edge, adding the length of the robot arm to the cable.

"Just a tiny bit more!" Kaizong's right eye showed that he was still thirty centimeters from the safe zone.

"Fucking hell . . ." Li Wen's swears came faintly on the wind.

The iron fist dropped again. Li Wen made the robot lean over the side as much as possible, and its two legs were now raised off the ground, balancing it precariously on the edge. Another inch and the entire steel hulk would tumble over. There was no airbag in the cockpit—not that it would have done much good.

The red indicator in Kaizong's eye finally turned green. He took a deep breath, and looked down at the sea, waiting for the right moment. He didn't want to strike the pier or land on top of some reef. His right eye busily estimated the water depth and the angle at which he would enter the water, and divided the sea into a grid of squares marked in different colors to help him decide.

Now! He let go and jumped down. Like a real diver, he adjusted his posture and put his hands together over his head, straightening his body as he fell. The robot, having been freed of his weight, dropped its legs back onto the bridge in a loud clang.

Kaizong plunged into the water like an arrow and disappeared beneath a cloud of spray. A few seconds later, he emerged at the surface like a big fish, hungrily gulping the precious air. After a brief rest, he divided the water with powerful strokes and headed for the capsized speedboat.

He could almost hear the faint cheers of Li Wen from high above.

"Don't come any closer!" Scott held a strangely shaped gun to the back of Mimi's skull. "I want a boat. Right now."

"Let her go." Kaizong tried to find his footing in the half-submerged cabin. "Don't harm her. I'll get you a boat, all right? Just don't harm her."

"Don't you understand that I'm the only one in the world who can save her? No one else! It's too bad that you don't believe me, and no one else does either. I think this gun is going to be used no matter what; that is its purpose, after all." Scott gave him an eerie smile. "This is a miniaturized EMP gun. Though it's not extremely powerful, it's more than enough to fry the circuits in your girlfriend's brain. If I can't get her, no one else will either. So, don't you dare to play any games with me."

"I don't think you will." Kaizong stared at him. "Listen to me, you're not an evil man."

Scott's body swayed as if Kaizong's words touched a nerve. But he had no choice left.

Mimi looked terrified. Her body was held up by Scott's dislocated right arm, and she swayed unsteadily. She gazed at the empty-handed Kaizong and silently warned him to not do anything stupid. Another voice spoke in her mind.

His heart, whispered Mimi 1. *I'll take over his heart.*

Mimi closed her eyes, eyeballs roaming rapidly under the lids. Her consciousness penetrated the chest of the man behind her and entered that tiny box. The protocol for synchronizing the data was easily cracked, and she possessed the lifesaving pacemaker as though she held Scott's damaged heart in her hand.

She sped up Scott's heart. The frail organ accelerated like a powered water pump: contract, relax, contract, relax . . . Blood surged through his arteries, disturbing the functions of his body like a flood.

Scott's face changed, and sweat beaded on his forehead. He tried to wait it out, expecting the pacemaker to do its job—not knowing that it was the source of the problem. A sharp stab of pain struck deep in his body like a steel needle. His limbs lost all strength and he couldn't help letting go of Mimi. The hand holding the gun was now at his chest as he leaned against the cabin wall, gasping. His breaths became uneven, and despair crept into his eyes.

"Nancy," he said. "Nancy."

Kaizong pulled Mimi over and interposed himself between her and Scott. Tentatively, he approached Scott, and pulled the EMP gun from between his powerless fingers as though taking away a poisoned apple.

Mimi stopped Scott's heart. The blood stopped circulating. Oxygen consumption turned the blood acidic. The smell of death.

Scott felt a chill at his back, as though some supernatural power had entered the cabin behind him. He twisted around and saw it was the steel cabin wall. His body convulsed uncontrollably and croaking noises emerged from his throat as though he were drowning. He looked down, searching for something, his lips muttering silently. Finally, he lost his balance and fell into the water. His pale face floated above the surface, staring up into the emptiness like a marble statue.

Kaizong understood his final, silent words. *I'm sorry.*

That's enough. A wave of disgust rose in Mimi 0. *I said that's enough!*
Your human weakness is going to be the death of you someday. Mimi
1 faded back into the darkness.

Mimi 0 stayed silent for a while. She knew it was time.

Kaizong pulled Mimi into a tight embrace. Two wet, trembling bodies pressed close to each other, sharing any residual heat. They kissed deeply, hungrily, as though this was their last kiss in the world. The water had risen above their waists, and the stench of the sea filled the air.

"Let's get out of here. The boat is about to go down." Kaizong pulled at Mimi, but she didn't move.

Mimi pulled up Kaizong's hand and aimed the EMP gun at her own head. "Pull the trigger."

"Are you crazy?" Kaizong couldn't believe his ears. "Why?"

"I'm no longer the Mimi you knew. I've killed many . . ." Mimi's face twisted as though she was fighting with another self hidden deep inside. ". . . I don't want to become a monster. I don't want to commit murder. I don't want to become a laboratory specimen . . ."

"That wasn't you! It wasn't. Mimi, we'll figure out a way. Believe me—" Kaizong tried to pull the gun away, but the girl, who looked as if she could collapse any moment, had impossible strength in her arms, and he couldn't budge the gun at all.

"You don't understand!" Mimi sobbed.

A series of images struck Kaizong's right eye, flashing by one after another: the experimental subjects for Project Waste Tide; Eva, the chimp torn to pieces; columns of smoke and bodies strewn around a battlefield; the thousands and thousands of fragmentary glimpses that made up a city; the prisoners rushing out of the jail like a flood; pileups of dozens, hundreds of cars; bleeding men and women desperately crawling through the wreckage . . . the images came quicker and quicker, overlaying each other, turning into a blinding ball of light that burned Kaizong's eye so that he could no longer bear to look at them.

"Do it now! Before she recovers!" Mimi's body convulsed as though she were a puppet using all her strength to fight the invisible strings.

Abruptly, her expression changed, and a crude, hoarse voice emerged from her throat. "Don't you dare! If you try, I'll kill her first, then you, then everyone!"

Kaizong's right eye felt like a red-hot piece of coal embedded in his skull. He felt his nerves burn, charring inch by inch. He smelled the odor of singed flesh. A million trumpets blared while a billion canaries cried. His trembling eye seemed like a bomb about to go off at any moment.

"I can't . . . I can't kill you . . ." Kaizong screamed in pain, and fell to his knees in the water. The skin around his right eye socket turned red, blistered, burned, and fragments dropped sizzling into the water, raising wisps of white smoke. The pain was like a drill on full power going straight into his skull.

Then, for a moment, all the pain and noise disappeared. Kaizong seemed to be floating in a sweet, serene vacuum, reminding him of that night when he and Mimi had lain on Tide Gazing Beach and looked up at the stars. But almost instantaneously, the pain returned with doubled strength, and devoured what remained of his consciousness like a tide.

"You can't kill me! You can't kill me!" Mimi's bamboo-reed voice overlaid the demonic screams like an eerie duet. The voices were entangled together, repressing each other. "I'm only a beginning! Only a beg—"

The voices stopped.

Kaizong's arm trembled in the air. He had finally pulled the trigger.

The instrument panel of the speedboat flashed brightly, and sparks emerged from every seam and gap like the fireworks for some wild party. The electronic whistle blared, piercing the walls of the cabin, and gradually faded, until all was silent again. All the light-emitting components dimmed, as though a giant beast had been trying to prove its existence with its last ounce of strength.

A look of astonishment froze on Mimi's face, as though she couldn't believe what she was seeing. She tried to touch Kaizong's deformed right eye. Her arm trembled in the air between them, but before she could reach her goal, her body stiffened and she fell backward into the water, making a loud splash.

The gun tumbled from Kaizong's fingers. He waded through the water and picked up the unconscious Mimi in his arms. Holding her tightly, he dove into the water, and the overheating right eye crackled in the sea, short-circuiting. Light disappeared, followed by a piercing pain. Relying on his remaining unenhanced eye, he looked for an opening, exited the cabin, splashed to the sparkling surface, and swam hard for the pier.

Behind him, air bubbled out of all sides of the sinking boat. Like an iceberg, the white belly of the speedboat finally descended below the surface, carrying with it Scott's ambition, leaving behind an irregular eddy. Typhoon Wutip, by now only a tropical storm, headed for Shantou, leaving a serene sea behind around Silicon Isle, as though nothing had happened.

EPILOGUE

It was July again. The sea south of the Aleutian Islands was in a trough of low pressure, and thick fog lingered for months, stretching westward to the Kuril Islands. From there, the cold, subarctic Oyashio Current originating in the Bering Strait flowed south, and met the north-flowing warm Kuroshio Current in the Pacific just north of 40 degrees latitude. The commingled current then headed east.

A man standing inside the bridge of *Clotho*, a scientific vessel, looked out at the vast sea. The skin around his right eye was marked with burn scars. Such injuries could have been easily repaired with cosmetic surgery, but he didn't seem to care.

"Mr. Chen, would you like some tea?" The captain, William Katzenberg, appeared by his side, holding a cup of thick, fragrant coffee.

"Thank you. I'll get it myself." Kaizong smiled at him. "Have you ever seen so much fog?"

"Of course. To me, it's no different from afternoon tea. If you live long enough, nothing will excite you anymore."

"I don't know about that. A year ago—" Kaizong stopped.

"What happened a year ago?"

"Oh, nothing." Kaizong changed the subject, and taking the hint, the captain began to tell stories about the blue fox of the Aleutians.

That golden dolphin.

The events of a year ago had left him half blind. The doctor suggested that he exchange his prosthetic eye for a new one, but he turned the idea down, opting instead to pay a higher price to repair the damaged eye. At his insistence, the optical defects in the eye caused by high temperature—barrel distortion and a tinge of yellow-green—had been preserved. The eye now saw everything through the filter of Silicon Isle, a hue that belonged to Mimi, an imperfect beauty. He hoped to forever remember everything that had happened, like the scars on his face.

In the end, TerraGreen Recycling had signed an agreement with the Silicon Isle government to construct a recycling industrial park over three years. Due to the sudden death of the head of the Luo clan, the project encountered few objections. Lin Yiyu convinced the Lin clan to no longer rely on its relationship with the government to manipulate the markets, and compete with the Chen clan fairly as two shareholders to promote modern management practices in the waste-processing industry, the free movement of labor, as well as better working conditions and social safety nets.

He still remembered Mayor Weng's rousing speech at the formal signing ceremony: *Win-win-win! A brand-new future for Silicon Isle.*

The brave deeds of the waste workers during the typhoon were duly recognized and rewarded. As a result of the heavy property damage and lost lives partially caused by the shutdown of network communications during the typhoon, the government, under heavy media pressure, announced a reexamination of the regulations for network monitoring and bitrate restriction. TerraGreen Recycling formed a special foundation to use part of the profits to aid those migrant workers who suffered damage to their health as a result of their work in waste processing. Mimi was the foundation's first aid recipient.

Mimi. Kaizong's heart clenched with pain. He would never forget the last time he saw Mimi.

It was a hazy afternoon. He entered the hospital ward and saw Mimi in her wheelchair with her back to him, looking at the trees outside the window. Kaizong walked in front of her, squatted, and carefully examined that blank face, softly calling her name, caressing her long hair with the same fingers that had pulled the trigger. Mimi gazed back at him as though looking at a lifeless thing. Something had been wiped from her gaze forever, leaving her a soulless shell. She opened her mouth, but no voice came out. Her face was expressionless, like a machine that had been restored to factory defaults.

The doctor told him that she had been lucky. As the electromagnetic pulse penetrated her brain, the heat had instantaneously incinerated the neural tissue around the metal particles. However, as the pulse had lasted only a few milliseconds, the damage wasn't life-threatening. The minefield in Mimi's brain had been eliminated by this carpet bombing, but the damage to her logical thinking, emotional processing, and memory was severe. Currently, she was the mental equivalent of a three-year-old.

But there is hope, whispered the doctor. *We're experimenting with trial medication. It requires patience, a great deal of patience.*

The trial medication was the legacy of Project Waste Tide, Kaizong knew. History certainly liked to make sick jokes.

Kaizong gave Mimi a light kiss on the forehead. Mimi responded with animal-like mutterings. A spark seemed to light up in her eyes for the briefest of moments before disappearing. He stood up, left the room, and did not look back. He didn't dare to look back. He was afraid that he would stay if he did, never leaving her side, living only on that shred of impossible hope. A hope would destroy the only remaining beauty between the two of them if he let it grow and fester and starve them both of the possibility of a real future that lay ahead, no matter how unlike the dreams he'd once had for the two of them.

"Kaizong! Look what we found!" his assistant called excitedly from the deck. Kaizong left his memories behind and climbed down onto the wet deck. The crew crowded around something that had just been fished out of the sea.

It was a crude but ingeniously designed machine, resembling a lotus flower made of metal and plastic.

The assistant demonstrated how it worked. Normally, the device floated at the surface, extending a flexible, LED-lit tube into the water to lure fish. When it sensed something living within range, the device snapped shut like a mousetrap and flipped over with the seized prey at the center of the lotus. Then the device sent out a positioning signal and waited for the fisherman to arrive for the harvesting.

A wonderful mimic. Kaizong was reminded of the prosthetic hand crawling along the ground in Xialong Village.

"Everyone, stay alert! I bet that thing is nearby!" Kaizong whistled and gave the order, and the crew hurried back into position.

"Mr. Chen, you've been searching the whole time since we started from the coast of California. What exactly are you looking for?" Curiosity was written all over the captain's face.

"You'll see. I have to warn you, don't get too excited."

After Silicon Isle, Kaizong had resigned from TerraGreen Recycling and traveled by himself for a while. Eventually, he returned to Boston and wrote freelance articles for small websites. This was an age that had little need for historians. Social networking, streaming media, and real-time computing provided more in-depth, data-driven analytical reports that were also easier to understand. In some sense, history had ended, at least as a narrative practice imbued with uncertainty. Kaizong sometimes even had the impulse to write a letter to the president of his alma mater, suggesting that history be eliminated as a department.

He recounted his experience on Silicon Isle in a calm voice to his parents—well, he told them what he was allowed to tell. For the first time in many years, he embraced his father. His father thumped him on the back a few times, his hand heavy and sure, as though they had reached some kind of understanding.

Kaizong thought a certain kind of urge in himself had vanished. He had once thought of himself as capable of changing things. Now he understood that it was but a fantasy. The world had never ceased to change, but it would also never change for anyone.

He still remembered the last words of the head of the Chen clan as he said goodbye to the elder.

People always think of themselves as playing with the tides, but in the end, they find out that the tides play with them.

Then he had received the call from a stranger in Hong Kong.

The caller introduced herself as Sug-Yi Chiu Ho, a project leader with the environment protection organization Coltsfoot Blossom. She was interested in Kaizong's background, especially his experience with the TerraGreen Recycling project in Silicon Isle. She was offering him an unusual job.

A chance to change the world, she said.

Kaizong shook his head and smiled bitterly.

Each year, hundreds of millions of tons of unprocessed trash were dumped into the world's oceans from coastal cities. The nondegradable refuse traveled the globe by riding ocean currents. As the pieces of litter traveled, they attracted each other, melded together, reacted, and even formed into giant floating islands that threatened the world's shipping lanes. Coltsfoot Blossom had always tracked these islands of trash closely. With RFID technology, they had built a map of the paths of the world's major trash islands that they offered to the shipping companies for free to prevent accidents.

But ultimately, someone had to pay. The efficient Asian woman smiled and added, *We are tracking some promising leads. There are strange things happening; for instance, the incredible frequency of lightning above the trash islands. We need you, and perhaps the people there also need you.*

There are people on the islands? Kaizong asked.

We don't know. But we do know the islands are not as desolate as Mars.

And so Kaizong had returned to the sea. The endless swaying nauseated him, but also seemed to become an addicting habit. The trash islands didn't merely drift with the currents. They seemed to take advantage of the complex interplay of various currents and played a game of cat and mouse with Coltsfoot Blossom. Kaizong and his crew chased from one patch of ocean to another, following the ever-changing directives issued by headquarters. Any slight change in the conditions seemed to suggest countless guesses, and the chains of deduction reached absurd conclusions.

Often, Kaizong lay on the deck to gaze at the stars as the waves rocked him to sleep. As he approached the border between dream and wakefulness, fantastical images would invade his right eye as though a giant eye glimpsed him from the universe. The clear gaze penetrated his entire being and elevated him into paradise. Like the gaze of Mimi.

I'm only a beginning.

Every time he recalled Mimi's last words, a bone-chilling sensation would crawl over his skin, like some incurable form of allergy.

Before leaving Silicon Isle, he had made a special trip to visit Luo Zixin, Luo Jincheng's youngest son. Other than his excessively proper Modern Standard Mandarin, the boy seemed no different from the other native children as they played and horsed around on the exercise grounds. Occasionally, however, the boy stopped and stared into the distance at nothing, looking thoughtful.

From time to time, Kaizong allowed himself to fantasize about meeting Mimi again. The visions were so detailed, specifying the season, light, temperature, the kinds of plants around them, the clothes they wore, their expressions, the type of birdsong, and their first words to each other. Then they'd reminisce, and like a regular couple, get married, have children, argue over trivial matters, hurt each other, annoy each other, and finally part from each other or live happily ever after. However, he knew that at least in this sublunary world, they would never meet again.

The fog over the sea seemed to grow darker, as though cocoa butter had been poured into a swirling mug of milk, dissolving unevenly. Kaizong climbed onto the bow and watched as the immense structure rose into view like a monster emerging from the mist. Gradually, the object solidified, grew clear, and loomed over the ship with an oppressive power. The sky began to flicker with uncertain arcs of pale blue light. An island of trash.

It's time to go onshore, he said to himself.

AUTHOR'S ACKNOWLEDGMENTS

I'm grateful to the following persons not only for making the publication of this book possible but also for guiding me in the grand world of speculative fiction: Ken Liu, Gray Tan, David G. Hartwell, Liz Gorinsky, Lindsey Hall, Han Song, Liu Cixin, Prof. Song Mingwei, Prof. David Der-Wei Wang, Prof. Cara Healey, Prof. Wu Yan, Prof. Yan Feng, Yao Haijun, Dong Renwei, Yang Feng, Shi Bo, Wang Meizi, Luo Yuhan, and my parents, Lijuan and Yingcheng.

TRANSLATOR'S ACKNOWLEDGMENTS

During the long but rewarding process of bringing Stan's haunting and moving novel to Anglophone readers, I was fortunate to have the help of many. I'd like to thank them here (though this is necessarily an incomplete list): Wang Meizi, Alex Shvartsman, Sarah Dodd, Carmen Yiling Yan, Anaea Lay, Kellan Sparver, Amy Franks, David Hartwell, Liz Gorinsky, Lindsey Hall, Desirae Friesen, Terry McGarry, Ryan Jenkins, Victor Mosquera, Jamie Stafford-Hill, Christopher Morgan, Bill Warhop, Russell Galen, and Gray Tan.